Praise for *Blood to Poison*

'A gripping, immersive story and a powerful vindication of
female anger, *Blood to Poison* is a stunning read'
Louise O'Neill

'I literally couldn't put it down! Watson builds an incredibly
vivid world oozing with magic, excitement and danger.
My heart didn't stop racing until the very last word'
Jasbinder Bilan

'I flew through this book. It's a gripping exploration
and vindication of anger'
Samantha Shannon

'Furious, beautiful and impossible to put down'
Katherine Webber

'Bold, visceral, and alive, from the hidden magic swirling
under the everyday and mundane, to the slow unfolding
of the depth of the curse and fight to break it ... an
absolute gut-punch of a novel'
Melinda Salisbury

'A compulsive read. It has everything a bestselling YA novel
needs: secret societies, deliciously evil villains, love and
enough twists to keep you gasping from beginning to end'
Sally Partridge

BLOOD
TO
POISON

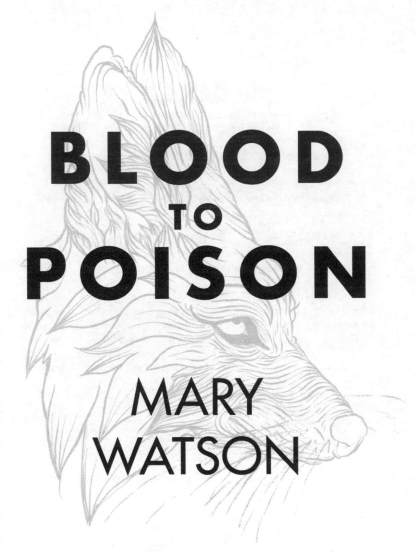

BLOOD
TO
POISON

MARY
WATSON

BLOOMSBURY
LONDON OXFORD NEW YORK NEW DELHI SYDNEY

BLOOMSBURY YA
Bloomsbury Publishing Plc
50 Bedford Square, London WC1B 3DP, UK
29 Earlsfort Terrace, Dublin 2, Ireland

BLOOMSBURY, BLOOMSBURY YA and the Diana logo
are trademarks of Bloomsbury Publishing Plc

First published in Great Britain in 2022 by Bloomsbury Publishing Plc

A catalogue record for this book is available from the British Library

ISBN: PB: 978-1-5266-1917-4; eBook: 978-1-5266-1916-7

4 6 8 10 9 7 5

Typeset by RefineCatch Limited, Bungay, Suffolk

Printed and bound in Great Britain by CPI Group (UK) Ltd, Croydon CR0 4YY

To find out more about our authors and books visit www.bloomsbury.com
and sign up for our newsletters

For my sisters' daughters, Zadie and Tracey.

*Remembering the women who came before us, those we loved
and those whose names we do not know.*

CONTENTS

AUTHOR'S NOTE

In my family, there is a story of a curse. My aunt died tragically when she was twenty-one years old and we came to believe that her rose-gold pearl ring was cursed, that it brought hardship, or worse, early death.

I realise now that cursed or not, the ring became the embodiment of a terrible trauma. It was more than just a ring; it stood for loss and grief across four generations. *Blood to Poison* was inspired by this cursed ring – the possibility of magic, of curses and devils, has been inscribed in how I see the world from a young age. But mostly because the ring connected my family in an intensely emotional way. When I held that ring, I felt the loss of my aunt, even though she died before I was born.

Blood to Poison is about a curse that forges emotional connection across generations. But the book reaches deeper into the past, to an enslaved ancestor, and the characters are linked by past traumas that reverberate in the present. Like Savannah, enslavement is almost certainly part of my own family history, and the book's underlying themes of trauma and historical rage resonate deeply for me.

Before I started writing, I had useful conversations about what it means to incorporate these very difficult real-life traumas into a story about a girl who discovers magic. What I heard was this: these are our stories and they should be told. It would be easier for me to explore these themes by writing literary fiction, a quiet reflective piece. But the challenge I took on with *Blood to Poison* was to take this story with all its implicit trauma and work it into a young adult romantic fantasy, and to do so sensitively and without compromising the real suffering that makes up the undercurrents of this book.

At the heart of *Blood to Poison* are two things: Savannah's anger, along with the understanding of this anger as something that links her to previous generations, and the figure of Hella, the ancestor who'd been enslaved during colonial times. When planning this book, I was feeling a constant low-grade fury – at lying politicians, disinformation, at how racism was becoming more overt, the way misogyny was manifesting as violence. While I was writing, angry South Africans took to the streets to protest violence against women and the high rate of femicide. I was researching slavery in colonial Cape Town, learning again about the appalling conditions that the enslaved endured, and finding connections between these two driving strands. Black anger is frequently dismissed or weaponised, women are branded irrational, and this story seemed an opportunity to open up conversations around anger. When I spoke to others about feeling angry all the time, I was surprised how often the response was, *So am I.*

For those unfamiliar with South Africa, it's a complex country with a difficult past. It is a vibrant, diverse place and the characters in the book reflect this diversity. I grew up during apartheid, the oppressive political system that entrenched white domination, where the small details of my life were determined by the colour of my skin – I was forbidden from certain beaches, benches, train carriages, living in the leafy suburbs, attending well-resourced schools and so on, because they were 'reserved for whites'. White was elevated, considered the norm – TV, magazines, sport, etc. were populated by white people, all in a country where white is the minority.

Like many South Africans, I am scarred by this past and it affects how I talk about race today. Some readers might find it strange that I don't explicitly label race in this book. It didn't feel right here. It's partly a resistance, from growing up in a time where everyone was defined by race, where these labels were used to oppress. Apartheid's strategy was to divide and conquer, to dehumanise through othering. I don't believe we can simply ignore race, not when there is so much to mend, but my instinct is to distance myself from the language of apartheid.

I find the terminology difficult: Savannah and her family, Inez and her family, Mama Daline, Quinton, amongst others, are all what is called 'coloured' in South Africa, the official apartheid term, and one that doesn't carry the same meaning outside of the country. It is the label applied to me. A complex term, it is both contested and embraced by people in my community, and I didn't feel there was room to explore the topic with any nuance here. Many of us identify as black (or Black – my preference when referring to myself is not to capitalise; both are used in South Africa) while acknowledging colourism and recognising those classified as 'native' were disadvantaged more severely during apartheid.

This is a book about magic and witches, self-discovery and love in its many guises. But, under the surface, it is also a story about how trauma is passed down through the generations. The story is inspired by the very real historical trauma and injustice of enslavement and discrimination in South Africa. Writing it required a careful balance between the need to tell stories sensitively and the need to tell stories. I have tried to find that balance and I hope you will enjoy the story.

Mary Watson

1

BABY

I am troubled by a memory that never happened.

We're running, Freda and I. She's ahead, her long hair streaming. The night is unnaturally bright, but not because of the stars. Freda turns to me, holding out a hand:

Faster, Savannah.

My bare feet beat the hard earth. Fear tightens my chest.

I glance behind me and see the world burning. The orange blaze, the hidden depths within the curling flames.

And from those depths, something comes for us.

I reach for Freda, grasping at her billowing nightgown. She looks back again and her face contorts with terror.

That is where the memory ends.

It feels real. But we've never escaped a fire.

Freda, my aunt, my second mother, was killed in a car accident nearly ten years ago. It is an impossible memory.

*

'Savannah, you gonna hang in the doorway there all day?' Solly says from behind the shop counter.

I ignore him. I have the devils in me today. Restless. That's what Minnie always says when I get like this: Savannah, you have the duiwels in you. Come here. Sit still. *Kry jou rus, meisiekind*. Get your rest, girl.

From the doorway of the corner shop, I look out on to the empty road. The sun is high in the afternoon sky and, in the distance, cloud covers Devil's Peak. I'm here for the sugar, to fuel me as I study for another exam. Just three more papers, then three glorious months of summer break.

I take a step forward, then hesitate. The memory felt more real today.

I'm holding the jelly babies I bought, but I can't eat with devils dancing inside me. I turn back to where Solly leans on his elbows, watching me. He's beginning to grey at the temples.

'All that sugar you eat.' He shakes his head at me, like he isn't the dealer who feeds my addiction. 'It's gonna kill you one day.'

'Can I return them?' I hold up the jelly babies. 'For a refund?'

'You opened the bag.'

'Small details, Solly.'

'You ate some.'

'Is that a no then?'

'Go home, Savannah.' He raises his newspaper, blocking my view of his face. On the front page is a picture of a smiling woman. *Stabbed seven times*, the headline screams.

I leave the shop. A car is parked beside the empty

playground, with two guys inside, smoking with the windows rolled down. Their eyes light up as they see me.

'Hullo, girl.' The words slide out, slick with oil.

I keep walking. Look straight ahead. I know how this goes.

'Sexy lady,' the man in the parked car sings. I make the mistake of glancing over.

He runs his eyes over my body, down my black cami, the short shock of grey tulle, my bare legs, red Converse. Makes a kissing noise. 'Mm-mmmm.' Like I'm something delicious.

I'm not angry. Not yet. But the duiwels want to play.

I step towards the car. He's young, this guy, twenty perhaps. Something about him makes me think of an insect. A cartoon bug.

A metal pipe lies on the tarmac, near the tyre.

'I like what I see, baby,' Bug-Face informs me.

'I don't give a fuck what you like.'

'You hear that?' Bug-Face jerks a thumb at me and he looks at his friend.

'Sies, girl.' The other man, full lips and a goatee, runs his eyes over my body.

'Can't you take a compliment?' Bug-Face tuts. 'Still, I like them a little dirty. You know, you really pretty when you're not so cross.'

He shifts in his seat, the hem of his T-shirt riding up. The shape of a gun is unmistakeable, even before I see the black handle at his waistband.

'You should be more careful around here. A neighbourhood

3

like this.' He shakes his head. 'You just never know.'

What happens next, happens fast. The metal pipe is in my hand. The jelly babies are scattered in the road. I bring the pipe down on the hood of the car. The damage is disappointing, barely a dent. I swing back and hit harder.

Shards of glass spray everywhere. I hit again. Bug-Face shields his face with his arm, eyes wide. And again.

The other man scrambles out of the passenger side, but he doesn't come any closer. He's too scared. I want to laugh. People are emerging from their houses.

Kyk die Tinkerbell. She's gonna moer him.

Arms grip me from behind, stilling me. The pipe is prised from my fingers.

'Let it go, Savannah.' The voice is gentle. Solly.

I'm trembling now. And embarrassed. Aunties have come outside. Small pieces of broken glass are trapped in my skirt. The skin on my inside wrist is red and mottled, even though I don't remember hurting it.

'The police are coming,' a woman says.

Bug-Face revs the car hard when he hears that; no one is sticking around for the police. His buddy jumps in.

'You'll pay damages,' Bug-Face shouts, jabbing a finger. 'Burns Road – you'd better bring the money.'

'I'll come,' Solly says to Bug-Face. 'Tomorrow.'

Their tyres screech as they drive away, burning rubber.

Walking home, Solly talks to me the whole time – about the shop, my exam the next day, if I'll resume dancing in the new year.

4

'Has Kim set her wedding date yet?' he asks, and I am so deflated that even this distant disaster, my mother marrying Quinton, doesn't make my stomach knot with anxiety.

The duiwels are quiet. They've had their feed, and now they rest.

The fear hits me later that night. After I've endured my mother's worried outburst, then her frightened silence. After I watched her seek comfort in Quinton's arms, barely able to look at me. He stroked Kim's slim shoulders, eyes on me, offering to take the money next door to Solly.

Lying in bed, in the quietest hours, I wonder if Kim ever allows herself to think: *My daughter is a monster. My daughter is cursed.*

There's a story that's been handed down the generations in my family. The story of a curse. The story of a woman so wronged that she burned with anger until it destroyed everything. The story of Hella, my ancestor, whose anger was passed down from mother to daughter.

I turn on to my side, rest my cheek on a cool spot of the pillow. In the glow of the outside light, the mottling on my wrist appears an orange red.

Hella had been enslaved, forced to work for a cruel family. Her anger grew until one day, it exploded out of her.

Hella cursed them.

You will die before you have fully lived.

She cursed them for every lash of the whip, every slap, every cruel word.

My anger will follow you.

She cursed the enslaver for his assault on her body, and his wife for looking the other way.

My anger will destroy you.

She cursed their ancestors, their children, the children of their line yet to be born.

You, your children, and your children's children. Until my rage burns out.

In the struggle, a fire had started. During the chaos, Hella fled, and around her the world burned.

She did not know she had his child growing inside her.

I think of Hella, running across hard earth, the dark night lit by the fire behind her. Running until she felt her heart would burst.

This story lives in my bones.

2

OLD WOMAN

Quinton drives with one hand on the steering wheel, the other on Kim's thigh. I want to slap it away, like an annoying fly.

We're heading away from the mountain, towards the Cape Flats. We drive through residential streets where tidy houses are fortified with burglar bars and barbed wire, through run-down roads where the shops badly need a lick of paint. People gather outside a church, hats and best dresses lifting in the wind. In the distance is a rise of council flats. I know these roads well, I've been coming this way for as long as I can remember.

Quinton parks on the road outside Minnie's house, a small rectangle with thick black bars on every window. The aunties, six women who have loved me my whole life, spill on to the stoep. This is the first time we're seeing them all together after Kim and Quinton announced their engagement weeks ago.

'They're going to fuss,' Quinton says. His lips are quirked in amusement.

'Oh yes they will.' Kim unclicks her seat belt, laughing. 'And you're going to have to suck it up.'

He gives a good-natured groan and gets out. The aunties are bouncing with excitement as they surround Kim. *Show us the ring*, they clamour.

Auntie Nazeema wags a schoolteacher finger at Quinton.

'Took you long enough.'

They've only known each other a year, I want to scream from the back seat.

'I wasn't sure she'd have me,' he says. 'I'm a lucky man.'

Hanging back, I let the happy couple go ahead. Then I scoop up the salad from the back seat and follow.

I'm grabbed before I reach the front door.

'Too skinny,' Auntie Chantie declares. 'It's all that dancing. You must eat.'

'Such thick hair.' Auntie Dotty tucks a lock behind my ear but it immediately springs out. My hair is more curly than wavy today. It's like the sea, changeable. Some days the long, thick weight of it pulls the waves straight, and then on others it twists into a semblance of curls. Kim likes to think it reflects my mood: straight when I'm calm, curling when the tempest inside stirs. But it was straight as a pin the day I beat up that car, so her theory doesn't hold.

'You've been eating too much chocolate, I can tell by your skin,' says Auntie Glynis.

Tietie pulls me into her arms, saying 'Pretty girl' into my hair.

I'm used to this, the customary dissection of my body. It's their way of showing me love, this circle of women, with their neatly pressed dresses and pink lipstick and recipes.

In the living room, a table is spread with food. There's always too much food at Minnie's. Auntie Chantie takes the salad from me and gives me a sly look. 'When you bringing your boyfriend, hey?'

'Don't have a boyfriend, Auntie Chantie.'

'Well, chop-chop then. You don't want to be left on the shelf.'

'I'm seventeen!'

'It's different for young women these days, Chantal. These modern girls, they don't need a man,' Auntie Dotty chides her, placing a tray of bread on the table. 'They just take what they want and put them out the door the next morning. Isn't that right, Savannah?'

'Exactly right.' I can't hide a laugh.

Auntie Chantie looks scandalised. And intrigued.

'A lady never tells.' Auntie Dotty flips her hair. She's worn it the same way since she was a beauty queen decades ago: long and extremely straightened.

'Who said I'm a lady?' I snatch a piece of bread from the table and Auntie Chantie smacks my offending hand while Auntie Dotty shrieks with laughter.

She stops abruptly. They're both looking at the red spots on my wrist. The red mottling that appeared the day I smashed up the car hasn't gone away. It sits beneath the surface, like damaged blood vessels.

'What's that, sweetie?' Auntie Dotty says.

'Just a rash.' I press my arm against my sundress.

They glance at each other. I know what they're thinking. It's the curse, making itself known.

When it comes to the curse, the aunties are divided. Auntie Glynis is undecided, but Kim, Tietie and Auntie Nazeema don't believe.

'You want to know why I'm angry?' Tietie likes to say. 'Look out the window.' She rarely elaborates, but I've heard enough to know she means 'the system'. The system that hasn't delivered housing, or addressed the high rate of femicide, or stopped corruption. And, further back, the system that divided people by race, elevating white to the detriment of everyone else. Apartheid ended before I was born, but the damage persists.

Kim says that by believing in the curse, we make it true. Women in our family have always been prone to outbursts of rage. Tietie served maggots in her cheating husband's rice and bredie. Auntie Glynis slashed Uncle Lester's tyres after he gambled his wages. They're not cursed, Kim says; they just have tempers.

But then there are the rare few whose lives are claimed by the curse. Hella's girls, whose fury turns their blood to poison. Kim finds this harder to explain.

My grandmother, Ma Stella, was one of Hella's girls. Cross and tired, she'd once sat on a 'whites only' bench. It took three men to drag her off, scratching and hissing like a cat. She died from a sudden brain haemorrhage at twenty-nine years old, and Minnie, her unmarried sister, cared for Kim and Freda as if they were her own.

Freda, the older daughter, was one of Hella's too. Family lore says that Freda was fearsome. A shrew, a harridan. Wild, wilful and sharp-tongued, she ran through a glass door in the middle of a screaming argument.

I remember Freda as the woman who loved me completely. When Kim found herself pregnant at sixteen, the aunties brought food and wisdom and hand-me-downs. But it was Freda who looked after me, so that Kim could finish school and train as a librarian. In those days, I had two mothers.

It was Freda whose bed I sought in the middle of the night, when nightmares tossed me out of my own. As a child, I was prone to loud, furious meltdowns, and Freda would hold my rigid body, whispering, 'Remember, Savannah, fear and anger are kin. And sometimes one comes when the other's been called.' She would wrap me in her arms and the scent of her perfume was my haven.

One April evening, during a bad tantrum, she slipped a cheap silver chain around my neck. On it hung her rose-gold ring with its jewelled star; the ring she wore every day. 'When it gets too much, touch this star and know that I am always with you.' Then we went outside to watch the shooting stars, just the two of us.

The next night, Freda lost control of her car on the highway. Her life ended when she was twenty-seven years old.

Because here's the thing about Hella's girls: they always die before they've fully lived. And the angrier they are, the younger they die.

When Freda died, my world bottomed out. And it's never been put right. I wear the ring with its shining star on my pointer finger every day.

In the cramped kitchen, I find Minnie alone, washing dishes in the sink.

'How you, my girl?' Minnie asks me. She holds out sudsy arms as she searches my face. Her hair is cut short, and her face is speckled with sunspots. 'Those boys trouble you again? The ones who pointed a gun at you?'

'No, Ma Minnie. And they didn't point a gun at me.'

She gives me a look: *Don't think you can hide from me.* 'Go on out, the boys are by the pool.'

Outside, my older cousins are actually *in* the water. Three young girl cousins drive tiny cars through their Lego town, their dolls tossed face down on the cement. More aunties are gathered under the awning on the patio. There are some in headscarves, my Muslim cousins who stop me to ask about my plans for next year. There are two aunties who passed as white during the apartheid years, and then a handful who aren't blood at all.

The men are gathered around the half-barrel, lighting the fire. At the centre of them is Quinton, talking loudly, gesturing. Showing off.

'Savannah!' The guys yell my name like a war cry. I go over to the small pool and they splash water on my sundress and leather sandals.

12

'You're going to regret that,' I say.

'Yeah, what you gonna do?' Harrison splashes me again.

'She'll bash our heads in with a metal pipe.' Donley holds up his hands, pretending to shield himself from me.

Harrison sees me wince.

'Wow, Donno, you can be a real tit sometimes.' Harrison smacks the back of his head.

'I'm going to change,' I say.

I take my time putting on my swimming costume in the back bathroom.

When I leave, I walk past the slightly ajar door to Minnie's bedroom and hear whispers.

'She has them, Kim,' Auntie Glynis hisses. 'The marks. You can't ignore *that*.'

'Enough.' Kim sounds tired. Like this conversation has been going on too long.

'What will it take to make you see?' Auntie Chantie says. 'That boy needed stitches from the glass. Savannah is one of Hella's. Just like Freda, and Stella.'

'The curse isn't real, for goodness sake,' Kim says. 'I won't tell her she's doomed at seventeen.'

'It was in her last months,' Auntie Chantie says, 'that Freda's marks came.'

No one says anything for a moment. I look at my wrist, at the deep red spots. Nearly a week, and they haven't faded.

'It's just a rash,' says Kim at last. Another pause. 'And even if it's not, what can I do about it?'

'There are people who know about these things,' Auntie Dotty says.

'Savannah,' Harrison says loudly from the opposite end of the passage, and a hush falls inside the room. He's olive-skinned, with curly hair, a wide nose and strong jaw. He has laughing eyes and his mouth is always slightly upturned, as if ready for fun. But now a shadow crosses his face. 'What are you doing?'

I walk away from the door. 'Eavesdropping. You interrupted.'

'They talking about you?' Harrison says, as I reach him. 'Because in case you were wondering, there is no curse. You need to be careful, though. Those guys could have—'

'Harrison, your mom said something just now,' I interrupt him. 'About people who *know about these things*. What does that mean?'

'You know. People *met die helm gebore*. Born with the second sight. They're open to …' He waves a hand. 'The other side. The supernatural.'

'They can fix curses?'

'Savannah.' He shakes his head. 'Don't do this to yourself, man.'

'Later, *Uncle* Harrison.'

I walk off, ignoring his tirade about being only three years older than me, not to mention better looking, so please not to call him that, thank you.

It's later, much later. I'm floating on a pink doughnut in the pool. As I float, the evening grows dark. I feel it inside me too,

14

something shadowed. Stirring. Slow and sure and biding its time.

The boys have disappeared to watch a match on TV and the smell of charred meat still fills the air. Barbed wire curls on top of the back fence. It feels like the surrounding houses are crowding in. Far above are the stars, which remind me of Freda. There, but distant. Always out of reach.

I think of Freda's face turned up to the night sky, her finger tracing patterns as she taught me the constellations. I see Taurus, then search for the Southern Cross, Freda's favourite. The Four Sisters, she'd called it, telling me the names of the four stars: the Jackal, the red star on top; the Arrow and the Worm at each side; and at the bottom, the Claw, the brightest of them all. The names of witches who'd once lived in the Cape.

Long ago, Freda would say, when there was still magic in the world, four girls were born on the night of the falling stars. The stars shed some magic that night and drops of it fell into the babies' eyes. They grew up to be powerful witches and when they died, they went back to the stars that had made them.

That scared me, the idea of witches in the night sky, but Freda would laugh. 'They won't hurt you. They're good witches. Except when they need to be bad.'

Good except when they need to be bad.

After a while, I notice Auntie Dotty watching me from the lounger. She has a colourful drink in hand, with a cocktail umbrella, and her high wedged sandals are studded with crystals.

'Coming in?' I call to her.

'You know how long this takes?' She makes a circle around her perfectly made-up face and immaculate hair. 'I'd have to be on fire first.'

Taking a last look at the sky, I ease off the doughnut and wade to the edge.

'You are so like Freda.' Auntie Dotty can't hide the sadness in her voice. 'She always had her face turned to the stars.'

'I was looking for the witches.' I pull myself out of the pool.

'I heard those stories from *my* aunties.' Auntie Dotty's red lips take a sip from the red-and-white straw. 'Proper church-going ladies all of them, but still they believed that seeing the Four Sisters was a good omen. That the witches would give them luck.'

'Funny that. My aunties are exactly the same.'

We both look at the sky.

'You're worried, aren't you?'

I nod. I'm dripping water on to the brickwork, suddenly chilled.

She considers me for a long moment, then puts down her drink. 'I have something for you, but you can't tell your mother.'

She tosses my towel to me, then lifts a book covered in pale pink, shimmery card from her lap and slips it inside the canvas bag where I stuffed my dress.

'What is it, Auntie Dotty?'

'Freda's notebook. All her research.'

'Research?'

She nods. 'Curses. Strange happenings. I found it in her

things a few years ago, when your mom was having a clear-out. Looks like she wanted to fix herself before she – well.'

'Freda believed in the curse.' I mean it as a question, but it comes out certain.

'She believed that something was happening to her. The marks appeared on her skin. She began to see things that weren't there. She remembered things that couldn't have happened.'

Dotty stops abruptly when she sees the look on my face. I've never told anyone about Freda and me running through the burning field.

'Kim won't like this.'

'She won't,' Auntie Dotty agrees, setting her empty glass beside her and getting to her feet. 'But I think you're looking for answers.'

She's right. But I hadn't expected them to come from Dotty, the youngest of my grandmother's sisters, the frivolous one, only interested in shopping, abhorring all serious talk.

She begins to walk back to the house.

'Do you believe in it?' I say, and she pauses, not looking at me.

'I want to help you, Savannah, in any way I can.' Then she calls over her shoulder. 'And for heaven's sake, wear a damn bikini. Nothing wrong with showing a bit of tit.'

3

QUEEN

Kim's late to pick me up. It's Harrison's birthday and I'm supposed to meet him at a park in Wynberg in five minutes. Instead, I'm on the low wall of the stoep, leg bouncing.

I've never been good at waiting.

On my lap is Freda's notebook. Every time I pick it up, fear collects in my chest and I think, *Later, I'll do this later.* Today was the day – exams over, no more excuses – but the cover remains closed.

Solly opens the gate next door, home from his shift at the shop. He lifts a hand in greeting, ignores my outfit. After living next door for years, nothing surprises him any more.

'Where's my sugar?' I give him my best smile. Solly reaches in his pocket and pulls out a bag of Skittles, tossing it over the Cape honeysuckle.

'It's a drug, Savannah, a drug.' Shaking his head, he disappears inside. Through the open door, I hear the excited chatter of his toddler daughter, the laughter of his wife and his brother.

I tear the bag of Skittles, knowing sugar is the last thing I need when I'm like this. Popping a red one in my mouth, I open the book.

Seeing her handwriting on the first page makes me pause. *Freda Visagie.* A lump forms in my throat as I imagine her at our old kitchen table, writing these words. Her reddish-brown curls piled on top of her head, her brow knotted with concentration.

I pick out a few more red Skittles and turn the page. There's just one line, written over and over.

They became Sisters when their blood first touched.
They became Sisters when their blood first touched.
They became Sisters when their blood first touched.

Like punishment lines, it fills the page. The hard candy is sweet and sharp in my mouth.

'I'm so sorry, honey-bun,' Kim calls from the road, slamming her car door shut. She is radiant in smart trousers and a violet blouse, and her hair is swishy after her blow-dry. Her eyes are so dark they're nearly black. Her skin is a warmer brown from sunshine days out with Quinton. I don't have to like him to appreciate that he takes Kim to new places, and it's been good for her.

'The traffic was terrible. You ready?'

'Just a sec.' I dash back to my room and put the notebook on a shelf. I text Harrison to say I'm on the way.

'You sure you want to wear that?' Kim runs her eyes over me as we get into the car.

I'm wearing elephant-print small shorts and a white tube

top. I've three skinny hair wraps threaded through my waves and I've touched my cheekbones with gold.

'Yup,' I say, clipping in my seat belt. 'How else am I going to pick up all the boys?'

'Savannah,' she warns.

'Relax, Kim. You know I dress for myself.' She's quiet. We don't argue about clothes so much these days, not since she started seeing Quinton.

It's slow going on the M3. Kim issues her usual instructions: one drink only, never from a stranger, no getting into a car with a drunk driver.

'Seriously, Savannah, call me or get an Uber.'

'No drunk drivers,' I say, trying not to roll my eyes. 'Do you think I'm stupid?'

'Just be careful.'

It was at a party that shy, careful sixteen-year-old Kim drank enough vodka to go with a boy called Paul into a quiet room, closing the door behind them.

They talked and talked that night. About what they wanted to do one day. See the Petrified Forest in the Namib Desert, cross a grassy plain with galloping giraffes, swim in a coral reef. Falling in love so deeply, so quickly, Kim had missed the boring details, like what school he went to, where he lived. What his last name was. Hours later, she woke to find Paul gone, disappeared into a city of Pauls with no surname. Leaving only the beginnings of me.

At the walled park, Kim pulls over to the side of the road, obviously holding back more words. I give her a cheerful wave.

Harrison is not outside. No surprise, since I'm forty minutes late. My earlier text is unread and my call doesn't connect. He must have run out of battery. Loskop, Auntie Dotty calls him. Scatterbrained. She says he would lose his head if it wasn't attached to his shoulders.

Around me, people cluster at the iron gates. My eyes widen with wonder.

Earlier this year, my drama class made a short film and I was the costume designer. The time spent sketching, making mood boards, finding the right textures, distressing fabrics, creating splendour, had been magic. For weeks, I'd been glowing.

This evening, I feel that same gleam. Like I'm about to step on to a full costume set. Sumptuously clad guests flash their tickets and walk through the gates. Their faces shine with delight. A poster with three large stars announces *CARNIVEIL* in circus lettering. *Expect the Unexpected!*

The unexpected. A thrill zings through me. *It's a spectacle*, Harrison had told me. *Music, street theatre, giant puppets.*

'The audience is part of the show, so leave your inhibitions at home,' he'd read from the leaflet, and waggled his eyebrows.

'Welcome to the Carniveil.' The woman behind the ticket office window wears a mass of peacock feathers in her hair and deep indigo eyeshadow.

'There should be a ticket for me. Savannah Visagie.' I give her Harrison's name too as she searches the box in front of her.

'I'm sorry. No Savannah or Harrison here.'

'He's inside.' She must see my face fall. 'Can I just go in and get my ticket? I'll come right back.'

21

'Can't, I'm afraid,' she sings, turning her smile to the group bustling behind me. 'Good evening, welcome to the Carniveil.'

Leaving the window, I try Harrison and groan out loud when the automated voice tells me again that my call can't connect.

Afrobeats pump behind the high wall, thrumming in my body. Through the trees, I glimpse bell tents and star-shaped lanterns. They draw me closer until, entranced, I'm right at the gates.

'Step aside, please.' A security guard gestures for me to make way for a couple with their shiny tickets.

I turn from the gate, and lean against the wall. My hand closes over my phone, but I resist the urge to call Harrison again. A car cruises past and a man leers out of the passenger window. The driver leans on the horn, and the men in the back seat cackle. I feel exposed, uncomfortable in my clothes. Maybe I should just go home.

Pushing off the wall, I look again through the gates at the dreamy white tents and soft white lights. A woman wearing black leather and springbok horns whispers to a man in brightly coloured robes and tribal markings. A juggler throws flaming torches. Sour frustration wedges in my throat.

Abruptly I step back, and into a woman. Stumbling, I grab her arm and she sucks in a breath.

'I'm sorry.' My hands fly up. 'Did I hurt you?'

She shakes her head, her eyes narrowing as she looks at me.

'Let's go in,' her friends call, but she ignores them.

'Have we met?' she says.

'No.' This isn't a woman anyone would forget.

22

She's magnetic, striking. Her large eyes are shadowed with shimmering silver. Her face is heart-shaped and while her russet-brown skin is smooth and radiant, she carries herself with the gravity of an older woman. She wears her silver braids half up, half down and her long ivory dress has a black pattern at the hem. The air crackles as she looks at me. I'm not sure if she's annoyed, or what it is that makes her stare so intently.

'Claw,' a man calls. 'We're late.'

'Coming.' She holds up a hand.

'Sorry,' I say again, awkward at her scrutiny.

'You not going in?' Her brow is furrowed, and I realise she's concerned. It will be dark before long and I am alone.

'My ticket's inside. They'll come out for me.' When Harrison realises the time.

She gives me a slow nod, then turns to join her friends, glancing back once.

They're enchanting, their clothes an explosion of colour, of texture and print. They are bold and glamorous. I can't stop looking. As they near the iron gates, a glossy square of cardboard flutters to the ground.

I go to pick it up. It's a ticket, emblazoned with a glittering silver talon.

'You dropped something,' I call, but they don't turn.

'No ticket, no entry,' the man at the gate says to Claw.

'Even me?' She has a quiet authority. Inside the gates, a man in a suit with an earpiece hurries along the tree-lined lane.

'Claw, of course. Please, go right in.'

They sweep through the gates and I'm left holding Claw's

ticket. It glints as I turn it in my hand. There's a name on the back: *Khetiwe Ntlali. Access all areas.*

It's worth a shot. Holding myself tall, I walk to the gate and hand over the ticket.

'Welcome to the Carniveil,' the gatekeeper says, and his white-gloved hand sweeps me inside.

Lanterns float above the shaded path. Awed, I take in the savage colour. A tapestry of things happens around me: puppet shows, dancing, a trapeze act. A guy winks at me and I realise I'm beaming, almost giggling, with heady joy.

'Tea?' A Mad Hatter appears beside me. With a flick of his wrist, he's holding a bunch of flowers.

'Oh,' I say. 'Wow.'

He takes a red zinnia and, bowing, he gives it to me.

Putting the flower in my hair, I wander between trees, scanning bars lit by star-shaped lanterns. In a corner, a DJ mixes Amapiano and the dancing crowd whoops when 'Amanikiniki' starts up.

I gawk at a man on stilts wearing a fox head, and a fairy with a green face and pink feather wings. I marvel at people wearing ball gowns made of Shweshwe fabric, suits from kente cloth, tribal dress reimagined in patent leather. Dresses are handwoven, embroidered, beaded, and tulle is matched with leather, silk with vinyl.

My phone rings with a number I don't recognise. It's Harrison.

'Sorry, Savannah.' He's merry. 'I didn't realise I was out of battery.'

I try not to sigh. 'Where are you?'

'I'm in a bar. With a devil and an angel.'

'You're going to have to be more specific.'

'We walked through a hedge, passed some mushrooms. Oh, there was a tall fox.'

Ahead, I see a clearing filled with giant papier mâché mushrooms.

'I'll find you.' I end the call.

Another fox on stilts turns to watch me as I step into the clearing, but there's no bar.

Then I see the woman with the silver braids emerging from a starlit aisle. Claw. She skirts the back of a crowd, moving with purpose towards a dimly lit cluster of trees. *Access all areas.* Wherever she's going is where the best party will be. And that's where I'll find Harrison.

I follow. The trees give way to a narrow, hedged path.

Two young women dressed in brown leather vests and leggings are stationed on either side of the entrance.

'Restricted area.'

I hold up the *Access all areas* ticket, with its shining talon.

I step into the hedged path. These are real plants with branches that reach up, roots that sink into the earth. I've been to this park dozens of times, and I've never seen this before.

It's never been here before.

I hesitate, studying the tops of the trees against the sky. Twigs reach out like skeletal hands.

You're being silly, I tell myself, and walk on. I walk away from light and noise.

That is when I realise that I am not alone.

4

SHADOW

'Hey, wait up.'

I turn back to see a stranger, not much older than me, slipping into the hedged path.

'My friend here,' the stranger gestures to me, 'has my ticket.' He smiles at the gatekeepers, smooth and charming. It's a game to him, I realise. He knows he's chancing, and that's why it's fun.

The gatekeepers glance at each other, one blushing. They're obviously not averse to a bit of eye candy.

'He with you?'

The stranger watches me, amused. The word is at the tip of my tongue: *No.*

But I stop myself. Why not let him in? After all, I'm sneaking in too. I nod and they turn away.

As he steps forward, his lips curve into a broader smile.

'Your ticket?' I put my hands on my hips and raise an eyebrow.

He looks at me with dancing eyes. 'Well, it's not yours, is it?'

I'm on thin ice here, so I say nothing. In the fading daylight, I study the stranger. He has strong features, tawny-gold skin and an athletic build. A white vest and an unbuttoned plaid shirt.

There's something else though, something elusive, that makes me want to turn to him. Faraway laughter and singing from the party we've left drifts over us.

'Thanks, I owe you.' His voice is low, American perhaps, and filled with mirth. Then he passes, continuing down the narrow path and leaving me behind.

'Not so fast, stranger.' I stalk ahead, overtaking him. I give him my under-the-lashes look, the one I keep for boys I like. He follows, watching me with amused eyes. Interested eyes.

'How do you intend to repay me?' My voice sparkles with invitation. What can I say? I studied at the Auntie Dotty School of Flirting.

'I could buy you a drink?' He walks behind me. The narrow path feels closer, the two of us enclosed by trees.

I give him a gracious nod but on the inside I'm grinning like a fool.

'Is that why you followed me?'

Behind us, the sound of the party grows distant. Inside me, caution rises.

'I followed you,' he says with mischief, 'because this is a restricted area, and I like to go where I'm not allowed.'

I smile, continuing down the path. It's longer than expected, with several sharp turns. Like walking in a maze, lit by the stars above. We're moving away from Carniveil. Away from the crowd. Walking into silence.

There are no more bursts of laughter from behind us, no more drunken singing. Just the rustle of leaves as we push on.

'Where are we?' I say, trepidation creeping into my voice. Kim would be so cross that I wandered off. I didn't realise we'd be so alone.

'I could go first, check for monsters?'

'I don't need boys to protect me,' I say loftily, and stride forward. Besides, who says the monsters are ahead?

Then I hear hushed voices. The faint beat of a drum. I walk a little faster. The stranger doesn't close the gap between us and I like him more for it. The path turns and in the distance is the orange glow of firelit lamps. The hum grows more distinct.

'Hand to hand, heart to heart.'

The words are murmured, an echo bouncing off trees in a secluded forest.

'They became Sisters when their blood first touched.'

Cold washes over me.

That line, over and over, in Freda's notebook.

Why are these voices chanting it? What does it mean? How did Freda know these words? Where are they from?

'Hunter, mother, lady, healer.

As Sisters, they united the children of the stars.'

I step into a clearing, surrounded by trees and a large pond. The water is like glass, smooth and shining. The clearing is filled with people clustered around small fires in cast-iron bowls. On their foreheads and arms, in white face paint, is a pattern of lines and stars. No one turns to look at us.

Stepping forward, I have an acute sense that I am intruding. That I don't belong here. Anxiety hooks its claws into my heart: *Go back to the party now, Savannah, go back now.*

But those words in Freda's journal. I want to know what they mean.

I glance behind me and see my disquiet reflected in the stranger's face. His eyes are steel, the alertness of his body tells me he's wary. *See any monsters?* I want to say, but I can't summon our earlier playfulness.

Between the knots of people is a single building, a tall, imposing rotunda with a domed roof. It has no walls, just thick pillars made of gleaming white stone, as if it were woven from starlight.

'The power that burned within drew them together.'

The air smells of herbs. No one notices me as I walk between them. All eyes are on the white stone building.

Within the pillars is a massive open brazier and three large chairs made of intricately carved wood. On the chairs are three women wearing headdresses of bone, metal and flowers. Firelight dances on their skin.

An unwelcome, dreamlike feeling settles upon me. I feel like I have stepped into a false memory and it makes me a little sick.

'They live on in the Constellation.

Lighting up the southern skies.

The Claw, the Arrow, the Worm, the Jackal.'

The three women in the temple stand. They hold tall, carved staffs in their jewelled hands. On their shoulders are heavy-looking robes made of stiff leather. Every face is turned up to look at them.

'The Jackal betrayed her Sisters
and crossed the Veil.'

I am a balloon released, drifting up, up and away. I look for the stranger, but he's nowhere to be seen.

'We reject magic from behind the Veil.
We reject the magic of the Jackal's children,
the veilwitches who clamour in the darkness.'

One of the three women steps forward and everyone falls silent. I recognise the ivory dress and the silver braids. It's Claw.

On her left is an older woman, short with rounded shoulders. The woman on the right is red-cheeked and stocky.

'We stand at the threshold of the summer prowling season.' Claw's voice is slow and melodic.

People around me mutter and hiss, making clear their distaste. Their fear.

'In the coming weeks,' the older woman says, 'the children of the Jackal will try to steal your magic. First magic, then your life force. We will stop them.' She drops dried herbs tied with twine in the brazier. 'This week, we Daughters forge protection for each one of our witches.'

'Do not be afraid.' The stocky woman feeds the fire with bones. 'We will protect you against veilwitches on the prowl.'

The women chant, their voices weaving in and out in an unearthly song, soothing and stirring. The audience is transfixed. I am transfixed.

Claw breaks away first. She holds a torch to the fire, drawing flame.

We watch as she glides down the wide steps, every inch a queen. In one hand is her staff, in the other, the burning torch. There's a faint smile on her face that promises mischief. She looks people in the eye. I feel the rush of love and adoration towards her. She winks at the woman beside me as she passes.

Claw stops at a second wide brazier in line with the one in the temple. It lights with an unexpected surge of flame, the heat warming my face.

'Children of the stars and shadows, I am the Claw.' She holds her hand out to the brazier. 'With the Worm –' she gestures to the older woman – 'and the Arrow –' a nod to the stocky woman – 'we have turned fire to starflame. It will help you resist the prowling.'

The Claw, the Worm and the Arrow. The names of the stars, the Four Sisters, in the stories Freda told me. Then where is the fourth, the Jackal?

The Claw smiles. 'Just don't go and pick fights, neh? They can still kill you.' There's laughter from the crowd which quiets when she calls. 'Zenande, will you try the starflame?'

A woman from the crowd approaches the brazier. She drops to her knees, staring into the fire. Claw stamps down her staff. Zenande raises her hands, holding them near the flame. Claw stamps the staff again.

And Zenande plunges her hands into the flames.

A gasp escapes my open mouth.

31

'This starflame is your armour.' Claw's words ring across the clearing.

The fire roars; the dancing flames lick Zenande's wrists, tease her arms, but she does not recoil.

Claw stamps the staff again and Zenande pulls back and holds up her hands.

They are completely unharmed.

A happy cry comes from behind me and the crowd ululates and cheers. Claw raises her arms and cries again, 'This starflame is your armour.'

She is triumphant, her face turned to the stars. The crowd chants her name: 'Claw, Claw, Claw.' Drumbeats thrum through the ground, and strings, horns and shaking instruments chase through the air. Around us, people sing, dancing towards the brazier, where they wait their turn.

Another woman kneels before the brazier. Claw's staff hits the ground. With a wild scream, she thrusts her hands into the fire.

The music grows louder, the dancing faster and more frenzied. Arms reach up to the sky, feet stamp the earth. Hands clasp mine and I'm drawn into a group of dancing women. I can't resist the pull; I never can with dance.

I see him then, the stranger. He's standing at the edge, watching.

I lift a hand, beckon him to dance with me. I like how his hair falls into his eyes. I like the look of his shoulders and arms in his vest. I like the shape of him as he stands there. He looks solid, grounded, the only still figure in a sea of movement.

He stares at me, matching my boldness with his own. I thought there'd been a spark earlier, but there's no smile now. There's nothing friendly about how he looks at me this time.

It is wrong, staring at him like this. A good girl would avert her eyes.

Neither of us looks away.

A girl bumps my shoulder as she dances by. She doesn't seem to notice, just raises her arms and laughs gleefully. Her friend waves and calls, 'Ekskuus,' and then the stranger is no longer there.

Instead, a scream: 'My hands! They're burning!'

The dancing falters; the music trails off.

The second scream comes immediately, a long agonised cry.

I'm too far away to see what is happening. I hear murmurs of horror, see hands clasped against mouths. Terror runs through the crowd.

'They're here.'

'How did they get in?'

There is shouting now, wailing, bodies pushing towards the brazier. A woman on the ground howls in agony.

I'm trying to make my way out when I'm stopped.

'Who are you?' The man's arms are folded as he towers over me, his face set with fury. 'I don't recognise you.'

He leans forward with hot menace. 'You're coming with me.' He yanks my wrist and pulls, my sandals slipping on the grass.

'Let me go,' I hiss.

That's when I see it. It's not anger on his face. He's afraid. He snarls at me, tightening his hand around my forearm. Fear and anger are kin.

I'm struggling to break his grip when I'm bumped from the side and drenched in cold, sour-smelling beer. It's on my shoulders, my top, and down my legs. Cursing, the angry man releases me; the beer has spilt on him too.

It's him, the guy from the hedge. I glare at him. 'What the hell?'

But while the angry man is distracted, the stranger, quick as a flash, whirls me around and sweeps us through the crowd.

'You should get out of here.' The stranger's mouth is grim.

'Maybe I'm not ready to leave.' I was born contrary.

He sighs, picking up pace. 'Things are going to get ugly.'

'Is that a threat?'

'A prediction.' We're at the entrance to the hedged path.

'It's my choice.' I pull away from him. I'm shivering, and my clothes are damp from the beer.

'Staying would be a bad choice.' He pulls off his unbuttoned shirt and slips one sleeve over my arm, his fingers brushing my shoulders. 'You don't want to get caught in a stampede.' The other sleeve goes on. 'Or a fight.'

I look up at him, trying to figure out how he can be both harsh and gentle at the same time.

'Go,' he urges, nodding at the path. Without another word, he turns and walks away.

Claw, her voice rough with anger and grief, calls from the temple: 'The veilwitches will pay for what they have done tonight.'

34

I hesitate. I've found something here and I'm not ready to let it go.

They became Sisters when their blood first touched.

Before I can make my choice, three large spotlights turn on, illuminating the pond. A line of eight people on stilts wearing large fox heads stand in the water.

I am in a place that can't exist. I've seen hands plunged into fire and emerge unscathed. And now, fox people rise out of the water.

They wait until there is silence. Then they speak in unison and the sound is robotic and distorted.

'For nearly three hundred years the Market has been run by the Claw, the Worm and the Arrow. They have ruled without the Jackal.'

They step forward together.

'This will change. A new Jackal has come.'

I see now that they're not foxes. The pointed ears, the slanted eyes, shaded cheeks, the hint of a smile.

'There is no Jackal,' someone yells. 'Not since she betrayed her Sisters and turned to veiled magic centuries ago.'

The jackals stare unmoving at the temple, where the three women stand.

'We are here to give you a chance, Claw. Will you welcome the Jackal as the Fourth Heir?'

'I will not,' Claw says, her voice loud and strong. 'The Market has been the beating heart of our community for hundreds of years. Veiled magic has no place with us.'

'Worm and Arrow, Daughters of the Stars, will you welcome the Jackal?'

'As Worm, I will not.' The older woman onstage folds her arms. Her voice is like gravel.

'Never,' Arrow shouts. 'The Nightmarket is yours – keep out of what is ours.'

'Then the Jackal will rule alone.'

Everything happens fast. A spotlight snaps on over a trapeze rig in the corner of the clearing. I turn with the rest of the crowd.

At the top of the rig, in the light, stands a figure wearing a leather robe and elaborate animal headdress. A creature of iron and fur and pointed teeth.

The Jackal.

My eyes are on her; every eye is. She raises her staff and points it towards the temple. As one, the braziers in the clearing flare.

The heat makes me step back.

'The stars will fall,' the jackals call. 'And when they do, the Jackal will rule the Nightmarket and the Market.'

There is a cry from the temple. I turn to see Claw, ripping off her leather robe.

'Get them out of me!' she screams, scratching at her skin. 'Get them out.'

'Claw!' someone yells.

Long streaks of blood are beginning to show on Claw's arms, chest and face as she tears at her skin. Her white dress is patched with red. Arrow holds her by the shoulders, but in her frenzy Claw is strong. 'Make it stop,' she sobs. 'Make it stop.'

She lifts her head and sees the brazier, the flame.

She tears herself from Arrow's grip and runs full tilt into it, flinging herself at the fire.

The air fills with cries as people rush towards Claw. And then the spotlights snap off and I can't see anything.

On the trapeze rig, the figure in the shadows turns its head. The face is a hungry darkness, just shape against shadow. Yet it looks right at me.

The distorted jackal voices speak from velvet black.

'Before the stars finish their fall, the Market will bow to the Jackal.'

I feel them moving towards me. First one, then a second menacing figure in the dark. Then a third, just about visible in the dim light.

My heart is wild. Panic tears through me and, clutching the stranger's shirt around me, I run.

5

DEAD MAN

It's after nine when I get home by Uber. Not even three hours have passed since I sat on the stoep eating red Skittles, but it feels like a lifetime.

I'm outside the front door when my phone rings.

'I'm getting worried about you,' Harrison says.

'Sorry.' I unlock the security gate. 'I couldn't find you.'

'You don't sound right. You OK?'

'Someone dumped a glass of beer on me. I'm soaked, so I came home.'

'Sorry, Savannah,' he says. 'I should have waited outside.'

'Not your fault, Uncle Harrison.'

'OK.' He doesn't sound convinced. 'Hey, the angel wants to take me to a club. Catch up tomorrow?'

Opening the door, I'm thinking about jackals on stilts. About the women inside the moonlit temple. Magic from behind the veil.

They became Sisters when their blood first touched.

Who were these people? Did Freda know them? Standing in the narrow passage, the evening is a half-remembered dream. Kim's voice carries from the kitchen and I try to shake off the strangeness.

It was all part of the Carniveil, I tell myself as I walk down the passage. An elaborate performance. They were all actors, and they're having drinks in a bar right now, laughing and flirting. The words are from a story, that's all. One of Freda's stories about witches who were stars.

'I think we should go for it,' Quinton says exuberantly. 'Live a little.'

'I don't know, Quinton.' Kim's voice is quiet. 'I never wanted a big wedding.'

'Big is beautiful.' I hear the soft release of a cork from a bottle. 'Big is bold, and the bold shall inherit the earth.'

Kim laughs. 'I'm sure it's the meek who inherit the earth.'

'Fine. Who wants the earth when you can have the stars?'

In the silence, I hear the wine glug from bottle to glass, and I am consumed with loathing.

'I shouldn't drink anything,' she says. The wine continues to pour into a second glass. I hope he chokes on it.

'You *think* you want a small wedding.' The glasses clink together. 'But you'll regret it. Come on, Kim. Let's throw a party we'll never forget. Invite everyone we know and then some. I want them all to see you in a moerse big dress. I want to dance with you to a corny love song while everyone watches. I want a massive cake with a tiny Kim and Quinton on top. I want the works.'

Even without seeing him, I know the expansive gestures that accompany his words. While Kim is hunched over the glass of wine she didn't want.

'Look, don't kill me,' he says. I can picture his boyish, bashful expression. 'There's a place past Kommetjie that looks incredible. They had a cancellation at the beginning of December, so ... so I made a provisional booking. Everything, the menu, music, cake, is lined up.'

December? I stiffen. That's just weeks away.

'Oh, Quinton.' Her voice is exasperated but indulgent. 'You did *what*?'

'You can walk down the beach on a red carpet. We can drink too much champagne and dance beneath the stars.'

'All the way out near Scarborough? I wouldn't want Minnie and the others driving that distance at night. They wouldn't like it.'

'It's not Minnie's wedding, now is it?'

'No,' Kim says. 'I suppose not.'

Kim hates being the centre of attention. She won't even have birthday parties. She's happiest blending in.

I sometimes wonder if it's because she was a pregnant schoolgirl. The endless staring and gossiping. The things they called her: *jintoe*, slut; *hoer*, loose. My father walked away, reputation intact. And hers was trashed. Auntie Glynis has warned me so many times: good girls keep their legs closed.

'I had to pay a deposit,' says Quinton. 'Twenty grand.'

40

'You shouldn't have paid the deposit without talking to me.' Her admonishment lacks conviction. 'But … I suppose I could take a look.'

'Right. No harm in that.'

I know how this will play out. In a few weeks, there will be a beach wedding with a red carpet, too much sparkling wine and dancing beneath the stars. A massive dress and corny love songs. Everything he wants.

And Kim will come to believe it was the wedding of her dreams. Because that's how it always works.

I go into the kitchen. They don't notice me at first. Kim's cradling her glass of wine, while Quinton has already chugged down half of his.

I concede he's objectively an attractive man: confident, well built, and with blue eyes that are striking against his golden-brown skin. He has vigour. The kind of man who demands your attention when he enters a room. Who can speak on anything in his private-school accent and sound like an authority. His light is so bright, it dazzles you. Kim lives in his shade.

'Savannah.' Kim sees me at the door. 'I didn't hear you come in, sweetie. You're back early.' She must smell the beer on me then, because she frowns.

'Someone spilt a whole pint on me.'

'Oh, that's unlucky.' Kim's mouth turns down in sympathy. 'Did you have fun, though? Is that Harrison's shirt?'

'It was like nothing I've ever experienced.'

'I want to hear all about it.' Kim beams. 'You hungry? Quinton's cooking.'

41

The kitchen counter is full of Quinton's cooking: mushrooms, garlic, butter, parsley. Raw steaks sit in watery blood and easy jazz fills the kitchen.

'Did I hear you talking about the wedding?' I shouldn't bring this up, not while I'm in this mood.

'We were.' Kim looks troubled.

'And?'

'There's something your mother wants to ask you,' Quinton says, then stops. I see the quick warning look Kim gives him.

'We'll talk later.' She stands up. 'Right now, I'm hot and sticky and need a shower. You should take one too, Savannah.'

She touches my arm as she walks by me.

Then Quinton and I are alone. It's physical, how much I resent him. I resent his bare feet on our kitchen floor. I resent his slightly crooked second toe, his hairy thighs in his shorts. The way he's crowded all the kitchen surfaces with his food, his keys, his wine. I hate how he's taken my home and made it his. Even though he doesn't live here, he's always *here*. Evenings, if he's not working. Sleepovers at the weekend.

We keep a fragile peace by not communicating much with each other. Quinton turns up the music, obviously not interested in talking to me while he chops garlic with fast, expert movements. I suspect it irks him that I'm immune to his charm.

'She doesn't want a big wedding.' I'm too loud. I hadn't meant to say that. But it's out now.

Quinton, large knife in hand, leans against the cabinets, watching me.

'She wants you to be her bridesmaid,' he says.

'I don't want to.' I sound petulant. Childish.

'Nor do I.'

'Why are you making her have this fancy big wedding? Do you even know the woman you're marrying?'

He puts the knife down with a precision that's frightening.

'Do you?' His control doesn't flag. 'Do you really know your mother as well as you think?'

'Of course I do.' I twist Freda's star ring.

'See, I think it's convenient for you to keep her in a neat, little box. To stop her exploring what else she could be. Tiptoeing around you, afraid to do anything that might set you off.'

'That's not true.' My jaw is clenched, teeth gritted.

What would Kim have been if it wasn't for me? Would she have travelled? Would she have seen giraffes gallop on a grassy plain?

He takes a step towards me. 'You hate that you're no longer the centre of her world. That's why you throw these little tantrums. For attention.'

The tension between us has always been subterranean. A leak, hidden poison. Now he's made it real.

'Smashing up a car, Savannah, that's the most hysterical thing you've done yet. But it worked, didn't it? It got your mother's attention.'

I could tell him that the word *hysterical* is often used as a misogynist smear to dismiss women. How it originates from the Greek for *uterus*, arising from the belief that women's wombs were moving around inside them, causing an excess of emotion and unstable behaviour. And I could tell him that maybe 'hysterical' women are simply pissed off at constantly getting the kak end of the stick.

Instead, I hiss, 'I know Kim better than you do.'

'Really?' There's a slight smile playing on his lips. It amuses him that I'm losing control. 'Do you know who paid the damages, Savannah? That guy's medical bill? The car repairs? I did. I fixed your mess. You fuck up, I pay for it.'

'I didn't ask you to.' The words explode out of me. I throw my hands into the air. 'I didn't ask for any of this.'

'Grow up, Savannah.' The disdain drips from his voice.

'I wish she'd never met you.' I'm shouting now, fury making me careless. 'You don't deserve her.'

Quinton's smirking at me, as if to say, *See? Hysterical.*

'And Kim doesn't deserve a daughter who manipulates her with hissy fits when things don't go her way.' He's louder now. 'Oh, wait, I forgot. You can't help it because you're *cursed.*' He sneers the last word.

It's too much. I need to get out of the kitchen.

He grabs my wrist. Hard. He holds it tight and it hurts. He speaks close to my ear.

'You will let your mother have the wedding she wants. You will wear a bridesmaid's dress, stand at her side, smile and behave yourself.'

I shake free from him and he steps back. I hold my wrist to my body. He blinks, like he's just realised what he's done.

'If you ever put your hands on my mother the way you just did there, you'll be sorry,' I tell him.

He goes back to the chopping board, calmly picks up the large knife. He holds it over the garlic. 'Yeah? What you going to do? Smash my car?'

I'm bubbling over then. Hot pot got too much in it.

'You're not good enough for her.' My voice is shaking. 'And *when* you hurt her, I promise you, I will hurt you back.'

'Savannah?' Kim's standing in the kitchen doorway, wearing only a towel. Her face is bare of make-up, and her hair is in a high, messy bun. She looks young, vulnerable. 'What's going on here?'

She looks from me to Quinton. I'm the one who's threatening violence. He's just there, chopping garlic.

'Nothing.' I'm deflated.

'Didn't sound like nothing to me.' Kim's voice is sharp.

'Everything's fine,' Quinton says. He goes to her, puts his hands on her shoulders. Fixing things like he always does. 'Savannah was just giving me a little pre-wedding warning.'

He kisses her forehead and then hands her the phone she left on the table.

'Looking for this?'

'How did you know?'

'You want your music. I know.'

I want to barf. Not in the way all kids mean it, when they see their parents getting romantic. I'm truly sickened at the sight of Quinton's hands on Kim's bare shoulders. The way he looks at her with utter adoration, like she's his delicate flower.

'Dinner will be ready soon,' he says warmly.

Quinton picks up the steaks from the counter. He smiles and it's obvious what he's thinking: this round to him.

I go to my room and sit on the edge of my bed. The red zinnia in my hair looks as wilted as I feel.

My eye falls on the framed photo of me and Freda on the bedside table. I pick it up and stare at my dead aunt, her arms tight around my eight-year-old body.

'I wish you were here,' I whisper.

Freda would know what to do. She would have seen through Quinton from the start.

In the photo, she's smiling, but her eyes are troubled. They seem to be looking right at me, and her words come to me suddenly: *Remember, Savannah, fear and anger are kin.*

Putting the picture down, I see something I'd never noticed before: on Freda's neck, the patch of angry red.

What were you afraid of, Freda?

I hear Quinton and Kim talking quietly as they pass my door. The deep sound of his chuckle. Letting out a low scream, I punch my pillow, hard.

Fear and anger, but there's something else too. Something new.

Sorrow.

I am overcome by a raw sadness. For the terrible things that have happened and the terrible things that are promised to come.

6

MASK

In our house are many self-help books. Except they're not really self-help books. They're *Savannah*-help books. Kim reads them not to work on herself, but to fix me.

I'd never been an easy child, but Kim handled my meltdowns in her calm, quiet way. Until the day five years ago, during a family party, when my then ninety-year-old great-aunt Bertha grabbed my shoulders with her gnarly fingers and whispered, 'Hella se kind.'

Hella's child.

The aunties paused their conversations. A tight-mouthed Kim pulled me out of Auntie Bertha's grip, saying there was no such thing as curses. The aunties took polite sips of their tea, avoiding Kim's eye. And that's when the Savannah-help books started.

An ardent believer in books, Kim is determined to cure me by reading. It's like she can ward off the scary dark things with pop psychology. She scribbles quotes on sticky notes, slaps them on surfaces around the house. Every day I find upbeat messages on doors, mirrors, the fridge.

This morning's fridge wisdom says: *What would you do if fear didn't hold you back?*

It's a good one. What would I do? My secret dream, if I didn't have curses and Quintons to contend with, is to be a costume designer. I haven't told anyone, not even Kim, who wants me to choose practical courses when I start my arts degree in three months.

I go off into a daydream and the next thing I know, Harrison's on the stoep, rattling the chunky steel security gate and yelling my name through the open front door.

'You're early.' I hurry to the gate, grabbing my bag from the living room, my phone, my ballerinas. Cool dude with his aviators. I roll my eyes at him.

'Early bird catches the moolah.'

Harrison continues obnoxiously rattling the gate even though I'm right there on the other side, fishing my key out of my bag.

'Stop, brat.' Which only makes him rattle it harder.

Harrison is a business student, but he also makes iron candlesticks that he sells at craft markets around the city. This summer, he's working two or three markets a week and I'm his sales assistant for the busy pre-Christmas period.

In the days since Carniveil, I've scoured the newspapers. A review declares it a *daring spectacle*. No mention of a performance gone wrong. If Claw really had been injured, it would have been in the news.

Doubt licks at the edge of my mind, but I push it away.

'So, tell me about your hot date with the angel,' I say once we're in the car.

Harrison just laughs and mimes zipping his lips shut.

'Sorry I was so useless.' He looks at me, sheepish. 'I missed you. Were you OK?'

I hesitate. 'I accidentally wandered into the VIP area.'

Harrison glances me. 'Accidentally? The VIP area was impenetrable. I know, I tried.'

'It was really strange, Harrison.' I don't mean to talk about it, but the words come pouring out. 'You remember that myth about the Four Sisters? Freda used to talk about it …'

'Vaguely.' Harrison prefers fact to story, the present to the past. 'Once upon a time there were four sisters who were witches. That one?'

They became Sisters when their blood first touched.

'Sisters through magic, not by birth.' I'm beginning to understand now what those words mean. But why did Freda write them in her notebook? How is it related to us being angry? 'When they died, they became stars.'

He indicates right. 'Good story, Savannah. Shame I'm not five years old.'

'There was, I don't know, I suppose it was a play? At Carniveil. Only this was different to Freda's story. In this one there were only three witches and then a fourth came … They said that the fourth would rule over everyone. That the other three would fall. *That* wasn't in the story Freda used to tell us.' I turn to him, expectant.

Harrison shrugs. 'So they took a bit of folklore and expanded on it.'

'I guess.' I see Claw leaping into the flames, hear her scream. It still makes me shudder inside. 'Harrison, I think I stumbled upon a cult. Everything was so strange. It really got under my skin.'

Harrison stops at a red light and turns to me. His expression is serious. 'Savannah, there's something I need to explain to you.'

'What?' I realise my hands are clasped tightly.

'There's this thing that happens sometimes. Sort of like a ritual. People put on costumes ...' Harrison's voice is hushed. 'And everyone gathers around to watch. Those in costumes, they, well, they pretend to be someone else. They make up stories which they tell the gathered crowd. To entertain them. It's called ... *theatre*.'

I whack him on the chest.

'Ouch.' He lays an open palm over his shirt. 'My heart.'

'You have no heart.' I nod at the green light. 'Drive on.'

Today's market is medium-sized, sheltered between a block of flats and a church in Claremont. It's not one of the posh markets with expensive cupcakes and exotic flowers, but it's smaller than the huge fairs where vendors sell knock-off handbags and deodorant.

Usually there is rowdy camaraderie, but today the mood is glum. Vendors keep their eyes down, ignoring Harrison's cheerful greetings.

Wheeling boxes on the hand truck, I search for our pitch. Afrobeats blast through a loudspeaker. People lay out their wares. Customers drink coffee, browse, chatter. Business is good, even this early.

Then why do so many vendors look miserable?

We find our stall. Harrison smiles at a woman sitting across, behind large folded squares of wax print fabric. She looks startled, like she's just woken from a bad dream. Opposite, a woman in a milkmaid costume and a blonde braid crown arranges cheese and organic fruit on her table.

It's only when I'm placing the smaller candlesticks on the table that I see the milkmaid is crying. She sees me watching, and turns her back.

'Harrison,' I say. 'How did you get the tickets to Carniveil?'

'You're not still on about that, are you?'

'Just curious.'

He eyes the display critically. 'I got them off Zenande.' Zenande? I've heard that name recently.

'Mama Daline's assistant. The psychic healer. Very friendly.'

I shake my head, smiling. Women are often very friendly with Harrison. Men too. Then I remember: the hands unburned in bright orange flame. Zenande.

A little after twelve, on my lunch break, I leave the stall in search of sugar and Zenande. I want to know more about that night. I want to know if Freda knew those people.

I wander past musical instruments, curios, masks and ceramics. One stall displays papaya, apricots and artichokes. Another sells boerewors rolls, and still another spicy chicken and injera. Clothes, textiles and fabric. Different languages, music and food. And somehow, in this city, it all fits together.

At the top of the path, I turn left and there, beneath a large wild olive tree, is a black tent-like structure taking up more than two plots. It is set apart from the other stalls. There's a poster tacked to the side.

MAMA DALINE
HEALER
Will cure any ailments.
Guided by the ancestors, Mama Daline sings over the bones.
Let her bone-song heal you today.

I remember what Auntie Dotty said. That there are *people who know things*. Could Mama Daline break my curse?

Either way, this must be where Zenande works. I step up to the entrance flap. I'm about to draw it back when I hear voices.

'… circles for hours,' a woman says impatiently, 'and getting nowhere. Claw might die. There is an axe over our heads and all we do is talk.'

The words send little shock waves through my body. Claw. So she *was* injured.

'What do you suggest we do, Arrow?' a second woman, older, gravel-voiced, says. 'Rush down to the Nightmarket with raised fists and get picked off one by one?'

The Nightmarket. I frown, trying to remember. Didn't the line of jackals say something about the Nightmarket?

But this isn't Carniveil. This is real.

52

'We need to act,' Arrow snaps. 'Even without Claw, we must continue armouring our people. We have to perform the star-flame ceremony tonight.'

'Prowling season started the minute they attacked Claw. Holding any kind of ceremony would be inviting the veil-witches to a feast.'

'Are you looking for something?' a voice behind me says. I turn to see a woman watching me with cold, searching eyes.

I swallow. 'I wanted to see Mama Daline.'

'Mama Daline isn't taking walk-ins today.' She has strong, bare shoulders, rich brown skin and her hair is coiled into buns. She's taller than me, and stands with her hands on her hips.

It's her, the woman who plunged her hands into flame. I glance down at them, and her skin is smooth and blemish free.

'Zenande, is that you?' a voice calls from inside, and a woman appears at the entrance of the tent. Her long, loose linen dress is creased from sitting. She has a halo of grey curls that fall to her ears, and her pale yellow-brown skin is pigmented at her cheekbones. I'd guess she's in her sixties, around Minnie's age. Her eyes are alert. This is a woman who doesn't miss much.

She is one of the three women from the moonlight temple. The Worm.

'Yes, Mama Daline,' Zenande says to her.

But it's me the older woman is staring at, her eyes wide. Soft as a breath, one word.

'You.'

7

BOWL

Even without the bone-and-flower wreath on her head, Mama Daline, the Worm, is quietly regal.

'So you've come looking for me.' She crosses her arms over her chest, like she's cold despite the warm day.

'Yes.' I have an uneasy apprehension that this woman has been expecting me. 'For a consultation.' I point to the sign, then dip my head with a small smile. 'Have we met?'

'In a manner of speaking.'

Mama Daline stares and stares, taking in every small part of me. After a long time, she gestures to the tent and says, 'Follow me.'

She watches me over her shoulder as we go inside. Zenande is a step behind.

It takes a moment for my eyes to adjust to the dim light. The smell is intense, smoke and burned herbs. In the centre is a small three-legged bowl where a fire has burned to glowing coals, and to the side, rows of animal bones. On a trestle table, three large shallow baskets hold hundreds of small brown bottles.

There's a third woman inside the tent. Fair with pink cheeks, she has kind Sunday-school-teacher eyes. I recognise her from the temple too, the Arrow. Today she's head to toe in activewear instead of leather robes, her brown hair in a high ponytail.

'We'll talk later.' Mama Daline gently ushers Arrow out of the tent.

'That's two fifty,' Zenande says to me. 'Pay now, extras not included.'

I can't afford this, I think as I unfold the notes. This will leave me short for the rest of the month. But Mama Daline stops me with a hand. 'This one is on the house.' I stuff my money in my purse, relieved but wary.

Zenande leaves and Mama Daline stands behind the fire bowl.

'Hello.' I sound nervous. 'I'm Savannah.'

'Do not give away your name so easily, meisiekind,' she chides.

'You seemed to recognise me,' I say. 'When we were outside.'

'I have seen you many times.' Mama Daline lifts a long bone from the row beside her. 'In my dreams. Many nights your face has troubled my sleep.'

'You've dreamed about me? Doing what?'

She holds the bone out, as if sizing it up against me, and frowns, putting it down in favour of another.

'In my dreams, you kill me.'

I recoil from her.

'Again and again, for many years. In a hundred different ways.' Mama Daline picks out a small animal skull. She weighs it in her hand, then changes it for a larger one. 'Sometimes a knife, sometimes a syringe. A cricket bat, a garrotte, a pillow. Often you hold my head underwater. Sometimes you kill me slowly, sometimes quickly and mercifully. But always you.'

The terrible words crawl out of her mouth and across the small space between us. They settle on my skin.

'I don't even know you.' I swallow. 'Why would I hurt you? I'd never hurt anyone.'

'You sound very sure.'

The thick haze in the room makes my head feel heavy, woollen. An image comes to me, of my hands around this woman's neck.

'Savannah,' Mama Daline says, and I blink. She's on the stool, across from me now. The bones lie on the ground between us. The coals in the fire bowl glow.

'You are not curious?' Mama Daline leans forward. 'About why you kill me?'

Obediently, through dry lips, I say, 'Why do I kill you?'

'Because of what is inside you, my dear.' She watches my reaction. 'Because of your curse.'

If I am being played, the game is a cruel one.

Mama Daline gestures to the bench. 'Sit down, meisiekind.'

I sink on to the low seat, feeling like I'm in a dream.

'I never met her,' Mama Daline says. 'The one before you. But I know she came to us, looking for help.'

'Freda?' I'm sitting bolt upright. 'Freda came here?'

'Freda came to the Worm who was before me. She tried to help your aunt. I'll explain if you want?' Mama Daline has both hands up, like she's soothing a spitting cat.

Taking a deep breath, I nod.

'When the curse was cast hundreds of years ago,' Mama Daline says, 'a fragment of the witch's magic was left inside it. That's how it always is with a blood curse.'

Blood curse does not sound good.

'As the curse was passed through the women in your family, so was this magic. Growing stronger with each new host.'

'Wait, you think the curse is real?' I interrupt. I should find it absurd, the idea of ancient magic passed down like some kind of warped inheritance. Instead, a warmth blossoms in my chest. A fierce, fleeting want.

'It's real and it won't end well,' Mama Daline warns knowingly. Her words are an unpleasant reminder of what happens to Hella's girls. 'It never does with blood curses.'

'Maybe this time it could.'

'But Savannah,' she says, 'you've been angrier lately, haven't you?' Those awful words are spoken so calmly, so reasonably. I feel like I am squeezed tight, a band around my ribs that presses too hard. 'You're finding it harder to keep control of yourself. This is what happens every time the magic stirs.'

The band presses tighter; my breaths are shallow. 'Because I am cursed to be angry?'

Mama Daline gives a short laugh and shakes her head. 'You're not cursed to be angry, Savannah.'

'But I thought …'

'You're cursed to die before your time. That is how your ancestor cursed the enslaver family.'

'Hella's girls are always angry,' I insist, 'because of the curse.'

'Many of us are angry.' Mama Daline raises one shoulder in a shrug. 'There are plenty of reasons why we should be.' She shakes her head, her curls shimmering in the dim light. 'Listen carefully to me. You're not cursed to be angry. But your anger is affected by the curse.'

Mama Daline gives me a Mona Lisa smile and reaches out one hand, palm up: 'As the descendant of the enslaver, you are cursed to die before your time.' Mama Daline holds out her other hand. 'But you also descend from the woman whose anger made the world burn, and Savannah, you are so very deeply connected to her.'

'Are you saying that when I get mad it's Hella's anger I'm channelling?'

'No.' Mama Daline is firm but gentle. 'Your anger, when you feel it, is yours and a valid reaction. The fragment of magic inside you binds you to your ancestor, and your anger holds echoes of hers. When you get angry, it reverberates with Hella's fury.'

Mama Daline's hands are still open in front of me. Like she's offering me something. The ancestor's rage, the enslaver's curse. One pill makes you larger, the other finishes you off.

Mama Daline continues, 'Anger can warn you when something is not right. It can be a powerful tool, but has to be wielded carefully and with precision. You have to control it, not have your anger control you.'

Maybe. Does it matter? I examine my shoes, the pale pink on the dull floor. I didn't come for the anger management lesson. I want Mama Daline to shake her bones and tell me what I need to do to make sure I don't die before my time.

'So I am connected to Hella and when I'm angry it cuts deep because of everything being messed up for centuries?' I try to direct the conversation back. I want a fix, not therapy. 'And there's magic trapped inside me?'

'That's right.' She sits back a little, a triumphant teacher who finally explained long division to a resistant child. 'This magic has been sleeping for years. It's stirring now, and when it wakes, it will search for a new host. The next angry girl in your family. Just as it did with your grandmother. Your aunt.'

I think about my girl cousins with their Lego and dolls, all of them still young and oblivious. My chest gets tight again.

'It's all changing now, isn't it?' Mama Daline says. 'It feels more intense, your anger? That's because as the magic rouses, your connection to Hella becomes stronger. Over the next few years –' there is apology in her eyes – 'or maybe only months, the magic will continue to stir until it fully wakes. This is death point.'

Death point. A piece of coal resettles, drawing my attention to the fire bowl. I'm relieved to stop looking into those eyes.

'This curse will kill you.'

'I know.' I always have.

'Unless …'

I look up sharply, a pulsing in my ears. 'Unless what?'

'Unless the Jackal gets to you first.'

Oh.

I remember the pure terror of Carniveil, my gaze locking on iron and fur and menace.

'Beware the veilwitches,' she breathes, 'for they will break you that the Jackal may feed. It is better to be killed by the curse than caught by the Jackal.' The older woman is grave. *They will break you, and so much worse*, her eyes are saying.

My hands are braced on my legs and I take a shaky breath. The curse will kill me or the Jackal will catch me. Two roads, both ending in darkness.

'But I can help you, Savannah.' Mama Daline's face is a small round moon, a distant light guiding me to safety. 'Just like the previous Worm tried to help Freda.'

'Freda died,' I snap.

'Freda wanted, more than anything, for you to be spared. Work with me,' she urges. 'This time we will beat the curse. We'll return the magic to where it belongs.'

'And where is that?'

'The stars, of course.' With her fawn-brown skin, the grey curls and all-seeing eyes, Mama Daline reminds me a little of Minnie. Like she should be telling me not to eat so much chocolate and cover my chest. Instead, we're surrounded by bones and talking about returning trapped magic to the stars.

'Market magic, good magic, draws power from the natural

world. From the earth, the sun, the sea, the wind, the moon, the mountain.' She smiles at me beatifically, the smile of a supplicant talking of her god. 'Here in this city, we honour the Sisters, and so we find special strength in the stars.'

Outside the tent, vendors call out to people passing. There's a cackle of laughter, a repeating cry. Business as usual.

'We first heard of this new Jackal a few months ago,' Mama Daline says. 'Before then, there'd been no leader of the Nightmarket, just a hierarchy of hordes who fought amongst themselves. In the spring, this stranger came out of nowhere. She declared herself the Jackal, ruler of the Nightmarket, bringing the hordes together under her.'

In the corner of my mind, something nags, but it stays just out of reach.

'The magic inside your curse is extraordinarily powerful. Rare.'

'Is that why the Jackal wants it?'

Mama Daline gives a slow, regal nod. 'Without it she is Jackal in name only.'

Again, I have that niggling feeling that I'm missing something important, but there's too much coming at me. I can't think it through.

'With your magic, the Jackal will have the kind of power no one person should. She has warned us,' Mama Daline continues, 'that she is coming to take the Market.'

I know, I think, *I was there.*

'You say you want to help me,' I say slowly, straightening my slumped shoulders, 'but isn't it really that you want to help yourself? To save your Market.' A surge of anger pushes me to my feet. The star ring is tight around my finger. 'You say it's better to be killed by the curse than caught by the Jackal, but what you really mean is that it's better for you.'

Mama Daline narrows her eyes. I've pissed her off.

'You have no idea,' she says sharply, 'how corrupt veiled magic is. Go to the Nightmarket and you'll find a spell for every twisted desire. But unnatural magic is greedy. It demands a price. And we will all pay.'

My legs are unsteady, like I've been dancing a long, difficult piece. I'm not sure they can bear my weight so I sit again, my mind in turmoil.

She's quiet, but I can feel Mama Daline watching me. 'If the Market turns dark, no one is safe. Not you, not your mother, nor the aunties you adore. Not your nice young uncle with his pretty candlesticks. Not your school friends, your dance friends, no one. This city will run on veiled magic.' She's angry now, and it's like I've infected her. 'They will take everything from us. Our love, our laughter, our spirit. Until we beg for death.'

I jerk my head up, startled that she knows so much about me. 'How do you know all this?'

'I've seen it. And more,' she says, her voice slow, almost chanting. 'In my bone-dreams, I have seen corruption spread through this city like a fire on a hot windy day. I have seen it overrun with veilwitches, tumescent as they feed on its people.'

'Veilwitches?'

'The witches of the Nightmarket, who practise forbidden magic. The Jackal's witches.'

'Do your bone-dreams tell you how to break the curse?'

'They have tried.' She gestures to the bones in front of her, the bones she selected while talking to me. 'I've seen a silver ticket with a talon. A pink notebook.'

And then, unexpectedly sprite, she's right beside me. 'To get real answers, I need to lay the bones on you.' She presses a hard hand on my shoulder, making me lie down on the bench. 'Relax.'

Surprise makes me compliant, and I let her arrange my hands palm up over my stomach, her cold, papery touch unfamiliar and unwelcome. I find a point on the ceiling, a pinprick where light comes in. I anchor myself with that spot.

'Hold this.' She places the skull in my hands, lays the long bone down my chest and another diagonally across. A delicate bone on my forehead.

Mama Daline sings. Her voice sounds through the tent, bouncing off the walls, the ceiling, my skin. The bones seem to vibrate. In my hands, the thin skull quivers. I hold on to the pinprick of light but it doesn't hold me. I am light-headed, adrift.

And in this twilight moment, I know only one sure thing: my world will never be the same again.

8

TEETH

When I said I wanted a hot-girl-summer, I didn't mean lying in a warm, stuffy tent beside a fire bowl. But here I am, draped in bones, while a woman who dreams I kill her sings over me.

Mama Daline's song stops and the sudden silence is almost violent.

'Three keys to seal the curse, three keys to unlock it.' Her voice is rich. 'The name. The manifest. The tormentor's blood.'

Mama Daline moves the bones from my face and chest. Holding the skull, I sit up. She takes the bones from me, returning them to where they belong.

'During the curse casting,' Mama Daline explains, 'three keys sealed it as a blood curse. The name of your ancestor, the creation of the manifest – that is the creature of the curse – and the death of the enslaver who tormented her.'

She leans forward as if she's trying to impress her words on me. 'These are the three locks on the curse. But locks can always be opened.'

'How?'

'You must turn the keys. Learn your ancestor's name, untether the creature of the curse, and –' she frowns – 'I'm not sure what you're supposed to do with the tormentor's blood.'

There is too much to unpack here, so I latch on to what I best understand. 'My ancestor's name was Hella.'

'You need her true name, not the one the enslavers gave her.'

'How am I supposed to find a name that was lost centuries ago?'

'Your dreams, meisiekind. Search your dreams.' Again, down the rabbit hole and into the strange. 'And with no delay, because prowling season has begun.'

'What happens in prowling season?'

'The predators go hunting.' I feel a small shudder at her words. 'Twice a year, the veilwitches pursue us to take our magic, our vitality, from us. Or, worse, they make us one of them.' I hear the heartbreak in her voice. 'This year, the Jackal leads them.'

She doesn't need to say it, that this year will be so much worse.

'Every prowling season ends with three nights of feasting,' Mama Daline continues, 'when the Nightmarket celebrates its steals. Newly turned veilwitches are initiated, amongst other horrors. There's a good chance the Jackal will claim your curse then.'

She walks to the trestle table, where she rummages among the small brown glass vials in the wide seagrass basket. 'The magic might not be at its peak, but the Jackal needs it badly.'

'When are these three nights of feasting?'

'Prowling season will end towards mid-December. Around the same time as our Summer Starfall.'

A month from now.

Mama Daline pulls a few bottles from the basket, reading the labels then discarding them on the table. 'I have something here that should help draw that name to you.'

Reaching deep into the basket, she extracts a vial and holds it in a stream of sunlight.

'Blood magic always leaves remnants.' She touches her heart. 'The story of how the curse came to be is in there, buried within the waking magic inside you. This will speed things up a little, prod the waking magic, and bring what's hidden to the surface. Your dreams will become vivid and that's where you'll find the name. But Savannah, this is a very precious potion, and the ingredients are hard to come by.'

'What do you want for it?' She so obviously wants something.

'This –' she closes her fingers around the vial – 'cannot be bought for cash.'

Her voice lowers a pitch.

'I want my death to be fast and merciful. Promise me that.' She speaks quickly and quietly.

My mouth falls open. 'I can't make a promise that isn't mine to keep. I don't know when or how you'll die.'

There's a look in those black bird eyes: *You kill me.*

'No? Then come back when you can.' Mama Daline puts the

vial on the table alongside the others.

'Mama Daline.' Zenande appears at the tent entrance. 'Mama Daline, it's the hospital.'

'I'll be back in a minute,' Mama Daline says, and follows Zenande out.

In a moment, I'm up and at the table. Beside the seagrass basket, Mama Daline has left four brown glass vials.

What would you do if fear didn't hold you back?

I turn one over and read the label: *Demon dispatch*.

That sounds alarming. I put it down and look at the others. *Possession. Serenity. Rouse.*

There's the sound of footsteps approaching the tent. I grab *Rouse*. Prod the magic. That has to be it. I hesitate.

I can't give Mama Daline what she wants. I won't make that promise.

There's a small opening between two walls, just enough room for me to squeeze out.

With the stolen vial in my pocket, I run.

The brightness of the day is startling after the dark, smoky tent. Head down, I walk fast, between the stalls.

I glance over my shoulder. Mama Daline emerges from the tent. Her furious eyes scan the market and she spots me.

'Savannah!' Mama Daline has her hands on her hips. Zenande appears beside her. 'Come back here.'

I see the two women talking urgently before I make a rapid left turn, then a right, and then another left. I try to lose myself in the maze of the market. Ahead, a lush pink bougainvillea adorns a high white wall. On the other side is a stone church, one that Kim and I briefly attended after Freda died. I head that way, ducking into the narrow alley between the back of the stalls and the bougainvillea-covered wall.

I peer around the corner, but I can't see Zenande. I close my hand on the bottle in my pocket.

I'll walk through the church garden. Just for a few minutes, to think through what Mama Daline said. Then I'll go back to her.

The bougainvillea is thick and untamed. I pick my way forward to the gate.

I don't see them, nestled between the startling pink flowers, until I'm close. She's dressed in tight black leather, with a long dark plait. Pressed against the wall, one leg hooks around his waist. His hand kneads her thigh as she devours him with her mouth.

The man grinds against her, his hands running from her thigh to her waist. She laughs and breaks the kiss. Places a hand on his cheek. He leans in towards her, but she holds him in place.

He's a vendor. I saw him earlier, selling imported coffee beans. Confident and self-assured.

'You feel so good,' he murmurs, aiming his mouth to her neck.

Her fingers, with many large-stoned rings, grip his cheek.

'What … ?' the man starts, but her palm covers his mouth and nose. His eyes are wide behind her splayed fingers.

His arms fall limply to his sides. She mutters something, fast and low, then kisses him deeply again.

A soft keening sound comes from him.

'Do I feel good now?' she laughs.

The wail grows into a full-on scream.

'Stop,' she commands.

He whimpers, then shuts up.

I am frozen in the narrow alley, watching as she withdraws her hand. The man slumps against her, and, irritated, she pushes him away. He stumbles, breaking his fall by holding on to the wall.

Hurriedly I press back into the bougainvillea.

She casts a quick look my way but doesn't see me. She struts down the alley, shoving branches aside, her heels echoing in the narrow space.

I take a moment to even out my breathing. The man's slumped against the wall, his head bowed.

Then there's a hand on my back.

I'm dragged from the narrow pink-petalled alley. Branches scrape my skin, tug at my clothes.

'Take your hands off me!' I shout.

'You don't like it? Too bad,' a woman's voice yells. She lets me go and I stagger. It's Zenande.

'Give me back what you stole from Mama Daline.'

I clutch the bottle inside my dress pocket.

She holds out an open palm. 'Give.'

I pull the bottle from my dress. *What would you do if fear didn't hold you back?*

Quickly, I pull out the stopper and raise the bottle to my lips.

'No!' Zenande shouts. I toss it down.

It's sweeter than I expected. My stomach contracts as I drink. I wonder if the liquid will come straight back up again.

'You stupid girl.' Zenande's lips are tight. 'Do you know what you've done?'

'Mama Daline said it would help.'

'One drop, Mama Daline would have said. Not the whole bottle.'

I'm light-headed, like I stood up too quickly.

'What will it do?' I can't hide the fear from my voice.

She laughs mirthlessly, and anger floods my body so quickly it startles me.

'A drop will lightly stir dormant magic. A bottle –' she laughs again, but it doesn't reach her eyes – 'will bring on the storm. That slowly stirring magic? You've just screamed it awake.'

'It's not funny,' I growl.

'No, it's not.' She shakes her head. 'You've just brought the death point nearer.'

I push the hair from my eyes, my stomach churning.

'Over the coming weeks, the magic is going to keeping stirring until it erupts out of you. Just in time for the veilwitches' feast.' She raises her eyebrows. 'It will draw veilwitches to you, like flies to honey.'

'How can I stop it?' I manage through gritted teeth.

'You can't. They're coming for you now, for sure. And remember, you drink, you pay. You owe Mama Daline.' She walks away, then glances over her shoulder. 'Get ready for the storm, Angry Girl.'

Furious with Zenande, Mama Daline, and most of all myself, I pick up a brick from the ground and hurl it against the wall. I find another and throw that too. I knock down a stack of crates. I kick at the wall, again and again, until pain shoots up my leg.

The pain makes me realise where I am, what I'm doing. I steady my breathing against the cold thing in my heart.

As I walk back to Harrison's stall, a sick feeling starts, like the early stages of a fever. A gust of wind lifts my hair, my dress. The wind is warm, unpleasantly so. A berg wind. Minnie always says that berg winds mean trouble.

The palm of my hand tingles. I look down. There, in the centre of my palm, are new cherry-red spots.

I pull myself straight, posture perfect, my dance face on.

Back at Harrison's stall, I surprise myself at how well I pretend. I flirt with the boys who stop to look. Wink as I suggest the delicate leaf-shaped candleholders for their girlfriends for Christmas. I ignore the nausea. The fresh marks on my hand. The swimming feeling in my head. The cold anger clenching my stomach.

I am so fucking charming. I'm smiling so hard my cheeks ache.

Inside, a storm begins to build.

9

ORANGE FLOWER

I'm running. Behind me, the world burns. Smoke fills my nostrils, closes my throat.

Faster, Savannah, a voice inside urges me.

I surge forward, fear driving me on.

There's a figure ahead, on the other side of the river. With her back to me, she's still, wearing a long white cotton nightgown. Dark, thick hair falls to her waist. She's familiar somehow, but I know she's not Freda.

I need to get to her, then I'll be safe.

From behind me comes the loud slobbering breathing of an animal. A sob catches in my throat.

Nearly there, Savannah, that voice urges again.

The woman turns her face just a fraction. Like she can hear me coming. Still facing away, she reaches out an arm behind her.

I'm near the rushing water when something snags my foot

and I stumble, landing hard on my knees. I glance back and see: glassy eyes staring at nothing. The short white fur and horns.

It's a goat.

I wake up suddenly, the sound of the river still loud in my ears. Then I realise: water *is* running.

I get up from my bed, my bare feet quiet on the floorboards. The water's stopped. No sound at all. I move cautiously to the door and into the passage.

Suddenly my dream feels close. The animal staring sightlessly. The woman on the other side of the river. Hella, I'm sure of it. The creature chasing me, the heavy sounds of its breath.

'Savannah, are you sleepwalking?'

Quinton is standing in front of me in the dark passage, wearing a robe, his hair damp.

'I heard a noise.'

'I was in the shower.'

'At two in the morning?' I narrow my eyes. 'Kim said you weren't working tonight.'

'I was at a party. Smoke got in my hair. Didn't realise I needed to report to the warden.'

He pushes past me and I stand there for a moment, trying to put a finger on what bothers me. Then I understand. It's so faint, it's almost not there. The smell of iron and smoke. Of animal. The smell of my dream.

The next day, I'm in a quiet upstairs alcove, surrounded by neat rows of books. I'm at the Nova College library, where Kim works as a librarian. I like it here in this nook; it's always felt peaceful beneath the large church windows and tall pillars. Not today, though. Today I am haunted.

When I look up at the high windows, I see the rig at Carniveil and the Jackal lording over everyone. Not theatre, but horribly real. The knowledge squats on my shoulders, bearing me down.

When I cast an eye over the other alcoves, at heads bent over books, I think only one thing: the Jackal wants to get me.

When I pick up my pen, I see the red marks, and with it comes the heavy, painful awareness that the curse is real. And unless I turn three impossible keys, it will kill me.

I uncurl my fingers and examine the red on my palm. My anger is leaving a mark. I compare them to the older marks on my left wrist, now a deeper red. Like a bruise that is never going away.

I've made everything worse by drinking the stolen potion. In drinking that whole bottle, I've brought my death date nearer. Over the years, Hella's girls have been a little angrier, died a little younger each time. Ma Stella at twenty-nine, Freda at twenty-seven. And now me, leapfrogging to seventeen.

On the table, bathed in a stream of light, is Freda's open notebook.

Her tight, looped handwriting is hard to decipher. The first few pages are all anecdotes of uncanny experiences. This auntie who saw a shadowy figure or that child who heard scratching in her wardrobe.

I've heard these kinds of stories before, many times. The aunties love a good story about a jinn or ghost or doekoem. They're of no use to me. I don't know why Freda wrote them all

74

down. Today my anger, a gentle flame, licks at my dead aunt. I twist my star ring.

If you wanted to help me, Freda, why didn't you write something useful?

I turn the pages. More anecdotes, more stories. I page on, until I find one with only a few lines in the centre.

A memory that can't have happened. I'm running in a field. I remember the heat of the night, the feel of my nightdress against my legs, the earth beneath my bare feet. My mother screams at me to go faster. But I know the thing wants her, not me. Not yet. I shout for her to run faster. Behind us, there's a fire.

I've carried this memory for years, but lately it's invading my dreams ...

I look up from the page with an urge to tear the books from the shelves, to fling them this way and that.

Instead, I stand up so abruptly that a heavy costume design book and my open pencil case fall to the floor. The sound echoes through the library and I feel the annoyed glances from the other alcoves. I go to the bathroom and splash water on my face. Take a deep breath. Angry Savannah stares back at me from the mirror. Flint in my eyes, hair wild and tangled.

Freda had the same impossible memory.

Pumping soap, I wash my hands. Remnants, Mama Daline had said. The story of the curse is there, buried inside me as it had been in Freda. Fragments of Hella's memories from that night.

Returning to the alcove, I look down into the large lending hall with its white pillars and stained-glass windows. Kim is at the front desk, scanning a pile of books. A librarian pushes a trolley with a squeaky wheel.

I see the back of a young man, reaching up to pull a book from the top shelf. Strong shoulders and arms. The way he moves, easy and fluid.

As if drawn by my scrutiny, he turns and looks up at me.

It's him, the stranger from Carniveil. It feels like a character from a story has stepped into real life.

I stare at him. The boundary between possible and impossible has worn so thin that I fully expect him to disappear before my eyes.

'Oh, for heaven's sake.' A voice, obnoxiously loud, comes from the loans desk. 'The sheer incompetence of this place is astounding. I've been waiting weeks.'

I tear my gaze away from the boy. There's a man in front of the loans desk, leaning forward, finger jabbing. Kim is trying to calm him.

When I look back to the stacks, the boy is no longer there.

I pick up my pens and the costume book, then frown at Freda's notebook.

I've been treating it like a storybook, with a beginning and middle and end. Maybe I need to try something different.

I flip it open near the middle and a loose sheet falls out. It's half a page. The uneven edges suggest it was torn from a printed book.

Types of curses

There are two kinds of curses: ordinary curses and blood curses.
Blood curses are rare. This is because they have a heavy
price.
A blood curse must be sealed three times. The final seal is
always the taking of a life.
The caster must also relinquish a piece of their magic.
The magic is then trapped inside the curse and, over time, this
magic will grow. If the curse is broken, the magic can be
returned to source. If the curse is unbroken, the magic may be
drained by a witch of particular strength. <u>Draining the magic</u>
<u>from a blood curse will likely kill the afflicted.</u>

Blood curses are alive. The magic that sustains them is
alive. They have a shape and form, a manifest. <u>The</u>
<u>manifest may be hostile to the afflicted.</u>

The growing magic, returning to source, the three locks.
Everything Mama Daline told me is there. Seeing this in print,
and not whispered in a smoky tent, makes it more real, and I
press my hand to my stomach, as if that could soothe the
gnawing anxiety.

What does it mean, *blood curses are alive*? There's still too
much I don't understand. I have to go back to see Mama Daline,
and even the thought of it makes my stomach twist more.

My phone buzzes with a message from Kim: *Ready to go?*
It's after five already.

We're going to a party at the Standers' this evening,

old friends we haven't seen in nearly ten years, who've just moved back from Canada. For forty years, our great-grandmothers lived beside each other in the now upmarket De Waterkant area. Until they'd been forced out of their homes so white people could live there. They stayed tight, even after they were resettled in different areas on the Cape Flats.

I gather my things, putting the loose sheet back in the book. When I glance back, I see my favourite pen still on the floor and pick it up.

The Stander return has Kim excited. Inez is older but they became close when they were new mothers, both single, struggling to make things work. Two months ago, Inez's mother died, prompting her move back here.

Kim is behind the loans desk, bag over her shoulder, briefing the evening assistant. Her colleague Fatima is doing up her jacket. The man I'd seen arguing with them earlier pushes past me.

'Still nothing? Your ineptitude is staggering. I insist on speaking to your superior.' His black-and-grey hair curls over his navy jacket collar and his face is pallid, his eyes a little sunken. He looks between Fatima and Kim and points with his stubby finger. 'This is what always happens with you affirmative action appointments.'

'OK, this conversation is over,' Fatima says.

Kim reaches for the desk phone. I hope she's calling security.

The man leans over the desk.

'It's not finished until I say it is.' This close, I can see the thick vein in his neck.

'Mr Meyer, please. I will investigate what went wrong with your request,' Kim says, and I hate how polite she has to be when he is so vile. Sometimes I wonder if Kim stays so composed even when she should be raging because she knows too well how women's anger is used against them. Her tone is calm: 'Or you can arrange to see the library manager between nine and five.'

Her composure further aggravates Meyer. He plants his feet wide, jabbing his finger right in Kim's face. 'Are you trying to get rid of me?'

I find myself stepping forward. 'You should probably stop now.' My pen is tight in my grip and the words come out louder than I intended.

Meyer turns to look at me, blinking. He looks me up and down. Takes in my wild hair, my skin as brown as autumn leaves. My cropped top, the heavy brocade silk skirt that falls to my feet. He looks at me a long time and his mouth twists into a sneer.

'This is none of your business,' he spits.

Just a girl. That's all he sees: just another dark-skinned girl with attitude. Sized up, then dismissed as angry and irrational.

'You should apologise.' This time as the rage fills me, it feels right. He was rude, and I don't have to just quietly accept that. While I can't know for sure, it's possible that with a white man librarian behind the desk, Mr Meyer might have found his manners.

Of course I'm angry. I've lived this moment, in other settings with different people, before. Of course Freda was angry; she was born into a world where the small details of living were determined by the colour of her skin. And of course

79

Ma Stella was angry, when her entire life had been walled in, with so many options denied to her.

In this moment, with Meyer glaring, it tugs at me, this long line of anger that connects the women in my family, all the way back to Hella.

Damn right I'm angry, Mr Meyer.

'Savannah,' Kim says. 'Go to the car right now.'

'You heard her. Savannah.' Meyer pokes my shoulder, one finger on the strap there. 'Run along.'

'Please,' whispers Kim, and I don't know if she's speaking to him or me.

'Your hot head is going to get you in trouble.' He jabs me again, fingers on my skin, and my anger is a swollen river.

'I am trouble.' It sounds like a demon's jumped out of my throat. My hand swings up and I stab the pen, my prize pen, into the flesh between his thumb and forefinger. He freezes, hand raised. The pen is stuck there, standing up like an extra digit.

There is murder in both our eyes. Then a security guard puts his hand on Meyer's arm.

'Please get Mr Meyer out of here,' Kim says, her calm tone at odds with her panicked eyes. Fatima's mouth is a perfect O. I want to apologise to Kim, I'm worried I'll get her in trouble, but my throat is too tight to speak.

Meyer shrugs out of the guard's hold and hesitates. Then he turns and walks out, cradling his hand. 'You haven't heard the last of this.'

Silence. Then:

'It was self-defence,' Fatima says. 'We all saw.'

Kim clears her throat, scoops up her bag and ushers me out, away from the stares and whispers.

Kim strides down the steps in silence. I scurry after. At the bottom, I see the glint of silver in some gathered muck. My pen. There's blood on it, so I wrap it in a tissue and drop it in a pocket in my bag.

She unlocks the car and we climb in. Only then does she speak.

'What possessed you to get involved, Savannah?'

I unwrap a nut bar, focusing on peeling back the paper. From the car speaker, a Savannah-help audiobook talks about finding inner peace.

I can't bring myself to look at her. She waits. Eventually, bar unwrapped, I say, 'He touched me first.'

'Men like that ...' Kim shakes her head and begins to reverse. 'You have to be careful. That man is a bully and bullies hurt.' Her lips press together. 'Don't poke the bear.'

What if the bear pokes you first?

We drive, stop at Pick n Pay for wine and flowers, and get on to the M3, our car tucked to the curves of the mountain.

The Savannah-help audiobook goes on about deep serenity. We pull up outside the Stander house in a fancy neighbourhood – high walls, tall trees, big houses down long drives. Large gates. I unclip my seat belt.

'Your skin,' Kim says quietly. 'Savannah, look.'

I flip down the mirror and look. There, on my shoulder, is a spreading red mark.

10

POISON

The house sits in a mature garden with old trees and flowers in full bloom. Smartly clad guests gather on the neatly trimmed lawn and the wide wraparound stoep. A long table covered with white cloth holds wine and food. Fairy lights twinkle in the early evening light.

I feel like we've stepped into a spread in a fancy magazine.

Walking up the path, heads turn to watch us. We stand out, I think, amongst so much elegance. The house is modern, with floating steps, wide glass windows. A burst of civilised laughter drifts across the lawn.

'Kim,' says a voice from behind. I turn to see a woman with large hazel eyes and cropped brown hair, the sleek pixie cut accentuating fine cheekbones. White shirt, trousers. A dash of lipstick. She's familiar to me, but in the way you recognise someone in a dream. 'It's you.'

'Inez.'

The women take each other in.

'I can't believe you're back.'

I think that Inez is in her late forties, though she is so groomed, so expensive-looking, it's hard to be sure. She pulls Kim into a long hug.

I stand there, awkward, till Inez releases Kim. 'Thanks for coming to my mother's funeral.' I'd been away on a dance tour in Joburg. 'I'm sorry we didn't get a chance to catch up properly.'

'It was a difficult time,' Kim sympathises.

'I hoped to see you and Savannah but before I knew, we were on a flight back to Vancouver.'

Inez turns to me and says, 'Savannah, look at you! When I last saw you, you were *this* big.' She gestures to indicate a child. She smiles. 'You were a terror.'

'Still am,' I say.

'Come on through.' Inez links an arm through Kim's and steers us inside. She glances back at me over her shoulder, eyes dancing. 'The twins are excited to see you. Rosie is beside herself.'

My memories of the twins, Rosaria and Dex, have long been packed away. We'd been close, and I'd been hurt when they moved so suddenly. There'd been an accident, Dex had been in hospital, and within weeks they were gone.

But I remember enough: a night-time game of hide-and-seek with cherry-flavoured sweets on my tongue. How safe and happy I felt when I was with them. A girl with sun streaks in her brown hair and pink jelly sandals. Her face, like the boy's, has blurred with time.

Kim and Inez pass through the wide arch and disappear among the guests. I stand there, scanning the living room. The aunties will be here somewhere.

'Savannah?' A girl appears in front of me.

A Canadian accent. Brown eyes with flecks of green. A black strapless dress revealing toned bronze shoulders, effortlessly tousled brown hair. Rosaria. My elaborate skirt with its silver threading feels like a costume. I'm the kid who's been at the dress-up box.

'Oh wow. It *is* you.' She hugs me, then pulls back and studies me. Her eyes are playful. 'You don't remember me, do you?'

'I do,' I say, trying to reconcile the child in my memories with the composed woman in front of me. 'Rosaria.'

She pulls a face. 'Rosie, please.'

She reaches out a hand and tugs at the shirt of a man holding a tray. Glasses wobble. 'Here's your old arch nemesis, Dex.'

'Watch it, Rosie,' he says, turning to us.

And once more I find myself looking into the face of the stranger from Carniveil. He must recognise me, but it doesn't show. Rosie's face is lit with unbridled delight, and I try to match her, hiding my fluster with a smile.

'Dex, it's Savannah,' Rosie says gleefully. 'Doesn't she look great?'

He holds my gaze, and it's like we're alone in the tree-lined hedge again. 'She does.'

I could say the same about him. Usually I would, with a big flirtatious smile, but I'm uncharacteristically tongue-tied.

'Hi, Savannah,' Dex says smoothly. 'We meet again.'

84

They're all three very alike, Inez, Rosie and Dex: sun-kissed skin with hair and eyes in shades of brown, like they're caught in a ray of sunlight. But it's him I'm drawn to most. It always has been.

'Go on, give her a hug. She won't bite,' Rosie teases.

Still carrying the tray, he pulls me into a quick one-armed hold. A brief, close clutch that makes me think of finding an old, long-lost comfort object. Rosie grabs a glass of wine and Dex offers the tray to me.

'Nah, I'm good,' I say.

'That's not what I've heard.' The words are spoken so low, I almost don't hear them. I glance at him sharply. Unsmiling, he gives a quick nod and says, 'Excuse me,' before disappearing through the wide arch.

I stare after him. I swear half the city has heard about the girl who went befok and smashed up a car. I'm surprised there wasn't an article in the *Daily Voice*.

Crossing the room, Dex doesn't bother to offer the wine, even though a couple try to get his attention. He disappears through the glass doors to the back patio.

'Nice place,' I say to Rosie.

'Yeah, rich stepdad.' She grimaces. 'Ex-stepdad.'

On the other side of the room, I see Harrison. He waves at me, then turns his attention back to the person he's flirting with. Through the throng, I can't see if it's a boy or a girl.

At the far end is Minnie in her dark pink lipstick and going-out earrings, Auntie Dotty in a tight dress with a plunging neckline, and Auntie Chantie, the only person in the room sipping a cup of tea.

'Dex wasn't keen to move back here,' Rosie says. 'He's been a little … troubled lately.'

'Hmmm.' I've limited sympathy.

'You'll help me get him settled in, right?'

'You guys have travelled a lot?' I avoid answering the question. I might think he's hot, but pandering to boys isn't my thing.

'A *lot*. Inez and Mike, ex-stepdad, they started *Wild Heart*. It's a magazine. You know it?'

'Of course,' I say. It's not just a magazine – it's a famous one. Luxury travel, but cool. For those planning a once-in-a-lifetime trip, or millionaires with taste. 'That must have been incredible.'

'It was.' She looks around the busy room. 'This has always been our end destination though. Come on, let's go find Dex.'

We make our way through the room.

'Savannah!' Minnie plants a kiss on my cheek as I pass her. Her fingers hover above the bright red marbling on my shoulder. Auntie Chantie frowns and even Donley looks glum. Auntie Dotty sighs. 'Ag, kind.'

Oh child, our scars tell our stories.

Rosie waves to me from the patio doors and, excusing myself, I follow.

'Rosie.' Inez stops her. 'Uncle Stan is misbehaving. Please help me rescue that poor woman.'

'There's always an Uncle Stan.' Rosie rolls her eyes at me. 'Back in a few.'

I walk through the glass doors. There's a bar on the patio and white paper lanterns hang from tall trees. A tray of wine glasses has been discarded on the half wall and I step past it, into the rambling garden. It's a world away from our tiny backyard, with its raggedy pot plants. I feel a prickle in my spine. A low-grade, ever-present simmering.

If I were a bird flying over, I'd see more of these houses enclosed in large leafy gardens. High gates, long drives. Moving away from the mountain, the houses and gardens would become smaller. I'd see children begging at traffic lights, people sheltering in shop doorways, beneath bridges, searching through rubbish bins. Further still, the tight rows of crowded flats, the sprawl of shacks. The remnants of apartheid.

I walk away from the house, away from the party. The path curves and I glimpse the blue water of the swimming pool.

'Sneaking around where you don't belong.' I turn. Dex sits in a leafy nook, stretching out his long legs and resting his feet on an iron table. He has a glass tumbler in hand. 'Seems to be a habit of yours.'

'What were you doing at Carniveil that night?' I step closer to the table.

'*Wild Heart* had a press invite.' He lifts one shoulder in a shrug. 'My mom couldn't go.'

He is so different to the boy I remember. The crooked teeth have been made straight; he no longer wears his hair in that 'too long for a boy' cut that had vexed the aunties. The round cheeks have been replaced by a strong jawline, defined cheekbones.

'You slipped in behind me. Why?'

'Told you, I was curious.' He takes a sip of the amber liquid, his eyes on mine. 'Never passed a restricted area I didn't want to explore.'

'You didn't know anyone there?'

'I've been away ten years. I don't know anyone.' Another sip. 'Except you.' He makes that sound so unsatisfying. 'My old friend.'

'When I said yes to that drink –' I sit on the table and raise an eyebrow – 'I didn't mean I wanted to wear it.'

He glances up with a slight wince. 'Sorry about the beer. I only meant to help.'

'You did help,' I concede. I lean over him, reaching for his glass. Honestly, I have no manners. I take it from his hand and he lets me. 'Why?'

His eyes are incredulous. 'You were clearly in trouble. You'd stolen that ticket and I intervened before things got worse.'

'I didn't steal the ticket.' I raise his glass to my mouth and taste. Whisky. The burn is pleasant.

'Then how did you get it? Why were you there?' He takes the tumbler from me. Leaning back in his chair, he lifts it to his lips. He's wearing a white shirt, his hair pushed back from his eyes, and it annoys me how much I like looking at this new version of him. How I suddenly wish this was just a school party where I meet a hot guy and kiss him by the pool. Dex swallows, then hands the tumbler back to me.

'I'm not sure,' I admit. 'I found the ticket on the ground.' It occurs to me suddenly that maybe I was meant to find it. That

Claw had deliberately dropped it for me. Intuitively, it fits. Worm had recognised the magic inside me; maybe Claw had too. Thinking about Claw standing over the fire, I take another quick drink.

'Did you see that woman throw herself into the fire?' I trace the silver thread on my skirt, how it curls through the indigo. The brocade is heavy, silky on my legs.

'I did,' he says at last, as he reaches for the whisky.

I look at his profile, the line of his nose, his lips. I'm trying to find the boy I played hide-and-seek with. But he's all grown up and a stranger to me.

'You want more?' He raises the glass in question. How easily we share, even after all these years. I shake my head, even though I do want, and he tosses down the last. I study him, how his throat works, the way he turns the empty glass in his hands.

'You're staring again,' he says.

'You were staring too, in the library. Did you know who I was?'

'Then, yes. Did you?'

'Not in the slightest.' I smooth my skirt. 'Just wanted to look.'

He gives a small laugh.

'Didn't you hulk out and smash up a car because of how some guys looked at you? But it's OK for you to stare.'

'That was different. They wanted me afraid.'

'I see.'

'Unless,' I taunt, 'I make you afraid?'

He doesn't answer, just reaches forward, placing the empty

whisky glass on the table, between his legs and mine. The silence is laden. Dex drops one leg, then the other, from the table and stands, now towering over me. He leans in, the side of his lips quirking up.

'Takes more than that to scare me.' His voice is low, amused. He turns to leave.

'There you are.' Rosie appears on the path, clutching a bottle of tequila, blocking Dex's exit. 'You're not going anywhere.'

There is a silent battle between them. She wins.

She raises the bottle. 'Let's get out of here. This old people party ain't it.'

Dex sighs. 'Fine.' He takes a few steps down the path, then glances back with a wolfish grin. 'The angry bird can come too.'

I'm pretty sure my mouth has fallen open.

'He did not just say that.'

'Don't mind him.' Rosie laughs. Her eyes sparkle. 'You two are going to pick up right where you left off.'

11

DRUM

We gather up Harrison and the pretty young man he's attached to, and then Donley insists on coming too.

'I'm Keenan,' says the young man, holding out a hand earnestly.

Harrison mouths, 'The angel.' He looks it too.

The mood is light as we walk down the tree-lined avenue. We reach a large park, one with old trees and picnic tables. A small stream in the distance and a pond. Nice, just like everything in this neighbourhood.

We sit beneath a tree, passing the tequila between us. After a while, Harrison sees a discarded rugby ball and insists we play. Dex and Harrison aside, none of us know the rules, so we make up our own version that involves tackling and scoring.

It's fun, even more so with the tequila. We're little kids again, playing like we've no cares in the world.

Harrison, Keenan and I score first. We're obnoxious with

our lead, doing victory dances and trash-talking. Rosie is laughing so hard it's easy to get the ball off her. My heavy skirt is hitched up as I run. The boys have their shirts off and trousers rolled up, and they're slick with sweat.

Somewhere in the park, a drumming session has started and the music carries over the trees.

'Savannah!' yells Harrison. Then I've got the ball, and drumbeats fill the park. I am stronger. Faster. I'm dodging Dex, outrunning Rosie, and who said sport isn't like dancing?

My bare feet move to the beat of the drums, pounding the patchy grass. My heart pumps to the bass beat. I'm near the goal line when a large body crashes into me, hard. Dex. We go down together, falling in a heap, and my head hits the ground.

Dex's arm and shoulder are on my chest, his body on my hips, and for a moment we just lie there, stunned. He gets to his knees. This close, I see the burn scar on his shoulder and some of his chest.

'You OK?' He leans over me. 'Sorry. I didn't mean to tackle you so hard.'

'But you did,' I snap. Ignoring his hand, I stand up.

'I didn't mean to.' He rubs his cheek. 'I'm sorry.'

'If you apologise again, I'm going to smack you.' The words are out of my mouth before I know what I'm saying.

'Dex, what the hell?' It's Rosie, hands on hips. Her lovely face is furious. 'You really hurt her.'

'Penalty,' calls Harrison. 'You get a free kick, Savannah.'

'You play.' I throw up my hands and walk away. 'I'm out.'

I make for the tree where we left the tequila, the boys' shirts, our shoes, my phone. The drum rhythms are louder here. I pause a moment, feeling the beats in the ground beneath my feet, all the way up my legs and to my heart. I walk closer, and even closer, until I'm standing right there watching them. The players – there are only three of them – are engrossed in the music, in their shared beats. It's a communion of sorts, a drummers' trance, and it's beautiful.

I am not surprised to see Zenande, Mama Daline and Arrow. It was inevitable they would find me. Players on a game board, manipulated by unseen hands. We are drawn to each other. We need each other.

They drum with their whole bodies, building the rhythm. Louder, faster. The music moves to a climax, and all too soon, it ends.

I clap. Their rapt audience of one. It feels like I've been allowed into something precious. A sacred space.

'You liked it then?' says Zenande. Her eyes are warm and I hope she's no longer pissed about me stealing the potion.

'I did,' I say. Through the trees, the makeshift rugby game seems to be winding down. Keenan's running after Rosie, who's about to score a try. Dex glances over at me, then away.

I reach out my hand and run it across the surface of Mama Daline's drum.

'It's djembe,' Mama Daline says. 'Do you want to give it a go?'

I sit on the bough beside Zenande. Arrow places the large drum between my legs, in the folds of my heavy skirt, tipping it outward. Crouching opposite me, she takes my hand.

'You're tense.' She smooths my flexed hand. 'Relax. Now, bounce it between the centre and the rim. Just like that. Keep going. Nice. There, you've got the bass tone.'

Through the trees, Donley lies on the grass beside Rosie. Harrison leans back against a tree, smoking; he likes his dagga. Keenan's head is on his lap, and Harrison lazily strokes his hair. He's talking to Dex. From the glances my way, I think they're talking about me.

Arrow and Zenande take me through the basic strikes. After I've had a few goes, Zenande beats a short rhythm on her drum, gesturing for me to try.

'That's right,' Zenande says. 'Doing great.' Arrow begins to beat around me and, hoisting a double-headed drum over her shoulder, Mama Daline joins in.

I lose myself so quickly, so deeply. The drumbeats carry me along in the gathering twilight. The rhythms change, taking us on a path we're discovering together. Louder, faster. It feels intense, magical. Like I'm being swept up in something I don't understand.

In my mind, a sudden image flashes: Zenande taking my hand, leading me into the trees. Whispering, *Come, Savannah.* It's so real, I can almost feel the touch of the beads wrapped around her wrist. Her hand, cool and slender. *Don't be afraid.* The image disappears.

Zenande's still beside me, beating her drum. Her smile is enigmatic.

Through the trees, I see Harrison. He shouts 'Savannah!' through cupped hands. Walks further, squints. Looks right at me, but through me.

My hands falter. Why doesn't he just come over here? Leaving the drum, I walk towards him.

A few steps from the drumbeats, I realise how muted Harrison's call is. It sounds like it's coming from far off, even though he's no more than fifteen metres away. Dex jogs over to Harrison, and they have a short, agitated conversation before going in different directions. Harrison comes nearer to me, calling my name like he can't see me.

'I'm right here, doofus,' I say to him.

But Harrison walks right by, as if I'm not there.

12

SNAKE

'Harrison, stop.' My laugh is lightly laced with panic.

Behind me the drumming comes to an end.

I turn and Harrison is nowhere to be seen.

It's impossible. He walked by me only seconds ago.

'Harrison?' I call. I sound afraid.

'Savannah,' Mama Daline says. The dark nudges in, recasting the park in shadow. I search for Harrison, but it's like he disappeared into thin air.

'Where are my friends?'

'They're here, in the park,' Zenande says soothingly. She gestures to the space around us. 'We're just a little ... apart.'

'Think of it as stepping into a secret room,' Arrow adds. 'One that we made, together, through our drumming.'

'We can talk here,' Zenande says, 'without being overheard. Harrison is fine, see, there he is.' She gestures to where he's reappeared, walking towards the road.

There's an almost imperceptible white haze over everything. A light opaque gauze, clouding my vision.

'We were concerned about you,' Mama Daline says. 'You drank that whole bottle.'

'I'm OK.'

Mama Daline gives me an arch look; she knows it's not true.

'May I?' She takes my hand and examines the mark on my wrist. It comes up from beneath the skin, like a blood spill just under the surface.

The sound of Donley crying my name is a seagull calling in the distance. Rosie appears at the tree where I'd left my phone and sandals. She picks up my phone and looks around, worry creasing her forehead.

I feel like I've been erased. I am a ghost, watching from the sidelines.

'You see her in your dreams now, don't you?' Mama Daline's finger circles the mark. 'The Jackal. You must approach her. Ask her name.'

'You said to find my ancestor's name.' I retract my hand, folding it into my skirt. 'Not the Jackal's.'

'I thought you understood.' Mama Daline frowns. 'The magic inside you, Hella's magic, is the first Jackal's magic. And without it, the new Jackal is Jackal in name only.'

I'm beginning to grasp what bothered me in Mama Daline's tent: why the new Jackal needs *this* curse. Why it could destroy the Market.

'Why would my family curse hold the Jackal's magic?' Did the Jackal help Hella escape? But anxiety rises inside me.

'Your ancestor, the woman you call Hella,' Mama Daline's voice is gentle, 'was the Jackal.'

'My ancestor is not your bad witch,' I say hotly.

'Hella wasn't bad,' Arrow sighs. 'She is a Sister and we honour her. She was the last to discover her power. Her life had been difficult. Hella had all this magic welling up inside her and she didn't know what it was or how to use it.'

'What happened?' There is a stone in my throat.

'The night Hella escaped was the night she learned to wield her power,' Mama Daline says. 'Casting the curse was completely intuitive, brought on by rage and desperation. Her magic burst from her that night, starting the fire, killing the enslaver and creating the manifest. She cast a binding blood curse without realising what she was doing.'

The women look at each other.

'Before long, she met the first Claw, who took her in and helped her birth her son.' Arrow gives a small smile. 'That's when Hella became the fourth Sister, the Jackal. Together, the Sisters led the newly formed Market.'

'This Market, where is it?'

'Wherever witches meet and trade magic,' Zenande says. 'It isn't one physical place. The Market is made up of witches and magic and bonds that run deep.'

'And Hella was part of this?' It warms my heart that she wasn't alone.

'She was. But the Jackal's magic had been malformed. Magic should not be claimed through rage.' Mama Daline's words hold a cautionary note. Like she's warning me.

'Hella came into her power through violence,' Zenande explains. 'Her magic was born in blood. It created, ah … cravings.'

Arrow picks up the story. 'She couldn't settle.' They share the telling between them, as they did with the drumming, effortlessly falling into each other's beats. 'She was restless, always hankering for something out of reach.'

'The Jackal went down a dark path.' Zenande takes over again. 'And it killed her.'

'How?' I'd so badly wanted Hella to live.

'She followed the call of veiled magic. In secret, she initiated a community of followers.' Arrow looks a little uncomfortable. 'The Sisters were heartbroken when they learned of this betrayal. They warned her to stop. But she didn't.'

'She was tried, found guilty of practising forbidden magic, and put to death.' Mama Daline's face is small in the growing dark. 'They had no choice – there's no place for veiled magic in the Market.'

'Her Sisters killed her? Because she didn't do what they said?' I am incredulous. Filled with sorrow, for the woman who escaped and found a family who then killed her. 'Because she was *restless*?'

'She died because she betrayed the women who loved her by giving herself to unnatural magic.' There is fire in Mama Daline's voice. 'The Jackal's death redeemed her.'

'Unfortunately, her veilwitches banded together and formed the Nightmarket, the shadow market, where forbidden magic thrives. They swore to avenge the Jackal.'

I can see why they would.

'Save your sympathy.' Arrow shakes her head. 'Because the veilwitches will come for you as they have come for us.'

The trees swish gently in the breeze. I think I hear Harrison call my name, or perhaps it's the wind.

'It wasn't her intention,' Arrow says, 'but the truth is that when Hella pursued forbidden magic, she created something monstrous.'

Monstrous. My heart is cold.

'We have to stop this new Jackal.' Mama Daline's words are urgent, desperate.

'Taking Hella's magic will make the new Jackal a true successor. A Daughter.' Arrow's face is etched with concern. 'And as a Daughter, the Market is hers, as it is ours.'

Hers, to turn veiled.

'If the Nightmarket eats the Market,' Zenande says, 'it will be prowling season all year round. Veilwitches will prey without inhibition. Everyone, not just witches, will be fair game.'

'They feed on witches? Like vampires?' I laugh, but it is because I am afraid.

'Do you remember me telling you that veiled magic comes at a cost?' Mama Daline moves closer until she's standing right in front of me. I nod. 'That's because veilwitches can cast living spells. Their magic can grow, reshape, multiply even after it's cast. As if it were alive.'

'Like my curse?' I swallow, suddenly certain I can feel wriggling inside me.

She nods. 'To cast a living spell, you need blood. Or stolen vitality, or human and animal parts.'

'But you use bones.' I'm trying to understand.

'The bones I use are long dead. Veilwitches prefer still-warm skin.' She touches my shoulder, the new marks there, then a light finger to my heart. 'Or a recently beating heart or contracting womb.'

I draw back from Mama Daline, my mouth turning down with distaste.

'To create living magic, veilwitches need life. And that's why they prey on Market witches. They steal our magic and our vitality to feed their unnatural castings.' Mama Daline's words are relentless. 'There is another way, through demon bonds, but it's difficult and only the strongest veilwitches are able.'

There's a ghost of a smile on her lips, as if she's thinking, *Not feeling so sorry for the Jackal now, are you?*

She touches a hand to my cheek. 'They will come for you too, Savannah. They'll drain you, maybe with a touch, maybe with a kiss. First the magic, and then all of your beautiful young life. All the while, you feel yourself slowly fading and there's nothing you can do to stop it.'

I think of the woman in the pink bougainvillea alley, how that man had screamed beneath her kiss. And it feels like I'm screaming too. A loud, hoarse roar that no one can hear.

'The new Jackal's success is bound to our destruction.' Zenande redirects the conversation – she can clearly sense my growing panic, and I'm grateful to her. 'There's an old prophecy that warns of this.'

Mama Daline speaks in her gravelly voice.

'The Claw will burn, veiled witches prowl.

The Arrow falls with the beast's howl.'

The words chill me, as if they themselves have power: the Claw has burned; the veilwitches do prowl.

'The vessel is cracked, old magic intact.

The Jackal rises with a smile.'

'We could just kill you, you know,' Arrow says, and I glance at her sharply, but there's no threat there. 'It would make things easier. The curse would go dormant. We'd be safe. For now.'

'Then why don't you?' How easy it would be here in their secret room. A knife through my heart; no one would ever know it was them.

'You are the first Jackal's descendant,' Zenande says. 'We owe you our protection.'

'The Jackal's descendant.' I test the words. 'But not her heir?'

'We don't pass our titles through bloodlines,' Arrow says. 'Each Daughter finds a worthy successor.'

Mama Daline hands a business card to me. 'This is Zenande's number. She will help you untether the manifest. Your dreams will reveal Hella's true name. Unfortunately, the tormentor key is more difficult.'

'It's all difficult,' I mutter.

'With the tormentor key, the discovery is part of the unlocking. There is something you must learn or experience, through the tormentor's blood.'

Mama Daline must see the bleakness on my face because

she squeezes my hand and says, 'Let the magic inside guide you.'

The living magic inside me.

I've had enough. I'm feeling uncomfortable, itchy under my skin. 'OK,' I exhale. 'I have to get back to my friends. I'll think about what you've said.'

'The magic is waking faster now.' Mama Daline glances at Arrow. 'In a matter of weeks, the curse will reach death point.'

'By the end of the Summer Starfall,' Arrow predicts, then sees how little her words mean to me. 'The meteor shower. It lasts ten days, peaking in mid-December.'

Mid-December, when the veilwitches feast.

Mama Daline nods. 'If you haven't turned the keys, you will die. Either at the hand of the Jackal, or by the curse itself.'

I can't listen any more. I can't hide my distress. I begin edging away.

'Wait,' Mama Daline calls, and I pause, looking back over my shoulder. 'You should know that for the Jackal to take the magic, she only needs to find one key.'

That doesn't seem fair. 'Which one?'

Mama Daline raises her shoulders in a shrug. 'Your guess is as good as mine.'

I leave. I hear them calling after me, but any more and I will drown in my despair. Each new piece of information is a heavy stone stitched to the hem of my skirt, bearing me down. Pulling me under.

The air feels thick around me and I force my way through it.

When I glance back, there's no one behind me. I'm all alone in the park.

It's dark now, and I'm more than a little nervous. From the distance comes the sound of barking dogs.

I begin retracing my steps through the empty park, finding my sandals in the grass; Rosie must have taken my phone. I'm not sure what I fear more, witches or ordinary men with a taste for violence. I walk faster.

'Savannah.' I turn to see Arrow, pink spandex gleaming in the dark. 'Wait, please. It's not safe. Let me see you to your friends.'

Behind her a man with blond hair, pale skin and a sharp nose walks his dogs. They snarl and strain at the leads, like they're taking him for a walk.

Without warning, the man releases the hounds.

I gasp as they run towards us. These aren't like any dogs I've seen before. They have dark, lean backs, sharp teeth and large ears.

In the moment the dogs surge forward I see that their legs, swirling into shadow, don't touch the ground as their bodies form and re-form. My heart is a drum. They're not dogs at all but creatures made of shadow.

'Run, Savannah,' Arrow hisses.

I sprint. Breathing heavily, I skid to a halt when I see a woman ahead. By the light of the park lamp, I make out close-cropped hair and a high forehead. I turn the other way, and there's the woman who'd been kissing the coffee vendor in the alley. She wears a long plait and leather, and, smiling at me, that same hungry look.

Arrow shuts her eyes. Around her, in a perfect circle, the grass smoulders. She holds a knife in her hands, murmuring inaudibly. She's safe, I realise, inside the circle of glowing grass.

The woman with cropped hair prowls nearer, and I am a mouse watching a cat advance. I search the trees, the benches, trying to plot a way out. Behind me is Arrow, but the blond man is behind her. To my left, is the alley woman. I think I see a man, tall and still, in the trees ahead.

The woman with shorn hair inches towards me. Arrow, eyes shut, sweeps her knife down, and, even though she is too far for the knife to touch, red stains the woman's shirt.

'Nice try, Arrow,' the woman sings, touching a hand to the impossible wound. She stalks nearer.

'That was a warning, Salomé.'

The leather-clad woman rushes forward and grabs my arms, holding them painfully behind me. I thrash but she is too strong. Unnaturally strong.

The dogs circle the smouldering grass around Arrow, their yips and snarls reverberating in my bones.

'Take down the circle, Arrow.' Her breath is hot against my face. 'Or the girl will die.'

'What kind of threat is that, Madison?' Arrow taunts. 'If she dies then the curse will be dormant again. Go on, kill her. It will solve my problems.'

Terror gives me strength. I buck and jerk, as wild as a beast. Madison grunts and her grip slips. I strain forward, but she holds me by the hair, winding it through her long fingers and sharp nails. She pulls viciously, and pain tears through my scalp. I cry out. Arrow brings down the knife again, her voice an animal roar. The tang of blood invades my nose. Madison pulls my hair harder, forcing my head down.

The dogs swirl, their pointed faces void of emotion. I have to make a break for it, no matter how much it hurts. Arrow is sweating now, her fringe slick from exertion. This magic is costing her. I don't know how much longer she can hold it.

Arrow slashes her knife through the air, a hard, brutal line. Madison screams. She releases my hair, stumbling. Arrow, now trembling, slashes again, yelling, 'Savannah, run!'

Salomé stands outside the circle, her arms outstretched and head bowed.

Madison falls to her knees and clutches her chest. Panting, her face is pale and she's streaked with blood. It's in her hair, on her arms. A criss-cross of cuts on her bodice, the brown leather stained dark. My legs buckle but I make them run.

A dog howls once. I look back to see it leap over the smouldering grass, yelping as it crosses the line into Arrow's circle.

'No!' I scream, my hands flying to my mouth. The dog is hunched down, ready to attack. Salomé raises her arms higher and looks up, her face set with determination.

From behind, a hand pushes me hard. It sends me flying, face to earth. I try to get up, but a foot on my back grinds me down. I'm sobbing, my tears mixing with dirt, as I watch a second dog break the barrier.

The shadow dogs leap, snarling and barking. Hands grab my ankles and drag me away, across uneven ground. A long, mournful howl fills the air. Through the grass and twigs, I see Arrow fall, a tangle of pink-and-black spandex.

The Arrow falls with the beast's howl.

'Arrow!' My eyes and throat burn. The hard ground grazes my skin and my ankles throb in that unyielding grip. The third dog crosses the line. My scream is hoarse: 'Arrow!'

Roots and stones dig into my stomach as I'm pulled into a darker area of the park. My hands grab grass, stones, anything, but it's futile.

'Stop.' There's never been a voice like it. It's entirely unnatural, hollow and echoing. 'Leave her there and go.'

It breaks me, that voice. Cracks me clean in half. It resounds with menace, power, mystery.

All my life, I've heard whisperings of jinn and of doekoems. Of the tokoloshe, the tiny man with a big dick, who comes for his victims at night. Of amagundwane, spiritual rats who bring money. They were just stories, I'd thought. Hoped.

Now I know, anything is possible.

The hands on my ankles let go. On my stomach and elbows, I inch away.

'Get up.' That terrible voice speaks.

I pull myself to a sitting position. There are no lights here, but I can still make out the figure wearing a long black jacket. And I can see her face. Strong cheekbones, high forehead, but what is human is melded to the features of a jackal. Those are jackal ears, jackal eyes and a jackal mouth.

'Who are you?' Fear leaks into my voice.

'I am the Heir of the Jackal.'

Such sharp teeth.

'What do you want?'

The huge slanted eyes devour me.

'To make you one of mine. Say yes to me and I will release you from the curse without hurting a hair on your head.'

The air fills with the sound of my breathing, loud and ragged. 'You want the magic.'

'That magic is mine,' the Jackal says, 'because I am not afraid of it.'

A chill runs through my body. I am afraid. So very afraid. 'You won't use this magic for good.'

'Oh! Good and bad, evil and pure. Such a dull way of thinking, Savannah. Say yes to me –' there's urgency in that voice now – 'and a whole new world, one you can't begin to imagine, will open to you. Wouldn't you like to do the impossible?'

Maybe I would.

'They punished Hella for being curious.' The Jackal's voice is lulling. 'For not staying in line. They killed her for wanting to know more. Does that sound *good* to you?'

'No,' I exhale. 'It doesn't.'

'They are threatened by me because I, like the first Jackal, am curious. I won't sit back and be satisfied.' The words are luring me now. 'Come, be curious with me, Savannah.'

I feel like I'm standing at the edge of a cliff. A hand closing over mine. Holding it tight.

'Jump with me, and I will make you fly.' Just a whisper in my ear.

I shut my eyes, like that could hold off the temptation. I remind myself of the terrors that Mama Daline and Arrow warned about. I grit my teeth. 'No.'

'Either way, I will take what is mine. With me, you thrive. Without me, you die.'

The dogs slink through the trees and press against the Jackal. They're calm now. *Satiated*, I think with a sickening feeling.

'How?' I say, 'Can you take the magic without killing me?'

'If I take the magic with one key, you will die. With two, you'll be as good as dead. With all three keys, I can take the magic without killing you. You will be weak initially, but I give you my solemn vow that I will make you stronger than before. Stronger than you can imagine.'

'Why?'

The Jackal's laughter is a pure animal sound. It echoes through the trees. 'You've nurtured the magic. Consider it a reward.'

I can feel it, the darkness within the Jackal. It seeps out, like moving shadows that hide rot and decay. I don't want to be that.

'No,' I say. 'I won't help you.'

'Then I will turn only the key I need, and you will die. Remember, before the stars finish their fall.'

The dogs cluster and pace around the Jackal. There's a sound of wild flapping. Dark shapes against a dark landscape. The Jackal's robe fans out, and the dogs turn to shadow.

Like dark burned paper swirling above the tree stump, the shadows rise and the Jackal is gone.

My hands, arm and face are grazed, my head throbbing. My top is crusted with dirt, my skirt stained. There are clumps of soil in my hair. It's dark and I'm limping down a dark road with no pavement. I don't know where the others are. I don't know the way back to the Stander house. I don't have my phone.

The houses around are hidden behind high walls, old oak trees. A car passes too close, making me stumble.

I stop at an iron gate and peer down the long drive, catching a glimpse of a huge house. I press the buzzer. It's a long while before anyone answers. Eventually, a tired voice says, 'Hello?'

'I'm sorry to disturb.' I'm stumbling over the words; I sound drunk. 'Please could I use your phone?'

There's silence on the other side, just static.

'Please,' I say.

'Don't bother us again.'

I walk on. Eventually, a car passes me and screeches to a halt a little way ahead. It reverses, and while it's moving, the passenger door opens and, in the street light, Auntie Chantie is half-running towards me. She has her arms around me, and Auntie Glynis is there too and then I'm bundled into the back seat with Minnie. I slump down, my head on her lap as she strokes my hair, and that's when I know I'm safe.

13

GOAT

I'm running. The world burns.

Faster, Savannah.

On the other side of the river, the woman faces away from me. Her hair is a black veil down her back. It's Hella. I know this with the certainty of dreams. And if I can just reach her, I will be OK.

Behind me, something follows. Gains on me.

She turns her head slightly. I still can't see her face.

Near the river, the ground is stony but I don't slow down.

I don't see the bundle until I've landed on the ground. I look at the thing that tripped me this time. A bundle of rags that heaves and shudders. I crawl towards it. A loud squall breaks the silence of the night. Leaning over the bundle of rags, I see.

It's a baby.

I wake up.

*

The next morning, Kim seems smaller than normal, frail. Her eyes are puffy and it's all my fault again. We're silent over our morning drinks, and the toast sits unclaimed in the toaster. Yesterday's message on the fridge mocks us: *Fight fire with your fists, and you'll get burned.*

'You really frightened me, Savannah,' Kim says suddenly. The kitchen doors are open, the sun shining on our small back-yard. The potted plants look thirsty and miserable.

We didn't walk in backwards last night. Minnie always says that if you come home after midnight you should walk back-wards through the door, so that the jinn and devils can't follow. But I suppose opportunistic jinn and devils are the least of my worries right now.

I examine my hands, knowing that Kim's staring at the bruise on my cheek, the scratches on my temple. The red marks spreading on my shoulder. She hasn't seen the grazes on my stomach.

I can still hear Arrow's screams inside my head.

I take a sip of too-hot chocolate, burning my throat.

'You can't just disappear.' Kim's voice cracks and she takes a moment to steady herself. 'You worried all of us. Why did you do it? Don said you argued with Dex?'

'We didn't argue,' I say feebly.

'There's a story,' Kim says, 'about a beautiful princess who was awful by day – mean, cruel and angry. At night, she turned into a mouse and she cried for all the terrible things she did.'

'It's not like that,' I shout.

'Then what is it?' Kim whispers. 'What's going on with you,

Savannah?' Her face is crumpled. 'You're angry, I get it, I really do. But lately, it's more. You are out of control.'

My breath catches.

'Freda's anger destroyed her.' Kim clutches her cup. 'I don't want yours to destroy you.'

'It's real.' My eyes are open so wide as I appeal to her. I need her to believe me. 'The curse is real. It killed Freda. And it's going to kill me.'

She doesn't answer. Her mouth opens, then shuts again. Her chin trembles, like she's trying not to cry.

The words are at the tip of my tongue: *I'm scared, Kim.*

After the longest moment, Kim puts her cup down and stands. 'I'm going to be late. We'll finish this conversation tonight.' She pauses by the door. 'Please,' she says wearily. 'Stay out of trouble.' She's scared too.

My shoulders slump as the front door closes. Kim's cup is still full.

I clear the dishes, knowing I should keep busy. Because when I shut my eyes, I see shadow dogs leaping. Arrow falling. When it's quiet, I'm sure I hear distant howling. I wish I was working, but Harrison is at the forge today. My school friends are back-packing in Australia and I have no one to distract me from my imminent demise.

I settle on my bed, making notes of what I remember from the park: living magic, prowling season, demon bonds. I write down the wild dreams I've been having, and as I write, I search the images for a girl's name. Then it strikes me: remnants from Hella's escape must have pushed into Freda's dreams too.

Maybe she wrote them down in her notebook.

My phone vibrates with a text from Kim: *Sorry I rushed off. We'll talk properly this evening. xoxo*

My mood lifts a little. Picking up Freda's notebook, I go through more anecdotes, looking for her dreams. It feels like Freda is talking to me, taking my hand and leading me. Not in a spooky way, but with the stories she'd written down. I read about cursed children, about a young woman who woke at 3 a.m. to find strange faces smiling from the edge of her bed. I read about a wife whose marriage suddenly went sour. The gardener dug up a Barbie doll with its face sawn off. When she destroyed the doll, all her troubles went away.

And I feel closer to Freda.

Freda took care with this book. She drew borders and boxes with a ruler and pasted inspiring quotes and meditations between the stories – clearly, she and Kim had that in common. The pages are thick and wavy with glue. Interspersed are recipes for pickled fish, daltjies, butter biscuits and more. Several shopping lists remind Freda what to buy: dhania, jeera, onions.

Then I see the word *dream* and I sit up straighter. On a page all by itself is an imperfect drawing of a strelitzia, the petals coloured orange. Beneath, Freda's written: *Slept so well last night. Dreamed I was on a bed of strelitzias.*

That's it? Where are the details of the dream, Freda?

As I lean back, the book shifts slightly. A chunk of pages flips over, revealing a folded square of thin writing paper tucked towards the spine. I unfold it and the writing is rust-coloured, spiky.

UNHIDING
Brings Hidden Magic to the Surface.
Opens the Eyes of the Star-Touched,
That They May See What Is Hidden in Plain Sight.

Beneath are instructions. A spell. *Opens the Eyes of the Star-Touched.*

There's a soft flapping sound. The beating of something small and delicate. Searching the room, I see a butterfly.

I read the instructions.

Make this offering to the Sisters: a bite of flesh, a pinch of salt, a drink of wine, a sprinkle of earth and a petal.

I'm going to do it, I decide. Freda had this page for a reason. She seems to have known more than I do. This Unhiding can help me see what I'm missing, maybe reveal Hella's true name.

I find a wooden tray in the kitchen, and search in the fridge for Quinton's precious steak. I cut a sliver, get the salt shaker and pour red wine into a brass goblet ornament. I go outside and scoop up a sprinkle of earth and take a fallen hibiscus flower from the ground.

'Hey, Savannah.' Solly watches from his stoep, the lines between his eyebrows even deeper than usual. 'What are you doing?'

'I'm picking flowers,' I say brightly.

He looks at the withered flower in my hand. 'That flower is verlep.'

'I find beauty in everything, Solly.'

'You're so strange.' He sighs and goes back to his phone.

In my room, I clear space on the floor and draw the curtains. From my bookshelf, I take an old wooden statue of a woman. It used to stand on Freda's bedside table, along with candles, crystals and her tarot cards. *It's magic*, she'd told me with a wink. *Shhh, don't tell Kim.* When Freda died, Kim threw the cards and crystals out, but I begged her to let me keep the figurine. I've seen others like it at the market – a power figure, they call it. For making magic.

I place the bite of raw steak and earth in its belly cavity. The instructions don't call for that, but it feels right. In a brass goblet, the petals float in wine.

My gifts to the Sisters.

I read the other instructions. Standing barefoot on the wooden floorboards, I circle five times, sprinkling salt as I turn.

Inside the circle are four lit candles. The Sisters. My reflection in the full-length mirror watches with quiet concentration.

I think of Freda, doing this same spell. Even if the spell worked for her, she still didn't break the curse before she died. Vicious determination tears through me. I will not let the curse take me too.

My arms are outstretched and the tips of my fingers are tingling. The house is silent, but I feel the walls sigh, the air prickle. A vague memory stirs, of Auntie Chantie, Auntie Dotty and Freda in a darkened room. Candles and something drawn on the floor. The hurried clear-up when Minnie's car pulled into the drive.

I check the instructions: *Taking your time, present yourself to each star using the words below. Feel yourself enter their presence. When you have the attention of all four stars, chant the invocation.*

I raise the goblet and say, 'I present myself to the Claw, who rules water and the willing.'

I lower my head and wait. I'm not sure what I'm waiting for, but it feels polite to leave a pause. Then I turn ninety degrees. 'I present myself to the Arrow, who rules air and the fierce.'

Lifting the power figure, I turn another ninety degrees and say, 'I present myself to the Jackal, who rules fire and the broken.'

Still holding the power figure, I turn a final time. 'I present myself to the Worm, who rules earth and the mundane.'

The butterfly lifts up, wings fluttering as it crosses the room. I read out from the paper.

'I gift my eyes. Two. You, open them.

Uncover.

Lay bare what was once unseen.'

The pageantry of it, the silent house and darkened room, makes everything feel immediate. I'm alert. My arms are stretched out like I am poised to fly. The prickling of something stirring, just beneath the surface of things.

Exhaustion hits me suddenly, like a blow, leaving me weak and light-headed. The room starts to swirl.

I sink into a crouch, dropping my head deeper to fight off the dizziness.

After a moment, I look up. In the mirror I can see, above

my bed, silvery symbols marking the wall. The marking is delicate, thin and light, but there.

Fear and anger tumble through me as I study the marks. Then I search the room, looking for more, but find nothing. My breathing is sharp and shallow, my head pounding. I'm glued to the floor studying the symbols above my bed, symbols that hadn't been there before I did the Unhiding.

Or rather, symbols I couldn't see before I did the Unhiding.

White-hot pain shoots through my head. I raise my hands to my temples, sinking to the floor.

When I come back to myself, I'm lying across the salt circle, one arm stretching towards the door, the other beneath my chest. The thin cotton of my sundress is perilously close to the candle flame. The symbols are still above my bed.

I get to my feet. The power figure has fallen over. I pick her up, her belly still stuffed with my offering. The petal floating in the wine.

When I return from the kitchen with a bucket and scrubbing brush, I stand on my bed and scrub. I scour the wall until it is clean. Then, methodically, I check every room, finding more symbols beside the outside doors, and clean those too. I don't know what they mean, or who put them there, but I am skeeved out. I need answers. And there's only one person I know to ask.

14

BLACK FEATHER

I'm out of the door, down the front steps and into the noon heat before I even know what I'm doing. I fumble for the card Mama Daline gave me. Before I can stop myself, I text Zenande.

You around?

As I'm walking towards the Main Road, my phone vibrates with a reply from Zenande. *At Greenmarket Sq. What do you need?*

I don't reply.

All my life, there's been a normal level of weird. Superstition. Don't let the duiwels in after midnight. A basic melody of strange.

This is another pitch entirely. The fire that did not harm at Carniveil, the smoke-hazed tent with Mama Daline and her bones, the drumming and the shadow dogs. The jackal-faced figure in the clearing, that terrifying voice. The writing on my wall. Like a descant that weaves in and out of the basic melody. Unseen till now, but always there.

This is how the curse plays out. Everything that is happening to me now has happened before. To Freda, to all the angry women who came before me.

Something inside me is taking root. And as it grows, I am able to see a world that's always been there. Waiting to receive me.

I reach the Main Road and flag down a minibus taxi. The van is nearly full. The gaadtjie yells 'Cape Town' and seats me in the packed middle row. My shoulder rests in the armpit of a man in a security uniform. He looks as unhappy about our proximity as I am.

Greenmarket Square is cobbled, and packed with colourful stalls. Centuries ago, the market here sold produce and people; now it's mostly curios and souvenirs. Now, as then, it's a place where people with different stories come together. Starting near the church, I work my way through the large, busy market, searching for Zenande.

Halfway down one of the rows, a man walking too fast crashes into me. It's Quinton.

'Savannah.' He blinks. 'What are you doing here?'

'What do people normally do at markets?'

'Look, Savannah,' he says. Quinton often starts his sentences with 'look' or 'listen'. 'I'm glad I bumped into you.'

I'm not, I think. But I behave. This time.

'I owe you an apology,' Quinton says, pulling off his sunglasses.

I stare at him; this is unexpected.

120

'I was out of line the other night and I'm sorry. I know it must seem to you like this is all moving too fast. I should have considered things from your point of view.'

I don't know what to say. I've nursed my resentment towards Quinton for a full twelve months. I need to hate him. Plus, I don't believe a word he says.

Still, there's no harm in playing this game for a while.

'Apology accepted.' I smile a liar's smile.

'Are we OK?'

'Sure.' I look at him. There's a frown creasing his brow, like he's genuinely concerned. I feel the faintest flicker of uncertainty. Kim's been mostly happy this last year.

I shut that thought down fast. He's scum. I'm just the only one who sees it.

'Listen,' Quinton says. 'Do me a small favour, would you?' He looks embarrassed, like a little boy. 'When we were here a few weeks ago Kim saw something she loved but she wouldn't buy it. You know what she's like.'

I nod; Kim rarely buys nice things for herself.

'She said no way was I to buy it, but, well, I just did. For our wedding. Don't tell her you saw me today, will you?'

Curious, I think. I hesitate. 'Sure. I can do that.'

He moves in for a fist bump. I hold up a hand. 'I don't fist-bump.'

He laughs but then his eye falls on the deep red on my wrist. His eyes darken with worry. He thinks he hurt me when he grabbed my wrist, I realise.

'That wasn't you,' I say.

'Oh. Good,' he says, his expression clearing. 'I'd better get to work.' He smiles at me. 'Truce, Savannah, remember?'

And then he's gone.

'Smile, girl.' A wiry man at a perfume-and-soap stall leans out. 'Why so serious?'

I roll my eyes. There's always one of these guys. Everywhere I go, they want me to fokken smile.

For no good reason, I answer his question, 'My mom's getting married to a doos.'

'Ja, shame.' He thinks. 'But is he a rich doos?'

I shrug. 'His car's nice.'

'Here, for you. Use on their wedding day.' He hands me a small spray bottle. It has the crying laughing emoji on it and the label says: *Though Your Heart Is Breaking.*

'Does it work?' I ask.

He nods slowly. 'For you, sure,' he says.

I thank him and put it in my bag. I walk on, passing a stall selling funky T-shirts with funny slogans. A jewellery stall. The man behind the display watches me with a broad smile.

'A pretty ring for a pretty girl,' he calls.

I pick up a ring with a deep blue stone.

'Go on,' the man says. 'Try it on.'

I push it on my finger. It's a little tight, but so exquisite. I want it, but I've been spending too much. When I try to take it off, I can't.

'It's stuck.'

'Don't worry.' He's polite. 'That happens, in the heat. I have some baby oil here. May I?'

122

Taking my hand, he dabs the oil around the base of my finger. The ring slides off and as I move my hand back, his eye catches the marks on my wrist. He frowns.

'You belong to the Market,' he says, emphasising the word. Market with a capital *M*. 'You should have said.'

'I'm new,' I say softly.

'Of course,' he says. 'Well, now that I know, I can show you some really special pieces.'

He reaches below the display and pulls out a large wooden box. 'Here we go. This ring, now – he who wears it will never leave you. This pendant will drain love from your enemy's heart – that one is popular. Or this hair slide, it's a blade, see? It can cut through anything. Bones, sinew, metal ...'

He holds the box out to me.

'Look,' he says.

I'm looking, but I only see rings, bangles, earrings. A gold chain with a red love heart. A hair slide made of small fake pearls. That's all.

His eyes narrow. 'Maybe I misjudged ...'

He moves the box away. Suddenly, I *have* to see inside. I lay my hand on the box, stopping him. In my head, unbidden, come the words from the Unhiding spell in Freda's notebook.

I gift my eyes. Two. You, open them.

Uncover.

Lay bare what was once unseen.

The silvery symbols on my bedroom wall.

Let me see, let me see.

I draw the box closer. It's a few seconds before I realise.

They move.

All the pieces inside move gently, as if they're alive. The ring has tiny razor teeth. Between two careful fingers, I lift it up and the teeth retract. I think about Ishaam, school head boy and my boyfriend earlier in the year. He ended it. Months ago, I would have been very tempted by this ring.

The mixture of delight and horror I'm feeling must show on my face, because the trader gives a sharp shiny smile.

'Will take more than baby oil to get that one off.' He chuckles as the teeth snap out. I put it down quickly.

The heart-shaped pendant is an actual human heart in miniature, with four chambers, vena cava and aorta. It beats with gentle throbs. Moving a hand over it, I feel its pull. The heartbeat speeds up. The stones on a pair of earrings whisper to me.

'What about this?' He lifts a bracelet from the box. 'The snake's bite will sedate the wearer, making them yours to control completely. They come in pairs, and I've only one set left.'

The bracelet shifts; the slim embossed gold bangle becomes a small coiled snake.

'No, thank you.'

'This, then. Please, a gift.' He leans over the table and holds out a vicious-looking red-stained blade; it swiftly retracts inside a hair slide studded with many tiny pearls. He pushes it into my hand. I close my fingers around it.

'Because of your affliction,' he says, looking at my wrist. There's an unpleasant edge to his voice. 'You will remember my kindness.'

Before I can stop myself, I say, 'These are bad, aren't they? Veiled magic. Like the Jackal.' So quiet, that last word.

He lowers his voice. 'It is not permitted to speak of that in the Market.' His eyes meet mine. 'You like my pretty jewels, don't you? Seems like you're drawn to *veiled* magic.'

I turn to go.

We'll keep your secrets if you keep ours.

The words are repeated whispers inside my head. They come from the stones in his box.

I drop the hair slide into my bag and practically run from the stall.

The market is swimming around me. The noises are loud and relentless. Too much.

I make myself look at the stalls. At the tie-dyed clothes, hand-painted kitchenware.

See, Savannah, I tell myself. *All normal. Nothing to worry about here.* I walk on, more calmly.

I've passed six stalls when I stop abruptly.

It's one of several stalls selling wax print fabric. The fabric is displayed in folded squares, pinned to the canvas wall. In the last row, the colours swirl and patterns dance. The blue rolls like a wave, whimsical and dreamy. Just looking at it lulls me into a sudden serenity. Beside it, the orange and red fight each other like tongues of flame. They're bold and brash. Wearing that cloth, I could take on anything.

'Looking for anything in particular?' the vendor calls. She knows.

'What do they do?' I ask. I am wary now.

'Depends what you need them to do.' She shrugs and her large hoop earrings jingle.

'Let's say I want to … persuade someone.'

She doesn't hesitate. 'The green with yellow detail. You need a Market seamstress though, to be safe. My lady won't try any funny business.'

I shake my head and step away. Somehow I can tell that the fabric isn't dangerous, not like the jewellery was. I move on to the next stall and the next. There is no magic there at all.

I pass the perfume stall, and the man who told me to smile reaches out his arm. He spritzes a scent, almost directly into my face.

Unexpectedly, I giggle. I feel silly, playful.

'That's more like it.' The vendor smiles with me. 'I also got: generous, no appetite, horny, and very sleepy. Buy one get one free. Today only.'

I hurry off, another giggle spilling from me.

'Look at you, bad angel.' Another man, his hand hovering just above my bare arm. 'Let me take you to the Nightmarket.'

I glide past him, grinning.

As I walk on, I realise that certain stalls have a light, almost invisible glow.

Magic.

Watching a vendor give a woman her change back, I see that she's handing over strips of newspaper instead of notes.

The woman glances at the pieces of paper, then puts them in her wallet, unsuspecting. She sees money, I realise.

'Wait,' I call to the customer. A giggle escapes me.

The vendor tuts at me.

'Mind your own business.'

Her eye falls on the deep red marks on my wrist. They're almost pretty, I think, like garnets under my skin.

'Or better yet, keep far away. We don't need any trouble here.' Her gaze meets mine. 'And you, girl, are trouble.'

15

SEASICK

I walk back to the taxi rank in a daze. I haven't found Zenande, but I can't stay another minute. I'll call later to ask about the writing on the wall. Now I'm in a fever dream, and I want to get home.

Waiting at the traffic lights, a leftover giggle falls out. The woman beside me gives me a skief look.

In the taxi back, I am again wedged beside strangers, but this time it's reassuring. The discomfort is grounding, familiar. A world away from the strangeness of the market. Is it, though? I steal a glance at the boy beside me. He looks ordinary. But how can I be sure? How can I be sure of anyone again?

Near my stop, I call to the driver. The walk home is only five minutes, but I'm so depleted. I stand on the pavement a moment.

'You all right, girl?' the gaadtjie says.

No, not all right. 'Just tired.'

Two men unfold themselves from the back row and step out too. On the pavement, they light up cigarettes. One nudges the other and winks at me. I roll my eyes and set off down the road.

At home, I drink iced water, then go to my room. I lie down and fall asleep in my dress. I dream of necklaces with beating hearts, and bracelets that snake around my wrists. I dream there is a storm in the house. It rattles and shakes the house. Pictures fall off the walls, books from their shelves. I dream there's a jackal in my room, sniffing my hand.

I wake up. There is a lingering feeling of wet on my hand.

Getting up, I feel strange. I stand dead still, as if that could quell the wildness inside. There's a loud, jarring sound from another room. Like something falling. Kim must be home early.

I check the time. It's only four.

There's another thud from Kim's room.

I go out into the corridor. Standing in the sunlit passage, my bare feet on the uneven wooden floor, I pause. My hackles up.

'Kim?' I say softly, walking towards her bedroom door.

It's slightly ajar and I push it open. Inside are two figures. They are so engrossed that they don't notice me. One rips a drawer from the chest, upends it and tosses the drawer to the side. The other pulls dresses, jackets, shirts from Kim's wardrobe.

They are monsters. Huge eyes rimmed with red. Horns protruding from wild hair.

No, not monsters; just men in masks. I duck out of sight.

Run. Call the armed response. I've read the newspapers, and there're too many bad ways this could play out. I could be assaulted, beaten, raped, kidnapped, murdered. Every woman's constant fear. I've never not been afraid.

And yet. I am trembling with rage. This is my home.

The men are in the far corner now, rooting through Kim's jewellery box. They have broken the lock.

My anger rattles its cage. I surge forward.

'Get out!' I scream. I leap over the bed and pounce on the man with the box in his hand. I take him by surprise and the box and jewellery scatters. Rings roll under the bed, earrings fall into the cracks between the floorboards. I fly at him with my fists.

'Get out. Get out. Get out.'

He grunts, trying to grab my arms, but I dance back. On the chest of drawers is a heavy candlestick, one of Harrison's, and I grab it. The man lunges for me and I hit him hard across the shoulder and run to the door.

Too late. A hand grabs the back of my dress.

He knocks the candlestick out of my grip and holds my wrists. I glimpse Kim's sheer black stockings balled up in his hand before he stuffs them into my mouth. I taste his fingers on my lips, in my mouth. Motor oil and salt combined with washing powder and a faint trace of Kim's perfume. He winds a pair of tights around my cheeks and mouth.

I've missed my chance to get away.

I'm kicking myself for not running when I had a chance. For letting my anger take charge.

Rough hands turn over my wrist, exposing the marks there. 'You were right,' he says, looking up at the second man. 'Oh, my girl. You are going to make my dreams come true.'

The second man strokes a finger down my cheek. 'You'll earn us a fortune at the Nightmarket.'

I jerk and squirm to break the first man's grasp. It only makes him grip me harder. He pulls my wrists together and binds them with a thin silk scarf.

Beneath the fear, that nub of anger burns. These men. These bastard men. How dare they?

The second man pulls the mask from his face as he examines a ring. I recognise him. One of the men who followed me off the taxi. In my home.

Without warning, my anger flares again. I kick out, hard. I must get lucky and cause some damage, because the first man grunts and his hold relaxes slightly. Breaking out of his grasp, I run, hands still tied in front of me.

My keys to the door and security gate are in the kitchen, so I sprint to the back of the house. Shoes sound on the floorboards behind me. The small courtyard, with its high walls, is a trap.

Veering into the kitchen, I find it upended. The toaster and kettle on the floor, dishes smashed to pieces. The portable panic button is on the counter, next to my keys.

The unmasked man is right behind me, the first still in Kim's room. I lunge for the button and miss, then scrabble for my keys – at least they are sharp. Instead, my fingers snatch up a small bottle. The spray from the market. Desperately, I turn and spray it full in his face. He cries out. Dropping the bottle, I inch forward and grab the panic button awkwardly in my bound hands, jab it hard.

The alarm screams through the house. I run from the kitchen, uproarious laughter sounding behind me. The man is on his knees, laughing. His eyes are red and streaming with tears.

Falling into the bathroom, I slam the door behind me.

I turn the lock with trembling, bound hands, dropping the panic button.

The men are just outside the bathroom, banging and rattling the door. One of them is still laughing.

The house is a hundred years old, the lock is flimsy. It wouldn't be hard to break it. In the uneven gap between the door and the floor, I can see the outline of shoes. I wait, barely daring to breathe.

After a long moment, they walk away. Laughter sounds down the passage.

Minutes pass. I tug at the tights wrapped about my face but they're tied too tight.

'Savannah?' I hear a voice from the passage.

I unlock the door. The knob turns and it flies inwards.

At the bathroom door are Rosie and Dex.

'Oh my God, Savannah,' Rosie says. Dex pushes past her as I sink to the edge of the bathtub.

'Are you hurt?' He runs an eye over me as I shake my head. 'Get a knife,' he tells his sister.

He works the tights from my face, careful with my hair. When they're off, I spit out the stockings, breathing heavily.

Rosie returns with a sharp kitchen knife and slices through the scarf. Stretching my wrists, I catch a glimpse of my reflection in the mirror: dark hair like a rat's nest. Eyes wide and terrified. New marks mottling the skin along my jawline.

'Are you hurt?' Rosie says. She smooths back my hair.

I shake my head. 'Will you turn off the alarm?' My voice sounds strange as I tell her the code.

'Hello?' There are voices down the passage.

'That'll be security.' Rosie looks relieved as she leaves the room.

'How did you get in?' I ask.

'The door and security gate were wide open,' says Dex. I get to my feet but my legs are shaking. I start for the door but he puts a hand on my arm.

'Savannah,' he says. He pulls a pen from his jeans pocket and scrawls something on a card, then hands it to me. Embarrassment and concern are at war on his face. The alarm suddenly stops ringing.

'If you ever need me,' he says. 'If you ever need help. That's my number.'

I look at him with surprise.

'Last night, during the game, I went at you too hard. I'm sorry.'

'It's fine, Dex. Really.' The game seems like a lifetime ago.

'I should have been more careful.'

'I'm still in one piece.' I touch his arm. 'It's not your fault. You didn't make me wander off.'

'Savannah?' a voice calls from the passage.

'The police are waiting.' I let out a loud exhale.

'Come, let's do this.' He takes my hand, giving it a squeeze. Together we walk out of the bathroom.

In the passage, Solly waits. He leans against the wall, worry deepening the lines between his eyebrows. 'Savannah.' He pushes off the wall. 'When I saw the police I thought ...'

'I'm fine.' I will be.

Solly sees our joined hands, his face blank as he studies Dex.

'This is Dex.' I retract my hand. 'He's an old friend.'

'I live next door,' Solly says to Dex. 'This neighbourhood can be rough, so we look out for Savannah and Kim.' He's upset, like he blames himself for not being here to prevent the break-in.

In the living room, I sit on the sofa. Men with guns are checking the house and I'm grateful that Kim's careful budgeting meant we could afford private security. Rosie places a cup of sweet hot tea on the table beside me. She squeezes my arm, and I feel her warmth, her solidity. I'm glad she's here.

'I'll need to take your fingerprints so we can rule them out.' A burly police officer takes my still-trembling fingers and smears them in the ink pad, then presses them one by one on the form on the table. 'They trashed this place good. Why?'

Maybe veilwitches like to break things. Maybe it's the petty cruelty of thieves. I've heard stories about burglars cooking themselves meals, trying on outfits, pissing on furniture. Maybe they wanted me afraid, maybe they were setting a stage – a break-in gone wrong, to mask the kidnapping and selling thing.

'Didn't take the electronics.' The policeman looks at the TV, the sound system. 'Unusual. You sure this isn't some jealous ex-boyfriend, getting payback?'

'Does it matter?' Dex says.

I realise in that moment that I am almost always angry now. Even when I'm afraid or happy or tired. It's my constant, this low-grade buzz of rage.

It's exhausting.

'It wasn't a boyfriend I dumped,' I say, slowly and clearly. 'They followed me from the Main Road.'

From Greenmarket Square, I think. They sensed the magic; maybe they saw the marks.

'They followed you?' The woman officer is alert. 'Any idea why?'

I shake my head. The truth is too much for them. Zenande's words echo inside me: *The rising magic will draw veilwitches to you, like flies to honey.*

'No,' I say. 'No idea.'

16

WAX

The aunties descend upon us with pots of food and vats of cleaning materials. I'm folded into arms, pressed against soft breasts that smell of musky perfume. Their eyes are red with held-back tears; they're haunted by dead Savannah, kidnapped Savannah. The bloody, injured spectres of those other Savannahs are there in the room with us.

Auntie Dotty touches a light finger to the new marks on my jawline.

'Savannah.' My name in three drawn-out parts. That's all she says.

Like a SWAT team, precise and efficient, they move through the house. Minnie, in her blue cleaning tracksuit, is commander. Rosie, her hair piled up in a messy bun, sweeps up broken glass, rehangs curtains, tidies the living room. They chat as they clean, and I hear Minnie's chuckle, Rosie's clear, infectious laugh. Auntie Dotty, insisting she needs a man's help, goes with

Dex to clear the broken furniture in Kim's room. Auntie Nazeema and Auntie Chantie, always reliable, work through the chaos in the kitchen.

There's comfort in the work, in the small repetitive tasks punctuated by familiar voices chatting and calling to each other.

'Lazy bums,' Auntie Dotty hollers through the window when she sees Tietie and Auntie Glynis sneaking a smoke on the stoep.

Kim rushes in. She finished her shift to a flurry of terrifying messages.

'I'm giving notice to the landlord right away,' she says, after asking me for the tenth time whether I'm OK. 'We'll find a flat in a gated complex. With security guards.'

'Let's talk about that later,' Minnie murmurs, steering her to my bedroom, which suffered the least damage.

I don't want to move. I like where we live, our community of families, students, hipsters and old hippies. I like that the Athaan sounds through the streets. That there've long been different skin colours here, even when it was against the law.

'Oh, thank the Lord,' Minnie says, seeing Inez at the front door. 'She can keep an eye on Kim.'

Inez comes inside, drawing me into her arms. 'You OK, honey?' She searches my face and I nod. 'Did they take anything?'

'Not sure. My keys.' They'd been on the kitchen counter and now they're not there.

When the work is done, we gather in the living room and eat dinner with our plates on our laps. The tomato bredie is comforting. Its spicy sweetness warms me from the inside. We're crowded in here, with aunties on every couch and chair. I'm on the floor, and the twins have drifted into the tiny adjoining room where the TV plays softly in the background. I glance over. A teen detective has just found a partially decomposed body.

I lower my loaded fork.

'Quinton's on his way.' Kim walks into the room, ending a call. 'We'll stay at his place until the locks are changed.'

My stomach takes a dive. I pop the last bite into my mouth, the tomato acid on my tongue.

'Good. Better to have a man around,' Minnie says. I strongly disagree.

'Where will I sleep?' I say to Kim. Quinton only has one bedroom in his Sea Point flat.

'Quinton's room, with me. He'll take the couch,' Kim says.

I do not want to stay in Quinton's room. I do not want to stay in his flat.

I can't ask Minnie. She shares a house with Auntie Dotty, Uncle Mervyn and Harrison, and space is tight. None of the other aunties have a guest room, but they won't mind if I sleep on the couch.

'You can stay with us, Savannah,' Inez says. 'If that's helpful.'

'I can?' I am unable to hide my relief.

'For as long as you need,' says Inez. 'We have plenty of room.'

138

Kim hesitates. 'I don't know.'

'Please, Kim,' I say. 'Quinton's flat is tiny and I'll just be in your way.'

I can see her weighing this up. Then she nods slowly. 'If you want to.'

'In fact ...' Inez smiles at me, then glances at Kim. 'I wanted to ask if Savannah could come away with us. I'm doing a feature on the Winelands for *Wild Heart* and we're staying in this gorgeous cottage. Rosie and Dex would be delighted if you joined us.'

Dex does not look delighted. Rosie's beside him, half watching the muted TV. It's the news now: another lying politician. I read the ticker, which says, *Senior cabinet minister denies harassment claims.*

'There's a spectacular mountain pool.' Inez's eyes shine.

'That would be awesome,' I say quickly, before Kim can raise any objection. 'Thanks.'

Inez smiles her lovely smile and Rosie squeals. 'Perfect. Get a bag ready for tonight, and we'll collect the rest of your things tomorrow.'

Kim isn't happy, but she's not going to protest in front of everyone.

Dex's face is tight.

'I'm heading off,' he says quietly. He stands and walks over to his mother. As he passes, I half expect the aunties to raise score cards. Auntie Glynis's mouth is downturned; she's not a fan. Auntie Nazeema's expression is sceptical, like she's thinking, *Yes, yes, fine to look at, but can he think?* Auntie Chantie smiles coyly. Tietie surreptitiously reaches for the smokes in her bag.

Auntie Dotty, sitting behind Inez, catches my eye and dramatically fans herself.

I wag a scolding finger at her before going to my bedroom to grab a few things. Thinking of the swimming pool, I throw in a costume. I'm on my way back to the living room when I see Dex trying to open the now-locked security gate with Kim's keys.

'You have to jiggle it,' I say, dropping my bag.

Unlocking the gate, I step outside, escaping the house for a moment. The stars are out and the night is pleasantly warm, so I walk down the path. Behind me, Dex is silent. Not rude, exactly. It's more like he's politely tolerating my company.

Quinton pulls up and, using only the palm of his hand, parallel parks. I am so not in the mood to see him right now. Not after this day.

Dex has opened the door of his car on the driver's side. Before I can think twice, I open the passenger door, and slip in beside him.

If he's surprised, he doesn't show it.

'What's up?' he says.

'I'll go back with you.' I don't have anything with me, no phone, no money, but I don't want to go back inside.

'I'm not going straight home.'

'Where are you going? Somewhere fun?'

'No. Just picking up something.'

'I'll keep you company.' I fret with Freda's ring.

140

He sighs.

'Why did you move back here if you didn't want to?' He's eighteen. He could have made his own way.

'I found an incentive.' He shifts in his seat to look at me. 'You should go back inside.' His voice is kind, which somehow makes this more embarrassing.

I hang my head. 'I don't want to.'

He is silent. Just as I'm about to open the door, though, he starts the car. He digs in his pocket and hands me his phone.

'You'd better let them know you're with me.'

We drive down the Main Road, stopping and starting at the many traffic lights. We pass fast food places, shops shut up for the night, a few sex workers looking for business. Dex is quiet, and the silence between us isn't entirely comfortable. On the radio, a therapist gives relationship advice.

'They struggle with discussing the *sex-sual* side of things,' she says.

'Are you starting university in February?' I say, so that I don't have to hear the radio doctor say 'sex-sual' again.

'Yeah, engineering at UCT.' He glances at me. 'And you?'

'Arts at Nova.' It's where Kim will get a discount on fees. Suddenly, it spills out of me, words I haven't admitted to anyone else. 'They have a costume design stream from second year. I'm really hoping to get into that.' But Kim will say it's not *practical*. Meaning, not a safe route to earning a safe income.

'Is that why you were in the library that day?'

No, I was researching curses. 'Something like that.' I mean, I

141

did flick through that one book. 'Why were you there?'

'My mom arranged access with Kim.' To my surprise, he elaborates. 'I was looking into the Four Sisters myth. After Carniveil.'

'Did you find anything?' I try to keep my voice casual.

'Nah, not much.'

'However, *sex-sual* intimacy is obviously important ...' the radio psychologist insists.

'Please can we change that?' I say, and Dex laughs. Finally. I didn't think his programming included laughter.

'Does sex-sual intimacy make you uncomfortable, Savannah?' he teases as he changes the radio station. 'Didn't take you for a prude.'

'Not a prude.' Just, it's a warm night and we're alone in the car.

'I'm not convinced.'

'Do you want me to convince you?'

I'd meant it as a mock threat but then I realise how it sounds, and my cheeks heat. A loud, delighted laugh falls out of him.

'I can't tell if you're hitting on me,' he says, still smiling, 'or trying to murder me.'

I give him a dazzling smile. 'If I was hitting on you,' I say, 'you'd know.'

That wipes his smirk right off. I let down the window, feeling the warm evening air. In the yellow street light, we pass a shop where a gang of friends hang outside beneath a flickering neon sign. They laugh and tease each other. Watching a girl my age, I am bitterly envious of her uncursed life. I want to flirt on a street corner and mess about with my friends on a hot summer night without a care in the world.

When I look back to the road, a signpost rises and Dex indicates left.

'That's where we're going?' I ask. This neighbourhood is known for gang violence, drug deals, and stories of children dying in crossfire.

'Yup.' Dex's eyes are on the road.

'What exactly are you picking up?' I ask. We drive past council flats. There's little green here. The street lights reveal a landscape of sand and cement, of chain-link fences and razor wire. 'A baggie?'

'No,' he says evenly, pulling up at the side of the road. On the opposite side, three large dogs snarl at us. 'That's my aunt's house.' He points a few doors down. 'We used to live in the small flat out back. My grandmother left something there for me before she went to the hospital.'

The house is a child's drawing. Box shape, two windows, the short path and a wire fence. I've seen it before, I think. The tiny patch of neatly cut grass and hydrangeas, which always remind me of old-lady church hats.

'In my dreams, this is always home.' He cuts the engine, picks up the keys. 'You can wait here if you prefer. I won't be long.'

At the street corner, a bunch of men are grouped around a bakkie, just talking. Still, I reach for the handle. 'I'll come in.'

As we get closer, I see the curtains are shut. The house is

cast in darkness. There's no flicker of TV.

'It doesn't look like anyone's here.'

'That's the idea,' he says, then starts down the weedy gravel drive towards the dark backyard.

The cement yard is filled with scrap, piles of tyres, rusted iron stacked with wood and scrap metal. In the corner is a tiny detached apartment. I've a brief flash of memory: Freda in this doorway, laughing. I move towards it, drawn by the memory.

'I've been here before,' I say.

'Many times.'

I hesitate, watch as Dex approaches the door. He tries the handle but it's locked, so he steps back, looking around. Suddenly I'm not sure about this.

'Where's your spirit of adventure, Savannah?' Dex senses my reluctance. He reaches into his pocket and pulls out lock-picking tools.

'What are you doing?' I eye the tools.

'Never met a restricted area I didn't want to explore, remember?' He examines the lock, then selects a slim metal pick.

'I thought this was your aunt's place?'

'It is.' He pushes the tool into the lock. 'There was a huge argument, years ago. We moved away shortly after. No contact for a decade.'

'Were you here in September?' I say. 'When your Ma Daphne died?' I know Inez was with her mother, but Kim hadn't said anything about the twins.

'Yeah, we came when we heard how sick she was.' He works the tool. 'It was really awkward and it ended in a screaming

144

fight between my mom and Aunt René at the funeral tea.'

Auntie René, whose property we're currently breaking and entering.

'What did they argue about?' I press. There's something to this story. I know from the hushed conversations between my aunties, the way they looked at each other whenever Inez's name was mentioned. Because of the accident. Nine-year-old Dex had been hurt when Auntie René and his Ma Daphne had been minding him. Boiling water fell on him, I think. I remember the hospital waiting room, drinking weak Oros with Rosie while Inez cried into Freda's arms. That was the last time I'd seen them.

'Family stuff.' He shrugs as the lock clicks. 'Aunt René accused my mom of stealing the family cookbook with generations of secret recipes.'

'Did she?'

'You know,' Dex says as he eases the door open, 'I think she probably did.'

He looks into the dark room. His face is hard. Then I realise the day of his accident is likely the last time he was here. His last memory of this childhood home.

'Ma Daphne left you something, huh?' I say in a lighter tone.

'She wanted me to have something of hers. When I visited her at the hospital, she told me where she'd hidden it.'

'A secret inheritance. Is it valuable?'

'Depends how you define valuable.'

He pulls a small torch from his pocket and we step into the

room, latching the door behind us. It's smaller than I remember, but the familiarity is immediate. Even in the dim light, I know this place. I know, beneath the lingering staleness of cigarettes, the smell of it. I know the shape of it. That to my left is a tiny bedroom with the double bunk, and in the corner right, a kitchenette. I didn't know where it was, but I've carried this warm, safe place with me for years.

17

PRIEST

Even in the near dark, they are there, the ghosts of happier times. Freda, Kim and Inez at the table, cackling like stage witches. The warmth of their togetherness. Me on the couch, eating buttery corn while watching cartoons, a twin on either side.

In the torchlight, I recognise the orange pine table pushed into the corner of the room, the brown couch that pulled out into Inez's bed.

The torch catches the coffee table, lighting up the remnants of a party. Empty beer bottles, full ashtrays. A bottle of Klipdrift and a two-litre Coke. Poker chips beside a pack of cards. A box of cigarettes with a Zippo neatly on top. Half-drunk glasses, like a party had been there just moments before and left in a hurry. Like they'd been interrupted.

Like they will be back any moment.

Dex catches my eye. 'This way.' There's speed to his

movements now, an urgency. He wasn't expecting this.

The door to the small second room is slightly ajar and Dex pushes it open. The double bunk, in the torchlight, is more worn and chipped than I thought. Stepping into the room, I'm gripped by a memory of Rosie and me giggling in a blanket fort on the bottom bunk. Dex, who liked to play the tyrant, holding us siege.

Dex walks to the built-in wardrobe and, setting the torch on the shelf, he crouches down. 'This was my secret hiding place. Only my grandmother knew about it.' He presses the thin panel between it and the floor and, after a moment, the white-painted wood swings out. He reaches his hand in and takes out a slim object wrapped in brown paper, which he slips into his back pocket. Reaching in again, he feels around, then extracts something else. It takes me a moment to recognise the long black hair, the brown plastic skin and impossibly proportioned body.

'That's my Yasmin!'

He stands up and I grab for the doll, but he snatches it out of my reach with a chuckle.

'You stole my doll.' My hands are on my hips but I can't conceal my incredulous amusement. 'You hid her.'

'In war, hostages may be taken.'

'I held a funeral for her! I made tiny sandwiches.' *And waited for you and Rosie to come.*

The Standers' leaving had been violent in its abruptness: one day we were together, Oros at the hospital. Within weeks, they were gone. I'd been devastated.

Moved to Joburg, Kim had said. *We'll visit them soon.* But soon never came, and after a few months they'd left for overseas.

Overseas. A single heavy word, not unlike *dead*, that pointed to absence. To the unreachable. Maybe the doll's funeral was my child's way of mourning the loss of my friends. And then, not long after, Freda was dead and this huge hole opened up inside me and ate everything, crunching through obedience, through patience. Leaving only fizzling rage.

Dex holds out Yasmin in a placatory gesture. 'After ten years, I guess we could start hostage negotiations.'

'What are your terms?' I eye Dex, then lunge for the doll. He laughs when he pulls her back, holding Yasmin out of my reach.

The games we'd played. Wild, long story games that sent roots into other worlds. That planted us there, twining us three together. We were best friends, but there was always a fight between me and Dex. Sometimes physical, where we'd wrestle each other on the ground until one of us got hurt. Usually him, because I fought dirty. But mostly our battles were mind games. One-upmanship, to see who would yield first.

'You really are the most infuriating boy.'

'I have many talents.'

I grab his arm, trying to pull Yasmin down. He laughs louder and I tighten my hold. It only makes him take the doll further out of my reach. Propelled by muscle memory, I dance my fingers up his rib where he was always so sensitive. He arches away, 'Aah, no. Please not that.' With a burst of laughter, I do it again. Squirming, he grabs my wrists. 'You're going to pay.'

Our grappling is interrupted by a sudden sound from the front door. A key inserted in the latch. Dex yanks me into the wardrobe, into the narrow hanging space beside the shelves. He kills the torch, closing the door behind him.

The space is tight, Dex stooping slightly because of the hanging rail above his head. There's a wall behind me, and I have to lean into it to keep from brushing Dex. My heart is beating so fast he must surely hear it. The living room light flicks on and the shadows of the slats paint a pattern on Dex's face. We peer through the slats, through the open door and into the other room.

The open door. My blood runs cold. It had been only slightly ajar when we came in. It's wide open now, revealing the group of men gathered around the coffee table. One lights up a cigarette, another pours a generous brandy and Coke.

The fourth man, the one who's standing, stares at the open door. He's young, in his early twenties I'd guess, and wiry, with buzz-cut hair. There are tattooed symbols just below his ear, down his neck and on his arms. Obsidian eyes and light brown skin. He looks strong. He looks a little scary.

Studying the door, he pulls a gun from the back of his jeans. The other three watch warily as he inches forward, gun in hand.

My heart hammers as he prowls towards the second room.

Then a black cat appears – it must have been sleeping on the window sill – padding to the door. He chuckles, tucks the gun away and picks up the cat, stroking its sleek black fur.

'There's your intruder, Jarred.' One of the others laughs as he deals cards with a fast hand.

Jarred turns to the table, letting the cat jump down to the ground as loud music begins to pump through the room. Do I imagine that his eyes linger at the wardrobe door?

'All right, julle naaiers, time to take your money.' Jarred rubs his hands as he sits. Someone whoops and the music is turned louder, swallowing their conversation. I feel Dex's body relax slightly. He leans forward, mouth to my ear. 'I think we might be here a while.'

He's not wrong. After ten minutes, I need to move. My knees are locked, my body stiff from trying to avoid brushing against Dex. The men playing cards give no sign they'll leave soon, so I might as well make this fun.

'You know I dance, right?' I straighten up, no longer hugging the wardrobe wall. 'I'm not the best in the company, but I enjoy it. One evening before a big performance, I was told that I, the understudy, would be going onstage. I quickly ran through a difficult piece, and of course, I sprained my ankle. Picked myself up, didn't tell anyone, and I danced onstage through the pain. It was the most uncomfortable hour of my life, but it taught me something.'

'What?'

'How to get through the uncomfortable.' I'm a little closer now. I can feel the heat off his body.

'What's your secret?' His voice is lower.

'Distraction.' I inch towards him.

'Any ideas how we distract ourselves from being stuck inside a tiny wardrobe?'

My chest touches his. The thin cotton of my dress falls on

the dark denim of his jeans. 'We play a game.'

He smiles. 'A game?'

'Only one of us can win.' I put my hands on his shoulders. He's wary.

'What do I have to do to win?'

'You have to take something from me,' I say.

'Why do I suspect this game is rigged?' Dex doesn't ask what *I* have to do to win. 'What must I take from you?'

I look up at him, deliberately coy. 'Guess.'

He's already distracted by how close I'm standing to him. By my hand tracing muscle through his T-shirt.

'I can't just take a kiss.' He's studying me carefully in the uneven light.

'You can, if that's what I want too.'

Now I've planted the image in his head. His hand comes up to my shoulder, lightly touching the bare skin beneath the thin strap. The other circles my waist, drawing me closer.

'Is that what you want, Savannah?'

His head dips. My hand trails down his back, hovers above his back pocket and the two treasures there. I tilt my head up, looking at him with wide eyes.

'Yes.' I'm a little breathless. Maybe I'm in over my head.

His eyes are suspicious. 'This is too easy.'

I hold his gaze, wishing I knew what he was thinking, and press into his embrace. One hand inches to his back pocket, the other down his shoulder. Dex is definitely distracted. Fingers gentle, I ease the doll from his back pocket.

Without warning, the wardrobe door is yanked open,

bright light spilling into the confined space. We quickly draw apart, me stuffing a hand into the large pocket of my sundress.

'If you wanted to visit, you could have called,' Jarred says. He doesn't sound pissed off, but his black eyes glitter with hostility. His friends are lined up behind him, aggression seeping from their bodies. 'Why are you here, Dex?'

Dex doesn't answer. There's a strange look on his face, warring emotions that I can't quite identify.

'Are you spying on us?' One of the heavier guys leans in and I roll my eyes. He looks like he's spoiling for a fight, as do the others right behind him. I step out of the wardrobe and stalk to Jarred.

'Hi, Jarred, you're Dex's cousin, right? I'm Savannah. We just came to get something. Got a little sidetracked.' I wave a breezy hand at the wardrobe. 'Sorry about that.'

'Savannah,' Dex warns as I try to push past Jarred. He blocks my way.

'You took something?' Jarred says in a menacing tone. 'If you found it here, it's mine.'

His eyes are fixed on mine. I'm uncomfortable with his intense scrutiny but I make myself smile. I lift Yasmin, giving her a little twirl. 'Yeah, you play with dolls?'

One of his friends laughs and Jarred glares at me. Dex pushes between us. 'We came to get the doll, OK? It's a dumb childhood prank. We're going now.'

'Check him,' Jarred barks at his henchmen. Two guys move forward quickly. One grabs Dex's arms and the other pats him down, checking his pockets. Dex hides his surprise when they say, 'Nothing.' One of them steps towards me, and I hiss, 'I don't have anything of yours. But touch me and I will go to the police.'

'Leave her.' Jarred sounds bored as he steps aside. 'Let them go.'

I've only taken one step when Jarred adds, 'Unless you want to come out with us? Cuz? Bring your girlfriend?'

If it's an invitation, it's a strange one. It's hostile, almost a challenge. I will Dex to say no. *Do not get drawn into your family drama.*

Dex doesn't answer. He's looking at the wardrobe and before he does or says anything stupid, I grab his hand and yank him out of the door. 'Time to go.'

His shoulders are stooped as we walk to the car. I don't look back, but I'm sure they're watching us from the darkened drive.

In the car, he starts the ignition and leans back against the headrest. 'I dropped my ma's gift in the wardrobe.' He looks back at the house. 'They're going to find it.'

I fish a hand into my pocket and lay the narrow parcel wrapped in brown paper on the centre console. 'I think we can begin hostage negotiations.'

Dex lets out a loud laugh. 'You distracted me, picked my pocket and stole both the prisoner doll and my inheritance?'

'We had a game.' I raise an eyebrow. 'I won.'

'You play dirty, Savannah.' He shakes his head.

'It passed the time. So win-win.' I'm curious, though. I want to know why the sons have taken on their mothers' fight. 'Your cousin Jarred is interesting.'

'He's not a good guy.' And it's clear that's all Dex will say about that.

Driving back, despite the day, I am oddly upbeat. Just over a week ago, I was flailing in the dark. Now I know what I need to do to save myself, to save future Hella's girls. There's not a lot of time, but I'm holding on tight.

I think about Kim, Harrison, Minnie and the aunties. I won't break their hearts by dying angry. I think about Rosie, my friend again, and cast a furtive look at Dex as he navigates the winding road. How I'd longed for him to come back.

I let the window down. I tell it to the night, the mountain, the stars: I will live.

Back at the Stander house, Inez meets us on the front stoep. She's been waiting.

'Everything OK, you two?' she says. 'You left so suddenly. Where were you?'

'Just out driving,' Dex lies easily as he goes inside. Inez looks from me to him. Her lips are pressed tightly together and she's holding back what she really wants to say. In the hall, she picks up the bag I'd packed earlier. 'Kim sent this. You need to call her. She won't go to bed until you do.'

I take my phone from the bag. Out the corner of my eye, I see Inez step towards Dex.

'Dex,' she says, and how loaded a single word can be. His name an appeal, but also a peace offering. One that's laced with something bitter.

There's a text message from Zenande, asking to meet in the morning.

'Savannah, don't you dare disappear on me like that again.' Kim's voice is so loud that they both glance at me.

'I texted,' I protest, turning away.

Kim is annoyed, but she quickly calms. 'We didn't have our little talk.' The TV blares in the background, some cop show.

'We will, Kim. I'll see you soon.'

She tells me to have a good time and to call her lots.

'Come on,' Inez says after I hang up. She's alone in the hall now. 'I'll show you your room.'

I follow her up the wide stairs. The fragrance of jasmine and leather hangs lightly in the air. Framed magazine covers adorn the feather-white walls.

'That's Rosie's.' Inez gestures to a shut door, saying apologetically, 'But she's out at a late-night movie. That girl loves nothing more than an empty cinema in the middle of the night. The more run-down the better. Romantic, apparently.' She nods to a second shut door. 'Dex.'

Beside Dex's door, Inez stops at a large room with hardwood floors and grey walls. The bed is huge, with magnolia cotton covers that match the simple muslin curtains. I want to sink in to it, cocoon, and forget that I am the girl with a storm inside.

'It's yours,' Inez says. 'Whenever you want it.'

'Thanks, Inez.'

'This is your and Rosie's bathroom.' She switches on the

light in a bathroom opposite and I see gleaming marble. Inez hands me a fluffy towel and I wonder about her, why she argued with her sister at her mother's funeral. I wonder about the woman who'd once slept on the sofa bed in her sister's flat, and how she became this one with her artfully designed earrings, her expensively maintained face.

'You'll feel better after a hot shower,' Inez soothes. Her gaze flicks to Dex's shut door and her shoulders square. She wants to ask me questions, she wants to know where we were. She wants me to tell on Dex.

We never did tell on each other. Even when I pinched him blue during our wrestling, he never tattled. When he urged me to jump from a tree and my face hit the ground, splitting my lip, there was *omertà*.

So whatever the argument brewing between Dex and Inez, she's not getting answers from me. But when Inez finally speaks, she surprises me. 'Was Dex … is he OK?' Suddenly she looks tired. Not even medical-grade beauty treatments can disguise the wearied experience in her eyes.

'He's OK,' I say, relieved that she's not drawing me into it.

After the shower, I find Inez in the kitchen, which is gently lit with candles. She has a line of them on the window sill, more on the tables and counters. There's an intoxicating scent in the room, woody herbs and sweet hot beeswax, but tonight the smell makes my head pound.

Inez is standing over a one-plate stove, watching something in a double boiler.

'What are you doing?' There's newspaper spread on the

157

island and on it are bundles of dried herbs, metal jugs and plastic moulds.

'I thought you'd gone to bed.' Inez watches the double boiler carefully as she inserts a thermometer. 'I'm making wax melts. I find it soothing.' She checks the temperature and when she looks up, her smile seems sad. 'Candles too. It's my way of making everything better.'

From the island, the newspaper headline catches my eye.

'The herbs are from places I've travelled and ...' I don't hear Inez's talk about candles and herbal infusions and heal the world make it a better place. The black-and-white print draws me closer.

WOMAN KILLED IN DOG ATTACK
The body of a woman was found this morning by dog walkers. The woman, thought to be in her thirties, had suffered injuries consistent with a dog attack ...

Arrow.

'Don't you think so?' Inez smiles at me, oblivious.

I'm thinking about Arrow, so regal in the temple, and my throat is raw with pain. I've no idea what Inez is talking about, but she's looking at me expectantly, so I say, 'Maybe.'

But inside I feel only a blank numbness. Arrow died.

Which means they'll come for Mama Daline next.

And then me.

Before the stars finish their fall.

18

HAT

After a night of restless sleep and storm-fuelled dreams, morning light spills into the room. I know with certainty that I'm not alone.

My fear is primitive. It's an icy hand in my gut, holding my body to the bed. From behind, a hand strokes my hair and I sit bolt upright and scream.

'Savannah!' It's only Rosie. Relief floods me.

'You scared me.' I press my hand to my pounding heart.

'You were having a bad dream. Calling out in your sleep.'

I shut my eyes, feeling her gaze upon me. 'What's the time?'

'Nearly seven. I'm sorry I missed you last night.'

'Did you have fun at the movies?'

'It was a blast.' She sits down on the bed. 'It's nineties month, you should come. Last night was *True Romance.*' She leans back and holds her fingers in what, with some imagination, could be called a gangster pose. 'Live fast, die young, have a good-looking corpse.'

The words bite, and I can't hide it.

'Savannah, omigod, I'm so sorry. That was incredibly thoughtless.'

'You know about the family curse, then.'

'My mom and Freda told each other everything, so yeah, I've heard. The curse doesn't have to affect you.' She sounds deliberately upbeat. 'I mean, I know you smashed up that car …' Her voice trails off. She looks down at the sheets and when she looks up again, she's determined. 'Curses can be broken, right?'

I laugh. 'Seriously? I thought you were going to suggest I try mindfulness.'

'You were my first best friend, Savannah,' she says. 'And I'm not about to let my first best friend die from some generations-old curse. So, let's do something about it.'

'Rosie,' I start. The urge to tell her everything is overwhelming but I hold back, settling for one thread of truth.

I reach out my hands, showing her the red on my palm and on my wrist. The thin line of marks on my jawline and the patch blooming on my shoulder. 'The aunties don't like to say it, but Freda had them too. They appeared in the months before she died.' I pull my hands back but she catches one and holds it in hers. 'I don't have a lot of time left.'

She touches a cool finger to the marks, then looks into my eyes and vows, 'We're going to end this, Savannah.'

My phone vibrates with a text from Kim doing her morning

check-in. I swing my legs over the side of the bed and memories of yesterday hit me like a body blow. The masked monsters in my house, the stockings stuffed in my mouth. Rosie's talking but I don't hear her.

'I'm sorry,' I say to Rosie, who's looking at me expectantly. 'What did you say?'

'I said, what have you tried so far?' In her butterfly pyjama shirt and shorts she looks suddenly formidable.

I hesitate, not sure what to tell her. It all sounds too crazy. Rumours and legends and half-truths.

'Freda was trying to find a way to break the curse before she died,' I say at last. 'She left a notebook but it's mostly spooky stories.' I rub my eyes. 'The one thing I do know is that I've got to find the true name of my enslaved ancestor in my dreams. And how am I supposed to do that?' My voice rises to a wail in spite of myself. Last night's dreams were wild and incoherent.

'OK, OK,' Rosie soothes. 'We can do this. But yesterday was a lot, so let's do something nice this morning. Maybe a spa? Or shopping?'

A slim, warm arm slips around my shoulders. *I've got you*, it seems to say.

'It's so easy to be with you.' I almost groan the words. Rosie feels like home and it's comforting and good. 'I'm so glad you're back.'

'I know,' she says. 'I feel it too.' Then she gives me a quick squeeze and shifts, pulling one leg up to the bed and facing me. 'You know the weirdest thing I missed about here when we were away?'

'What?'

'That I never have to try to explain what I am or where I'm from. I feel more … connected?'

I look at her curiously, wondering what she's getting at.

'Do you ever think about your ancestors?' Rosie says, then quickly adds, 'Not just Hella. All of them. I do. I think about how they came from all over – from here and other countries in Africa, from Asia and Europe. I think to myself, Rosie girl, that's a lot of stories. So many stories.' She circles her finger. 'Entwined like a double helix inside me.'

'Yeah.' I smile. 'So many stories.'

'When I'm here, I feel closer to those stories. And that makes me feel, I don't know, part of something.' Then she returns my smile and says, 'I know – the beach. We'll go to the beach.' She flops back on the bed. 'But first, more sleep.'

Rosie stays in the bed and falls back asleep in minutes. I ease out of the room. Downstairs, Inez is in the kitchen, typing on her laptop with a cup of tea in front of her. The glass doors are open and birds sing in the trees.

'Morning, Inez. Have you been here all night?'

She gives me a broad smile.

'Morning, you're up early. What can I get you?'

'Maybe a hot chocolate? I can make it myself.'

'I want you to feel at home here with us.'

Inez tells me where everything is and then I sit at the table beside her as she shuts her laptop.

'You look so much like Freda,' she says as she studies my face. 'So, can we talk about the marks, Savannah? Because I do believe in your family curse, and Freda wouldn't want this happening to you.'

'She spoke to you, didn't she?' I glance at Freda's ring and Inez does too. 'About what she was doing. How she hoped to break it.'

'Freda never explained why, but she was searching for the farm where Hella was enslaved.'

'Did she find it?'

'No.' She gives me a small smile. 'But I have.'

'Inez.' My voice is higher with excitement. 'Do they have any records or documents?'

'Everything from the original farm burned down. Even so, I think you should visit. It might contain a trace of Hella. Especially given what happened there.'

OK, didn't expect this turn of the conversation, but going with it. 'But where is it? When can I go?'

Let the magic inside guide you, Mama Daline had said. I don't know if it's the magic, but I have to go to this place. I know it in my bones.

I'll see the place where the tormentor's blood was spilt. Where Hella found her power. And that's where I'll turn the tormentor key.

'We're going tomorrow –' Inez gives me a brilliant smile – 'to Nietvergeten. That gorgeous cottage for the Winelands feature I was telling you about? It's on the farm where Hella was enslaved.'

'That's why you asked me along.'

Inez nods. 'That's why I'm doing the feature.' Her eyes are

filled with sympathy. 'It's always plagued me. That I left, and soon after, Freda died.'

'It wasn't your fault, Inez.'

Inez looks at my face, tucks a hair behind my ear. 'You're a fine young woman, Savannah.' Her gaze is searching and it makes me uncomfortable. 'Can I ask you one thing?'

'Sure.'

'Promise me you won't say anything about Hella and Nietvergeten to the twins. I don't want Dex to know, and Rosie tells him everything.' Seeing my frown, she adds, 'He won't understand.'

Her words bother me, because I've already told Rosie things I'd rather she didn't share with Dex. Inez is looking at me expectantly. I don't want to add to whatever's brewing between Inez and Dex, so I smile.

'I promise.' I take a sip of my hot chocolate. 'How does it feel,' I say in a lighter tone, 'to come back after all these years?'

'It's a little different, I suppose,' she laughs, drawing back and picking up her tea, 'but mostly the same.'

'Must be good to see your family again,' I probe. 'I'm sorry about Ma Daphne. That she died, I mean.'

'I am too,' Inez says. 'We didn't have a good relationship, but her dying made me realise what's important. Things that seem big and insurmountable don't always matter as much as we think they do.'

She looks sad, like she's thinking about nearly ten years of not talking to her mother and sister. It looks like she regrets it a lot.

'I've carried a lot of anger over the years,' Inez says. 'Lately I've been wondering if it's time to let go. And what has to happen so I can do that.'

I feel the weight of her words, particularly of what she doesn't say. How anger can be a burden, how it wears you down.

'If there's a way to be free, you should take it.' I reach for her hand on the table and close mine over hers. 'Talk to your sister.'

'Dex.' Inez shifts her gaze to over my shoulder. I turn around to see him on the threshold of the glass doors and I know at once that whatever ground we'd regained last night has been covered over. He's back from a run and takes a long drink from his bottle. Snapping down the lid, he doesn't look at me, but casts a hot look at Inez as he walks past us.

'Good morning, honey,' she says. 'Did you go far? Can I get you something?'

'I'm fine, Mom.' He's pissed off, but I've no idea why.

'Dex,' I say tentatively. He's halfway to the door. 'Rosie and I are going to the beach later. Do you want to come?'

'Can't.' Beside me, I can feel Inez cringing at his abruptness. She calls after him again but he's left the room.

Inez lets out a sharp breath. 'I don't know what I'm going to do about him.'

19

DARK CLOUD

Rosie sleeps soundly in the guestroom, barely stirring when I go in to change. After calling out to Inez that I'm going for a walk, I leave for the park.

Zenande leans against a picnic table, watching a group of nannies and children in the shelter of some trees. It's a little after nine, and it's already hot.

'You not working today?'

'No,' she says. Seeing my concern, she adds, 'Mama Daline isn't alone. I'm not her only apprentice. But I have a meeting with my master's group soon, and our professor gives shit to anyone who comes in late.'

'I'm sorry about Arrow.'

'Me too.'

We walk between the trees, away from where the children play, and I tell Zenande what happened at Greenmarket Square.

'The Market hides behind what is plainly visible,' she tells me. 'All over the world, behind the selling of candles or fabric or wooden giraffes, you'll find the secret trade of spells and enchanted objects.'

'Is it the same everywhere?'

'There are similarities.' Zenande stops between a cluster of trees. Ahead, a group of women do yoga. 'But you know this place, it's a kaleidoscope. Magic from different parts of Africa, Asia and Europe have threaded together over hundreds of years.'

She waits until two joggers pass.

'The Market has only two absolute rules. First, you can't tell anyone. People have to discover it for themselves or not at all.'

'And the second?'

'Veiled magic, and all it entails, is forbidden. Has been since the time of the Sisters.'

I'm about to ask about the man and his whispering jewellery at Greenmarket Square when I notice how drawn Zenande's face is and I hesitate. She's grieving; now isn't the time to be worrying her with rogue traders.

'I found magic in my house,' I say instead, remembering why I'd gone looking for Zenande at Greenmarket Square. 'Silvery symbols were drawn on the wall above my bed and the outside doors.'

'Symbols?' Zenande's mouth turns down. She hesitates. 'Did anything bad happen there?'

'Nothing. Not even a break-in, which is unusual in our area. Until –' my face crinkles with confusion – 'until I wiped them off.'

'It sounds like a protection spell,' Zenande says reluctantly.

167

My stomach plummets. 'It's veiled magic, isn't it?'

'Yes,' she exhales, 'but why would the veilwitches want to protect you?'

'To ensure I'm nice and healthy for when they do kill me?' I say, my finger twirling around the star on Freda's ring. 'I mean, they'd be pretty pissed off if I'd ended up murdered by ordinary criminals.'

Zenande gives me an inscrutable look.

'Was it a living spell?' I do not want to hear that I've been sleeping beneath dark, living magic cast from blood and body parts.

'No.' She thinks carefully. 'I'm no expert on veiled magic, but I'm fairly sure that you can't just wipe away a living spell. You'd have to kill it.'

Kill it. How my world has changed.

'So, you're here to help me untether the manifest?' I have to keep positive.

'I am.'

'We don't have much time.' Three impossible keys in just a few weeks.

'We have enough,' she says firmly. 'How's the name coming along? You haven't told me about your dreams.'

'My dreams are mad.' I think of the glassy-eyed goat. 'Unclear. But I have news about the tormentor key.'

'That's good!'

'I'm going to the place where Hella was enslaved,' I say. 'Where her tormentor died. We leave tomorrow, for a week.'

'This is huge.' Zenande claps her hands once, her eyes shining.

'What do you think I need to do there?'

'The farm will remember Hella and her tormentors. There will be echoes of the people who lived there. Connect to the farm, and see if you can find its memory of the curse.'

'The farm burned down.'

'Then connect to the land.' Her thumbs fly over her phone as she makes notes. 'I'll organise a package for you, with directions on making the connection and whatever instruments you'll need.' She looks up at me and her happiness is infectious. 'Oh, Savannah, this is a game-changer.'

I really hope she's right.

Zenande slips her phone in her pocket. 'Great. Now let's get to work on untethering the manifest.'

I step away from the tree, feet in a loose second position, arms in a relaxed *bras bas*. 'OK.'

'So, the manifest is the physical expression of your curse. With this key, we're breaking the connection between you and the curse by undoing the bond between you and the creature. Does that make sense?'

'Physical expression of curse. Break the bond.' I nod. 'Clear as a bell.'

'To untether, you must first learn to summon the manifest. It may take a few goes, so don't be discouraged if you don't manage to call the creature immediately. Now, start by taking deep, steadying breaths.'

I inhale, exhale, just like the Savannah-help books taught me.

169

'Close your eyes,' Zenande says. 'That magic inside you is preparing. I can feel it. You need to try to feel it too.'

I close my eyes, empty my mind. Inhale, exhale.

I search inside me for Hella's magic.

Auntie Dotty told me that when she was pregnant with Harrison, she first felt him as a muted fluttering and curling from within.

That's what I feel inside my heart. A quickening. My mouth twists up with satisfaction.

'Stay focused,' Zenande says. 'Once you tune into Hella's magic, call to the creature of the curse. Ask it to show itself to you.'

'What does it look like?' My eyes snap open. 'I mean, what am I calling? Is it the size of a rat or a lion?'

'I don't know.' Zenande doesn't hide her irritation very well.

'Where is it now? Is it invisible?'

'It's a curse. You can't see a curse. Not unless you summon it into its physical form. Which is what we're trying to do here.'

'So I must take this black cloud of curse –' I shape my hands into a puffy cloud – 'that's inside me somehow, and play-dough it into a tiger or similar? Gotcha.'

Zenande mutters under her breath in isiXhosa. I don't catch everything she says, but I'm fairly sure it's a request to the Sisters to give her patience with annoying cursed girls.

But when she speaks to me, it's with kindness. 'Will we try again?'

'OK.' I take a deep breath and shut my eyes again. I look for the magic but this time, that feeling stays out of reach. I'm kinda hungry though. Maybe I should try this after I've eaten?

'Concentrate, Savannah.'

I push all thought away. I feel my feet on the grass, the sun muted by the shade, the sound of birds, of children playing. I search for that tangle inside. If I can find one thread, then maybe I can unravel it all.

There's nothing. Even the dark thing, my anger, sleeps.

'It's there, but I can't reach it.' I open my eyes.

'This is going to be harder than I thought,' Zenande groans.

Rosie is a terrible driver.

She's at the wheel of the car she shares with Dex. Music blaring, we're going a little faster than we should over the narrow mountain pass and it's brilliant.

We stop at a beach on the False Bay, dumping our things on the fine white sand.

'What's up with Dex and your mom?' I ask.

'It's nothing serious,' she says. 'He's angry with her for leaving our home, our friends, our lives. Our stepdad, Mike, who he adored. Dex will be OK. He'll come round.'

'He hates it here that much?'

'Not hates, no. He'd just rather be there.'

'Was there,' I start tentatively, 'someone he left behind?'

'Dex likes girls,' she laughs. 'And they like him, you know?' Unfortunately, I do know. 'He's got a rogue's charm, when he's not in a funk, and he's fundamentally decent. But Dex is a terrible boyfriend. Never manages more than a week. I always warn my friends away.'

She's warning me now, as she stands there looking out to sea. We're at the edge of the water, the wind dancing around us. The beach is quiet, just a few older women getting sun, one swimming in the sea.

'A great white was spotted here a week ago.' Enough about Dex. 'First time in ages.' The water laps over my red-painted toes. I don't turn back. Today I'm wearing a red bikini. Today I want to ride in fast cars and see sharks.

Rosie looks at me. The wind whips her hair into her face and she pushes it away. 'You're everything I dreamed you'd be.'

She grabs my hand and we run into the water. She's screaming as we head straight to a large wave. Within minutes, we're dunked and soaked and laughing our heads off.

'Hello, girls,' says an old woman leaving the sea. She's wearing a one-piece orange costume and a vintage white petal swimming cap. Her blue-green eyes are troubled as she looks at us. 'Be vigilant, OK? The sea is in one of its moods today.' The water's completely calm. I don't know what she means, but she moves on before I can ask.

The sky is so blue, so high. The sun is warm on my skin. I can smell the salt water, hear the cry of gulls. Rosie was right. I needed this.

'I'm heading to shore, OK?' Rosie says after a while. I stay, bobbing on the gentle waves.

Despite the sea, the sun, the sky, all of a sudden I can feel my anger squatting inside me. This dark, ugly, constant thing.

172

Maybe it's because the sea is in a mood, but right now it feels like a power. An unfamiliar potency thrumming in my body. Maybe I can use this.

I concentrate hard. 'Creature of the curse,' I say into the blue. 'Show yourself to me.' The strangeness inside me blooms and I say it again, shifting from my back to tread water. 'Creature of the curse, show yourself to me.'

I repeat the words again and again, as if I can do this. As if I can make magic. Because today, alone in the ocean, a vigour I've never experienced before courses through me. Like there's a tide rising inside me, calling out to some unknown thing.

And I feel it respond.

'Savannah.'

I turn to the shore where Rosie calls me, cupping her hands around her mouth. The old woman is beside her, her petal cap bright in the distance. *Not now, Rosie.* I turn away.

'Savannah.'

It's like staring at the abyss full on. My skin pricks as I search the horizon.

Then I see it, on the long body of rocks that juts out into the water. An animal.

Its face is sharp and pointed; the ears are long and upright and the eyes, which are looking intently at me, are slanted. The fur is reddish gold with patches of black.

A jackal.

Of course it's a jackal.

Blood curses are alive, the torn sheet said. *The magic that sustains them is alive.*

The jackal opens its mouth and all I see are sharp teeth. *They have a shape and form, a manifest.*

It snarls.

The manifest may be hostile to the afflicted.

I did it. I summoned the manifest. Wild excitement rolls through me.

'Savannah!'

I glance around to see Rosie wading into the water. When I look to the rocks, the jackal is gone.

I swim out to meet Rosie. The old woman is on the shore, her blue-green eyes watching my every move.

'She started getting really agitated,' Rosie murmurs. 'Said you're angering the sea.'

The old woman watches me as we leave the water. 'You OK, darling?' She holds out my towel and wraps it around my shoulders. In my ear, she hisses, 'Your kind are not welcome here.'

Drawing back, I'm shocked by the venom in her words. Rosie's bending over our things, taking two Grapetisers from her bag, oblivious to the unexpected turn of our conversation. 'Your kind?' I say the words with disdain.

'I can sense bad magic,' she declares. 'And the air is thick with it this morning.'

Rosie's frowning at us now and the old woman takes careful steps on the wet sand. 'Oh dear, the sea is in one of its moods. Better stay away when it gets like this.' She gives me a final look with those startling blue-green eyes. 'Better stay away.'

20

EGG

I'm running but I am so tired. My lungs are squeezed tight and my legs ache. The creature behind me does not fatigue.

On the other side of the river, the woman waits. She turns her head, showing a little more of her face than before.

I'm near the river when it comes slithering out from behind a rock. A large, thick dark snake. I skrik, falling back.

The snake slithers towards me. I scramble away, but it slinks over my leg, up my stomach, reaching for my wrist. When it reaches my marks, it opens its mouth wide and—

I wake up.

When Harrison collects me from Inez's house the next morning, I'm puffy-eyed from lack of sleep.

'Wild night?' He raises an eyebrow.

'Only wild dreams, *Uncle* Harrison.'

The magic is stirring. At night, I am a small boat, battered at sea.

'I'm glad you're taking a holiday.' He reaches over, squeezes my hand. 'I've been worried about you.'

'You'll be OK without my help?'

'*Pfft.*' He waves a hand as he gets on the road towards Tokai.

We unload at a craft and curio market, and after a while I do a coffee run. This time, as I wander from stall to stall, I'm looking for magic.

It's there. Not at every stall, but at the few with that slight glow. Today I watch. I watch a man buy a money charm, note the grim set of his mouth. I see a girl buy a beauty potion at the handmade soap counter.

I watch these interactions carefully. Ordinary folk know something of the hidden Market, I realise. There is the odd nervous outsider, brought here by word of mouth, buying a charm or locket or piece of enchanted fabric. They don't know much. They don't fully understand what lies beneath.

No one is going to tell them.

This Market is built on secrets. Hands cover whispering mouths. Spells are passed down families and never shared.

A man with a narrow face and navy baseball cap walks up to a stall with handmade sculptures. Some figurines have super-long dicks; there's one with two heads; one that's half man, half hyena.

'I'm picking up,' the man says. 'I rang earlier.'

The vendor whistles. 'Oh yeah.' He leans forward, conspiratorially. 'Are you sure you can handle this?'

'None of your business,' the man snaps, dropping a wad of notes on the table.

The vendor shrugs, then reaches under the stall and hands him a figure with a belly cavity and its face spiked with nails. He nods and walks off.

Curious, I'm following him through the crowd when my attention is caught by Mama Daline's large black tent. I push away the memory of our bargain: *fast and merciful.*

There is a queue of people on the bench outside today. Two burly men are stationed at the entrance.

I think of the dogs leaping for Arrow. I don't know if two strong men can save Mama Daline from the kind of magic that killed Arrow.

When I look back, I have lost baseball-cap man.

I buy koesisters from the woman who sells samoosas, curry pies, and salomies. I can see now that she also sells spices to make boys notice you, or to help you do well at school. I get Harrison's coffee and am heading back when a flower seller calls to me.

'Hey, girl, buy some flowers for your mommy?'

I stop. I'm meeting Kim for a dress fitting this afternoon and she loves fresh flowers. I go over, examining the stems in their buckets.

She watches me. 'You're a dabbler. Yes?'

I don't know what to say to that. She moves a heavy bucket of flowers from the sun to beneath the shaded canopy. 'You're no witch, but you're sensitive to magic. And you've just started to see. Am I right?'

'Yes.' That sounds *so* much better than cursed.

The woman stretches out her back. 'Just tread carefully. The Market isn't always kind to newcomers. Especially now.'

'Especially now?'

I notice then that her face is pale. Sickly.

I put down the coffee and koesisters. 'Here, let me do those.'

Lifting the rest of the heavy buckets, I move them into the shade. She watches me. Her breathing is heavy, laboured. After I'm done, she says, 'Go on, take a bunch. You earned it. I've fresh roses today. Red roses. They will make romance more intense.'

That's the last thing I want for Kim.

'Or these white roses have hidden thorns, if you need something with more bite.' She touches a petal, and razor-sharp thorns push out from the long stem.

'What about the gerberas?' I point to the brightly coloured flowers beside the dark red roses.

'Those improve a mood.'

'Perfect.'

I walk back to Harrison's stall, juggling flowers, coffee and the bag of koesisters. Before Harrison can complain about my long break, I tuck a gerbera behind his ear.

'You're a terrible assistant,' he says.

'What I lack in diligence, I make up for in charm and beauty.'

He laughs, taking his coffee and a koesister, handing the bag back to me.

He looks around. 'Is it my imagination or is the energy here a little low today?'

178

Dusting coconut from my dress, I glance up. People bustle from stall to stall.

'It's your imagination.'

It has to be. The marimba band plays a happy tune. It smells of herbs, soaps and candles. Of hot spiced food and fruit.

'No, look.' He points to the flower seller way down the row, now sitting slumped in a chair. 'She's totally out of it.'

'Not everyone is as exuberant as you.' I bite into the light, syrupy dough, tasting cardamom and cinnamon.

'And that guy.' He points to a man at the candle stall, who is twisting his hands together, face heavy with fatigue. 'And him.' He nods to a man selling coffee beans. 'Name's Khulani. I see him all the time at a Milnerton market. Usually the life and soul. Look at him now.'

It's the man I saw in the bougainvillea alley, kissing Madison, the veilwitch. Confident, tall, handsome.

He has changed almost beyond recognition. His hair is beginning to grey. His face looks weathered. His frame is hunched and shrunken.

'Is that a berg wind?' Harrison says, and I feel the sudden gust of warm wind, and with it the nausea.

The wind is unexpected and fierce. Stalls rattle, wares fall from their display tables. Harrison secures the canvas that separates us from our neighbour.

Then I see them. Four people standing at the top of the row. They are dressed as if for Carniveil. They start a slow swagger forward and several vendors go rigid. The flower seller flinches.

I recognise the blond man from the park, the man with the

dogs. Today he wears a top hat and a snakeskin waistcoat with matching trousers. Madison has a strip of orange print fabric across her breasts, matching pantaloons and large velvet ribbons in her hair. Salomé, in a leather bodice, full cotton skirt and Marie Antoinette wig, tucks her hand into a second man's elbow. He's tall with dark brown skin and wears wire-rimmed glasses, a long pink-velvet duster coat and black-and-white checked trousers.

'Jaco, I'm starving. What will we have for lunch?' Madison says loudly.

Their skin is painted in the same red-and-black design. Three downward strokes on the forehead, a spiral on the cheek and a circle on the chest. Patterns on their hands and wrists.

Madison stops when she sees the coffee seller.

'Hello, handsome. Miss me?'

'No, please,' Khulani whimpers. 'You took too much last night.'

She leans over and gives him a soft, sweet kiss. 'I like to draw it out.' Then she stands tall, placing her hand over his face. She chants something under her breath and he twitches and groans.

Harrison nudges me.

'Will you just look at that goddess?'

His face shines with admiration and I don't understand why he isn't terrified.

'What's happening there, Harrison?' I try to keep the panic from my voice.

He gives an exaggerated sigh. 'I've neglected your educa-tion. Flirting: when humans feel a pull of sexual attraction, they emit certain cues ...'

'Harrison,' I warn. 'Please. What do you see?'

'They're just flirting, Savannah. You know, talking, but with hope.'

'Right.' My voice sounds strangled. I watch Khulani whimpering beneath Madison's hand. No one does anything. Maybe no one dares.

When she takes her hand away, he falls to the ground, weeping. Madison laughs. 'To think you could have stopped all this. Shame your armouring was interrupted.'

'What do you see now?' I say to Harrison, who has gone back to fixing the display.

'Seriously, Savannah?' Harrison shoots an uninterested glance at the man, then frowns. 'He's fallen over.'

He looks thoughtful. His eyes are on Madison as she approaches us. She gives him a wave and I go rigid.

'I like your sticks.' She runs her eyes over him admiringly.

He grins. 'I can show you more?' She smiles, but she doesn't stop.

I exhale shakily. 'Stay away from that woman,' I hiss as Harrison checks her out from behind.

'Why? You think she's trouble?' says Harrison. 'Because I like trouble.'

I ignore him, watching as Jaco and Salomé stop in front of another vendor, a man selling spices. 'Where's the Worm hiding?' Jaco says.

'I don't know,' the vendor replies, fear in his voice.

Jaco grabs him by his collar and lifts him effortlessly a metre off the ground. 'I don't think that's true.'

'Look,' I whisper.

'Savannah, what is going on?' he says. 'Do you need your eyes testing?'

'Please,' I beg. 'Tell me what you see.'

He takes a deep breath. 'Fine, I'll play.' He glances over at the two men, one still in the air, legs dangling. 'I see two men talking.'

'What about their utterly fantastic clothes?' I say, looking at Jaco's snakeskin waistcoat and top hat.

Harrison stares at me. He gives a nervous laugh.

'Utterly fantastic? A brown suit?'

He doesn't see it, I realise. They've masked themselves, with magic, to blend in. Jaco pulls the vendor out of his stall and manhandles him down the row. The Market vendors shrink from them.

'Be right back,' I say, darting out from behind the stall.

'Hey,' he calls. 'You do know I pay you, right?'

As I walk quickly after the foursome, I hear the whispers, borne on the dry wind: *veilwitches.*

I turn the corner in time to see them dragging the man into the area behind the stalls. The wind is strong, shaking the stalls, lifting my dress. I duck back so I can watch unseen.

'Tell us.' Madison slaps him hard, a sharp crack that jolts me out of the scene. And, for a brief second, I see all four of them differently – four friends, chatting to one of the vendors. They are wearing a brown suit, a floral dress, jeans. No one's hurting anyone.

The picture blurs, and Jaco's right arm pounds the vendor

182

like he's a slab of meat on the chopping board.

'Stop that.'

Mama Daline stands on the grass, away from the stalls. Short, stooped shoulders, she's just an auntie in her pale blue linen dress.

Her words have authority. Calm and certain.

She shifts her gaze to the stall I'm hiding behind. 'Come then,' she says, and I am sure she's talking to me. She turns and starts walking towards a field. The four veilwitches follow and so do I.

Zenande runs out from between the stalls.

'No, Mama Daline,' Zenande cries.

Mama Daline speaks over her shoulder. 'Remember our agreement, Zenande?'

The younger woman gives a choked sob. 'Yes.'

'Then you have a job to do. Stay here and do it.'

Mama Daline ambles forward, humming. The veilwitches could kill her now. They don't. They follow her away from the market, across the field. She glances over her shoulder once, as if to say, *Well, are you coming?* Then walks on.

I inch after them. At the edge of the field, Mama Daline disappears beneath a nearby bridge. The veilwitches follow.

When I reach the bridge, I peer into the tunnel. Mama Daline is on her knees. The four veilwitches form a semicircle around her.

Mama Daline is speaking. 'By the light of the Worm, the Pale Star, I curse you. I curse each one of you: Madison, Salomé,

Jaco and Skull. From this minute, your clock will begin to run down. From this minute, your violent death hastens to meet you. When the Worm decides, your lives will end in pain and despair.'

'Careful now, Mama.' Jaco smiles with too much gum. 'I didn't think your kind were allowed curses.'

'It's frowned upon.' Mama Daline sounds cheeky. 'But only blood curses are banned.'

'Just as well.' Salomé sounds bored. 'Because only blood curses matter.'

Mama Daline looks straight at Salomé. 'You should remember, Salomé, that people are reckless when they have nothing to lose.'

It's Auntie Nazeema's schoolteacher stare. The one that can freeze the worst troublemaker in their tracks.

Then, still on her knees, Mama Daline raises her arms. I don't know what I'm expecting. Sparks to fly out, the ground to turn to liquid.

Nothing happens. Just a small woman, holding up her hands. A Daughter, on her knees, making empty curses.

Get up, I scream inside my head. *Use your magic.*

'Who's going first?' The veilwitches glance at each other. Skull runs his hand down his jaw. He gives a little chuckle.

'Let's do it together.'

They circle her like a pack of wolves. Then Salomé pounces, touching her hand to Mama Daline's face. She flinches. Madison dances forward, laughing. Then Jaco, then Skull. They take turns. A long caress of Mama Daline's cheek, a stroke

184

of a hand up a bare arm. The lightest press of fingers on her shoulder. A kiss on her forehead. Gracefully, methodically, the veilwitches feed.

By the light of the Worm, the Pale Star, I curse you. I curse each one of you: Madison, Salomé, Jaco and Skull. Mama Daline repeats the words over and over.

Get up, I urge her, *get up.*

As if she can hear me, Mama Daline looks right at me. And slowly, pointedly, she looks down to my feet.

I look down. There, beside my sandals, in a clump of weeds, is the shining blade of a knife.

I look at Mama Daline and she gives an almost imperceptible nod. Carefully I pick it up by the carved wooden handle. Symbols are etched into the handle. This is no ordinary knife.

A magic knife, I think. I can stop them with this.

Mama Daline mouths two words, and I hear her voice inside my head. 'Kill me.'

My eyes meet hers. The words echo again. *Kill me.*

The veilwitches taunt her, mock her, touch her. My anger stirs.

Mama Daline looks grey. She's wailing now, a thin high sound that echoes under the bridge. The knife is heavy in my hand.

I step inside the tunnel, slowly raising the knife. I creep by the faded graffiti, the stale smell of smoke from quenched fires. Four of them, against a defenceless woman.

Kill me.

I want to make them hurt.

Fast and merciful. You owe me this. The voice is fainter now.

'It's prowling season. We will drain your witches dry, just like this,' Jaco says as I inch forward behind him. 'It's a shame you won't be around to see your witches turn. It's a shame you won't live to see the Jackal rule the Market.'

Mama Daline's bird eyes are on mine.

Madison turns, sees me. She lets out a delighted laugh when she sees the knife in my hand.

'Today got even better.'

My anger comes racing through my veins. Today it's a snake, rising, ready to strike. I charge forward, screaming. But I run past them. With all my strength, I plunge the knife into Mama Daline's heart. And something inside me shatters.

But always you.

'*Now* it's a blood curse,' Mama Daline murmurs.

The air around us thrums. She falls to the ground. In the silence that follows, there is only the sound of my hitched breaths.

'What have you done?' Madison screams. My hand, still holding the knife, is shaking, wet with blood and sweat.

Madison pulls out a curved blade. The others draw behind her. As one, they advance.

I hear it then. It comes from behind me, a low rumbling sound that echoes across the space. The growl of a wild animal.

Madison's step falters. A strange expression crosses her face. Fear, almost. The others pause too.

It's the jackal from the beach.

The creature of the curse is beautiful, with thick reddish-gold fur, black markings on its back and slanted yellow eyes.

Did I unleash that? I think wildly. *Did I summon it?*

For a second, I feel power.

It dips its head, sniffing the ground, like it's tracking magic. Then the creature sees me and bares its teeth, a loud snarl ripping from its throat. It rolls its head and its body stiffens.

I scramble away, terror ratcheting up. I stumble over the uneven ground, run, but the jackal charges at me. I see its open mouth, all those teeth. Throwing my hands over my face, I wait for the impact, for sharp teeth. Just as it leaps, there is a dull thud and the animal seems to disintegrate. A bit of broken brick strikes the tunnel wall behind me.

A siren sounds in the distance. Jaco jerks his head to the exit. 'The Worm is dead.'

'We'll be back for you,' says Madison. 'Once that magic is ready for us.'

They walk away. I lean against the wall, my legs suddenly boneless.

From the other direction, a voice yells my name.

21

FALLING STAR

Harrison is at the entrance to the tunnel. He reaches me in three long strides.

'Jesus, Savannah.' He runs worried eyes over me. 'Did that thing hurt you?'

'I'm OK.' My mouth is dry. 'Did you see it?'

'I saw it. Market shut early. I was looking for you when I heard a scream, like – a bad scream. I get here, find you with a knife in your hand facing off some gang, and then that *thing* leaped at you.'

'You stopped it,' I realise. 'You threw a brick at it.'

'Luckily I've always been good with balls.' He smirks only a little and then his face falls. 'Savannah, that was some scary shit. Who are those people?'

He pulls me into his arms and I am hungry for the contact. The feel of his cotton T-shirt, the skin of his forearms. He says, 'You're safe now,' and I hold him tighter.

When I let him go, he smooths my hair from my face and, with a strained smile, says, 'Your eyes are still bugging out.'

'Harrison,' I start, about to warn him about Mama Daline.

'What's that?' he whispers, squinting down the tunnel.

'Mama Daline. The healer. Those people you saw, they—'

'They killed her?'

I killed her, I want to say. The knife in my hand, the feel of it going through her skin, between her bones. My breath catches.

'You saw how the people at the market were tired and sickly?' I say, and he nods. '*They* do that, those four and others like them. They drain magic out of them.'

Harrison looks as queasy as I feel.

'Can you call Zenande?' I pass my phone to him, trying to quell the sickness.

He nods, dazed. 'Savannah, man,' he says softly as he pulls up my contacts. 'What are we going to do with you?'

Zenande is there in less than two minutes. She'd clearly been waiting for my call. She rushes up to me, pulls me into a tight hug.

'This is what Mama Daline wanted. It's what she'd fore-seen.' She's vehement, and tears prick at my eyes. 'This is how it had to be.'

She pulls a brown vial from her pocket. 'For the shock. Only one drop, Angry Girl.'

I hold back a choked sob and take the bottle. One drop. It feels like months since I drank the stolen potion.

Zenande gestures to Harrison to drink too and I am surprised when his long fingers lift the bottle from my hands.

The effect is immediate. It doesn't mute my sorrow or guilt, but I feel able. Like I can go on, rather than curl up in a ball and weep.

Zenande gives me a nod. 'Go on, I'll deal with the police. I'll tell them how Mama Daline was robbed, then killed.' She hands me a brown paper package. 'This is for your Winelands trip. Use it to call Hella's tormentor.'

'Are you sure?' I say, taking the package. 'We can wait with you.'

'You'd best go. They won't ask too many questions.' Another day, another woman killed.

She turns away from us and walks slowly towards Mama Daline. I brush away a tear. We leave the tunnel, Zenande bent over the older woman's body, sobs racking her shoulders.

Harrison and I are in the car. Late for the dress fitting with Kim, I'm cleaning my bloody hands with an old towel. The silence is uncomfortable, which is a first. It's never been anything but easy between Harrison and me. I'm already teetering at the edge, and this might push me over.

'Why did the market close early?' I twist my star ring, miserable. We're nearing Hospital Bend now, five minutes from town.

'The wind went crazy, like a mini tornado. Stalls blowing everywhere.' He glances at me. 'C'mon, out with it. Tell me this hateful story.'

'I don't understand how you could see the jackal. You can't see magic. Can you?'

190

He looks sheepish. 'My mom always used to say that I was, you know, met die helm gebore. Psychic, spoke to ghosts when I was a kid, dreamed about stuff before it happened. I don't remember.

'What I do remember is that one day, just after Freda died, I saw this shadow around *you*. Like an aura, but black. It frightened me, and it wouldn't go away. So I made myself not see it. Blocked it out. Not seeing became habit. I forgot all about it, or I wanted to.' He rubs the back of his neck. 'But this afternoon after you disappeared, the wind was going mal and suddenly I could hear all these whispers. They said someone was being executed.'

'You thought it was me.'

'I ran between the stalls, looking for you. And, it was like a light had been switched on. The stalls were glowing, I saw patterns moving on fabric. A statue turned and looked at me. Something made me run to the bridge ...'

'You came for me.'

'I will always come for you.' He speaks so fiercely, it's a growl. It rumbles through me, and I keep my eyes down in case of rogue tears. Harrison checks his blind spot and changes lanes. 'I thought that animal would kill you.'

'It will kill me,' I say. 'That creature is the curse. The manifest.'

'Savannah,' he says weakly. I'm quiet. 'All this stuff happening, and you didn't say anything?'

'It started the night of Carniveil.'

I tell Harrison about the starflame protection ceremony

that turned bad. About the line of jackal-headed figures and their warning. The Jackal who wants to unite the Market and the Nightmarket under her rule.

'What's this got to do with you?' Harrison says. He's listened quietly so far, which is another first.

'Our Hella was the original Jackal. I'm ninety per cent forbidden magic and the new Jackal wants it. You know that night I went missing in the park?' He nods. 'She came to me. Offered to protect me if I joined her.'

He looks ahead, thinking. 'They found a body the next morning,' he says. 'Not far from where we'd been.'

'That was Arrow. The veilwitches killed her.'

Two women, dead within days. Harrison gives me a worried look. 'I'm glad you're out of town next week.'

'Me too.' Though something tells me the veilwitches will find me wherever I go. That there is nowhere I can hide.

'Did you think about accepting?' he says gently.

'The Jackal is dangerous.' What would she be if she had more? 'I'm not going to help her get stronger.'

I quash the wriggling anxiety inside. Three weeks to the Summer Starfall peak.

He pulls up at the wedding dress shop and we sit for a moment in silence. I never imagined that Harrison of all people would be the one to understand.

'You want to come in?' I say, stuffing Zenande's package into my bag.

'Isn't it enough that I slayed a beast for you this afternoon – now you want me to face death by bridal wear?'

It's nearly there, the usual jokey tone. Not yet, but almost. I smile and he returns it.

'I'll call you later. And Savannah – please, no magic, no witches, no curses and no animals. Just for the rest of the afternoon, OK?'

I get out of the car, holding the now-bedraggled gerberas that Harrison packed with my things. The doorway to the wedding shop is thickly arched with fake flowers and foliage. The bell tinkles when I go in. Along the walls, the dresses wait. A hundred virgins in shades of white. Ghosts ready for a dance.

The sales assistant glides over to greet me, and leads me to a room at the back, lined with cream wallpaper. There, Minnie and Auntie Dotty sit on elegant chairs. Lilies stand in a tall vase, their scent too sharp.

Rosie is at the window, a shaft of sunlight touching her face. She smiles when she sees me and widens her eyes just slightly, as though to say, *Where have you been? This is boring.*

Kim and Inez are in the middle of the room, frowning at a line of dresses. This is a serious business. Their heads are close together. Like sisters.

'Savannah, you're here,' Minnie says, and I go to kiss her cheek. She holds my arm, wrapping her cool fingers around my mottled wrist. It is soothing.

'Sorry, I'm late.' I drop a kiss on Auntie Dotty's cheek. 'A woman was, ah, mugged near the market. I called for help.'

'Oh, Savannah.' *There's always something,* Kim's face says. I can see her mind ticking over the possible dangers I avoided. 'That's terrible. You OK?'

'They didn't mug *me*, Kim,' I snap, and she looks down at the floor.

'Sorry,' I exhale. I drop the flowers on a chair. Even apologising makes me cross. Make nice. Stay in line.

The sales assistant brings out another rail of dresses and the aunties descend.

Rosie takes my arm. 'I found something,' she whispers. We sit on the chaise longue.

From her small, quilted designer bag, Rosie pulls out a sheet of paper. It's so old, the blue ink has bled through the page. Rosie unfolds it along worn crease lines.

I follow her neatly manicured finger as she traces the rows. It's a table, written in shaky capitals: *Widow's Words.*

A	1	BABY	O	15	SEASICK
B	2	OLD WOMAN	P	16	WAX
C	3	QUEEN	Q	17	PRIEST
D	4	SHADOW	R	18	HAT
E	5	DEAD MAN	S	19	DARK CLOUD
F	6	MASK	T	20	EGG
G	7	BOWL	U	21	FALLING STAR
H	8	TEETH	V	22	BLOODSTAIN
I	9	ORANGE FLOWER	W	23	DARK ROAD
J	10	POISON	X	24	BLUE EYES
K	11	DRUM	Y	25	BEES
L	12	SNAKE	Z	26	BLUNT KNIFE
M	13	GOAT		27	GOLD
N	14	BLACK FEATHER		28	BAD MAN

	29	BIG FISH		35	WATCHMAN
	30	BITE		36	LADDER
	31	CAGE		37	COIN
	32	FULL MOON		38	THRONE
	33	KEY		39	GRAVE
	34	DEVIL			

It looks familiar. Like the list of Fahfee numbers and dream symbols that Minnie uses to bet on the horses and play the lotto. Dream of an old woman? Place a bet on number two. A code for interpreting dreams.

'My mom got this years ago when she was travelling, from a village witch.'

I look over at Inez, browsing the rails. She's wearing another one of those dresses that look more like sculpture. Her cropped hair is swept back, her face is bare of make-up except for a dash of red lipstick. She's unspeakably elegant. It's impossible to imagine her consulting village witches or reading dreams.

'Rosie, did you say *village witch*? Your mom? Inez?'

'Uh-huh,' Rosie laughs. 'You haven't spent enough time with my mom, obviously. There is nothing she loves more than a village witch. You've seen her herb candles, right? Learned from the village witch.' Rosie leans in closer. 'Anyway, this is really old, and eerily accurate. We can use it to find this name in your dreams.'

'Rosie …' I hesitate. 'Has your mom said anything about witches *here*?'

Rosie frowns. 'Here? No. Why?'

'No reason.' I look down at the page again.

'Oh my, you look stunning,' Auntie Dotty says, clapping her hands together. I look up to see Kim step from behind the curtain, wearing an enormous white dress with a lace bodice. 'Yes. That's the one.'

'Savannah,' Kim says. Her expression is tentative, hopeful. 'What do you think?'

I think that when you've seen one big white wedding dress, you've seen them all.

'It's … big,' I say.

Kim's face falls. The older women close around her in a circle, muting the blow of my lack of interest with a flurry of compliments.

'How does it work?' I ask Rosie. 'This list.'

'Um. Well, you have to look out for a really striking object or image in your dream. See if it matches a letter and collect the letters to form a word. Has anything stood out?'

I watch Inez undo the tiny pearl buttons with careful concentration. 'A goat.' The dreams are mostly the same, what is most striking is where it changes.

She squints at the list. 'Goat is M. Anything else?'

'A baby.'

'That's A. So M-A. That's a start.'

'Savannah.'

Kim is standing before me.

A snake, I'd almost forgotten the snake. I run my eyes over the letters. L.

'Savannah.'

'What?' My head is still in my dreams; the creature, hard earth, the bones, the letters. M-A-L. A shiver runs down my spine. This feels *right*.

'It's time to try on your dress.'

I blink at the rail of peach dresses, which were surely sewn with the devil's thread and created in my nightmares. My horror must be evident on my face.

'Not a chance.' I'm too blunt, but— 'No way, never.'

'Won't you at least try them?' Minnie says, getting up from the chair. She's stiff from the arthritis in her knees and moves with difficulty.

Minnie, in her trousers and knit top and pink lipstick. She is my constant. A guiding star in the tumultuous waters of my life. 'They might look beautiful on.'

Because it's Minnie, I take two dresses. Inez follows me into the dressing room with the rest.

She hangs them up while I pull off my dress. I'm not self-conscious, not after years of dancing with quick costume changes in the wings. Inez picks it up from the floor and frowns. Near the waistband is a smear of blood.

I reach for it. 'I got a paper cut.' I look down, feeling the heat in my cheeks. It's a stupid lie.

'Ah.' Inez's face tells me she's not satisfied. 'Here, step in.'

She zips up the dress. I stand back from the mirror in a cloud of peach chiffon, hating my reflection. For a second, I imagine the fabric unravelling, slithering around my neck and choking me.

'What do you think?'

'You look beautiful,' Inez says dutifully. 'But it's not you, is it?'

'No.' I wish I could be the daughter Kim wants me to be.

'Do you want me to talk to Kim?' Inez says gently, like she knows how itchy-under-the-skin I'm feeling. 'About getting something else?'

'Would you?' I say, and Inez chuckles at my sudden enthusiasm.

'Sure. But in turn, can you show just a little interest in the wedding?'

'I'll try.' Ashamed, I look at the hem while Inez puffs out the dress.

She straightens, takes my hands in hers. 'I'm really looking forward to spending more time with you over the next few weeks. This trip is going to be special – and then we have ten days when Kim's in Zanzibar.'

'Zanzibar? No, they're driving up the Garden Route.' Kim and Quinton are taking a few days away after the wedding.

'Oh, honey, did she not tell you there was a change of plan?'

'She's got a lot on,' I say feebly. The mirror I'm facing reflects another, and within is an infinity of Savannahs, all of them sore and cross.

'Quinton only told her last night,' Inez says.

Where is Quinton getting the money for all of this? An expensive wedding and honeymoon abroad? He likes nice things, I know that. But this dress shop, the venue he's chosen … how is he paying for it all?

I step out of the dressing room in the peach puff and Kim touches her hand to her chest.

'Oh, my girl.'

I twirl for Kim, for Minnie, for Auntie Dotty. I spread out the dress, do a little princess curtsy and present the battered gerberas to Kim. They beam and clap, and for once I've done something right.

22

BLOODSTAIN

Two days later, Dex is in the driver's seat and Inez navigates as we set out for Nietvergeten. Rosie is beside me, zinging with anticipation as we leave the city.

I can't stop thinking about Mama Daline in the tunnel. How the veilwitches danced around her. What I had to do to stop them.

'Savannah?' Rosie says and I turn from the window and look at her. 'Do you want to listen to music? What do you like?'

'Sure.' I make myself smile. 'You choose.'

Arrow and Mama Daline are both dead. Claw is still in hospital. I have to stop the Jackal. Which means I must find the tormentor key this week. Of the three keys, this one worries me the most. I summoned the manifest easily enough and with the Widow's Words, I have a map to navigate my dreams. I exhale, wishing to hear Mama Daline's calm, soothing voice telling me to listen to the magic inside. But she's gone.

'Louder, Dex.' Rosie bounces forward as Taylor Swift begins to sing. 'This one's my favourite.'

Packed in my bag are the tools Zenande gave me. A shallow wooden bowl, a vial labelled *See*. Instructions for calling a spirit bound to the land. She'd talked me through it on the phone last night, saying, 'You'll know when the time is right.' I'd groaned at this vagueness, but she'd been adamant. 'You'll feel it.'

Table Mountain disappears behind us, and new mountains rise ahead. Rosie chatters beside me, pointing out landmarks she remembers. Inez teases her for being a tourist.

It's afternoon when we reach Nietvergeten, an old wine farm off the beaten track. Driving through the tree-lined entrance, into the sprawling estate, a bud of apprehension unfurls. Following the curve of the road, we pass neat lawns and beautiful Cape Dutch buildings beneath ancient oaks. These give way to rows and rows of neat vines. Red roses bloom at the end of each, a splash of colour against brown earth, the green vines, the high blue sky.

Hella lived here, I think. She walked these fields, was sheltered by this mountain. A sunbird calls, and I think to myself: how pretty it is, this place where terrible things happened. How in this country, beauty is often the *mise-en-scène* for trauma.

Beyond the vineyard, four guest houses are scattered among the foothills. We stop at a Cape Dutch cottage nestled into the mountain. It has a rounded gable, whitewashed walls and a thatched roof. Dark green shutters frame the windows.

'I'll be working most of the week,' Inez says as I take my bag from the car. Dex carries two large suitcases through the front door and Rosie's investigating inside. 'It's a big feature. I've booked a few things to keep you busy – horse-riding, quad biking. There are hiking trails around, and the mountain pool is off the trail behind the cottage. Plenty to explore.' There's a slight emphasis to her last words.

'Inez.' I want to tell her how grateful I am. How much this means. But what comes out is, 'I've no idea how to ride a horse.'

She laughs, but she must read something in my eyes, because she gives me a hug, pulling me to her. I relax into her arms, into the expensive perfume and cool linen.

'This week is for learning new things.' She squeezes my shoulders, then releases me, saying, 'Come on,' as she turns to go inside.

The cottage is luxurious, decorated in calming whites, with thick walls, sash windows and half doors.

'Savannah, you must see this,' Rosie says. She leads me down the passage, and I glance at the main bedroom with its four-poster bed. We put our things in the mountain-facing room with twin beds and a window seat. 'Isn't it gorgeous?'

'Beautiful,' I say dutifully.

'Swim, hike or chill?' Rosie looks out of the window. The mountain looms behind her and all I can think about is Hella. 'Savannah? Hello?'

I turn to her and blink. 'Sorry, what was that?'

'Do you want to go for a swim?'

I want to find Hella. 'Sure.' I say and Rosie's still looking at me strangely so I make myself fun. 'That would be great.'

We change quickly and Rosie calls out for Dex, who's looking out the front window, pensive.

'I'll catch you up,' he says. 'I'm going with Inez to meet the manager.'

The afternoon sun beats down as Rosie and I follow the mountain path.

'Do you hear that?' Rosie says, gleeful at the loud, rushing sound of water. Down the steep embankment, tucked into the rocks and trees, a waterfall crashes into a sparkling pool.

'Hell yes,' Rosie calls, running down the path and dumping her backpack on a wide flat rock.

We strip to our costumes and jump in, gasping at the difference in temperature.

After a while, I swim to the waterfall. Rosie's floating and staring up at the sky. I stand right under the rushing water, enjoying how it kneads my shoulders.

'Incoming!' Dex yells. On a high rock, he pulls off his T-shirt. His body is a neat line, the sun dancing on oak skin.

Dex jumps, letting out a gleeful roar. He lands in the darker, deep water.

'I want to do that!' Rosie claps her hands.

I move from the spray and lean against a rock as I watch Rosie pick her way barefoot up the path. With graceful strokes, Dex swims towards me.

At the top, Rosie holds out her arms like Jack on the *Titanic* and yells, 'I'm the queen of the world.'

'Nineties month at the cinema has a lot to answer for,' Dex laughs. His walls are down again, like the night we broke into his aunt's flat. It's easier here, in this secluded pool away from everything.

With a savage, happy cry, Rosie jumps.

'You're way too comfortable there.' Dex gives me a wicked look and, tugging my wrist, he pulls me back under the waterfall. Water rushes over us, and we're laughing so hard as we clutch each other to keep from slipping. I grab his arm, my hand close to the scarred skin on his shoulder.

'Do you remember how it happened?' I brush a finger over the scarring. It feels uneven.

'I'll never forget.'

'Savannah,' Rosie calls, 'come! You have to try this.'

'I'll watch and applaud,' I shout through cupped hands.

'I hated the afterwards,' Dex continues, to my surprise. He moves away from the cascading water towards the centre of the pool and I float with him. 'Inez was furious. There were loads of arguments. Hospital, pain. Being away from everyone.' He smiles apologetically. 'I didn't return your Yasmin.'

'You did. Eventually.'

Rosie's reached the top again. This time she holds out her arms, but doesn't shout. Just stands there, reaching to the sky.

'When we moved, things were really difficult.' The light dances on the rippling water, on his scar.

Rosie jumps, her body straight and falling, then disappearing beneath the dark water.

'We couldn't afford much. I'd cry for my grandmother almost every day –' Dex gives a quick laugh – 'which Inez hated, but it was Rosie who really struggled.'

Rosie surfaces, letting out a jubilant cry.

'She couldn't make friends, was teased a lot.' He speaks quietly so she can't hear. 'For her accent, for being shy, for being different. I felt like it was my fault. If I hadn't been burned then we wouldn't have left.'

'Did it get easier?'

'It did. Rosie can be determined, and I guess she decided she wanted to make things work. We changed schools, and after a while, we were happy.'

Until he had to move back here again.

Rosie's wading towards us now. In the afternoon light she is golden. She laughs and never have they seemed more like twins. Sleek, beautiful.

'Wasn't I amazing?' she preens. She is, very much.

For the first time since their return, it feels like Dex is truly here with us. This afternoon, we're together. Three of us, as we once were.

In the early evening, while Dex is in the shower and Rosie watches something old and violent on her laptop, I go in search of Hella.

I leave from the back of the cottage and, at a fork, I take the flat, narrow path that winds along the bends of the mountain.

As I walk, it feels like I'm being drawn along the path, a thread gently tugging me forward. It's comfortable, like taking the route to an old home. I know the curve of this overgrown path, the sway of the watsonias dancing in the breeze. The gleam of the early evening sun, the woody scent of fynbos.

Rounding the corner, I see a sheltered spot resting in the folds of the mountain, and I know I must leave the path here.

Stepping away from the trail is like walking a knife edge, somewhere high and dangerous, but with no fear. I move through heathers, white ericas and pincushion flowers. I roam between them until I come up against a low wall that juts out of the ground. My eye traces the stone, connecting the pieces until, with growing excitement, I realise it's the barest remains of a building.

'There was a house here once.'

I jump, my heart pounding in my chest.

Dex moves through the shrubs towards me.

'Could you not,' I yell, my voice echoing off the rock face, 'sneak up on me like that?'

'Sorry.' He moves closer. He smells nice. Clean.

I take a deep breath and look around. 'The original farmhouse?'

Zenande had said to be as close as possible to the place where the enslaver died when I make the connection.

'Yeah.' He nods at the leftover walls. 'I read about it down at the office.'

'This is where they died.' I'm speaking more to myself as I try to map the house from its remnants. 'Inez said that He ...' I start, and then press my lips shut. She asked me not to tell Dex about Hella and Nietvergeten.

'What did Inez say?' Dex says in that slightly dangerous voice.

'Nothing.'

'Did she tell you about the enslaved woman who'd been whipped? About the fire that broke out after?' He sounds bitter.

I don't answer.

'What did my mother tell you, Savannah?' He's pissed and I don't understand why.

I turn away from him. I want to tell him, but I promised Inez I wouldn't. I feel the weight of his gaze. He's gone cold again, a cloud blotting out our sunshine hour in the mountain pool. I stay silent.

Birds fly overhead, crying out as they pass. The sun is lower, its light softer, golden. There's a dull ache in my heart.

Hella.

'It was about your family curse, wasn't it?' He comes up behind me. 'She's obsessed with your family curse.' He shakes his head. 'She brought you here because she thinks the runaway woman is your ancestor, didn't she?'

I am not getting drawn into his fight with Inez. Dex drops his head. He seems defeated.

'You can tell me, you know. Whatever you want.' When he looks up, there's a shadow in his eyes. 'Whenever you're ready.'

I nod, and Dex takes a step to stand beside me. His arm brushes mine as if to say, *Truce.*

'What else did you learn?' I veer away from his mother. 'In the office?'

He doesn't answer immediately. After a moment he sighs. 'How badly the enslaved people were treated. Our history is filled with stories like that.'

'Men and women, chained. Tortured to death on the wheel,'

I say. 'Mutilation and branding. Their time, their labour, their bodies, their lives, their names. All stolen from them.'

We're both quiet, thinking about the people who were taken from their homes, from their countries, forced on to boats for horrendous sea journeys. Sold, as if they were property. Made to work.

I don't know where Hella first called home. She could have been born here to an enslaved mother who gave her a secret name, one remembered from long ago. Or Hella could have been taken from Madagascar or India or Indonesia or another Asian country. So many stories, Rosie had said, entwined like a double helix.

We look out over the valley, the distant vineyards. Nietvergeten: do not forget.

I think of the children born to that life. How, over time, we still feel the echoes, the aftershocks of injustice. It's always there, this shadow. Stories we can never fully know. The people whose names are lost to us.

Rosie brings me hot chocolate in the morning. I feel confused and tired. My heart hurts for a reason I can't remember.

She takes her drink to the window seat and looks at me through a curtain of honey-brown hair. 'You were tossing in your sleep again.' The storm grows wilder.

Always the same dream: the fire, running, the river. Hella on the other side, waiting. Impatient? Then it fizzles into nothing.

'What did you dream?' Rosie says.

'I can't remember with you constantly asking me about it,' I snap. I take a hot sip and it burns my throat. Rosie flushes.

'I'm sorry,' I say. I go and sit opposite her and look out at the mountain. Our toes touch. 'You're just trying to help. I'm scared. I feel like a sitting duck, waiting to be picked off.'

Rosie rolls her eyes. 'Savannah, there's something you need to know about me. I don't give up. Not when I set my heart on something. It's why I'm first in my class every year – except once when I had flu and missed a whole month, and even *then* I only missed out by one mark. I don't quit. There must be something we can do.'

'Like what? Hold a séance?'

Rosie's face lights up.

'Rosie. That was a joke.' I shiver. No way am I bothering the dead. Minnie would kill me.

Except, I realise unpleasantly, that's exactly what I am doing, trying to connect to Hella's tormentor. I hide my obviously stricken face with my hair, keenly aware of the grim task that awaits me. When the time is right, whatever that means.

'OK, OK. I might have an idea.' Hugging her knees, she looks serene in her butter-yellow sleepshirt. 'But I can't possibly think clearly until I've had breakfast.' She unfolds from the window sill, and takes my hand to tug me up.

'Rosie,' I warn, following her into the corridor. 'What's your idea?'

'Good things come to those who wait.' Rosie dances through the kitchen to where Dex is at the table and gives him a quick hug from behind. Inez has left for the day, and I'm relieved. The tension between her and Dex has become substantial. An unpleasant thickness that occupies the room when they're together.

'Someone's in a good mood,' Dex says as Rosie sits beside him, pinching a strawberry from his bowl.

It's me he's watching, though. I feel his eyes on me as I walk into the room, slump in my seat. I stare at the large fruit bowl like it's an oracle that will give me answers.

'You sleep OK, Savannah?' he says, something clouding his eyes.

No. Because there's a storm inside me. Because I drank that stupid remedy. Because I'm cursed.

I choose a plum. 'No rest for the wicked.'

I'm almost touched by the concern on his face. Except pity isn't what I want from Dex. I stop myself there. I don't want to think about what I do want from him.

23

DARK ROAD

Running. Always running. Behind me is the roaring flame. The heavy panting of an animal.

And ahead, the river. As always, the woman waits there, her back to me but her face in profile. In the light of the fire, she seems ethereal. Otherworldly.

Approaching the river, I stop running. I look around to see what might trip me up this time. There's nothing, so I step carefully, placing my bare feet between the smooth river stones.

I'm about to put my foot in the river when I hear the scream. It's a loud and furious cry. I turn, and there, precariously positioned on a rock, is a baby boy. His mouth is a large angry gash, his eyes scrunched with fury. He begins to slip off the rock and I reach forward, trying to catch him, and I grab—

I wake up.

And feel the softest brush of fur against my uncovered calves.

I leap out of the bed with a shuddering gasp. I look over to Rosie's bed, but she's fast asleep. I search the dark corners of the room. There is nothing there.

There's no way I'm going back to sleep after that.

Another baby. That's A. I now have M-A-L-A.

I peer around the room, checking the shadows. Nothing. Leaning on the window sill, I look out, and the same draw I felt on the mountain path tugs at me, but stronger. *You'll know when the time is right.*

I have to go out there. I want to.

Rosie sleeps on as I open my drawer and pull out Zenande's tools and instructions. I ease the drawer shut and slip out of the room.

I don't turn on any lights as I ghost from the bedroom, down the passage and into the kitchen, where I fill my bottle with water. In my sleep shorts and vest, I go outside.

The stars are pinpricks in the velvet night. The beam of light from the small torch barely cuts into the darkness. It is so thick, so complete, and yet I'm not afraid. I follow the path behind the house, then on to the narrow trail hugging the mountain bends. I take one resolute step after another, until I reach the ruin.

Setting three candles on the broken walls, I light them. Cross-legged, I place the remaining four around me. I'm exposed, vulnerable. But I'm swathed by an inexplicable conviction that I will be fine. It feels like I've tuned into a strength that is not my own.

Tonight, I am not afraid. Not of men nor monsters.

I empty my bottle of water into the shallow wooden bowl

and then the vial labelled *See*. The water turns cloudy.

A light scent lifts from the candles and I stare at the flame, emptying my mind. Minutes pass, a light breeze picks up, but I'm not cold. I could sit like this for hours.

Watching the tapering light, I speak the words Zenande had written down: 'I call to those bound to this land.' My voice is deep and loud, and something like power zings through me.

At the fringes of the light, the black seems to shift shape. Perhaps I hear the softest murmuring sound.

I am dissociated. I am here, but also not. In my body, but spilling out. Me, but connected to something bigger. 'I call to those bound to this land.'

I feel them gather in the darkness. Their presence is wary, watchful but not malevolent. In the shifting black at the edges of the candlelight, I imagine I see a young man, an old woman, a middle-aged man. They shimmer into form, smudges in the dark, then disappear.

In the bowl, the cloudy water ripples gently. My feeling of detachment, the conviction that I am in some strange dream, grows stronger.

Let the echoes of this earth show me the way forward. The words are the dry rustle of leaves. I repeat them: 'Let the echoes of this earth show me the way forward.' I say the words again and again.

In the water, I see the shouting face of a long-ago neighbour, *you horrible, naughty girl*. The picture shifts and two small blonde girls taunt, *you can't be a princess, Savannah*. Me sitting alone on a chair in front of the class, for bad behaviour. Then standing at a camp fire as a boy whistles at me from behind. When I turn to face him he laughs, *oops, wrong colour*. My old dance teacher who'd weigh us and say, *Have you been scoffing chocolate, Savannah?* The laughter of the other dancers. The boys who'd call mockingly when I walked home from school, leering and reaching as I passed. The scenes continue, on and on.

I don't realise I'm crying until I touch a hand to my face. The images play on, as if by some invisible mini-projector: the man who'd flashed me at the station, the one who put his hand up my school dress on a crowded train. My first boyfriend telling sixteen-year-old me, *If you won't then you don't love me.* The time he took a topless picture of me and showed his friends. Their crude, suggestive comments. The shunning.

The onslaught is relentless: scene after scene of bitter memories from my life. I am wrenched out, hollow.

Make it stop, I plead, but the scenes continue: the guy at the party who'd cornered me, the best dancer in the youth company laughing at my mistakes.

Bug-Face showing me the shape of his gun. Meyer's finger on my skin. The masked man grabbing me in Kim's room.

I'm surprised by an image I don't recognise: me roaring into a man's face. A second one follows quickly, where strong hands shake me until my teeth rattle. They drag me, my thin shoes burning against carpet.

Suddenly it stops, this brutal playback of humiliations. The daily torments I've lived through. A solid ball of rage is wedged in my chest and I am breathless with it.

Blood. I hear whispers in the dark. *Three tormentors.*

And then, the sound of raging fire: crackling, hissing and burning through wood and turning stone to dust. I close my eyes, and I am in my dream. I can almost feel the heat of the fire.

I open my eyes and it stops. Just seven candles in the dark night. I'm cold now. Shoulders slumped, steel no longer runs through my veins.

I haven't turned the tormentor key. I came out this evening prepared to connect to Hella's tormentor. To glimpse the hardship she endured, an intense suffering I can't ever really know.

Instead I connected to these small brutal moments. My own torments. And I realise with sudden clarity that to lift this curse, I needed to look my own past in the eye; to observe the story of *my* anger.

The cloudy water showed people who deliberately hurt or intimidated me. It made me inhabit how useless, afraid and broken I felt. How furious.

Except for the last two scenes. Those haven't happened. Yet.

I pack everything up, thinking carefully as I walk back to the guest house. It's a step closer, but how?

Blood. I hear the echo inside my head. *Three tormentors.*

I return to the cottage in a daze, half running in the dark.

I'm trembling a little when I stop outside the kitchen door. Unsettled and upset. I can't go in to bed just yet, so I wander to the patch of lawn beside the house. That's when I see him, stretched out on the grass at three o'clock in the morning. Dex. He rests his head in his hands, looking up at the stars. I drop the bag on a lounger and go over to him.

'You can't sleep either?' His voice brings me back. Anchors me.

I lie down beside him, tilting my face up to the sky. I'm relieved he's here, outside in the deepest part of the night. That I'm not alone right now.

'You OK?'

'Yeah, it's just …' He trails off with a small head shake.

Inez. It's clear he doesn't want to talk about her now. 'Look.' I see the four bright stars low in the sky. 'The Four Sisters. That's a good omen.'

'You know much about the Four Sisters?'

'My aunt Freda did. I can't remember the stories.'

'I know a little,' he says.

'From the library?' I glance at him.

'Four girls from very different families were born on the night of the falling stars. A shard of star touched each one and as they grew, so did the magic inside them. The magic drew them to each other.'

'I wonder how they met. They couldn't exactly hop in a car.'

'Magic, Savannah, keep up. They could manipulate distance. Step through one door and emerge from another twenty kilometres away.' His voice is playful. 'They would meet under the cover of darkness. The general's lady wife, the enslaved woman, the hunter and the healer.'

'That day in the library,' I say, 'I thought you were magic.'

'Savannah –' his lips quirk up – 'you have the worst pick-up lines.'

We laugh and the strangeness from earlier further loosens its hold on me.

'It was so weird, seeing you there after Carniveil. It felt unnatural, somehow. Like other forces were at work. Like you were a jinn, following me.'

He turns on his side, head propped up by his arm.

'So that's why you were staring at me,' he says.

'I was curious. You seemed like a book I wanted to read.' I laugh.

He sighs, a small sound. 'That book doesn't end well.'

'What do you mean?'

He looks at me a long moment, and then he says, 'I can still see you, that day in the library. In that insane skirt and your hair tumbling down like snakes. You were, I don't know – wild. Terrible and magnificent. Like a wrathful queen.'

Maybe it's the brilliant sky above us. Maybe it's being outside at three in the morning, when nothing feels real. Maybe because I just relived my worst experiences and seeing him has been a salve.

Maybe it's because he just called me a fucking queen.

I touch his arm, my hand on skin and muscle.

His eyes are fixed on mine.

I move closer. Too bold, I brush against his body. I wait a moment, giving him a chance to stop me, if he wants to.

Above the moon looks down; the stars, the Sisters themselves, are shining on us. In the cold light of day, we can pretend this was a beautiful dream.

'Savannah,' he says, and I can see his throat move.

I kiss him. And yes I am brazen and no I am not sorry. For a moment, he seems to hesitate. Then his hand touches my back, pulling me on top of him, and we fall into the grass.

The night is electric. There are secrets beneath the sky; anything can happen under the cover of darkness. I throw back my head and chest, stretching out my arms with my face to the moon. I'm seconds away from howling at it.

Dex laughs softly, but I think he gets it. He runs his fingers up my bare arm and he pulls me down again, his face inching towards mine.

His fingers stop. He glances at the curse mark on my shoulder, and in his eyes, I see pity.

I don't want pity. Anything but that. I pull back and stand up, my bare feet on the grass.

He gets to his feet too, not meeting my eye. 'This probably isn't a good idea,' he says. Behind him, the stars glint and gleam.

Waiting to fall.

'It's just a kiss, Dex.' I smile. 'Doesn't have to mean anything.'

I walk back to the house, grabbing the bag from the lounger, before he can say anything else. My exit is graceful. My dance teacher would approve.

Inside, I'm trembling.

In our room, Rosie sleeps, her thick hair spread out dark against the white pillow. Her arm is stretched out, as if reaching for me.

24

BLUE EYES

Kim's wedding day is everything Quinton dreamed it would be.

The ceremony takes place on the beach, with the mountain looming over us. The bride, wearing a massive dress that makes her look like a bag of marshmallows, holds hands with the groom as waves crash upon the shore. The bride speaks so softly as she pledges herself to a snake.

I wear a long, heavy red silk skirt embroidered with gold thread. I'm on my best behaviour. The aunties, delighted to be in their fancy hats, dab at their eyes.

After the ceremony, we follow the flower-marked path back to the boutique hotel.

On the vine-covered terrace overlooking the sea, guests sip sparkling wine. Hundreds of paper lanterns hang from the pagoda and there are flowers everywhere, orange and red, Kim's favourite colours.

'Just like the movies,' Tietie says.

'She looks radiant,' Auntie Nazeema sighs.

'She's happy.' Auntie Chantie beams. 'At last.'

'You should see the sexy panties she's wearing. Somebody's getting lucky,' Auntie Dotty sings, gleeful.

Quinton is the cat who ate the cream, accepting congratulations. The perfect wedding.

Through the dining room doors, I can see the massive tiered cake with the triumphant smooching couple on top. I want to rip the head off the groom.

Quinton stalks across the terrace, his eyes on his bride. The aunties nudge each other, smiling.

'Kim,' he announces, interrupting her conversation with Fatima from the library, 'you've made me the happiest man in the world.'

He swoops her into his arms, dipping her so that her veil hangs to the ground, and gives her a dramatic kiss.

All the guests whoop and cheer. When Quinton lifts Kim up again, her earlobes are red with embarrassment.

I can't bear it any longer. I slip out of my heels and go down to the beach.

Back on the terrace I can see smiling guests bathed in a glow from the low, golden sun. It's a happy day. A celebration. Then why does it feel like something bad is beginning?

I try to quell the rising dread about our new future. I can't afford to move out while I study over the next few years. I'm stuck with Quinton as much as she is.

It's done now. They're married.

I allow myself five more minutes, then head back. Coming up the path, I see Quinton talking to Rosie, standing slightly too close, letting her know that he's bigger, stronger. The one with all the power.

'Hey, Rosie. Quinton,' I say. Quinton turns and gives that smile that never reaches his eyes. Rosie, beautiful in pale pink lace, catches my eye and hides a laugh by taking a sip of her drink. I'm not sure he intimidated her, even though he might think he has.

'You having a good time?' I say.

'The best.' Quinton looks around, pleased. 'Dinner in five minutes.' He waves at someone further up the path. 'Excuse me, girls.'

He squeezes my shoulder as he leaves. I can't repress a shudder.

Rosie laughs, but there's sympathy in it. 'You hate him, don't you?'

'Well …' I hesitate. 'Yeah, OK, I do. What were you two talking about?'

'He was telling me how to win at poker,' she says. 'Gaming and probability. He always wins, apparently.'

'Sounds right.'

'Anyway, thanks for rescuing me.' She slips her arm in mine.

We walk to the dining room with our arms linked. It's a small thing, but it makes me feel better.

'Right,' Rosie says, 'so, we're going to play Quinton bingo. Every time he says something excessive and ridiculous in his speech we have to drink.'

'You're on.' A little fun, to help me through this dark night.

In the dining room Kim and Quinton are alone at the top table, like a king and queen presiding over us. Kim looks longingly to where Fatima and her friends from work are laughing and chatting.

I take my seat at a round table with Harrison on one side and Donley on the other. They are both wearing suits and ties. Harrison looks good and he knows it. So does the woman on his other side who eyes him hungrily. 'You OK?' he asks me.

'No cars have been damaged tonight, no magical creatures summoned.'

'Yet.'

The room sparkles with fairy lights and every table has a huge red-and-orange mixed bouquet. I take a gerbera and put it in my hair, thinking of the flower seller in the market. I wish this one could magically improve my mood.

Quinton taps his glass with a spoon and the room goes silent.

Across the room, Rosie lifts her glass from where she sits beside Dex and mouths, 'Game on.'

'Friends and family,' Quinton says, his voice carrying throughout the large room. 'I am beyond excited to have you with us to celebrate today. The day I finally made this goddess, this angel sitting beside me, mine.'

Rosie puts up two fingers. I lift my glass and take two tiny sips. As tempting as it is, getting drunk would be an exceptionally bad idea.

Quinton continues in this vein, and Kim looks at her lap,

eyes downcast and cheeks pink. Rosie drinks a lot. I pretend to. Dex rolls his eyes at both of us. Then I realise that Quinton is taking Kim's hand, trying to get her to stand.

She's smiling, saying no, really no. Quinton laughs. 'Come on. Just a few words.'

He tugs her upright. Kim is visibly shrinking.

All the rage that has been welling up through the day suddenly bursts. All day he's pushed Kim, had her do things that make her uncomfortable. Red mist descends and I can barely see straight. Not this. I won't let him have this. I clench my fists. I grit my teeth. It takes *everything* to not scream at Quinton. Pummel him with bread rolls. Fling myself across the table and strangle him with his stupid fucking bow tie. Harrison turns to me, like he can see steam coming out of my ears.

How dare he. Before I know it, I've pushed back my chair.

Everyone turns to me. Now that I'm standing, I'm not sure what to do. Quinton's expression darkens. A hand slips into mine and squeezes. I look down. Harrison. His eyes say lots of things, including *Are you OK?* And *Don't do anything stupid.*

They ground me, Harrison's eyes.

'I'm not one of the scheduled speakers this evening,' I begin, worrying Freda's ring on my index finger. Kim sinks gratefully to her seat, into the puff of white dress.

'Speak louder,' someone yells through cupped hands. Phones are raised.

'Kim has been the best mom I could have had, these nearly eighteen years,' I say. 'She gave up a lot for me, and I appreciate it so much. I just want to welcome Quinton into our little family.' I struggle to sound warm. 'And to say that I'm trusting Kim's heart to him and … if he hurts her, I'll make him sorry.'

It's a joke, or at least I'm trying to pass it off as one, but as I speak, a mic is thrust at me by a keen hotel worker, and the last words are blasted across the room.

'Jesus, Savannah,' Harrison whispers beside me.

'Just kidding,' I force a laugh. 'But, look after her. To Quinton and Kim.'

There is a smattering of applause and glasses are raised. Kim smiles at me, but Quinton looks straight ahead, his jaw tight.

'Where did you get that?' murmurs Harrison as I sit down. 'Shitty wedding speeches dot com?'

'Wine.' I push my half-empty glass forward. I should have just chucked the bread rolls. Harrison pours a little and shakes his head when I gesture for more.

'You're in a mood. Wine is the last thing you need.'

'How bad was it?' I whisper. 'If ten is good?'

'Two? Three?'

There is laughter in his eyes but there is pity too. More pity. I hate it.

I force down a mouthful of yellowtail and salad.

A few minutes later, the lights dim and Quinton and Kim take to the dance floor as 'Unchained Melody' begins. There are cheers as he swings her, then draws her close. I push my plate away. Kim hides her head in Quinton's chest but when she looks up, she's beaming.

I watch them sway, Quinton singing the words as they dance, looking into her eyes the whole time. Their perfect day.

25

BEES

A fast song comes on and everyone storms the floor. After a while, it's only me and ninety-five-year-old great-aunt Bertha still sitting in our seats. Auntie Dotty dances over.

'Why are you sitting down, Savannah? When over there is that delicious young man.'

She nods at Dex, who's dancing with Rosie and Harrison.

'Just look at those hips. Your boy can move. You know, the way a man dances is the way he fu—'

'Auntie Dotty!' I yell, cutting her off. But I'm laughing, which is what she intended.

'Have you kissed him yet?'

'A lady never tells, remember?'

She's watching me too closely.

'You have,' she cries triumphantly. 'Good. You need some fun. Let's get him over here.'

'No, please—'

'Dex,' she yells through cupped hands, while I sink down in my chair, trying to become invisible.

'What can I do for you, Auntie Dotty?' Dex says. He looks utterly fine in his suit, I have to say.

Auntie Dotty takes his hand. 'Dance with me, gorgeous. Savannah, come on, don't be such an ou vrou.'

Laughing, Dex lets her lead him on to the dance floor. I stay sitting.

It's the stage of the evening when the aunties get down to 'Jerusalema', their favourite party song. I'm usually there with them, leading the way, but tonight, I can't. When I think of Quinton and Kim, together forever, it's just too grim.

Auntie Dotty shakes her hips, swaying her arms above her head as she dances with Dex. Auntie Chantie, laughing her head off, tries for a twerk, while Auntie Glynis does her chicken arm sidestep. Even Donley's there, doing the robot and missing all the beats, while Harrison, who really has them, shows his moves.

'What you waiting for, Savannah?' Auntie Dotty hollers, holding out her hand.

'Fine.' For Auntie Dotty, I will pretend. She dances with me for a minute, shaking her hips, then twirls me around so I'm facing Dex. With a little bow, she withdraws.

When the next song is a slow one, I look to the DJ and, sure enough, Auntie Dotty is strutting away from his deck.

Dex watches me. There's something in his eyes – a challenge. He thinks I'm going to bail. *Let's play a game.* To prove him wrong, I put one hand on his shoulder and the other around his neck. Wait for him to pull back.

He doesn't. Instead, his hand circles my waist, drawing me nearer. He raises an eyebrow and I repress a smile. I don't pull back; instead, I run a hand down his back, tracing the muscle beneath his shirt.

A radiant Kim slips back into the room, into Quinton's waiting arms and my heart sinks. She's changed out of her marshmallow into a simple sleeveless pale blue dress. They're catching a late-night flight to Zanzibar. It's almost time for them to go.

'Savannah.' Dex inches his hand higher, his fingers beneath the silk.

My eyes drift over to the cake, at Quinton dropping a kiss on Kim's head. They giggle in the corner as he slices the cake without any fuss or ceremony. Their quiet intimacy makes my stomach twist.

Dex's thumb makes little circles beneath my top. I like it. I want him to continue. I have to stop peeking at Kim.

I tighten my arms around him, press my body closer. Hand on my nape, he arches over me. My heart cartwheels in anticipation. He's going to kiss me, here. Now. I give him the come-hither eyes.

But then Kim turns and I can't help stealing a last look. Now that she's facing me, I get a better view of her wrists. Of the bracelets around each wrist. They are roping delicate bands of gold. I frown. I've seen that bracelet before.

'Sorry.' I pull away from Dex. The song ends. 'I have to talk to Kim.'

I'm walking towards Kim when I see it: the bracelet slithers. Its head moves.

I freeze on the dance floor, watching in horror. Around me, guests laugh and dance. The aunties are forming a circle with Rosie, now singing along to 'Umqombothi'. People drink wine and talk, *such a good party*. Quinton holds a slice of cake to Kim's lips.

At Greenmarket Square. That's where I saw those bracelets. *The snake will bite and sedate the wearer, making them yours to control.*

Quinton was there. *A little wedding present for Kim*, he'd said. I push through the dancers.

When Kim sees me her eyes light up. 'There you are!' she says.

'Can I talk to you for a second?' I ask. Force a smile. 'Say a proper goodbye.'

Her lovely smile breaks out. 'Of course, sweetie.'

Quinton nods benignly. I take Kim's arm and we walk through the doorway into the hotel reception.

She squeezes my arm. 'I'm so pleased you've hit it off with Rosie,' she says. 'I always hoped we'd all be friends again. Me and Inez, you and the twins.'

'I'm sorry my speech wasn't great,' I say. 'I should have practised.'

'It was just fine.' She smiles at me. 'I know you're adjusting. But it's going to be good. We're going to be happy.'

'Where did you get the bracelets?' I stare at them. There is a tiny bead of blood on one wrist.

'Wedding gift from Quinton. Aren't they gorgeous?' She beams, holding them out.

'Kim, you can't wear those,' I say.

She glances down, surprised. 'Why not? I love them.'

I don't have an explanation. Or at least not one I can give her. *Kim, I think the bracelets are enchanted. With forbidden magic. No one other than me, and presumably Quinton, can see that they're actually snakes.*

One of the snakes moves. It opens its little mouth wide and sinks its teeth into her arm.

'Did you feel that?' I sound strangled.

'What?' She stares at me, confused. 'It just pinched a little.'

'Take them off. I'll look after them for you.' I'm babbling. 'They'll be uncomfortable in the heat. I'll keep them safe.'

'Savannah, stop. You're making a show of yourself.'

'Take them off.' My voice is loud and heads turn our way. I don't care. I grab her arm and try to pull the bracelet from her wrist. It won't budge. Kim is struggling. At this point, everyone in the hotel reception is watching us.

Quinton pulls us apart, looking at me with disgust. 'What on earth are you doing?'

Kim is breathing heavily, her chest heaving as she stares at me.

'Kim—' I begin, but she holds up a hand. A single tear runs down her cheek.

'Could you not have given me today, Savannah? Just one day?'

It's not Quinton who made my mother cry. It's me.

229

'Our car's here,' Quinton says quietly. 'We should go.'

I stare at Kim, helpless.

I have to let her go.

'Just be careful.' I sound shaky.

'Of course I will.' She pulls me into a hug but all I can feel is the cold metal of the bracelets against my bare back. '*You* be careful. I'll call you, OK?'

And then Quinton puts his hand on Kim's hip and they walk away.

I lean against the wall, holding back tears. Everyone will be talking about me. More evidence of the curse in action, is what they'll think. The angry girl.

'Are you OK?' It's Dex. He hands me a tissue.

'Can we get out of here?' I wipe my face. 'I can't stay another minute.'

He watches me for a moment. 'If that's what you want.'

I nod and we begin to walk. 'I let her down,' I say.

'That's part of our job,' he says lightly. 'We're supposed to frustrate and worry our mothers.'

'What is it between you and Inez?' I say. 'Why are you so hard on her?'

A shadow crosses his face. He holds out his car keys. 'I've had a few drinks,' he says. 'Are you happy to drive?'

I love driving. I love the control. I love going as fast as I safely can. Harrison taught me and as soon as I could, I got my learner's licence. But apart from occasionally driving Kim's car, I don't get to do it much.

Dex leans back in the passenger seat. 'You buzzed?' I say.

'A little.' He smiles. 'Your aunts are great.'

'Yeah. They like you too. You know they're planning our marriage, right?'

He laughs. 'They're not very subtle.'

We drive away from the beach, along the folds of the mountain.

'What do you think of Quinton?'

Dex shrugs. 'Not a quiet man. Likes to be seen.'

'That's an understatement. He isn't good for her.'

'We have to let people make their own mistakes.' He speaks gently and it pisses me off.

'Did you see the bracelets he gave her?'

'No, why?'

I don't answer. We're beginning the ascent on Ou Kaapse Weg, the narrow, winding mountain pass.

'It's not me you're pissed at,' Dex sighs. 'It's Quinton. And your mom.'

'Please.' I sound nasty. 'Spare me the cheap psychology.'

I pick up speed as we continue to climb.

'You're going too fast,' Dex says quietly.

I drive faster. The dark road twists as it elevates, and I accelerate around the bends, the beast inside roaring.

Nearing the final hairpin bend, Dex says, 'Savannah, please slow down.'

The beast doesn't like that. It doesn't care for his tone of voice. I press my foot to the floor as I accelerate around the corner. It's reckless, but I know what I'm doing. I won't lose control. The bend is sharp, and I'm managing it like a pro.

Then, on the other side, another car appears. I am approaching too fast. Too close. I'm seconds from crashing into it, forcing us both into the rock face of the mountain. Swerving hard, I screech to a stop on the wrong side of the road, the sharp drop horribly close. The other driver blasts their horn before descending into darkness.

'There's another car coming.' Dex is unnervingly calm. I see the approaching headlights.

Wheels spinning beneath me, I turn the car. We drive down the hill in silence. At the bottom, I pull over and get out under a tree. I smash my fists into the trunk again and again and again like that can stop the heartache. They're raw and bleeding but I keep punching. This pain is easier to bear.

Dex pulls me away from the tree. I kick out at him, legs flailing. I'm crying, raw with rage and sorrow.

I could have killed us both. And the other driver. I am badly, badly out of control. I am a danger to myself, to other people.

I haven't cried like this in a long time, but I feel so broken. The tears stream and I'm making these awful noises. Wailing. I'm fucking wailing in the dark, on the side of the road.

Dex puts his arms tight around me and at last I let go. Give up. I lean against him. Soak the front of his nice shirt. I think of Kim's story, about the princess who raged during the day and wept as a mouse at night. I am the mouse now.

'I'm sorry,' I say at last. I wipe my tears.

Dex takes my hand and leads me back to the car. Without

saying a word, he gets in the driver's seat and we drive the rest of the way to Inez's house in silence.

In the street lights, I can see the bare skin of my waist. And, just under the hem of my top, the new marks.

26

BLUNT KNIFE

I'm being watched.

A man with a flat cap pulled low over his eyes leans against a wooden beam. His eyes track me as I walk past a handmade chocolate stall. We're at an evening market, and a posh one, with jazz music and craft beers, exotic flowers, handmade shampoo bars with twigs inside and candles with names like 'cedarwood and leather'.

It's a bustling, relaxed scene but beneath, unease stirs. Vendors, those who trade magic, are nervous. Unsettled.

The man watching me is not the first. They were watching when Rosie and I went shopping at the Waterfront yesterday. They were there when we stopped for ice cream in Camps Bay, and I spotted one in the studio mirrors when I visited my old dance teacher this morning.

I know they're veilwitches because of how they look at me, like a cat playing with its food. They don't come too close;

they're just there to let me know they're watching.

The man gives me a nasty little smile and I duck down a row, out of his sight. I almost bump into two women talking quietly at a ceramics stall.

'They came for Naledi last night,' a woman mutters to her friend. 'Look at her.'

The panic in her voice is infectious. I follow their gaze to a woman with long dreads standing bolt upright at the organic produce stall. Tiny little needles prick at me as I study Naledi. She has the full, smooth cheeks of a young woman but there are deep lines around her mouth. Around her vacant eyes. She stares ahead, oblivious to the child trying to pay for a bag of plums. Naledi has left the building.

I reach out and touch one of the women on the arm. She turns, frightened.

'The veilwitches did that to her?' I say quietly.

She gives a short nod. 'It's that or join them,' she says.

'Will people join them?' I ask curiously.

'Why are you asking me this?' Her eyes narrow with suspicion. 'If you're Market, you'd know.'

'I'm new.'

She examines me, and then that awful knowing settles in her eyes. 'You're the cursed girl.' She draws back from me.

'Please,' I say. 'What will happen to Naledi? To the others like her?'

The woman relents. 'Depends how desperate they get.' She leans closer, whispers, 'The veilwitches move in hordes, you know. At the top is the Jackal's horde, at the bottom, the poor hordeless souls with the weakest magic or those desperate enough to turn.'

'How do you join a horde?'

She glances around. 'You can be initiated, for a price. You have to do something bad, though. You be careful, you hear? It's not worth it, so don't even think about it.'

The women move on, glancing behind them as they leave.

'Sorry I'm late.' Zenande comes up behind me, a heavy-looking backpack dragging her down. 'Had to talk to my supervisor.'

Her eyes are still wrong, the only sign of the grief she's carrying. A load even heavier than her bag.

Impulsively, I give her a quick hug and to my surprise, she squeezes her arm around my back.

We walk towards the Liesbeek River before she speaks. 'So, you summoned the manifest?'

'I did.' I don't hide my pride. 'Twice.' Then I remember how it snarled at me after Mama Daline died.

'Can you do it again?' We sit on the grass.

'I think so.'

'Then the next step is to break the tether between you.'

'How?'

'Ask it.' Zenande pulls an avocado salad roll from her bag and begins to unwrap it. Then she places it on her lap and stares at the bread. A tear splashes on to her jeans.

'Zenande,' I say tentatively.

'Don't, Angry Girl, please don't.'

We stare at her bread for a minute. Then she looks at me with a watery smile. 'Can I tell you a secret?'

'Of course.'

'Before she died, Mama Daline initiated me as her successor. I am the new Worm. We're keeping it quiet for now, for obvious reasons.'

'She chose well.' I feel my throat tighten.

Zenande senses my distress and her voice is gentle when she speaks. 'It had to be this way, Savannah. Mama Daline knew her time was up, she'd seen it in the stars. Better she died at your hands than have her life drained by those monsters.'

She picks up her roll and takes a small bite. 'Everyone is afraid. Some vendors are keeping away, but most can't afford the loss of income. Without Mama Daline, and Claw and Arrow, we are so much weaker. If veilwitches decide to set up stall in the Market, I don't see how we can stop them.'

'I think it's already happening.' I have to tell her. 'There was a jeweller in Greenmarket Square selling forbidden magic a few weeks ago.' Currently wrapped around my mother's pretty wrists.

'There's always a bit of veiled magic creeping in,' Zenande says, 'but Claw kept a lid on it. We have to. The Market has a far reach, politicians, business leaders, bankers, all source magic from us. Imagine the level of corruption if they used veiled magic.'

'Yeah. Disaster.'

'You've no idea,' Zenande sighs, putting the mostly uneaten roll back in the wrapper. 'They bury the hearts of fertile women beneath new businesses to ensure success. Dead bodies are stolen for money charms. The spelled blood of young virgins is drunk to stave off old age. Young men are held captive to increase a rich man's physical prowess. It's grim, Savannah.'

'Who *is* the Jackal?' I say. 'If we knew who she was, we could find out where she lives. Stop her.'

'Only the Jackal's horde knows. At the Nightmarket, she's only been seen wearing the Jackal disguise. My guess is that she's lying low until she has your magic and is so strong that no one can hurt her.'

'You're certain the Jackal is a woman?'

Zenande shrugs. 'There've only ever been Daughters, but there's no rule about that.' She stands. 'I have to go, I'm dropping something to Claw at the hospital. You can come if you want?'

'I should get back to Harrison.' I jab my thumb in the direction of the market stalls in the distance.

'I'll walk with you.' She checks the time and looks down the river path. The evening is getting on but it's still bright.

'You don't have to. They won't hurt me.' My voice sounds small. 'Not yet.'

She gives a quick nod. Then she hoists her bag on her shoulders. I watch Zenande leave, her tread heavy, and my heart hurts.

As I walk back to the market, I wonder how I ask *my* jackal to untether itself from me.

I stop and shut my eyes.

Creature of the curse, show yourself to me.

238

I repeat the words like a mantra and when I open my eyes, about ten metres away, the animal waits.

'Let me go,' I say to it. 'Please, will you let me go?'

I glance behind me, and see a large, muscular man checking his phone. A woman with her hair in two buns scurries to catch up with him. I turn to the jackal and say quietly, urgently, 'Please.'

The jackal watches me with those knowing eyes. Then it turns and takes a few steps. It looks back at me, and seems almost to be laughing. At me. The jackal lopes along the river path, fading out the further it goes.

I swear under my breath and without warning, my arms are grabbed from behind, a hand clasped over my mouth. I struggle; he is too strong.

'What are you doing?' a woman's voice hisses at my assailant. 'We're supposed to watch, not grab her! The Jackal has claimed that one.'

'Not if I get her first,' he chuckles, hoisting me around his neck like I weigh nothing. His grip is like iron and the ground bounces as we move. I'm screaming but we're alone out here, just grass and reeds and river. 'Think about it, we can take the magic and with it we'll· be stronger than the Jackal. Why let someone else take what could be ours?'

The woman is silent, clearly appreciating the logic.

'The magic isn't full awake yet.'

'So? She called the manifest. I saw with my own eyes. It must be close to ready. We'll lock her in the garage until then.'

He has one meaty arm clamped around my thighs, the

other around my arms. He smells of sweat and onions. He grunts as he jogs on the grass. 'Quick, open the car. She's making a helluva racket.'

Grumbling beside us, the woman says, 'Put her in the boot, OK? And she'd better not vomit.'

We stop at an old boxy white Toyota parked on gravel. The woman unlocks the boot and a bolt of fear rips through me. The angry thing snarls and springs.

The man slides me down, legs first, but before he can toss me inside, I elbow him hard in the stomach. He grabs my arm I am filled with raw hatred. I want him hurt. No; I want to claw off his skin, gouge out his eyes. I want to make him bleed. I scream.

The scream is loud and feral. It's loaded with anger and fear and hate and I hurl it into his face. I feel the storm inside me, and it's rough and turbulent.

He doubles over like he's been punched, clutching a hand to his ear, and I fall on to the gravel. The man cries out in a low, tortured voice. Blood and sweat pour down the side of his face. He looks at me with surprise, his eyes accusing.

I scramble to my feet, backing away. He falls to his knees, cupping his bleeding ear. My heart is wild in my chest. I don't know how I did that. I don't know what I did.

I turn and scarper, but the woman is fast and within seconds she leaps on me. I grab her hair and yank.

'Help me,' she yells to the man. I hear him lumbering over, cursing me with every breath.

He pulls me, locking my arms behind me. I scream at him

240

again, but whatever had powered it earlier is gone. The frequency is scrambled and I can't tune in.

Then I remember the cloudy water at Nietvergeten. The image of me screaming into a man's face. I'd seen this moment in the cloudy water.

'Mind if we join you?' a deep voice says. Ahead of us, blocking the path to the car, is one of the Jackal's four. The tall man with wire-rimmed glasses, Skull.

'Looks like you're planning a party.' Coming up from the river is Madison. 'Or at least, that's what I hope you're doing.' She stalks closer. 'Because if you were thinking of taking Savannah here for yourself, that would be very stupid.'

'You, come back here,' Skull barks. The woman, who'd been slinking away, halts in her tracks. I'm watching the line of tension between Skull and the woman, and I don't see what Madison does to the man. But suddenly, my arm is wet with blood. The man's hold slackens and he slumps against me. With a shriek, I try to move away but he brings us both down, falling on top of me. I wriggle out and roll away from him, seeing his glassy stare. Frightened cries escape me and when I clamp a hand over my mouth to stop them, I see it's red.

A few metres away, the woman has fallen to the grass in a pool of blood.

Wild with terror, I get to my feet, watching Skull and Madison.

'Tell your Jackal –' my voice shakes with fear and rage – 'to call her witches off. No one else follows me.'

'You can't command the Jackal.'

241

'Does the Jackal want a repeat of this?' I gesture to the fallen pair. Madison and Skull stare at me, then without a word, they walk away.

I am trembling violently, suddenly cold. There's nothing around here, only the river and reeds and gravel. In the distance is the parking area and beyond that, the market. I run towards the parking area, stopping before I reach it. My arms and legs are streaked with blood. There are red smudges on my pink terry shorts and my top is drenched. I can't go back to Harrison like this.

That scream, though. I hurt him with my scream. That momentary power, the thrill of it, that was magic. Hella's leaked magic.

It's gone eight, which means that the live jazz band will be playing. Harrison will be busy, but would pack up if I asked. I have other options though.

If you ever need help, Dex had said. The phone rings three times before he answers.

'Dex, I need a lift, please.' He must hear something in my voice because he tells me he'll be with me as soon as he can.

I send Dex the directions and text Harrison saying I'm OK but had a run-in with veilwitches, conveniently omitting the nearly kidnapped and accidentally making magic thing, because I don't want him freaked out.

Even in the twilight, Dex sees the blood as soon as he pulls up. He gets out and strides over to me. His face is set, his eyes glittering with anger and concern. 'Are you hurt?'

'It's not my blood.'

He reaches inside the passenger door and retrieves a cloth lightly marked with grease and a flask of water. 'That's the best I have, I'm afraid.'

I take it gratefully and, wetting the cloth, I clean the blood from my arms and legs.

'You can wear this.' He takes a long-sleeved sweatshirt from the back seat. I pull off my bloodstained top and ball it up.

Blood. Three tormentors. The sound of fire.

The sweatshirt is long enough to be a short dress. Beneath it, my pink bra is stained red with my tormentor's blood, and that will be enough.

I know what I must do to turn the tormentor key.

I need blood from three of my tormentors. This shouldn't take me long at all.

'We need to bin this somewhere.' I sound calm as I hand over the bloodied cloth and clothes, like I'm not disposing of evidence of a crime.

'I'll sort it.'

He starts the car and only once we're on Liesbeek Parkway does he ask, 'What happened?'

'You know I'm cursed, right?' I can't stop moving my hands, fidgeting with the cup holder, twisting my hair. I desperately want Dex to understand.

'I've heard the story of your family curse.'

'It's not just a story. It's real.'

My fingers work a loose thread from the hem. Dex catches my hand. I feel a sensation like a hot liquid pouring over my insides. 'You knew all along. You knew what happened that night at Carniveil was no performance. You knew it was bad magic.'

He doesn't deny it, just exhales. 'I've heard things. Talk me through this evening.'

'Two veilwitches grabbed me,' I say. 'They tried to put me in their car boot.'

'How did you stop them?'

I poured my fury into him through a scream until his ear bled.

'Someone came along. I don't know exactly what happened. I ran.'

He knows there are gaps in the story, things I'm not telling him.

'Is this the first time something like this has happened?'

'No. The break-in.' I take a deep breath. 'They're coming for me.'

He lets out a low whistle. 'Hell, Savannah.'

'What do you know about veilwitches?'

'That they're very dangerous.' He glances at me. 'That it's better to keep away.'

'They need to keep away from me.' I mean to sound vicious but it comes out scared.

'They're after you, huh?' Dex stops at a red light, meeting my gaze. The worry in his eyes makes it so much harder to press that lid down. The one that keeps everything from bubbling over, leaving me a sobbing wreck. 'Let me help you.'

'I don't think you can.' The stone-cold truth of those words. A lump forms in my throat.

'I could try.' The light changes and he shifts the car into gear. 'Tell me what you need and I'll do it.'

Break the curse. Save me. But no one can do that for me.

'Come when I need you. Like tonight.'

'Of course.'

'And it helps to talk.' There's so much more to say, but this is enough for today. I have to think through how much I can say, how much I trust him.

'Could I ask one thing of you?' Dex says. 'It's really important.'

'What's that?'

'Say nothing to Rosie or my mom. Leave them out of this. It's dangerous. I don't want them involved.'

'OK,' I say, thinking about what I have already told Rosie. That she was helping me look for the name. Dex wouldn't be happy about that.

'Savannah,' he says. 'You can trust me, you know that, right?'

'What about you?' I say. 'If it's dangerous, then you should keep your distance too.'

He closes his hand over mine for a moment. 'You need someone on your side.'

Back at the house, we find Rosie watching TV in the den. It's the news. A man stands on the steps of a courtroom, flanked by lawyers. I recognise him as the cabinet minister accused of sexual harassment. A crowd of journalists surges forward, cameras flashing.

'Where have you been?' Rosie glances at Dex. She does a double take when she sees me in the doorway. 'Savannah, I thought you were with Harrison?' She's hurt, I realise. She feels left out.

'I needed a lift so Dex picked me up,' I explain. 'Going to have a shower and call Kim. We could watch something afterwards?'

She brightens. 'Sure.'

'Not this though.' I jerk a thumb at the TV.

I watch the politician's lawyer holding up his hands for quiet. 'All right, let's keep this brief. My client has had an exhausting few weeks.'

Dex is sticking porcupine quills into Rosie's perfectly messy bun. 'Get off,' she says.

He pokes her with a quill. 'Seriously,' she says. 'I'm going to kill you.'

'You can try.'

I look more closely at the screen. Behind the politician and the lawyers, I see someone familiar. Someone I've seen before – not on the news, in real life.

Then it comes to me; he was at the market, wearing a blue baseball hat. He bought a power figure. He'd seemed dodgy.

'As you know,' the lawyer goes on, 'all the women named have withdrawn their accusations. My client will now give a short statement.'

The politician steps forward. He looks kindly, like someone's grandfather. 'I have done nothing wrong,' he says, his voice full of righteous indignation. 'But my good name and reputation have suffered damage. I want to thank my wife and children for standing by me these last few months …'

'Hello?' I realise Rosie is trying to get my attention.

I nod at the TV. 'Looks like he's off the hook.'

She shrugs. 'Another man gets away with it. No surprises there.'

This man is not the only powerful person to use the Market to magic away his problems, in exchange for a wad of cash. The Jackal had scoffed at my outdated ideas of good and evil, but what happens to ordinary people when those in power don't care about right and wrong? When they can do what they want and get away with it?

'Do you want popcorn?' Rosie says. The porcupine quills are sticking up in her glossy hair. She looks at me and frowns. I glance down nervously, wondering if I've still got blood on me.

I realise what she's looking at. I'm wearing Dex's sweatshirt.

'I spilt something on my shirt. Dex had this in the car.'

'What do you want to watch?' Dex says, scrolling through the TV. 'There's a new horror about this kid who gets possessed—'

'No,' Rosie and I say together.

'What about that one?' I say, recognising an art-house film. 'A woman falls in love with a statue—'

'No,' Rosie and Dex shout together.

Rosie grins. 'Something funny. Relaxing. I want a happy ending.' She brightens. 'We could go to a late-night screening? It's noughties month now.'

'Nah, I'm wrecked,' Dex says, and I'm grateful because really, it's me who's wrecked. 'Savannah, have your shower so we can watch *Legally Blonde* for the eighty-seventh time.' Then, surprising me, Dex picks me up, swoops me over his shoulder and runs out.

I can't help laughing as he climbs the stairs before dumping me on my bed. He's grinning as he stands above me.

I throw a pillow at him and say, 'Out.'

Standing beneath the spray of hot water, I think about what I've been told. Hella's magic will kill me, I've been warned. But this evening, screaming into that man's ear, it saved me.

Let the magic inside guide you, Mama Daline had said. I want it to. I want more of that vigour I'd tasted so briefly this evening. It wasn't the first time either; I'd felt it that night at Nietvergeten, when I called spirits in the dark.

Time is ticking too quickly. If I am to beat this curse, I need to figure out how I can draw on Hella's legacy again.

27

GOLD

After the movie ends, Rosie and Dex disappear to FaceTime their friends, and Inez, wearing an embroidered shawl, finds me in the kitchen.

'We haven't had a chance to talk, after the wedding. How are you?'

'OK.' I give her a weak smile. 'You heard about the argument with Kim?'

She looks at me kindly. Everyone heard about the argument with Kim.

'Come,' she says impulsively, stopping to grab candles and matches. 'I know something that will help.'

She leads me through the garden to a corner near the back. She lights three of her candles.

'Now, dig a hole.' She holds her hands a little apart. 'Maybe this big.'

I glance through the trees at the house, at the lights from upstairs.

'With my hands?'

She nods and I sink to the ground and dig my hands into the soft, chunky earth. It smells damp and rich. I burrow deeper, seeing the quick slither of an earthworm. The soil is under my nails.

When I've scooped out a hole bigger than my head, Inez says, 'That will do.'

She hands me her heavy, embroidered shawl.

'Lie flat on the ground on your stomach and cover your head. Whisper your fears about Kim into the hole.'

I do what she says. I don't feel even a tiny bit silly.

'I am afraid that Quinton is not a good person. I am worried he will hurt Kim.' The whispered words sink into the earth.

I pause, then plunge beneath the shallows to the murkier depths.

'I am afraid that Quinton will make her hate me. I'm afraid she already does a little.'

I sit up, pulling the shawl around my shoulders.

'All done?' Inez says. 'Now, bury them.'

Heaping the soil into the hole, I bury my fears about my mother, about Quinton.

'Is this another thing you learned on your travels?' I ask Inez, sitting back on my heels.

'Yes, it is.' She smiles indulgently at me.

'You're interested in witches, right?' I look at her curiously. 'In magic?'

'For much of my life, I've collected herbal remedies, sought out rituals around sickness, birth, death. I've travelled to many different countries.' Inez's features are sharper in the near dark. 'All over the world. And one thing is sure: wherever you go, there are always witches.'

I wonder how to break it to Inez that she need not have travelled so far. That magic was always right here.

'This is to help you manage the fears you have no control over.' Inez holds out her hand and helps me up.

Standing, I see the figure over her shoulder. Dex. His mouth is in a tight line, his body rigid as he looks at the freshly covered earth, the candles. 'What are you doing?'

'It's nothing, Dex,' Inez says. 'Just a charm to help Savannah.'

He glowers at me, then turns on his heel. I start after him, to tell him that this has nothing to do with curses and veil-witches, that I didn't say anything to Inez. Inez stays my arm. 'He doesn't like my little charms. It will blow over.'

But her lips are pressed and she's quiet as we walk back inside.

In the morning, the house is silent and empty. Finding no one around, I check Inez's office, then go back upstairs. I get ready, choosing to wear my short grey tulle skirt, a black tank and red Converse. The same outfit I wore the day Bug-Face suggested my wayward behaviour could get me shot.

Today I am after blood. My tormentors' blood.

After breakfast and talking to Kim, it's a little after eleven. Before I leave, I peer into Rosie's room, where she sleeps.

Quietly, I shut the door and knock at Dex's.

When no one responds, I open it slightly. The bed is untidily made, his bathroom door open. He's not there. I'm about to shut the door again when brown parcel tape on the desk catches my eye. Moving closer, I recognise the slim package we collected from his Aunt René's flat. Dex's inheritance. The top's been snipped, and a silver tip sticks out. I frown, wondering why Dex hasn't bothered to take it from the paper; he doesn't seem to care for his inheritance. I pick it up and slide the object out of the brown paper. It's a knife. The handle is an intricately carved dull silver and the blade sharp and fine. It looks antique. Hearing a sound from the passage, I leave the package as I found it and slip out of the room.

In the kitchen, Rosie's yawning as she scoops a granadilla for her smoothie. 'I'm so not a morning person,' she grumbles when I enter the room.

'What did you see last night?' I laugh. Rosie went on to a late-night screening.

'*A Knight's Tale.*' She waves the small sharp knife at me. 'You should have come, it was so good.' She grabs berries from the fridge and says, 'Working today?'

'Chores.' I roll my eyes. I have the blood of one tormentor upstairs. I should have another back in our house. And today I will get the third.

'I can keep you company?'

'I have to leave soon.' I pull a face. Rosie won't be ready for another hour at least. 'Catch up later?'

'Begone, you strange creature of the morning.' She shoos me

252

away. I smile but it doesn't feel good, lying to Rosie.

In town, I go to the Adderley Street flower market. I look among them for the slight glow, the one that tells me magic is sold there. I move slowly between the flowers until I see it.

'I'm looking for white roses with long stems and sharp thorns.' I describe the roses I'd seen at the Tokai market.

'This better not be for blood magic.' The seller regards me warily.

'It's for lifting a curse.'

Her face softens. *She's heard of me*, I think. The Jackal's prey. She lifts three white roses and wraps the stems. 'The thorns come out when you touch the petals. Careful, they hurt.'

I pay for the roses and then take a minibus taxi back to my old neighbourhood. I make a quick stop at our house, which is packed up, with our things still inside. It's strange to walk among boxes and abandoned rooms, my childhood come to an abrupt end. After the break-in, Quinton made a few calls and rented a house in Claremont, where we'll move on their return.

I go to my room and find the box I'm looking for. Then I lock up again, and wave at Solly's wife, who's sweeping the stoep. I walk in the direction of their family shop.

Burns Road, Bug-Face had said. I pass the shop, the faded lettering saying *A. Soloman and Sons*, the red Coca-Cola sign and a note on the door announcing, *CLOSED FOR LUNCH*. He'll be in the courtyard out back, eating with his brothers.

I walk for ten minutes, until I see the old Toyota Tazz parked outside a small row house. The car has been fixed, but the paintwork doesn't quite match up.

I take a deep breath. I really don't want to go in there. They have a gun. This could go badly wrong. I dial Solly's number because someone needs to know where I am.

'Hey, howzit?'

'I'm in the hood. About to visit Bug-Face. See you later, maybe?' If I make it out in one piece.

'Savannah,' Solly warns as I hang up on him. Taking a deep breath, I walk down the short path and knock at the door, white roses in hand.

Music blares from the house, mixed with sounds of talking and laughing. The door is slightly ajar and I push it open. From the living room I can see a group of people in the small yard, chatting in the sun. I watch from inside the glass doors.

One of the women notices me first. She tugs at Bug-Face's arm, drawing his attention to me. His laugh turns to a scowl. He marches towards me and I step back from the glass doors. We don't need witnesses for this.

'What the fuck are you doing here?'

I hold up the flowers. 'Consider it a peace offering.'

I catch him off guard. He inches towards me and I have to make myself stand still. 'You come in peace, hey?' That oily voice again.

I don't answer. Let him come closer. When he's right in front of me, I slip the roses from the foil wrapping and extend them to him. The look on his face seems both bewildered and a little playful. He takes the roses, closing his hand around the stems. I touch the silky petals.

'Heyyyyyy,' he hisses, dropping the roses. His hand is bleeding and it spills on to the floor. I pick up the bloodiest rose and put it in a ziplock bag which I drop into my tote. Then I turn and leave.

'That's a kak peace offering,' he shouts as I turn away. I smile. It's the perfect peace offering. From him to me.

He's muttering, something about me being a psycho bitch, but I don't look back, just walk out of the house and down the road. Not running, just walking. The blood of my tormentor in my bag.

I've only walked a few metres when a car stops beside me.

'What's going on, Savannah?'

'Solly.' I beam and open the door to get in beside him. 'Got any sweets?'

There's a white souped-up Golf in the Stander drive when Solly drives me back to the house. Solly eyes the car as he parks on the road.

'Thanks, Solly.' I unclip the seat belt.

'You're not going to tell me what you were doing there, are you?'

'I just needed to face him again.'

Solly shakes his head. 'You're up to something and—' His words cut off suddenly. 'Who's that?'

I follow his gaze to the man who's just got out of the Golf and leans against it, cupping his hands to light a cigarette. Jarred. Dex's tough-guy cousin who carries a gun. I open the door and get out.

'What are you doing here?' I say. Inside the car, two men and a young woman laugh at me.

'It's Savannah, isn't it?' Jarred blows smoke from the side of his mouth. 'Who's your friend?' He jerks his head to Solly, who's standing behind me.

'Why are you here?'

'I'm visiting my family.' He smirks at me. 'Come to see my cousin Dex.'

'I don't think a big reunion is on the cards,' I say, looking at the tattoos on his neck and wondering if they're gang symbols.

'Maybe you should think again.' Jarred's eyes are laughing as the gate buzzes open. Dex steps out.

'Dex,' I say, relieved as I walk towards him. 'I've been looking for you.'

Dex holds Jarred's gaze. 'I'm going out.'

'Wait, Dex.' I step closer, touching his arm. He smells of mint and aftershave. 'You're going with him?' I lower my voice. 'I thought you said he's not a good guy.'

'He's family.' Dex won't meet my eyes. 'I want to get to know him.'

'C'mon, Dex, it's party time,' Jarred yells loudly.

'Are you angry about last night? About me and Inez in the garden?'

'I'm late.' He pulls his arm away. One of the guys in the car says, 'Ooh, trouble in paradise' and the others laugh. I hold myself tall, I will not let them see my embarrassment. Dex's eyes soften. 'Later, OK?'

256

'You can sit next to me, Dex.' The woman pats the seat beside her.

From inside the gate, Inez watches. As he moves to the car, she calls, 'Dex.' He gives her a hard look, then gets in. Jarred revs unnecessarily and then they're gone, the engine roaring down the road.

Inez's face is a mask. She stands a moment, then, registering me and Solly, she remembers herself. She paints on a smile and strides over.

It's burned into my memory, though, how lost she seemed for that moment. Her vulnerability as she watched Dex leave with Jarred. If Dex is riding out with his wild cousin to punish Inez, my guess is that it's working.

28

BAD MAN

In my dream, she's waiting for me at the river. She turns slightly, giving me more of her profile. I'm faster tonight, more agile.

I can outrun the beast that chases me. I'm going to reach her this time. I'm sure of it. I pick up speed, pounding down the path. Before the river, I step on something thin and wet. I look down and see a cracked egg, the yolk oozing between my toes. I try to move on, but I can't. It's like the yolk has glued me to the ground.

I can't move. The woman ahead lifts her arm and I want to call to her, but my voice won't work. I am frozen, a statue, and she slowly turns to face me—

I wake up.

There's a weight on my chest. Hot breath in my face.

It's after one in the morning. Putting on the bedside lamp, I reach for the Widow's Words beneath Freda's book. I run a finger over the words until I find egg. Egg = T. M-A-L-A-T. That's what I have so far.

I get out of bed. Like at Nietvergeten, now feels like the right time. Maybe it's because I still feel Hella with me. I lean down to the bottom drawer and pull out the ziplock bag.

The blood of my tormentors.

Now I'm going to listen to the magic inside me to see what comes next.

In the dim downstairs hall, I startle at the reflection of a girl in a white slip nightdress. Me. In the glow of the outside light, I examine the marks on the underside of my jaw. On my chest is a new red cluster, where my would-be kidnapper held me. My shoulder, my wrist, my hand, my jawline, my stomach.

I light candles in the iron candelabra, one of Harrison's, on the coffee table. Then I push open the glass doors to let in fresh air. The night is clear and bright, and a star travels across the sky. Anxiety twists my stomach. The meteor shower has started. The Summer Starfall. I have less than ten days.

I open the woodstove and start a small fire. *Let the magic inside guide you.*

I've no books to follow, no one to tell me what to do. But intuitively, I know this is right.

Watching the fire, I sit cross-legged for many minutes, clearing my mind. Finding Hella's power.

When that inexplicable strength courses through me, I open the bag and take the piece of my bloodied bra that I'd cut out. The stem and thorns with Bug-Face's blood. My good pen wrapped in tissue that I'd collected from my house earlier. I scrape Meyer's blood from the nib on to the bloodstained tissue.

Here, the blood of my tormentors.

I put everything into the stove, watching the flames catch.

Across the room, the jackal has appeared, drawn to the blood, the magic. It watches me expectantly. *Good*, I feel the thought from it. *More*.

Maybe there are words I'm supposed to say, a chant or spell. Shutting my eyes, I search inside. *Good. More.* The beating of my heart. Nothing to clarify what the *more* might be.

Opening my eyes, the jackal has gone.

I raise my leg and the stretch is pleasant, a little painful, but in a good way. My back arches, my arm sweeping back. My silk nightdress, from Auntie Dotty of course, is soft on my thighs.

Here, the blood of my tormentors.

I dance. There is no music but for the storm inside me. The wild wind of my rage, the stormy waters of my sorrow. The lashing anxiety, the fear raining in my heart. My movements are jagged, broken, and they take over where my words aren't enough.

The fire burns and with it the blood of my tormentors.

This feels like a spell. This feels like magic. It must be working. I am turning the tormentor key.

A dark figure at the open glass door watches. I stop dancing, heart hammering.

'Dex.'

He steps into the candlelit room. There's enough light to see the grazes and filth on his face. The split lip and blood on his clothes. He looks at me a long moment, then turns away and walks up the stairs.

I hesitate. The fire has gone out, the blood burned away.

It worked, I think with a burst of joy. I confronted my

tormentors. I burned their blood. I did it.

One key turned, the other two in reach.

My phone vibrates with a message from Kim. At this hour? It's a photo of Quinton in an infinity pool, staring at the camera. His eyes shine with unnatural light. His teeth bared in smile, he looks menacing. Feral. The picture unsettles me.

Something falls upstairs. Grabbing the candelabra, I make my way up.

I knock on Dex's door, hesitate a moment, then turn the handle. In the dark, he sits on the floor against the bed, head in hands.

I go to the bathroom and search for cotton wool and disinfectant. Back in his room, I kneel to clean the cuts on his face. His knuckles are split and bleeding.

'Can I?' I tug at his bloodstained T-shirt. He nods. Pulling it over his head, I see large bruises across his torso. The old burn scar on his shoulder.

'Were you mugged?' I say.

He shakes his head, then seems to notice his filthy jeans. 'I'm going to take a shower.' He grabs clean joggers and disappears into his bathroom.

When he comes out, his hair is wet and the bruises and cuts look like an abstract design.

'Tell me what happened.' I sound sharper than I intended. 'Was it Jarred?'

'Taking it to the grave, Savannah.'

We scowl at each other. 'What do you want?' I say crossly, my buzz from the spell fading.

'To not think.' He exhales.

I turn away, striding to the door, saying, 'I'll be back.'

In my room, I search for the spray I was given at Greenmarket Square. *Though Your Heart Is Breaking*. I close my hand around it, thinking: *I need answers from Dex*.

Back in his room, I get on his bed, legs criss-cross, and pat for him to sit beside me.

'Let's play a game,' I say.

'Another game?' He glances at me, sighs, then sits. 'What do you want to play?'

'I'm going to try to guess a truth about you and every time I get it right, you get a blast of this.' I hold up the bottle. In the mirror, my eyes glint.

'I get to guess too.'

'Fine, but me first. And you have to tell the truth.' I take a breath. 'You want to prove something to Jarred.'

His smile is brief and sad. 'Wrong. My turn.'

'I've nothing to hide.' I hand him the bottle. He thinks for a moment.

'You're angry with Kim, and you hate yourself for it.'

I incline my head and he presses the nozzle. The lift in my mood is quick, uncomfortably so. I find myself grinning.

He hands the bottle back.

'You were in a fight this evening.' It's more than that. 'You hurt someone.'

Dex shuts his eyes and I give him a good puff. He drops his head.

'You really hate Kim's self-help books.'

I nod. The spray wafts over me and a soft giggle escapes.

'You want to hurt Inez and that's why you're running wild with your bad boy cousin.'

He gives a brief nod. This time when I release the spray, he smiles. I'm starting to feel lighter myself. Happy. Silly.

'You feel bad that you let your family down.'

'*You* feel bad that you let your family down.'

This tickles us and we're sniggering like naughty schoolkids at the back of the class. Soon we're both laughing so hard that we've fallen back, lying beside each other on the bed.

I turn to him. 'You worry about Rosie, that she's too eager to please.'

'You've been having bad dreams since the burglary. Wait, since before.'

The darkness inside tugs at me. I'm still laughing, though. A frenzied kind of laugh. Hollow.

'You liked it when I kissed you at Nietvergeten.' I want to know.

'It meant more than you let on.' He wants to know.

We look at each other for a long moment.

Then we're laughing again. We can't help it. Tears run down my face. It hurts.

The empty bottle is discarded on the bed. We might have overdone it. The room is covered in a light mist. It smells of overripe apples, sweet, fresh and a little sickly.

I sit up, and turn to Dex, holding my hands like they're claws, like an animal. Dex doubles over, howling.

'Make it stop,' he gasps. I put my hand to his mouth to hold in the laughter, but this only makes him laugh harder.

I'm looking at his lips. We both know what we're going to do. And because we're basically goefed, it makes complete sense.

When he kisses me, the laughter doesn't go away immediately. But it's confined to an occasional shoulder shake or shudder, which might not be the potion at all. He kisses me until the urge to laugh fizzles out.

'Let's play a game,' I whisper.

'I'm enjoying this one.' His hand touches my face.

'Hide-and-seek. Outside.' Like we used to.

'What does the winner get?' Interest sparks in his eyes.

'What the winner wants.'

'Counting to ten. You better run.'

I'm off the bed, running quietly down the stairs as he starts counting. I'm falling out of the glass doors and into the moonlit garden, with laughter spilling out of me. It's after two in the morning, and something not unlike magic stirs as I run through the lush garden, between the sleeping flowers and shrubs.

I hide behind an old thick tree, watching Dex step outside. He ambles down the steps, torchlight searching the trees and bushes.

I slip away from the tree, wild exuberance chasing through my body as I run barefoot towards the blue light of the pool.

Looking around, I try the handle of the pool house. It opens and I go inside. The room is large and mostly empty. The floor is polished cement. There's a bed on one side, an armchair near to where I'm standing.

Flat against the wall, I peer out of the window, watching Dex move down the path. Once he passes, I'll sneak out, return to his room, call him to announce my victory, and have him serve my every whim for a week. There'll be no time for Cousin Jarred.

But Dex leaves the path, moving with purpose to the pool house. How, in this enormous garden, does he know to come here? I duck behind the armchair as the door opens. His footsteps move closer.

'I know you're in here, Savannah.'

I watch his shadow grow on the far wall and I dash out of my hiding place. I chuck an armchair cushion at him – *Take that, Dex Stander* – then sprint. I've reached the door when he lifts me off the ground, takes three huge strides and drops me on the bed. He turns on the lamp.

I leap off the other side of the bed and dash for the door. He's blocking my path, watching to see which way I'll go. I feint left and bolt right but he catches me again, this time pushing me against the wall, knocking the hanging picture askew.

'I won.' Smug bastard.

'You cheated,' I say. 'You couldn't possibly have known I was in here.'

'The white dress was a bad call.' He laughs. 'You were practically glowing in the dark.'

'Nightdress.'

Dex brushes his knuckles down my shoulder. The strap falls with his hand. 'I like it.'

'Gift from Auntie Dotty.'

'Can we not –' his hand runs down my ribcage, pausing at my hip – 'talk about your aunts right now?' His hand moves down to my thigh, his eyes searching mine. They're shining, like he too is high with euphoria.

When he kisses me, it's different to before. It's rawer. Truer. I tighten my arms around him, drawing him closer.

'Savannah.' He breaks away, his voice low. 'I don't want to play any more.'

'What do you want?' That tight squeezing inside me.

'No more games.' His hand covers my thigh, inching up. The twisting inside intensifies.

He lifts me again and we fall back on the bed, bodies entangled. Fingers edging beneath elastic. The heat of his hand through silk. The feel of him against me.

I touch a familiar shape in his back pocket and pull out a foil square.

'Presumptuous.'

'Nah, just hopeful.' He smooths back my hair. 'Forget it's there.'

'Maybe I'd rather we used it?' I trace my fingers over his burn scar. There's a long fresh cut on his chest and I touch it, again wondering what happened this evening.

'In that case –' he gives me a heated smile – 'less talk, more action.'

His mouth on my skin, I forget about parties and wild boys, about fights, witches, anger, curses. I think about this infuriating, secretive boy instead.

Maybe we're all a little cursed, I think.

Then I stop thinking.

29

BIG FISH

I'm in the kitchen, drinking hot chocolate with Rosie, when Dex comes in wearing his running clothes. Heat blooms in my chest as I think of how we'd woken up at five, the sun streaking across the bed, and snuck back into the house. It's just after eleven now.

'You only up now?' Rosie raises an eyebrow. 'What's this about you and Jarred hanging out?' Then she sees his face, the grazed temple and busted lip. 'Dex, what happened?'

'It's nothing, Rosie.' His tone is light, gentle. 'Don't fuss.'

But Rosie is troubled. Dex comes towards me, a small smile playing on his lips. I am hyperaware of him as he walks to the sink.

'What are you doing today?' Her eyes track him.

'Going for a long run. Seeing some friends later.' He runs the tap to fill his water bottle.

'What friends?'

'Rosie,' he warns.

'Are you working today, Savannah?' Rosie shifts her attention to me.

'No. Harrison's taking a few days off. Hanging with his pals, catching some waves.' The tension at the Market is getting to him.

'Do you want to grab lunch later?' Rosie says. 'Inez is at her beauty clinic and I'm meeting her there. Join us later at the Silo? We can check out the art museum.'

'Perfect.' I stand up, pushing out my chair and glugging the last of my hot chocolate as Dex leaves for his run.

Rosie drops me off in Rondebosch and I walk up the hill to the university, where I'm meeting Zenande. She's on the Sarah Baartman steps, bent over a book, and I sit beside her.

'We lost more witches this week. They're turning to veiled magic.' Zenande sips from her travel cup. 'Can't blame them really.' Her eyes have smudges beneath them. 'But there is some good news.' She gives me a look that's half a smile, half a frown. 'It's a steep learning curve, becoming the Worm, but I'm getting stronger.'

Our eyes meet. Hers are filled with grief and it pulls at the awful tangle of guilt and sorrow I carry since the day in the tunnel.

'I think about her all the time,' I confess. I don't need to say Mama Daline's name, Zenande knows. 'It's like I carry her inside me. In my heart.'

She squeezes my hand and we look out over the rugby fields, the sprawl of suburbs beyond. Eventually, I break the silence. 'I summoned the manifest again but it's still tethered.'

'You'd think the creature would be fed up of you by now.'

There's a hint of amusement in her eyes and I'm relieved to see it. 'If it were me ...' She gives me a shoulder bump and laughs.

'And ...' I draw out the word and add a dramatic pause. 'I've sorted the tormentor key.'

Zenande nearly chokes on her coffee. 'What?'

I tell her about burning the blood, the dance and the jackal.

'Did anything unusual happen?'

I crinkle my face. 'My mom sent me a picture of my stepdad?' Ugh, I can't get used to that.

'No, I mean, was there lightning or a wild wind or something?'

'It felt like there was a storm inside me, Zenande. I could feel the power surging through me. That was magic last night, I know it.'

'Hmmm. Good. Now let's step up the others. The Summer Starfall started a few days ago. It will peak next week.'

Next week. Still, Zenande's caution doesn't faze me. Today, hope surges through me, from deep in my bones: I will live.

My mood must be infectious because she grabs my hand and says, 'We're going to do this, Savannah. We're going to save the Market.'

I have five letters of the name. I've burned the blood of three tormentors. The creature comes when it's called. Zenande tells me that Claw has taken a turn for the better; all going well, she will leave the hospital in a few weeks.

'Wear this.' Zenande closes something cool in my hand. I look down and see a hand-painted bead bracelet.

'It's beautiful.'

'I made it. It's magic. Wear it all the time, it will help me find you.'

If I find myself lost or snatched.

As I walk down to the Main Road, I think about Dex. Maybe it's time to tell him the whole story. He gave me space, didn't push for answers when I wasn't ready to share.

Maybe I'm ready now. He was right, I do need someone on my side.

I'm near the Main Road when Rosie calls. 'Can we push lunch out an hour or two? Mom's running late and they've talked me into getting a massage and the woman with the amazing hands is busy right now so ...'

'Rosie, don't rush. We can visit the museum tomorrow.'

Relieved, Rosie rings off. Outside Pick n Pay, I hold out my hand for a minibus taxi. Dex said he's meeting Jarred later, and I want to catch him before he goes. I will tell him everything that's been happening these last weeks. He wanted the games to end. It's time to give him the truth.

There's a van with dark-tinted windows parked on the street outside the Stander house. The writing on the side says *JANSEN SECURITY GATES*. Neither of the Stander cars are in the drive.

I let myself into the house.

Something's wrong.

I know this feeling. I had it the day of the burglary. This time, I'm not going to be taken by surprise. I hold my phone, finger hovering over the keypad, ready to call for help if necessary.

The alarm's not on. And yet there doesn't seem to be anyone

home. I take a small sharp knife from the kitchen, then check all the rooms downstairs before going up. There's no one in my room. I knock at Dex's room and push the door open. Empty. His joggers from last night are on the bed, and I can't look at them without feeling heat.

I peer inside Rosie's room. The delicate scent of her green tree body lotion lingers. There is a jumble of lip gloss, necklaces and hair slides in a little clay pot on the window sill.

I stand at the open door to Inez's room. Thick books on architecture, travel and design and precisely folded bedcovers. I think of her herb candles, her worn scrap of paper with the Widow's Words. So incongruous in this elegant house.

Everything is fine.

Leaving Inez's room, I stand on the landing overlooking the garden. This carefully curated wilderness. The mountain looming over us, majestic, always watching.

Down the far end of the garden is the pool house partly hidden behind trees and shrubs. From the landing, from this angle, I can see that the door is wide open.

There's someone in there.

Maybe it's Dex. Rosie might have told him I was heading back to the house. Butterflies flutter in my stomach as I walk outside.

The birds sing. Leaves rustle in the breeze. There's a skip in my step as I pass the table and chairs where we shared his whisky that first night. Oh, the things we will discover on a summer's afternoon beside the pool. Past the three oaks, past the sparkling blue water, to the pool house.

The noise alerts me first.

There's a low hum, the sound of a man's voice chanting. It doesn't sound like Dex. Pressing myself flat against the wall, I peer through the partially open white wooden blind.

I can't see everyone, but I know there are several people in the room. In the centre stands a young man, his face marked with a white V on his forehead. There are three red lines across his cheek and large swirling marks on his chest.

Horde marks.

Dex.

He raises the dull silver knife with its decorative handle, his grandmother's knife, to his waist. His face is impassive as he slices the knife through the skin near his rib. Blood spills, and he catches it in a bronze cup. Three large symbols are drawn on the polished cement and he bends to smudge each one with his blood. At the centre is a bowl with liquid in it and he drops the cup in there. Then he stands and looks ahead. The picture we knocked last night still hangs askew.

The chanting and drums stop, and a man with salt-and-pepper hair speaks.

'Complete the summoning, Dex.'

Dex's body trembles slightly with strain.

'Dex, be careful, you're calling something very powerful.' The man speaks urgently but Dex ignores him. He's standing tall, no longer strained, facing something on the other side of the room. 'Stay in control.'

'I'm not afraid.' His eyes gleam.

I back away from the pool house. Bile rises in my throat.

Dex is a veilwitch.

272

30

BITE

My rage wants out. I walk out of the gate, knife still in hand, not knowing where I'm going. I walk down the street, then down another. *You need someone on your side*, he'd said. The filthy liar.

When I look up, I see them. Three of them, standing at the far end of the road, tall and menacing. Skull's panama hat is adorned with small bones, Madison's in a long patchwork leather skirt and an animal-skull headpiece and Salomé wears an ostrich feather jacket and platform heels. I look around at the high walls, the houses hidden in large lush gardens with old trees. No one can see us. I am alone.

I turn and leg it down the leafy suburban road.

I'm putting a good distance between us. But then, suddenly, they're in front of me again. Still in the distance, but closer than before.

'We're coming for you, Savannah,' Madison sings.

They have black and red markings on their faces and hands.

The different hordes must have different patterns.

I veer down a side road, only to see them ahead of me again.

'We're always closer than you think.'

Playing with me, like a cat with a mouse.

'We're there when you least expect it. When you think you're safe.'

Like Dex, who sleeps in the room beside me. *You can trust me, you know that, right?* My hand tightens on the knife.

'It's nearly time, Savannah.'

I hear wild screaming and realise it's me. I'm running at them, knife raised.

I don't see the SUV until I'm nearly on top of it. The car screeches to a halt, inches from hitting me. The driver, a mom with a headband, shouts furious curse words at me. Three wide-eyed children watch from the back seat.

I stand, my breath coming in gasps. My legs are shaking. The woman finishes her angry tirade and drives off.

The veilwitches are gone.

I walk until my legs stop shaking. I reach the park and leave the road, wandering between the trees. A group of young teens laugh in the sun, older women in tracksuits walk with purpose. I sit beneath a tree and think.

Dex lied to me from the start. It was no accident he was at Carniveil that night; he was there working for the Jackal. Then he pretended to help me. Gained my trust. Why?

So I could tell him the name. That's all he wanted from me. The magic.

I am in deep, deep trouble.

I close my eyes.

Let the magic inside guide you.

I hold on to the anger I feel for Dex. How badly he's hurt me. How I want nothing more than to lash out at him. I let the anger course through my body. Flowing through me like hot lava.

I claim this magic. The words come from inside me, from somewhere beyond thought and logic. *I claim this magic. It is mine. I will wield this magic to defeat evil.* I repeat the words in my head.

I am running out of time.

I open my eyes, and there, a few metres away, is the jackal. Its yellow eyes regard me with contempt.

I stand up, watching it carefully. 'Untether me at once.'

The creature yawns. My anger curdles.

'You are mine to command.' I raise my voice. 'You will listen to me.'

It watches, unaffected.

'I am your master.' I'm screaming now. 'Do as I say. Let me go. Now.'

The animal gives me no warning before it attacks. I raise my arms to shield my face. It closes sharp teeth on my forearm and I cry out in pain.

'What's going on?' a man calls out in Afrikaans.

I look at my arm. There are deep puncture wounds. The skin has been torn away and I'm dripping blood on to the grass. The jackal is nowhere to be seen.

Nothing. I've achieved nothing. I want to scream up at the sky.

The man runs over, followed by a child walking two large huskies. He examines my arm and shakes his head. 'You have to get this looked at. My wife's a doctor, her surgery is down here.'

'Is that really necessary?'

He glances again at the wound. 'It's necessary. Come.'

When I get back to the house in the evening, the van is gone. The pool house is empty, with only a small feather and an almost invisible trace of blood on the polished cement floor.

I sit at the kitchen table, my mind turning over what happened in the park. Thinking through my options. My head throbs.

I can't stay here.

Inez and Rosie come in, with sushi and shopping bags. Rosie sees the bandage around my arm and her mouth falls open.

'Savannah. What happened?'

'Dog bite.'

She examines my arm and says, almost with admiration, 'You have the worst luck.'

Inez reaches for her keys. 'I'll drive you to the hospital.'

'There was a doctor nearby. She treated it. All fine. Just have a headache.'

'You don't look OK.' Inez frowns.

'Where's Dex?' I ask.

'Out with Jarred again.' Rosie's disapproval is evident. Inez clearly isn't happy either.

'It's so unlike him,' she says. 'I wish he'd talk to me.'

'Inez.' I keep my voice calm. 'I've been thinking. Kim's back soon and I'd like to spend these last two days with Minnie.'

Your son is a veilwitch and I'm too afraid to stay here.

Inez looks at me with such sympathy and I realise she knows, not the details, but that lines have been crossed. She presses the back of her hand to my forehead. 'I promised Kim I'd look after you so I'd rather you stayed here, but obviously it's your choice. You're a little hot, and you need to rest. Take tonight to think on it, and we can decide in the morning.'

After we eat, I excuse myself and go upstairs. Sitting on the bed, I'm troubled. I haven't untethered the creature, I still don't have the full name. The hope I'd felt earlier has completely disintegrated.

Through the window, the stars are a cruel reminder of how little time I have left.

A few minutes later, Rosie's at the door juggling tea and a large shopping bag.

'Rooibos and honey.' Rosie puts down the tea. 'Mom's fix for everything.' She sits on the rug, placing the bag on the floor. Patting the spot beside her, she takes out a bag of jellies and opens it. 'These are for you. So you can focus.'

Lured by the sweets, I slide off the bed and slump beside her.

'We're going to do this, Savannah.' Her face is determined. 'When I put my mind to something, I always get it right.'

Overcome by a swell of affection, I sit up straight. 'I bet you do.'

'Here.' Rosie pulls a binder from her bag. We can file your dreams according to theme and colour-coded recurring images with corresponding letters and numbers from the Widow's Words.'

I'd love to live inside Rosie's head. What a clear, organised place her mind must be. A high-rise office block with lots of glass and chrome and lifts that work. Mine is an old, badly kept Gothic mansion with secret rooms and things that bite.

'This is ... organised.'

'I know.' She pushes her hair from her eyes. 'I'm sorry. I'm that kid.'

'Don't apologise.' I whisper-shout the words.

'You're right. I apologise too much. Sorry.' She claps her hand over her mouth and we both laugh.

She reaches for a pen and turns to a fresh page. 'Have you had any more dreams?'

I hesitate. Freda's notebook is on the nightstand. I *have* dreamed of more letters since we last spoke. I trust Rosie, but Dex is her twin. *Rosie tells him everything*, Inez had said.

'Nothing new.' My cheeks burn with the lie.

'Oh.' Rosie deflates, then brightens. 'Let's go through the notebook again.' She retrieves it, then settles in beside me, picking through the jellies and passing me the red ones. We turn the pages. There are indecipherable scribbles, appointment times, the name of my childhood dentist. 'No offence to your aunt,' Rosie says, 'but if I was cursed and making notes that could save my life, I'd be a lot clearer.'

'I don't think Freda realised she'd die so soon.' I flick past a recipe for akhni, then pause at the badly drawn strelitzia: *Slept so well last night. Dreamed I was on a bed of strelitzias.*

Rosie groans, 'Hate to say, but your aunt was no artist.' She turns to me, giving me big eyes. 'OK, I'm going to suggest something I don't think you'll like. Remember that idea I had at Nietvergeten?' She reaches into the bag again and pulls out a wooden board and planchette. She places it on the bed between us, looking at me anxiously. 'Don't be mad.'

A Ouija board.

I don't want to do this. I really don't. But the stars are falling this very night. Everyone, Market and Nightmarket witches, has told me my days are numbered.

I give the slightest nod.

'Yes!' says Rosie. 'It's worth a shot, right?'

I don't reply. Rosie gets up from the bed, closing the curtains. Consulting instructions on her phone, she lights candles and arranges them in a circle around us. Taking a mirror from the bag, she places it at the centre of the candles.

Rosie sits on the floor and pats the spot beside her. I sit so that our knees are touching, then she takes a pin, pricking her finger. She drops the blood on the mirror.

'I read about this online. It's supposed to make it stronger.'

I let her prick my finger and a small bubble of blood appears. Holding my finger, she drops it on hers, then smears the blood on the mirror, which she places opposite us.

We put our hands together on the planchette. Rosie's eyes

are wide and serious. Shutting mine, I say, 'I'm Savannah and this is Rosie. We respectfully call upon the spirit world to guide us to an answer.'

'Is there anyone there?'

We wait. I shift, getting pins and needles in my leg. Beside me, I can feel how hard Rosie's concentrating.

There's nothing. Relieved, I open my eyes.

The curtain lifts slightly, as if from a breeze. The window is closed. The room feels different. Heavier.

Then the planchette moves, startling me. My fingers are a reluctant passenger as it swishes across the board to YES. Beside me, Rosie gasps.

'Can you help me break the curse?' I say.

It moves immediately, definitively, to YES. The planchette glides faster now, swinging from R to E and then L-E-A-S-E. It pauses and then continues at speed. T-H-E M-A-N-I-F-E-S-T.

Release the manifest. 'How?' I say, frustrated. I know I have to untether the creature.

'Ask about the name,' Rosie nudges. 'Quick, before it goes.'

'How can I find Hella's true name?'

The planchette takes our lightly pressed fingers to N-O-T. And that's when I realise he's there, watching. Dex. He's pushed the door ajar, taking in the scene: the candles, the Ouija board, the blood-streaked mirror. His eyes are hard and cold.

E-B-O, the planchette says.

Dex makes the smallest gesture with his hand and I see his mouth move. The planchette falls off the board, like whatever was guiding it has let it go. Something unseen, a disturbance in the air, moves across the room. The heavy presence lifts.

N-O-T-E-B-O – I glance at the notebook just outside the circle of candles. It's open to the drawing of a strelitzia. Freda had coloured only the orange petals, leaving the stem and leaves blank.

Orange flower, I realise. That's on the Widow's Words, I'm sure of it. I try to remember which letter corresponds to orange flower.

'Notebook,' Rosie says excitedly. Dex is in the corner, his mouth moving, but I can't hear what he's saying. He's livid as he looks at me.

Then I know with that uncanny certainty: orange flower is *I*. I'm sure of it. Before I can reach for the list of Widow's Words to confirm, there's this wild twisting inside. In my head, I add the *I* to the letters I already have. To form the word I need.

Malati.

The wringing feeling intensifies. The turning of an ancient, rusty lock.

'Oh no!' Rosie cries. But she seems so far from me.

I'm cheek to floor and as the skin on my back burns, so does the fury in my chest. Through the window, the stars shine with a fierceness I've never before seen. They shine for me. The light grows, spilling into the room. And inside me, a spark ignites. I feel it inside me, the steady beat of a drum. Across the room, her skirt begins to burn.

That spark inside. Violently, it chases through my body and the ground beneath me trembles.

'It's burning.' Rosie's alarmed voice brings me back to where

I'm sitting beside her in the shaking room. 'Is that an earthquake?'

Tapered candlelight dances on black wicks, the flames licking and hungry. Behind the candles, Freda's notebook burns with magnificent intensity.

'No,' I cry, jumping to my feet, emptying the tea on the fire just as Dex throws a heavy blanket over it. The fire goes out. The ground stops moving.

'What the fuck are you doing?' Dex's face is tight with anger. 'Leave my sister out of your mess, Savannah.'

I glower at him. I don't know where I'll start when I tear him apart, limb by limb.

He slams the door and we listen to his footsteps all the way down the stairs. Inez calls out, asking if we're all OK.

Rosie and I look at each other. Her face is red and pinched. She's frightened, I realise. Dex is right. I should never have involved Rosie. She has no idea of the danger. It was stupid and risky and I should have known better.

'It's not like Dex to lose his temper like that.' She looks at the door, like she wants to follow. 'Do you think he's been acting strangely?'

Using forbidden magic can change a person. 'I don't know,' I say cautiously. 'I don't know him as well as you.'

She sighs. 'He's been ... off, lately. He's hiding something from me, and I hate it. We tell each other *everything*. I should probably check on him.'

'Go on, I'll clear this mess.'

At the door, she pauses. 'You felt them, didn't you? The

282

tremors?' I nod. 'The candles weren't even near the book. What happened?'

'Weird, right?'

Rosie looks like she wants to say more, but she leaves. I put the remains of Freda's book into a cardboard box. The floor is scorched, the pages charred beyond repair. Freda's notes, her handwriting, her stories, are gone.

And in its place, I have Hella's true name.

Malati.

Two keys. I have now turned two keys.

I'm running. Ahead is the shallow river, and beyond the woman with long black hair.

In the early dawn light, I recognise the woody stems and flowers, the slope of the mountain at Nietvergeten. The river is filled with strelitzias, the orange flame like petals bobbing in the water. I cross the path of stones, and the woman turns slowly. She's standing in a circle of strelitzias.

'You learned my name,' the woman says. 'I knew you would.'

Malati. I want to take her hand, feel her smile warm my face. I want to ask her questions, to know her story.

Walking between the flowers, she comes closer, and closer still. She leans to me and whispers in my ear, 'I've watched you, from your earliest days. I stood with you when you felt angry.'

I feel a hum through my body. Something like power. She's watching me, a knowing look in her eyes.

'But I don't want to be angry,' I say.

She touches a hand to my cheek. 'Child, you are so much

more than your anger. It is a tool, sometimes necessary. Your anger does not define you.'

Urgency pumps through my body. The beast still chases. I need help.

'How,' I say, 'do I end this?'

She leans in again and whispers but her words become wind and swirl. I try to catch them, frantically gathering the words that are scattering around me.

I grasp only three: *at the Nightmarket.*

I wake too soon.

I wake up thinking about Mama Daline. About my hand holding the knife as it cuts her skin. I cover my face with my hands and take three deep breaths. Then it hits me with a savage freshness: Dex is a veilwitch. He'd knocked on my door in the small hours of the morning. Tried the handle, but I'd locked it.

'How are you this morning?' Inez says when I enter the kitchen. She's in her yoga clothes, looking relaxed and healthy as she drinks rooibos.

'Better.' I take a grape and pop it into my mouth. 'Where's Dex?'

'Went for a run.' Rosie reaches for a rusk. 'He was out late, I'm not sure he even went to bed last night.'

The sweetness of the grape is at odds with the bitterness inside.

'Shall we go to the museum this morning, Savannah?' Rosie says. She stirs sugar into her coffee.

'I have to visit Minnie.' I can't be here. I can't be here with him.

'You'll come back, won't you?' She looks so sad.

'I haven't packed up my things.' I avoid the question. I don't tell her about the rolled-up change of clothes, my toothbrush tucked into my bag. But I'm afraid. I'm out of time. I want to be with Minnie. And I need to persuade Harrison to return to work, so I can find a way to the Nightmarket.

I meet Dex in the driveway, clearly just back from his run.

'Hey.' He stops close to me. Closer than necessary. 'You going out?'

'Yeah, can't talk now.'

'I'm sorry I blew up like that last night,' he says.

'You were right,' I say. 'We shouldn't have messed with the board.'

'You're upset.'

'You know me,' I say. 'Always angry.'

'But now you're angry with *me*.'

'Not now, Dex.' I start walking.

'Savannah.' His voice is soothing and I hate it. I've heard that tone all my life, *easy now, calm down, steady girl*. 'We need to talk about your curse.'

And there it is. The interest in my curse. 'Just stop!' I explode. My voice is too loud, too ugly in this quiet neighbourhood. A woman walking by gives me a dirty look.

'Dex, Savannah.' Inez stands at the front door. 'What's going on?'

I stare at Dex angrily.

'Conversation over,' I say. 'I'm out.'

I march out of the gate and down the leafy streets, fuming at the huge houses, the fancy cars. I glare at people in their monstrously sized vehicles who don't stop at the zebra crossing.

This is the thing about persistent anger. Ordinary civility becomes harder and harder. I'm impatient. Rude. I want to snap at the couple who walk slowly on the pavement in front of me, the boy who drops a chocolate wrapper on the ground. I want to swear at the man talking loudly and importantly on his phone. I want to stand in the middle of the road and scream, 'What's your fucking problem?'

I do elbow the guy who sidles up too closely in the minibus taxi. He turns, bristling, and I give him a look: *What you going to do about it?* He looks away.

When I get to Minnie's, she's in her cleaning tracksuit.

'Savannah,' she says when she sees me. Looks closely at my face. Then she pushes back her short grey hair and says, 'I need someone to get on a chair and clean inside the top cupboards. You know my knees.' I'm grateful for what she doesn't say.

'Can I stay here tonight, Ma Minnie?'

'Of course, kind. You sleep in Harrison's room, he'll take the couch.'

In the kitchen, we take everything out of the cupboards and wipe down the insides. Harrison comes home, wind in his hair, sand crusted at the nape of his neck after spending the morning surfing. He heats a salomie, the smell of hot curry and buttery roti filling the kitchen.

'You could help, you know.' I swat him with the cloth as he bites through flaky roti.

'Let the boy eat,' Minnie chides me, and Harrison gives me an angelic beam.

No wonder he's in no rush to move into his own place. The boy is treated like a king.

When Minnie's not looking, I make cutting throat signs at Harrison, who stands up, stretches lazily, then picks up a cloth.

'We need to get back to working the markets,' I say when Minnie leaves the kitchen.

'I thought we'd take time out.' Harrison wipes a clean surface vigorously. 'Just for a week or two.' He rubs at an invisible stain, refusing to meet my eye.

'I need to go back.' I close my hand over his. I need to find a way to the Nightmarket. 'As soon as possible.'

'OK.' He sighs. 'I've been thinking about Freda.' He leans against the table. 'About her stories of the star witches.'

'You *do* remember them.'

'I've been trying.' He presses a hand to the back of his head. 'She always said they were good witches except when they needed to be bad. I think I understand what she meant. Sometimes we need to be bad in order to do good.'

I stare down at the cloth in my hands. 'What do you mean?'

'That you shouldn't judge yourself too harshly for your most desperate acts. I know I wouldn't.'

Minnie comes back and tells us to work smarter, that I missed a spot, and slowly the knot of sorrow and anger begins to dissolve.

When Harrison disappears to take a call, Minnie suggests we stop for a tea break. As the kettle boils, she looks at me with those keen eyes. 'It was terrible what happened to that boy. Dex.'

Dex. I glance up at her. Minnie knows I've scuttled here because of Dex. 'What happened to him?'

'It was when he was eight or nine. Just before they fled the city.'

'Fled?'

'He'd been badly scalded. Boiling liquid all over his poor little body. Inez told everyone that a kettle fell on him when her mother and sister were minding him, but that wasn't what really happened.'

'What happened?'

'I overheard Inez and Freda talk just before they left. I've never breathed a word, because it's not my secret to tell, but I think you should know.'

'I won't say anything.'

'Inez told Freda that her mother was a witch.'

'A witch?' I practically shriek the word.

'René too, but her mother was very powerful. They used dark magic, calling demons with blood and bones. Inez said she wanted none of that and they all rumbled along fine for a while. Until they realised that Dex had the gift, though not much of a gift if you ask me.' Minnie shakes her head. 'Inez's mother and sister wanted to teach him magic and Inez refused. They did it anyway, on the sly. They made him one of theirs.'

'Without Inez knowing?'

'She said she didn't have a clue what they'd been doing until a spell went wrong. Hot liquid, hotter than boiling, spewed out of their cauldron, or whatever pot they used, and landed on his body. Inez knew the only way to keep those children safe was to get them as far away from her family as she could. So she ran.'

'Only coming back when her mother died.' It explains why she never returned for a visit in ten years.

Minnie nods. 'What happened to that child.' She tuts. 'That boy will have scars, Savannah.'

She doesn't mean the physical. And that's why Minnie, who always sees, is telling me this.

'Come, pass me that dish here,' she says as Harrison comes back to the kitchen.

Minnie feeds us malva pudding and ice cream, and tells us to scrub the front stoep. As I scrub, I think of Dex learning dark magic as a child, his body scalded by a spell. I think about how unhappy he was to return here. I think about the stars that will fall tonight. If ever there was a time for desperate acts, it's now.

I wonder just how bad I'll need to be.

31

CAGE

There's a coil of dread and agitation in my stomach as I stand on the Stander stoep the next day. I don't want to see Dex. My clock is running down.

'Hello,' I call. The door is wide open. The klezmer music that Inez loves is upbeat and joyful, and light streams through the house.

I'd called Inez yesterday evening saying I'd stay the night with Minnie and she asked if we could chat when I returned. I haven't told her that I'm here only to collect my things.

I walk through the hall, crossing my fingers that Dex is out. No such luck; he's in the kitchen. Barefoot, he's clearly just out of the pool. A trickle of water runs down his back.

'Hey.' He glances at me, water jug in hand. 'You're back.'

'Where is everyone?' I'm hella awkward. Exactly how do you behave with the guy you've hooked up with, who also wants to kill you?

He puts the jug back in the fridge. 'Rosie's taking a shower. My mom is catching up with work.'

'Right. Thanks.'

'Savannah.' Dex steps towards me. I step back. The kitchen island digs into my back.

'What's wrong?' He moves closer. His hands touch my bare arms. His fingers are cold, but that's not why I shiver. I'm too aware of his chest, his face near mine. 'Why won't you talk to me?'

I want to talk to him. I want to scream at him. *I trusted you, Dex.* But it's all been lies and deceit and pretending to be on my side. I press my lips together so that my rage stays contained. Better he doesn't know that I know. Why give him a chance to adapt his plan?

'Savannah?' He places a hand on my hip, tugging me towards him. 'Can we go somewhere and talk?'

Minnie's words nudge at me: *That boy will have scars.* But I won't let Dex's scars be my weakness.

'Like the pool house?' *You want my trust*, I think, *so you can use it as a weapon against me.* He nods.

I leave it a moment. Savour the nearness of him. One second, then another. Last one.

'Stay away from me,' I whisper. And then I walk away.

I find Inez in her office. She's in charcoal silk, looking over the photographs from Nietvergeten while on a call. She smiles and signals for me to wait. I perch on one of the mid-century chairs in front of her desk.

'That's right, a double-page spread,' she says. 'Thanks. Yes. Send it over when it's done.' She rings off and removes her glasses. 'Savannah, glad you're back. How's Minnie?'

'She's good. You wanted to talk?'

She keeps her eyes on mine, like she's choosing her words carefully. Fishing. 'You seemed really upset yesterday.'

I really don't want to talk to Dex's mother about Dex, so I say in a light, easy tone, 'It's tough being cursed.'

'That's why I wanted to talk. Rosie told me that you're worried? That you think time is running out?'

I straighten, wishing Rosie had kept that to herself.

'Oh, darling, she was really careful in what she told me, but we both just want to help you. And you know I've picked up a few things from my travels. What I have in mind is a simple protection ritual, much like what we did in the garden with the shawl, except this will form a shield around you. I learned it from a woman in this village near the east coast of ...'

In the mirror behind her, I see Dex's reflection as he stands just outside the doorway. I want to make him hurt. He doesn't like Inez doing her kitchen witchery? Too bad. So I say, 'Thanks, Inez, that sounds like a good idea.' I feel vicious. 'Can Rosie come too?'

'You'll do it?' Inez smiles.

What's the harm? This afternoon, I will meet Zenande to untether the manifest, the last key. I told her on the phone last night about the Ouija board, and that I'd discovered the true name. Early this morning, she'd texted saying she'd figured out how to untether the manifest. She'd used a string of emojis, distinctly out of character for Zenande, and I am amped to get to it.

'OK, I have the instructions somewhere here, give me one minute.' Inez searches through the stack of papers on her desk.

'I know just the candles we'll use. And Rosie will be so happy you want her there.'

In the mirror, Dex's eyes harden. He turns and walks away. Good. I hurt him. Then why do I feel so bad?

'Now where did it get to?' Inez mutters to herself. 'Aha.' She pulls out a typed sheet and stands up. 'Come, let's go.'

'Where to?'

'A special place. Really magical. It's not far.'

'But you're working.'

'Work can wait.' She grabs her light jacket, bag and the instructions. In the hall, she says, 'Will you get Rosie?'

I run up to Rosie's room, where she's doing her make-up. She gives a loud squeal of excitement when she hears the plan. 'We're going to fix this, Savannah, I told you.'

Downstairs, Inez's things are waiting on the console table but she's not there.

'Mom,' Rosie calls, and Inez comes rushing, her phone on her ear. 'Yes, I'm just stepping out for an hour. We'll deal with it when I'm back, OK?' She ends the call, gives a small impatient shake of her head, and minutes later, the three of us are in her car, driving towards the university.

We park at the foot of the mountain and set out through long grass. The southeaster wind whips around us.

After a few minutes, a brown stone building comes into view. Everything is overgrown and marked with graffiti. I know where we are: the old Groote Schuur Zoo, long abandoned. I see the lion enclosure, the remains of the amphitheatre, the pale green cages.

We walk through the cages and into the building. 'This is really eerie,' I say. There's a strong smell of damp and urine. Discarded rubbish in the empty cages. Shafts of sunlight through glassless windows.

'It is,' Inez agrees, her silk dress rippling as she moves. The wind sweeps her fringe away from her eyes. 'But beautiful in its way, don't you think? I'd forgotten all about this place until recently. It's one of those power sites, where energy gathers. That will make the ritual stronger.'

Rosie follows behind, looking around. 'I'll just wait here. Don't want to get in the way.' She hangs back at the door, watching us continue down the passage.

On one side of the passage are cages made of stone and bars; each cage has a gate on one side and a metal slide-down door on the other. Inez stops at one. Outside the cage, she lights three candles and places them on the floor.

'So what do I have to do?'

'Not much. I'll follow exactly what it says on here.' She waves the crisp sheet at me. It looks new, recently typed, not like some ancient ritual. My wariness must show because she touches my arm.

'Nothing can go wrong, so just relax, OK?' she says. Her eyes are more green than brown today. 'It's a really simple ritual.'

I nod as I take her hand. Her skin is smooth and cool. There's a plain, raw sapphire ring on her finger.

She sees me looking at the stone. 'It was my mother's,' she says. 'I still wear it. It reminds me of a time when I had nothing. It reminds me what matters most.'

'And what's that?'

'Family.' She smiles and something prickles inside me. 'Would you mind taking off your dress and shoes? Sorry to ask, but I'd rather follow the instructions to the letter than make any miscalculation.'

I feel some trepidation at her words, then push it away. Inez isn't a veilwitch, though I'm still mildly stunned that her mother was. I'm almost happy for Inez, that on her travels she found a tamer, gentler kind of magic. From down at the doorway where she waits, Rosie gives me a little wave.

I pull the ribbon of my wrap dress and hang it over the rusted green bars. Step out of my sandals and on to the cool, dirty floor. Barefoot, in my underwear, I feel unguarded.

'Shut your eyes, Savannah.' Inez comes closer. 'Trust me.'

I close my eyes. She takes both my hands and starts murmuring words in a language I don't recognise. That prickling inside me grows stronger.

'Keep still,' she warns. 'Whatever happens, do not open your eyes until the end. Or else it won't work.'

She holds out my hands, positions my face upwards. 'Spells are articulated through words and body.' She presses the arch of my back, so that I push out my chest. She lightly touches cold sharp metal to the mottled skin on my stomach and it's uncomfortable. A blade, I think. It curves and dips with her hand as she forms symbols on my skin. She does the same to the mottled skin on my shoulder, my chest, my palm, my wrist, my jawline. It tingles. If I looked now, I think, symbols would be glowing on my skin.

Inez moves away from me. Her chant comes harder and

faster. My eyes are shut, and I feel vulnerable. Cold. Frightened.

I'm tied to a post, the whip on my bare back. The sudden flash is almost dizzying.

'Just keep still,' Inez murmurs. I feel something tugging and shifting around me. My skin tingles. The air is changing. Something is there.

I squeeze my eyes tighter. Something else is in the passage with us. Eyes watching me as I shiver on the cold stone.

Panic floods me.

Then a wet nose against my bare leg, the brush of fur. It's comforting, this touch. It feels safe, a haven in this gaping darkness.

'Mom?' Rosie sounds frightened. 'What's happening?'

I open my eyes. The manifest is there, right in front of me, in the holding cell.

'Oh,' Inez gasps.

All by itself, the gate slams shut. The door at the back of the cell slams down. The creature is trapped behind bars. It lets out a high-pitched cry. Inez looks startled and murmurs, 'I'm not sure how …'

The creature looks at me with hurt eyes, like I've betrayed it. 'No,' I gasp, rattling the gate. I don't understand what happened, but intuitively I am certain it isn't good.

This isn't untethering. It's something different. The manifest is trapped: I can't get to it. The connection between us feels dulled. How can I untether from it when I can't feel it?

'This is wrong.' I'm almost in tears.

'But I did everything according to the instructions.' Inez

sounds shell-shocked. 'This isn't what was supposed to happen.'

Rosie is beside me now, pulling my dress from the rail. She looks around, like she too can feel the residual menace. 'Let's get out of here.' She hands me my dress and I pull it on.

The jackal sits in the cage, eyes on me. I move towards it and Rosie says again, 'I don't like this, Savannah. We really need to go.'

I feel wrong as we leave. Hollow. Rosie slips her hand in mine, quietly leading me back to the car. That was strong magic. A world away from lighting candles and whispering my fears into a hole in the ground. Inez is looking at the page again, and suddenly I get it. She left it on the console table when she answered the phone.

That's the only thing that makes sense. The protection ritual got switched with this entrapment spell.

Dex.

But how did Inez, who isn't a real witch, get it right?

A chill runs down my spine. I don't know how he did it, but he's making sure I can't break the curse. He's making sure that the Jackal can get the magic. Maybe the manifest is the key the Jackal's been after all this time. And now, thanks to Dex, she has it.

Like a match to kindling, I expect my anger to flare.

But it doesn't.

All the way home, I have the sense that something is missing. I am dull. Detached. Like it wasn't the animal manifestation of the curse that I left behind in the cage. It was part of myself.

32

FULL MOON

I stay a second night with Minnie and, in the morning, Harrison drives me to my new home. The honeymooners have returned.

'You've lost your spark,' he says as I stare at the house. 'Is it Quinton or Dex?'

'Neither.' I sound flat.

He casts me a worried look. 'Are you still OK to work the Claremont market tomorrow?'

With the manifest in a magical trap, I can't untether it. I cancelled on Zenande yesterday afternoon; she'd been dejected when I told her what happened to the manifest, calling it sabotage. The Jackal knew I was getting close, and I was stopped.

'I'll be there.' I have to find a way to the Nightmarket. Dream Hella said I would find answers there.

Harrison pulls me into a tight hug, like he can squeeze spark back into me, and declines my invitation to come in.

The house is cute and has a little garden with a syringa tree, rose bushes and a hammock. Walking down the path, it feels like I'm made of stone. There's no excitement, no trepidation.

No storm.

Inside, it's immediately evident this isn't my home. It's Quinton's. It's his glass table in the dining alcove, his stiff black leather couches in the living room, his bland art on the walls. His cups and plates, his toaster and his fugly coffee machine in the kitchen.

'Don't you love it?' Kim beams. 'You just missed Quinton. He had to take care of some urgent business.'

'When did you unpack?' I say, looking around.

'We got back yesterday and worked late into the night.'

'Yesterday? You didn't call me?' It should upset me, but I feel … nothing.

'We wanted to surprise you. Have everything ready. Here, let me show you your room. You have your own bathroom!'

In my room, the fairy lights and red-and-silver bedcovers are familiar and comforting. My photographs of Freda and the aunties. Me and Harrison laughing. My moon chart and the hanging crystal at the window throwing rainbows on the walls and floor.

I follow Kim to the kitchen, which is adjoined by a small bright sunroom.

I look around for our things, the small ordinary details of home, like the chipped mugs with silly messages that Kim would cradle as she drank her morning coffee. The worn red-velvet couches and fresh flowers.

'Where's our stuff?' I sit down at the kitchen table and Kim pours tea into shiny black cups. The snake bracelets curl around her wrists.

'In storage,' Kim says.

One snake shifts and I see her skin underneath.

So many bites. Little puncture wounds decorated all over her wrists, some faded and others fresh. The bracelets themselves are faintly tinged with red.

'Savannah? I was saying, do you want to go shopping at Cavendish Square?' Kim's favourite mall. 'And then Inez booked us tickets for the sunset concert at Kirstenbosch this evening.'

I force a smile. 'Sounds good. Who's playing?'

She tells me and I'm pleased. They play cheesy pop songs that Kim knows by heart, but I secretly love them too.

The snake opens its mouth and takes a bite. She doesn't even flinch.

'Listen, honey. Now that we're all living together, just … don't bottle up your feelings. You know what happens when you do.'

'*Boom.*' I smile, making an explosion with my hands.

But I haven't felt angry since we locked the jackal in a cage.

I look around the kitchen. The sunroom. I picture myself smashing everything in a fit of rage. Taking a cricket bat to the kettle, the cups, the ceramic salt and pepper shakers. The coffee machine squatting on the counter. Shards of glass flying as I tear it all down.

But I have no anger.

'Can we put the Christmas decorations up before we go?' If

I can't take a bat to it, I'll cover it with tinsel. It's our ritual to go overboard with the decorations. 'Or are they in storage?'

'Have them here.' Kim claps her hands. 'I knew you'd want to put them up today.'

We spend the next hour hanging tinsel and lights, setting out the garden reindeer, the beadwork stars. I unwrap Freda's star from its tissue paper and place it beside Ma Stella's heart on the plastic tree.

'I like it,' I say when we're done. It still doesn't look like home, but it's better. Kim puts an arm around me and kisses my temple.

Even though it's hot, we decide to walk to Cavendish. Crossing the bridge over the railway line, Kim talks about the honeymoon – the hotel, the scuba diving, the beaches, the food.

'We were at this amazing restaurant,' she says, 'and Quinton puts his hands over my eyes. And when he took them away, all the waitstaff had come out with this huge cake and champagne and they sang to us. Everyone was staring. I felt like the luckiest woman in the world.'

Sounds like torture to me, but I guess we're all different.

At the mall, we browse the shops, Kim looking for a Christmas present for Quinton.

'He said something small,' Kim says, running her hand across a row of shirts, 'but does that mean *physically* small, like cufflinks, or does it mean cheap?'

'I mean, who wears cufflinks?'

Kim shakes her head fretfully.

'He means a token gift,' I say, because she looks genuinely

worried. 'It's been an expensive year, with the wedding and the honeymoon.' The smashed car repairs. 'Here.' I hold out boxer shorts drizzled with tiny snowmen.

Kim laughs and even her laughter sounds off.

'What's the matter?' I ask.

'Nothing. I just want to get it right.'

A little later, leaving Woolworths, we run into Inez and Rosie.

'Kim,' cries Inez, enveloping her in a hug. 'You look incredible. Tell us everything.'

Kim begins again the summary of the honeymoon. I listen as she runs through her description of the hotel, her scuba-diving lessons.

'… this amazing restaurant and he put his hands over my eyes. When I opened them, all the waiters had come out with this huge cake. Champagne too. They sang to us and I thought, I'm the luckiest woman in the world. Everyone was staring.'

A chill runs down my spine. It's almost word for word what she said to me and sounds even more mechanical the second time.

Inez flashes me a quick, concerned look.

'Enough about me,' Kim says. 'How are you? Did Savannah behave?'

'Of course.' Inez smiles. 'We're good.' She hesitates. 'I've been seeing my sister. We're patching things up. It feels good, coming back into the fold.'

As the women talk, Rosie tucks her arm in mine.

'I miss you already. Come for a swim?' she says. Avoiding my gaze, she adds, 'Dex is out for the day. If that's what's troubling you.'

But I don't feel troubled. I am wondering about Dex, about what he will do next, but I can't make myself feel afraid.

'If Kim doesn't mind.' I don't care either way.

'Go on,' Kim says. 'Quinton's on his way to pick me up. Said he misses me.'

Her smile is wide and fixed.

In the car, Rosie talks excitedly about a trip they're planning to Namibia in January. If she notices I'm a little dull around the edges, she says nothing. She talks faster, brighter, like this is the balm I need. And maybe it is.

I change into one of Rosie's swimming costumes – sensible navy one-piece – and we spend the next hour at the pool. I smile at videos with Rosie, cool off in the water as she talks about some hot guy who packs shelves at Clicks. Inside me, there is a tug. Through my numbed emotions, there's an awareness that I am hurtling towards disaster. And I can't feel any urgency at all.

We step back in the cool of the house and head to her bedroom.

'Rosie,' I say. 'I know the name.'

She shrieks, yanking me into her room. 'But that's amazing! I knew you'd find it.'

I remember Dex furious in the doorway. *Leave my sister out of your mess.* If my life were a horror movie, Rosie is the nice, pretty girl who dies in the final act.

'What do we do next?' Her eyes are shining with excitement.

'I'm not sure you should be involved,' I tell her. It's too dangerous.

303

'Oh, please. Don't let what Dex said get to you.' She takes my hands in hers. 'I'm stronger than I look, believe me.'

'Girls.' Inez appears briefly at the door. 'Grab a shower, a snack. We're leaving in forty minutes.'

After my shower, I sit at Rosie's mirror and she says, 'Will I do your make-up? I could do your hair too.'

I don't usually wear much make-up. 'Sure, why not?'

Rosie touches my face with a brush. She does my eyes, paints my lips. She blow-dries my hair straight down my back. 'It's so long,' she murmurs. The heat of the dryer is unpleasant. The brush pulls at my hair.

'Omigod,' Rosie says as she finishes. 'I love your hair like this.'

The girl in the mirror stares back. Smooth, sleek, burnished.

'It doesn't go with my outfit,' I say. I'm wearing old work trousers I stole from Harrison, rolled up and belted, and a worn tank.

'I can help there,' says Rosie, flinging open her wardrobe. I find myself looking at clothes hanging pristine on hangers, shoes in racks.

'I'm taller, but these should fit,' says Rosie, handing me a pair of jeans. 'And this.' I try on the clothes. Skintight white jeans and a cami. More make-up than I'm used to.

'Smile,' she says.

As I smile for Rosie in the mirror, panic creeps in. I am trapped in a room, banging on the walls, and no one hears me. A butterfly hitting against glass.

'You look glorious.' She strokes her fingers through my

hair, soothing me. 'You look perfect.'

I look like her.

I am remade. I am a different girl. A nicer, un-angry girl.

Rosie is proud of her creation, so I thank her, and we head downstairs together. Inez and Dex are talking with quiet anger in the kitchen. He's looking good, in black jeans and a smart shirt, and smells so nice. Seeing him, an uncomfortable mix of fear and muted longing halts me in the doorway.

Veilwitch.

'What do you think?' Rosie says, ushering me into the kitchen.

Dex glances at us. He takes in my new look with a scowl, and I feel a small ripple of laughter break out. It's brittle. Mirthless.

'I think we're running late,' he says.

Inez shoots him an irritated glance. She stands, smoothing her cream tunic.

'You look beautiful, both of you,' she says. 'Shall we go?'

We drive to Kirstenbosch, and walk across the sprawling gardens nestled under the sloping back of Table Mountain to where we'll meet Kim and Quinton. The band is popular and the garden is buzzing. People of all ages carry picnic baskets, chatting merrily while kids run screaming across the grass.

'New look?' Kim says when she sees me. 'Very glam. I like it.'

'Yes,' says Quinton, raking his gaze over me. 'Nice to see you dressed up for a change.'

'Hi, Quinton,' I say. 'Welcome home.'

He nods affably. He has no reason not to. He's won and he knows it.

On the grass, beneath the towering green-and-grey mountain, we set up our picnic. Inez has packed berries, figs, crunchies, cheese, sun-dried olives, rock-salt chips, and sour mebos.

'This was my favourite band when I was your age,' Kim says. 'I was so in love with the drummer.'

Inez grins. 'Kim tormented us with these songs on repeat.'

'Lies. You loved them too.'

Inez, on a blanket with Kim and Quinton, fills two glasses with sparkling wine. She whispers something to Kim that makes her burst out laughing, loudly. Quinton, eyes hard, takes a swig from his bottle of beer.

Rosie, Dex and I sit on a rug together, Rosie with her legs tucked neatly behind her. I am already uncomfortable in the skintight jeans. Dex keeps his distance. 'Squeeze in,' Rosie says, holding out her phone. 'I want a picture.'

We dutifully shuffle closer. I feel the warmth of Dex's arm on mine. Rosie takes a flurry of selfies. As soon as she's done, Dex and I scoot away from each other.

'Nice,' says Rosie, scanning through her phone. She shows a picture to me: Rosie, her smile bright and happy. Me with my resting bitch face. And Dex. In the picture, I see it. His expression isn't cold. It's sad.

I look up at him quickly. He returns my stare.

The band walks on to the stage. Cheers and whistles go up from the audience, and still Dex holds my gaze.

He's trying to tell me something, there in the evening garden, in this strange, wordless conversation.

'I know what you are.' The hushed words spill out of me. I

hadn't planned to tell him. The crowd gives a loud cheer.

'We need to talk.' His face gives nothing away. 'Not here.'

The band plays the first notes of a fast song, and the audience whoops. Rosie nudges me and laughs, 'Look at them.' She's pointing to our mothers, the two women squealing and roaring with laughter. Kim says, 'Do you remember … ?' and Inez says, 'Remember when Freda …' at the same time. They burst into fits of giggles. Quinton looks like he's tasted something unpleasant.

'Tonight?' Dex whispers.

I do not want to meet a veilwitch at night.

'No, tomorrow. The Claremont market.'

He nods.

The lead singer belts out the first line of the next song, a crowd favourite, and Inez and Kim, along with most of the audience, jump up, shouting the words at the top of their lungs. Rosie pulls me up to dance. Kim throws up her arms as she sings. Wine sloshes out of her glass.

Quinton dabs at his shirt, annoyed, and takes the glass from her. He speaks in her ear. Her arms drop to her sides.

Inez holds out the bottle of wine. Kim catches Quinton's eye and shakes her head.

For the rest of the evening, instead of watching the band, I watch them. When the next fast song starts up, Quinton wraps his arms around Kim in a lover's embrace. Holding her still.

That's how she spends the rest of the concert, bound by his arms, while everyone else dances to the music she loves.

I'm not even angry.

33

KEY

After another dreamless night, Harrison and I return to the Claremont market. The same market where I first met Mama Daline.

On the koesister run, I see how much it has changed. Next to the ordinary traders, the remaining Market vendors are thinner, visibly worn. Hair that was black is peppered with grey; cheeks are sunken. They shoot me resentful looks as I pass. I don't see the tired flower seller or Khulani, the man Madison drained with her kiss. New faces look out from familiar stalls. Strangers who seem sleeker, stronger, radiating vitality. Veilwitches.

Prowling season has taken its toll.

'*Psst*, girl,' one of the new vendors calls to me. I stop at the stall, a display of muddy-looking candles.

He grabs my hand, too quick for me to stop him. He sees the curse marks and laughs. I snatch my hand back and his eyes linger on my jawline, my shoulder.

'It's true, you're the cursed girl. A spell before the Jackal comes for you?' He pushes a brown candle forward.

'I *am* looking for a spell. Something to break a magical entrapment.'

I have only one key left to turn: untether the manifest. But I need magic to break Dex's spell first.

'For that, you'll have to come to the Nightmarket,' he says slyly. 'There you'll find what you're looking for, and more.'

'How do I get to the Nightmarket?'

'I can't tell you that.' The man laughs, loud and obnoxious. 'No one will. But girl, don't worry. The Jackal will make sure you get there.'

I draw back with distaste.

'Maybe I'll see you there tonight.' He winks. 'Big party, not to be missed.'

Walking away, I feel eyes on me. This time they're not even pretending. The veilwitches chuckle as I pass, calling to me, whistling. A man walks after me, whispering to me as I pick up step. A woman joins him. Market witches fold their arms, look away.

Abandoning my search for coffee and sugar, I return to Harrison.

'It's different today,' he says, looking around. 'It's not so hidden any more, you know?'

I hide my face with my hair. 'They're too aware of me.'

'Let's get out of here.' He begins packing candlesticks in boxes. I protest; I don't want him losing any more sales because of me.

'I have to meet Dex.'

Harrison keeps busy. 'Look behind you, Savannah,' he says quietly. 'No way are we staying. Call Dex, make another plan.'

I turn slightly. Too many people watch. Some are veil-witches, some angry Market witches. Even the ordinary vendors are wary.

We leave and get into the baking-hot car. Harrison lets down the windows and starts up the engine. 'Where do you want to go?'

'Just drive.' I can't go straight home. 'The beach.'

The seat belt burns my skin as I clip it in and call Dex but it rings out.

Tonight is the second-to-last night of the Summer Starfall. The curse will reach death point by the end of tomorrow night. Or the Jackal will take me.

I have to get to the Nightmarket tonight.

This is urgent, Savannah, I tell myself. But I can't feel it.

Then it dawns on me: I could follow Dex. I sit up straighter. This will work. I could take Kim's car, wait outside their house. When he leaves, I'll drive behind Dex to the party at the Nightmarket. There, I'll sneak in and buy the magic to untrap the manifest. Zenande will meet me afterwards, and we'll go to the zoo for the untethering.

I shut my eyes with relief, turning my face to the hot sun. I have a plan. All going well, I could break the curse by morning. I run through the steps in my head, testing for weakness. Dex could lose me on the road to the Nightmarket. I need to track his phone.

My phone rings. Dex. I stare at it, thinking. I could distract him, like I did in the wardrobe that night. I could get to his phone then.

'You going to answer that?' Harrison nods at my phone on my lap.

'Dex,' I answer before it rings out. 'Change of plan. Can you come over later?'

'Sure.' He sounds wary.

'In two hours?'

'Can we make it three? Say five thirty?'

'See you then.'

Harrison and I stop in Hout Bay and eat fish and chips on the beach. I can barely taste the food. Harrison doesn't have much of an appetite either.

When I get home, after dropping my things in my room, I find Kim in the kitchen, sitting at the table. It's only three thirty; she should still be at work. Something is wrong.

'Savannah.' Kim smiles. 'I wasn't expecting you back.'

I do live here, I think. I wait for something inside to ignite, but it's all damp wood.

'You're not at work. Did you take the day off?' Lipstick-marked cups line the sink.

She keeps smiling. 'I wanted to finish sorting the house.'

'What happened to the decorations?' I suddenly realise what bothers me. All the tinsel, lights and ornaments we put out the previous morning are gone.

'We changed our mind about them. It looked a bit cluttered.' Kim gets up from the table. Her tea is untouched.

'Now, Quinton wanted steak. Should I make them with corn? Mushroom sauce? He'll be back soon, bringing some friends for a braai.' She looks at the clock and freezes. 'Oh, look at the time. I don't know where the afternoon went.'

'It's just a braai, Kim.'

'He said to have everything ready.' She's pulling the chopping board from the drawer, bustling to the knife block like a frantic little mouse.

This is the point where I should lose my shit.

Instead, I yawn. I'm suddenly very tired. Exhausted. Almost dizzy with it.

Kim takes spinach and fresh herbs from the fridge. We hear a key in the front door, and she stops dead at the centre of the kitchen.

'We're home,' Quinton calls. I hear him talking with his friends as they walk down the passage, then they come through the kitchen door.

A woman in a pinstriped suit and heels, and another in a floral dress. Two men in chinos and shirts. Utterly ordinary. No elaborate costume, no horde marks. Salomé and Madison in my kitchen, Skull and Jaco standing behind.

'Savannah,' Quinton says, smiling. He drops a kiss on to Kim's head. 'So pleased you could join us.'

'Well, hello there,' Salomé purrs, canting her head as she looks at me. 'Aren't you a pretty little thing?'

This is a nightmare, a waking one.

'I've to sort the food,' Kim says. 'Get our guests their drinks, will you?'

I consider refusing. Quinton's hand is on Kim's arm, still watching me, and I open the fridge. 'What do you want?' I sound ungracious, but I get their drinks.

'Let's go through, shall we?' Quinton says, gesturing to the sunroom.

The veilwitches drape themselves on the soft chairs. Skull folds his large frame into the armchair. Madison slips out of her heels, tucking her bare feet beneath her as she takes a glass of red wine.

'We've heard so much about you from Quinton.' Madison sips her wine, eyes laughing. 'I'm Madison.'

'And I'm Salomé,' Salomé says. 'Nice to meet you officially.'

'That's Jaco and Pascal, but we call him Skull,' Madison says. 'Say hello, boys.'

'I want a Coke.' Salomé hands the bottle of beer back to me, holding it a beat too long before letting it go.

At the kitchen table, Kim is peeling husks of corn. She doesn't lift her gaze. I grab a can from the fridge.

'Why are you here?' I say, handing the drink to Salomé.

'Don't be rude, Savannah.' Quinton sits in the biggest chair, legs splayed and fingers steepled.

'We're just here to collect the name,' Skull says.

'Is Quinton one of you?' I say. 'A veilwitch?'

'Quinton?' Jaco laughs loudly and Quinton's mouth tightens. 'Quinton is a con man. He likes to buy trinkets and potions so he can persuade casino owners into giving him a cut of their winnings.'

Skull smiles and speaks in his surprisingly gentle voice. 'He simply opened the door. For a fee.'

'That's enough,' Quinton interjects. 'Savannah, tell them the damn name.'

'What will you get?' I say to Quinton. 'For selling me out.'

'How about pretty things for your mother?' he says nastily. 'Maybe some earrings to match the bracelets.'

Where is my rage? Where is my indignation?

I turn to the veilwitches. 'I'm sorry, but he's wasted your time. I won't help you.' I stand up.

I've only taken a few steps back into the kitchen when Quinton calls out, 'Kim, babe. Do something for me?' His voice is light and easy.

She looks up, her expression anxious. She steps forward, holding the knife.

'Slice the knife through your finger, will you? Just a little cut. Please.'

Before I can speak, she has deftly nicked her finger.

My mouth opens, but nothing comes out.

Quinton says, 'Now, a nice big cut on your palm for me. I want you to smile and tell me how much you love me.'

Kim smiles at him. The knife is poised over her palm. 'I love you, Quinton.' Blood gathers in her palm and trickles down her wrist. 'So very much.'

'Stop doing that,' I say to Quinton.

He doesn't look at me. 'Now, Kim, I want you to place the point of the knife just there beneath your eye.'

Kim frowns. She lifts her bloody hand and rests the sharp tip of the knife on the thin skin under her eye.

'That's enough,' I say.

'Shhh. I'm only just getting started. Keep the knife there, Kim. Now, very slowly, make a small cut. And keep smiling, beautiful.'

A prick of red appears. 'Hold it there.' Kim lets out a whimper, but she is smiling.

Quinton's voice is rough as he turns to me. 'Tell these witches Hella's true name. Now. And don't even try lying – they will know and Kim will be punished. There are worse things than death.'

My mother holds the knife beneath her eye, quietly crying as she smiles.

I shut my eyes. With this name, the veilwitches can kill me and take my magic. Destroy the Market. Corrupt the city.

But I have no choice.

'Malati.' Just saying the word, I feel the power of it.

I open my eyes.

The four veilwitches are standing. Salomé is giddy with excitement.

'Tonight,' she says, 'at the Nightmarket, the Jackal will claim your curse.'

'Tonight?' I rasp, alarmed.

'It's the first of our three feast nights.' Madison flashes her teeth. 'We will celebrate the spoils of prowling season. And you, my dear, are the guest of honour.'

She sees the horror on my face and laughs.

'Keep her locked up,' Jaco tells Quinton. 'We'll be back for her in a few hours. Do not fuck this up.'

315

They leave and the house is suddenly too quiet. Kim still holds the knife beneath her eye, as if she's frozen in position. Quinton moves towards me.

'Let me stay here with Kim,' I tell him, backing away. I can't let him lock me up.

'Not a chance.' He looms over me.

'It's not going to work.' I square my shoulders, fight back. 'I'm going to break the curse. They'll be so pissed at you.'

'You're going to be locked in your room.' He grabs my arm. 'Like the little brat you are.'

'You're a coward,' I hiss at him. 'A fake. You think you're the big man with your connections to veilwitches, but you're just a cheat. A bottom-feeding scrounger.'

He grabs my shoulders and shakes me so hard that a high ringing sounds in my ears. He drags me out of the kitchen, down the passage, the thin soles of my shoes burning into the carpet. He shoves me against the wall.

The shaking, the dragging – it's the final image I saw in the cloudy water. I look up into the eyes of my last tormentor.

But I turned that key, I think to myself. *That's done.*

'Get in there.' He points to the door.

'No, please. Let me stay with Kim. I won't run out.' My words tumble out too fast. 'You can lock all the doors.'

Quinton yanks my arm hard and shoves me into my bedroom. He grabs my bag and empties it on the desk, taking my phone.

He slams the door shut and turns the key.

34

DEVIL

The house is a prison. The metal bars on the windows, meant to keep us safe, make it impossible to get out.

With shaking hands, I scrabble through my drawers and wardrobe, looking for a screwdriver, scissors, a knife, anything with a strong edge.

Nothing.

'I have to step out for an hour,' Quinton says, his voice coming from the passage. 'Do not let Savannah out. Do not open the door or answer the phone to anyone. Stay in our bedroom and watch TV.'

The front door shuts. I shout for Kim through the door. I call for my mother. I hear a soft tread down the passage, stopping outside my door. I say in my calmest voice, 'Kim, please let me out.'

After a moment, the footsteps walk away. Then, from her bedroom, I hear the sound of the TV. The opening music of a soap opera.

I hit the door with my flat palm, slide down to the floor. The veilwitches have strong magic. Demons at their call. They have Hella's true name. They have the manifest trapped. Everything is lined up for the Jackal to strike.

The end is drawing near, and I am not ready. I straighten my shoulders.

If I must die, it will be on my terms.

Picking myself up from the floor, I study the clothes in my wardrobe. I choose a cropped tank and the long, deep red silk skirt with gold threading I wore to Kim's wedding. I put on make-up, shake out my curls. When I'm done, I cast an impassive eye over my reflection in the mirror.

I look fine. I look ready to die.

That's when it catches my eye. My old hat box, filled with hair pins, combs and slides. I scrabble through them, tossing grips to the floor. I find the one from the Market, with the tiny fake pearls. *It can cut through anything*, the vendor said. *Bones, sinew, metal.*

At the window, I turn the slide in my hands. A thin steel blade emerges from the side. It has a reddish tinge. I don't want to know how this thing was made.

I examine the bars carefully. There are four places I need to cut through. The blade goes through the first bar without trouble. Positioning the blade to the second, I see that the red tinge has darkened to black. My palms are lightly rouged. A barely audible whispering sound emanates from the blade.

Slicing through the third bar, the blade begins to dull. Three of the four corners removed, it's enough. Slinging a small

318

bag across my body, I slip between the bars and the window and jump the short distance from the ledge to the ground.

I crouch for a moment, listening. Everything is still. I steal round to the front of the house. Quinton's car is gone. Kim's is here, but I don't dare go back inside for the keys. It must be nearly five thirty now.

I run down the road. After a few minutes, I see a woman with a baby strapped to her. I'm about to ask if I can use her phone when I see his car. Dex. I wave and he pulls up beside me.

'I thought we were meeting at your house.' Then he sees my face and his jaw tightens. 'Get in, Savannah.'

I hesitate. It would be very stupid to get into a car with a veil-witch. But I'm out of time, low on options. Quinton could come back any minute. If I call Harrison, it increases the danger to him.

'I'm not risking you taking me somewhere I don't want to go.' I take a deep breath. 'Let me drive.'

Dex raises an eyebrow, but opens the door and gets out. From the passenger seat, he takes in my elaborate outfit. 'What happened?'

'Not here.' I shift the gear and pull away. My heart is hammering. Maybe I should just put my foot down and go. Dump Dex and disappear into the Karoo. But there is no hiding. Mama Daline's grim prediction remains unchanged: I will lift the curse, or die trying.

Within minutes we're at the old zoo. Outside, the south-easter has picked up again. It tugs my skirt, pulls my hair as I run down the path to the cages.

'What's going on?' Dex catches my arm at the door. He is

such a good actor. I glare at his hand and he lets go. 'Savannah.'

I push past him, inside the building, and there, in the cage, is the creature. It looks thin and unhappy. It might not need food and water, but locked in here, the manifest has been deprived of whatever gives it strength.

'Let it out,' I command Dex. 'You trapped it, now let it out.'

I reach through the bars to touch the animal's rough fur, feeling its warm body beneath my hand. There's blood on its fur. Neat lines have been cut into the skin.

'I didn't trap it,' Dex says. 'Whatever happened here, it wasn't me, I swear.' He examines the cage, looks at the jackal. 'Let me guess.' Realisation dawns on his face. 'The protection ritual you did with Inez.'

'Which you sabotaged.'

A muscle works in his face. 'That's not what happened.'

Before he can make excuses, I say, 'Can you do it?'

He touches the gate. 'I can try.'

I don't want to watch Dex practise forbidden magic so I leave the building, out into the sunshine and wind.

I feel it, the second the animal is freed. A giant swell, an uprising. Every numbed emotion from the last days hits me. I sense Dex behind me, the wind rising around us.

I am *furious*. My cure is pure, molten rage.

And I'm glad to have it.

It courses through my body, pumping through my veins, and I am so alive. I ball my hands into fists, clench my muscles and scream up to the mountain.

Then I turn to Dex. The jackal stands behind him, and I feel a surge of strength as our eyes meet.

'Why didn't you tell me you were a veilwitch?'

'How did you find out?'

'I saw you in the pool house.' The words are shaky with anger. 'The pool house, Dex? Seriously?'

He looks away. 'I was going to tell you.'

'Sure you were.'

'I needed to know,' he says, 'that I was doing the right thing. I wanted to gather more information first.'

'Don't.' I hold up both hands. 'Save your excuses. I know what I saw. Was it fun? Was it another game for you? Dupe Savannah and take the magic for your true master.'

Devil's Peak looms behind him, large and majestic.

'A game?' His voice is hard as he stalks towards me. 'How's this for a game, Savannah?'

The jackal moves closer to me, standing at my legs.

'Imagine you've known magic from your earliest memories,' he says. 'Imagine you've been told by the women who care for you, your mother, your aunt, your grandmother, that it's the biggest secret you'll ever have. You can tell no one, ever. Imagine the shadows in the dark corners of your home begin to whisper to you, but you can't tell your best friend or even your twin, because it's *secret*. Imagine your mother becomes spooked, decides she won't practise veiled magic any more because she's worried about the spirits gathering around her child. They're drawn to him, see. Something about him calls to them.'

He moves closer. 'And it terrifies him.' His eyes seem darker.

'Imagine your grandmother ignores your mother's wishes. Secretly initiates you, only a child, as a veiled witch. Uses your strength to augment her spells. She tells you: Dex, this is your nature, your destiny. This is who you were meant to be.'

He looks broken. I want to tell him that he's more than this, but anger catches the words in my throat.

'The secret spells continue,' he goes on. 'You're not terrified any more. You might even enjoy it. And then one day, something goes wrong and you're grabbed by a hostile demon whose touch burns through layers of your skin. You nearly die. Your mother is distraught. Realises that she'll never escape the grandmother's hold unless she runs. So she does.'

He drops his head, like he's suddenly exhausted. And then I'm madder than before. That he's manipulating me to feel for him, when he's one of them. 'You're a veilwitch because it's in your nature? That's your explanation? That's why you serve the Jackal?' My voice is strained with rage. 'That's why you're trying to kill me?'

'No,' he says, frustrated. 'I don't serve the Jackal and I'm not trying to kill you. I'm trying to help you.'

'You have a really strange way of helping, Dex!' I yell.

'I haven't told you what happens next.'

I'm holding my body rigid in an effort not to scream, not to kick the wall, pound my fists. Not to fly at him, shove him hard. My anger is alive. At my feet, the jackal growls slightly.

'Imagine that years later, your mother regrets what she's done. Maybe she misses the magic, and her herbs and candles aren't enough. She's hungry for the thrill, the high, the trip of mastering

something dark and dangerous. She tells you she wants to reconcile with her family. There's a deathbed reunion. She steals the
book of family spells, causing another fight with her sister.'

I vaguely recall Dex telling me about how Aunt René
accused Inez of stealing a book. Recipes, he'd said. He'd meant
spells.

'One afternoon, you find remnants of blood magic in the
basement. You don't want to move to another country, but
you're the only one who knows. And you have to stop her.'

I found an incentive, he'd said when I asked him why he'd
moved back here. But Minnie had said that Inez never practised
veiled magic. That it was her mother and René who did. Maybe
Inez didn't want to admit to her darker side around Freda.

'Your mother reconnects with her magic that's been
dormant for so long, but it's not enough. She's always been
competitive with her sister. She has to be best. After denying
her true desire for so long, she is ravenous. She grows her magic,
but it's still not enough.

'There's a perfect solution right in front of her: the curse that
killed her best friend. If they're going to die anyway, what harm
if she takes the magic? It will make her stronger than her sister,
her mother, anyone she's ever known. She wants that magic so
badly. So she begins to plan.'

'You think Inez is the Jackal.' The realisation is a body blow.
Inez.

She was so careful. Telling me who she really was, but
presenting it as safe, hiding her darkness behind stories of her
travels, her herbs and candles. Never quite admitting how

powerful she was. Her pretended innocence when she trapped the manifest.

'She's obsessed with your family curse,' he says. 'Has been for a long time.'

'You blamed me.' It's all falling together now. Dex's initial frost, Inez taking me to Nietvergeten because she too was looking for Hella's true name. Why Dex was so angry when he realised Nietvergeten was where Hella once lived. Inez taking me to the zoo, and removing my ability to break the curse under the pretence of a protection spell. That's why she wanted me to stay, so she could keep an eye on me. How she sent her veilwitches to get Hella's true name after she overheard me tell Rosie I'd discovered it.

'Honestly? Yes, I resented you and your curse.'

He takes a step, narrowing the distance between us.

'Then I got to know you again. I found out that you're brave and funny and that your anger is difficult, but also beautiful and true.'

'You haven't been true with me.'

'I needed to know what I am first.' I almost miss it, the note of anguish in his voice. 'For ten years, I've shut myself to magic. And now ...'

'You've let it in. Why?'

'The only way I can stop Inez taking your magic is by embracing my own. My grandmother left me her athame. She wanted me to practise again.' The parcel we retrieved from his aunt's flat. 'I wasn't sure it was the right thing to do. But then you called me that night, deep in shock and covered in blood, and I saw first-hand the danger you were in.' He exhales. 'I decided to do it. Be a veilwitch again. Despite the utter hypocrisy of not wanting my mom to make up with her sister even though I was reconnecting with Jarred.'

'Why *did* you turn to Jarred?'

'I need his help. I needed to join his horde.'

'Jarred's a veilwitch too?' A different kind of gang entirely. 'You're part of his horde?'

He looks away. 'I had to fight …' The night he came home with cuts and bruises. 'I earned my place. And Jarred's going to help me stop her. Not everyone is keen on the new Jackal becoming stronger than she already is.'

'What about Rosie?' It occurs to me suddenly. 'Does she know? Is she a witch too?'

He gives a short laugh. 'Rosie would be horrified. She had no gift for magic, didn't experience what I did. After we moved, she forgot magic was a part of our childhood here.'

'Forbidden magic, Dex?' I say, thinking of the spells Zenande told me about. 'Calling demons and using blood and body bits in your magic?'

'You've learned about forbidden magic from those who hate it. There are more ways of thinking about veiled magic than the Market allows. You've been told how it's used for riches, or maybe revenge. For some, sure. But there are enough of us who pursue veiled magic for the knowledge of it. For the art.'

His eyes shine. It calls to him, this magic.

'You've been told that the first Jackal's magic was damaged because it was born in anger. What if they're wrong? What if

325

her magic became *more* because of how she'd suffered? What if her magic was bigger and stronger, better, for the scars she bore? If the Sisters hadn't been so close-minded, if they'd accepted who she was, let her explore how her rage added to her power instead of condemning her, then maybe things would have turned out differently.'

'Forbidden magic comes at a cost,' I say, trying to resist the allure of his words. 'You need life to make living magic.' Or demon bonds, I remember Mama Daline telling me.

'There are ways around that. Any cost is mine to bear.' His voice sounds different. 'It's only been a few days, but I crave it now. It comes so easily to me.' He is so still. 'If I surrendered to it, it could consume me. Change me. But I can control the urge.'

'Is that what happened with Inez?' The jackal watches Dex, still at my feet.

I try to imagine wanting magic so much that you'd take it from your friend's daughter, knowing it would kill her.

'She could have used her magic to help you.' Dex echoes my thoughts.

'I have been helping myself.' I straighten my shoulders. 'I have two of the three keys and I will get the last.'

The jackal stands now, watching me. I feel a flood of warmth towards it. Even though it's no longer locked up, it's still not free. It is my ruin, but I am its cage.

'You said you wanted to help,' I say to Dex. 'Tell me how to untether the manifest.'

'I've been trying to tell you,' he says sadly. 'These last few days. You already know.'

I frown at him, but before I can ask, he explains, 'Remember the message through the Ouija board.'

'Release the manifest.'

'Untether it from yourself,' Dex says.

'You think I haven't tried?' I snap at him. 'I've asked it nicely. I've commanded it, begged it. None of that's worked.'

'Savannah,' he says with marked patience, '*you* need to let *it* go.'

I am its cage.

Oh. I squat down. The jackal regards me, its eyes locked on mine. The wind whips my hair in my eyes and I push it away. I reach out a tentative hand and touch fur.

My hand on its warm, beating body, I realise that this jackal is no longer simply the creature of the curse. Nearly three hundred years of magical existence has given it substance. The slanted yellow eyes tell me they know a thousand stories, that they've seen more than I can dream. That Hella's magic and the curse have become so entwined, they are no longer distinct.

'Creature of the curse, you were born of rage and injustice.' The words just come, words I never knew I had. 'You have walked with the women of my family a long time.' The wind dances around us. 'Your work is done. I release you.'

A blinding pain shoots through my head. I groan, holding my head in my hands and squeezing my eyes shut.

I'm in a room with heavy furniture. I'm tied to a post, my wrists raw from rope burn. I twist, and behind me, a woman holds a sjambok. No, I cry, but her face is emotionless. She hasn't struck yet, but my body already hurts. Something terrible has already happened. She raises the whip and it licks my skin. Lazy. *She lashes again.* Indolent.

But that's not why she wants to hurt me.

With each strike, the anger grows. It's whirling around inside me. It's wild and unstoppable. I scream and scream, twisting my hands out of their constraints. The whip lands again, and I fall, cheek down to the ground. Bright light shines in through the window.

'Savannah.' *I barely hear the voice calling my name. All I know is pain and blood and fury. The room spins. A wind of rage spills out of me, making the dinner dishes, the half-eaten meal on the table, rattle. It bursts into the room, shaking the window frames, the flaring of the fire in the grate.*

'Savannah.'

The vision loses its hold. The anger swirls. The wind is wild. I've fallen, face to the ground, though I don't remember it. The sun has disappeared and the zoo is covered by thick mist, as if we were right at the top of Devil's Peak, cocooned in cloud. Fighting the gusts, I get to my feet.

'Savannah!' I can barely hear Dex through the howling of the wind. It stings my face; the cages clatter and clang. This is no ordinary wind. I can't see the building any more. I can't see anything more than a few metres in front of me.

'Dex!'

A wooden board flies by and I duck before it hits me. A strong gust pushes me forward. 'Dex?' I call out, but the wind snatches my words away. I'm muddled by emotion, like the vision I've just had was the real life and this the dream. And in both, turmoil. I think of the whip lashing down on the bound woman and I stagger with the force of the churning inside me. A gale rushes through the zoo, nearly lifting me off my feet.

That's when I realise: I'm causing the wind. When I tapped into Hella's pain, I tapped into the magic. Her pain, my agitation.

I have to calm down. I try taking deep breaths, willing the roiling to stop. Count to ten, all the tricks Minnie taught me to cheat the anger. But if I started the wind, it's now developed a life of its own. I can't control it.

I'm pushed again, running blindly with the force of it. A tree in full leaf groans, crashing heavily to the ground in front of me. I turn, moving against the wind, and a board hits the side of my face. I fall to my hands and knees, Hella's pain and my own pain tangling together.

Then I feel his hands on my arms. We're both on our knees in the raging wind.

'I can't make it stop,' I gasp. I don't know if he hears me.

His hands clutch my arms. We're the only steady thing as wind and sand and debris swirl around us. His head is cast down, as if he's gathering himself.

When Dex looks up, there's something different about him. He's somehow luminous, radiant. More. It both draws and repels me.

Dex chants words I can't catch. He releases my arms, reaches into his pocket for the athame. My hair whips into my eyes. He lifts his shirt and draws a light line down from his heart to his stomach. His hand stills there and then moves down towards his hip. The cut is shallow, fast. With the blood-ied tip, he draws symbols into the ground. His arm trembles.

The wind surges, dancing around Dex now. It nudges his arm, trying to throw his hand off course. Dex's eyes, red around the rim, are focused on some distant point as the wind tugs his shirt, his hair.

He takes more blood, feeding the symbols on the ground. He's shaking violently now, shoulders beginning to slump. With trembling fingers, he feeds the symbols, and I know that whatever he's giving is too much.

I touch my hand to my temple, to where the board hit me. It's just grazed, but the skin is broken and my fingers have a trace of blood. I touch my fingers to his symbols. First the circle with the line drawn through it, and the wind feels a little less aggressive. Then the upside-down Y, and it settles to gusts. Last, I trace the one that looks a little like an eye.

The sudden calm is eerie.

Dex slumps to the ground.

'No, no, no!' I scramble over to him, raw terror making me clumsy.

His eyes stare blankly ahead. His shirt has lost some buttons and something must have whacked his unscarred shoulder because a bruise is beginning to form. His eyebrows are knotted and his breathing is shallow. I am cold with dread.

I try to connect with the magic again, but frustratingly there's nothing there. Not even my fear can summon it. I exhale slowly, trying to restore order to the chaos inside.

Reaching into his pocket, I pull out his phone and hold it over his face. When it's unlocked, I go through his contacts, and find the name I'm looking for: Jarred.

'I need help. It's Dex.' My voice is shrill with panic.

'Where are you?' Jarred says, and I tell him, briefly explaining what happened. 'Give me twenty minutes.'

'Wait,' I say before he rings off. 'What's wrong with him?'

'He went in too hard. The magic inside you can't be battled by one person.'

'How serious is it?' I say. It looks bad. He's lost colour, and his skin looks clammy. 'What can I do?'

'He could die.' Jarred hesitates. He's walking fast, worried. I can tell from his breathing, the texture of his silence. 'This is why veilwitches prowl, so they have plenty in reserve. But you know that Dex wouldn't do that. Wouldn't ask that of you.'

'Tell me what to do.'

When Jarred rings off, I touch Dex's hand to my face. Dex can't draw strength from me, but I could give it to him. I open myself to him, the way Jarred told me to. But there's no spark, no connection.

I try to calm the agitation inside me, placing both my hands around his face and willing him to take from me. After a moment, there's the slightest tingle. It's too weak. I lie beside him, body to body. I hold my hands to his face. Better.

He begins to stir slightly. I reach for the storm inside, push it into him. His eyes are a little more focused. 'Savannah.'

I kiss him, holding his face in my hands, giving magic to him. He kisses me back, and the pull is harder. The kiss grows more urgent. Every dark thing – my heartbreak, rage, fear – rises to the surface. I feel him stronger in my arms, alert, awake.

He presses me down to the ground, and inside me, the magic responds.

Dex breaks away. He looks down at me and there's pink in his tawny cheeks; his brown eyes sparkle like a mountain pool. He holds my gaze. 'I took too much.'

I touch his cheek. 'You nearly died.' Then I kiss him again, a cleansing kiss to chase away traces of magic. 'Jarred's on his way.'

We get up, looking at the damage around us. I look for the manifest but it's nowhere to be seen. The cloud is lifting, and broken wooden boards are littered everywhere. Several trees have fallen. But I did it, I have the last key.

'I've turned all three keys.' A tentative jubilance runs through my body. I did it. 'Dex, I've broken the curse.'

Dex shakes his head and the sympathy in his eyes is terrible. 'You can't have. It's unchanged. The curse is still sealed. I can tell.'

'I released the manifest. I was shown how Hella suffered.' I pace as I try to keep the panic down. Think it through. 'It caused a reaction in me, which made the wind go wild.'

'The tremors and the fire in your room.' Dex catches on immediately. 'What key did you find then?'

'That was the name.' Then I know. 'There was no vision, no fire or wind or tremors when I burned the tormentor's blood.' I look at him with dismay. 'Because it didn't work.'

'Did anything happen after you burned the blood?' Dex says. 'The burning was a step, the information must be there.'

'You came in, hurt from that fight.' And then I followed him upstairs. 'Wait, Kim sent me a picture.' I freeze. That awful, unsettling photo of Quinton.

332

Quinton's furious face in the passage after he shook me. My last tormentor.

I think about Hella, inadvertently casting a blood curse through the death of her tormentor. The words on that torn-out page in Freda's notebook: *The final seal is always the taking of a life.*

I think about Zenande in the shade of the trees saying, *You can't just wipe away a living spell. You'd have to kill it.*

Horror ripples through me so violently that I nearly vomit. Of course breaking a blood curse, just like its casting, would carry a heavy cost. I was naive to think burning the blood would be enough.

To break a living blood curse, I have to kill. And burning the blood told me who must die.

I have to kill Quinton.

'What picture?' Dex says, but then his phone rings. 'It's Harrison.' He answers, then says, 'She's here with me.' He hands the phone to me.

'Oh, thank God, I've been calling and calling,' Harrison says. He's upset, and talking too fast, both cursing Quinton and telling me something important.

'You need to slow down.'

'Quinton's looking for you. He's gone completely befok, said he's going to the Nightmarket but he's really mad at you and—'

'We had an argument.' To put it mildly.

'Savannah, don't get angry,' he pleads. 'I have to tell you something. Quinton said that Kim's missing. He said the Jackal has taken her.'

333

35

WATCHMAN

'Your hair,' Dex says quietly. Guiltily. His eyes are on the road.

I unfold the passenger mirror and see the slight tinge of grey just above my temple. I don't feel any different. Whatever Dex took from me before Harrison's call, it wasn't much.

I am still alive. I still hold the Jackal's magic.

We drive behind Jarred, following him into town. Dex parks outside a blue house, Jarred's digs.

We walk up the front steps and inside. Jarred grabs a beer from the fridge, Dex and I decline. He holds it up to me and says, 'You did well.'

I nod at him, and look through the glass doors. There's someone outside, smoking a cigarette. I frown; I know that shape.

'Solly,' I gasp, seeing my old neighbour and long-time sugar supplier. He stubs out his smoke and waves, then steps inside.

'Heard you were coming,' he says.

'I didn't know you smoke,' I say stupidly. Solly is all about cycling and green smoothies.

'I don't. Gave it up years ago.' He sits, patting the chair beside him. 'Come, sit with me.'

Jarred glances at Dex. 'Talk upstairs?' And they leave the room.

I sit down. 'You're one of them?'

'Yes and no. I'm not part of their horde. I only met them because of you.'

'But you are a veilwitch.'

'Does it bother you?'

Only this morning, it would have. But things have muddied since. 'I don't know.' I'm playing with the gold thread on my skirt. 'It depends what you've done. What you will do.'

'It's easier to think in absolute terms, black and white, good and bad, right and wrong,' he says. 'The reality is that all of us have good and bad within us, can be both right and wrong. What matters are your actions. Do you cause harm? Are you interested only in power?'

'Some things are just wrong, though,' I say. 'Objectively speaking.'

'Probably.' He sighs. 'Not all veilwitches prowl. Not all of us hurt others.' He glances at his hands. 'I looked out for you. Placed protection spells in your house.'

The silvery writing above my bed and the outside doors. 'I cleaned them off.' And that same day, the house was broken into.

It is surreal, having this conversation here with Solly. In the room with its matching couches and folded Trellidor, the humming fridge. A bowl of fruit and a screwdriver on the table.

'I recognised at once that Dex was a veilwitch. He was out of practice, but still he saw it in me too. He came to the shop, to talk to me after the break-in. We realised we had your safety as our first common objective.'

'There's a second?'

'To stop the Jackal from getting stronger.'

'Is it difficult, being a veilwitch but not prowling?'

'The more adept you are, the harder it is.' He glances at me. 'Dex is a powerful witch. He will need to stay strong.'

I sit in silence for a while. Solly slides a bag of Skittles over the table.

'Sugar for the shock.'

'Now I know you've been taken over by aliens.' I tear open the bag and pop one into my mouth. I'm rooting in the bag for the red ones when Jarred and Dex return.

Dex looks pissed off.

'Your mother will be at the Nightmarket tonight,' Jarred says, without preamble.

'I'm going,' I say, mouth full of sugar.

Jarred smiles wolfishly. 'That's what they want you to do.'

There's a knock at the door and I nearly jump out of my skin.

'Don't worry,' says Dex, going to the door. 'I know who it is. He was very insistent.'

I turn back to Jarred. 'I'm going tonight,' I repeat.

'The Nightmarket's vicious,' Solly says, his expression serious. 'You need to know what you're walking into. There are no rules there.'

I wink at him. 'Sounds like my kind of place.'

'Tonight is the first of three feast nights,' Jarred says. 'The newly turned veilwitches will be initiated. The Jackal will reveal her true identity for the first time. Dex and I mean to stop her taking your magic.'

'What are you going to do? Lock her in her room? Slip her a pill?'

'Oh, you sweet summer child.' Jarred shakes his head, laughing. 'A locked room won't hold Inez. She has already increased her strength by a lot, probably through prowling, likely through bonds. Once she has your magic, she will be unstoppable.'

A familiar voice sounds in the passage and I hurtle out of my chair. 'Harrison. What are you doing here?'

'You're in trouble. Where else would I be?' He looks around. 'What's going on?'

'Savannah wants to walk into a trap,' says Dex, his jaw set. 'She wants to go to the Nightmarket, where the Jackal will be waiting for her, to save Kim.'

'I'm going,' I say. Dex opens his mouth to argue, and I slip a red candy inside. 'You can't stop me. So help me.'

I am still wearing my skirt, but I've cropped the tank to just beneath my bra. My hair is wild, slithering down my back. I place a wreath of white flowers and red feathers on my head. Hair wraps trail over my shoulders.

In my skirt pocket is the screwdriver I've swiped from the kitchen.

Solly paints my face with a design similar to the red-and-black pattern of Jarred's horde: three red stripes on my left cheek, the V on my forehead. One swirl on my chest. He does the same for Harrison.

'You'll stand out without marks.' Solly admires his work in the mirror. 'The hordeless are easy pickings.'

I look up to see Dex in the doorway, watching with a troubled expression. 'We need to do a muting spell on you before we go. Any decent veilwitch can sense your magic even before they see you.'

I narrow my eyes at him. 'That night in the garden, you knew where I was hiding.'

His smile confirms his guilt. 'It's how Jarred knew we were in the wardrobe. I'd forgotten what it was like, being able to sense magic.'

I take a last look in the mirror, at my disguise. Then I turn to Dex and we speak quietly.

'What's the plan for tonight?'

'Jarred, Harrison and Solly will find Kim. You and I will turn the last key. The tormentor's blood.'

'I have to kill.' I look him in the eye.

'That doesn't surprise me.' He reaches for my hand. 'Blood curses are demanding.'

That last image in the cloudy water vision. The picture on

my phone after I burned the blood. I know, deep in my bones, that it has to be Quinton. The thought fills me with dread.

'Quinton's definitely going to the Nightmarket?' I say to Harrison. Dex stiffens. I hadn't told him it was Quinton who is my tormentor.

'That's what he said.'

'Quinton?' Dex lowers his voice.

I nod unhappily.

He exhales. 'I'll help you as much as I can. We have to turn that last key. You won't be safe until we do.'

'I'll be safe.'

He wants to say so many things, I can tell. But instead he gives me a once-over and says, 'You look convincing.'

Solly shakes his head. 'Stop ogling and get dressed. We're leaving in ten.'

We've long since left the highway and now we drive along narrow, unlit roads. In the darkness, I have little sense of where we are.

My stomach twists with fear and anticipation. Because of the unforgiveable thing I have to do.

We pull up beside Jarred's Golf, on a wide patch of gravel. The night is clear, stars shining.

And then we walk across the vast, empty expanse to the Nightmarket.

Harrison has borrowed a black shirt from Jarred's wardrobe which he wears unbuttoned, a wreath of flowers on his head. Dex wears jeans and a wine-coloured velvet jacket, open to reveal the swirls and lines marking his chest. His hair is slicked back, and his eyes darkened with kohl. His horde marks are bold and exaggerated.

'OK, let's split up,' Dex says. 'We'll meet back at Jarred's when it's done.'

'You'll look after Kim, won't you?' I say to Solly and Harrison.

The centre of the wasteland is lit by fires in metal barrels and braziers. Colourful tents, stalls, tepees, marquees and shacks all cluster together. Floating above us are trapeze wires and boxes.

It's Carniveil, the nightmare edition.

Dex takes my hand as we walk between the stalls. I'm trying hard to keep my face neutral, like I've seen all this before. But inside, I am struck with awe.

I catch small snapshots. Two men wearing hoods haggle in a dark corner. Something wriggles in a bag. Two girls pass a cigar back and forth, clove-smelling smoke hooding their eyes.

My pulse quickens as I take in colour and texture, different scents mixing with each other. This place lures you in through your senses, and then, I think, it devours you.

I am enchanted by the costumes. Headdresses of bones and flowers, long flowing cloaks in indigo, purple, yellow. Leather and silk, feather boas, satin bodices – I want so badly to touch. A woman saunters by wearing a brown-and-yellow dress, and the pattern wriggles like worms, making me recoil.

We pass a fire-eater and a woman dancing on a tall box. Her entire body is covered in tiny blue-green scales. Her

340

movements slow down, become jerky and she stops. A small man appears beneath her and winds the crank; she lifts her arms and begins her dance again. Her scales shimmer with each sensuous move. I watch, aching to dance with her, until Dex breaks the spell by nudging me away.

Fireworks explode. Suspended high above us in a birdcage, a man sings. His voice washes over me, like rain after a drought.

Inside open tents, I catch glimpses of limbs entwined on lush silk cushions and, flustered, I avert my eyes. A woman walks a man on a leash. Inside a marquee, a hushed group is bent over a card game. From the sweat on the man's brow, he's about to lose big, and I feel a pang of sympathy.

From the corner of my eye, a woman with silver eyes smiles and crooks her finger at us. She is beautiful.

'No thanks,' Dex declines.

'Maybe another time,' I say, edging away.

A viper tongue slips out of her mouth and my eyes widen. She winks at me.

'Watch what you say,' Dex murmurs as we walk past a pair on stilts wearing long red robes. 'Words have power here. They can be interpreted literally and you'll be held to them.'

A woman sits on the ground with tied bundles of dried plants, and calls, 'Try my special root mixes. Drink that one, girl, and you'll fly when you dance.'

How does she know I dance? The sly smile on her face tells me the answer: *I just know.* That's how it works at the Nightmarket.

We've reached the heart of the Nightmarket, and right in

the centre, between the stalls and tents, is a large stone platform. A theatre in the round. People have gathered, looking expectant. They're animated as they talk to each other, clearly excited.

'What are they waiting for?'

'The entertainment,' Dex says. I shiver.

On the far side of the stage, I see a large group of people who aren't dressed like the others. By the light of the flaming torches, their clothes appear ordinary, drab even. Then I see the bars holding them. They're trapped.

'Those are the initiates,' Dex says. 'The Market witches who've turned to veiled magic during prowling season.'

The initiates stand upright, without emotion. They face straight ahead, and their blank rigidity makes me wary. There's easily more than a hundred of them.

'They're enchanted,' I realise, and Dex gives a grim nod. 'What if they change their minds? Decide they don't want to go through with it?'

'They can't. That's why they're enthralled.'

'We can't leave them here like this.' Rage so strong that my skin feels tight.

'Hold your anger, Savannah.' He looks at me with troubled eyes. The night will be difficult enough. 'We will help them.'

36

LADDER

Dex and I stroll hand in hand like we haven't a care in the world. No one would guess the anxiety that rages as I smile up at him.

He wraps an arm around me, dropping his lips to my neck. A man watching gives us a sly look as Dex steers me around the side of a marquee with a devilish look in his eyes. Just two young people looking for a secluded spot to steal a few kisses. Away from the bustling crowd.

Out of sight, we don't stop. We continue around the back, where there are fewer people. Now scurrying, we cross the empty space towards the place where the initiates are being held.

They're still standing with that eerie blankness on their faces. I recognise Khulani, the coffee bean vendor. The tired flower seller. The milkmaid, a fabric seller. They're in a wooden enclosure, not unlike an animal pen.

'Can you lift the enchantment?'

'It will take time.' He tugs my hand. 'Come, we should be undisturbed here.' We go around the back of the enclosure.

There, in the empty space behind the enclosure, I'm startled to find a figure bent over a fire. A woman, with her face covered by a heavy scarf. Dex is about to pull back, conceal ourselves, when I realise who it is.

'Zenande?' I whisper as I approach. There's no one else behind the pen; just the dark expanse of a field stretching to nowhere. It's quiet here, but for the muted buzz of the Nightmarket.

She drops the scarf. 'Savannah.'

'What are you doing here?' Any Market witch would be in danger at the Nightmarket. Zenande, the new Worm, *really* shouldn't be here.

'I have to help them.' She straightens up, casting a searching gaze at Dex. She knows he's a veilwitch. 'Who's this?'

'I trust him.' I tighten my hand around Dex's. She's still suspicious, but she nods.

'How are you here? Only veilwitches know the way to the Nightmarket.'

She touches the hand-painted beads she'd given me. 'I knew you'd be here.'

'What's this for?' I gesture to the fire.

'I'm completing what we started at the starflame ceremony,' Zenande exhales. 'Or a watered-down version of it. If my witches are to have any chance, they need armouring. I don't know if it will be enough.' She sounds deflated. 'I didn't expect the enchantment. I can't break that.'

'Can we help?'

'I don't know. To armour them, they have to touch the flame with both hands.' Zenande reaches into the fire. Her hands pull at the flames and when she raises them, I see a small glowing ball of flame. 'I can move quietly between them, get them protected. But it's no good if they remain enthralled.'

'I can lift the thrall,' Dex says.

'Savannah, you could do the armouring with me.' Something like hope passes over Zenande's face. 'It will be faster.'

'We should stay together,' Dex objects. 'This isn't the plan.'

'I have to do this, Dex.'

He gives me an exasperated look but nods.

Zenande hands me the ball of starflame and says, 'Unfortunately, all the starflame in the world can't protect you.' She takes a second ball. 'Come then.'

I give Dex's hand a quick squeeze, and then, leaving him at the fire, Zenande and I stealth-move towards the enclosure. When I glance back, Dex is focused, drawing symbols in the earth.

At the enclosure, we slip into the back row, agreeing that I'll take one half, and she the other. I step between the rigid Market witches, touching the starflame to their hands. *This starflame is your armour*, I murmur each time. Just as Claw did all those weeks ago. I hold the flame low, keeping it close to the folds of my skirt so we won't be seen. The enclosure is away from the stage and there is plenty to delight the veilwitches at the Nightmarket. The Market witches standing stock still with unseeing eyes present little interest.

A crowd is beginning to gather around the stage, the buzz of noise growing louder. I've done half my section and am getting closer to the front row. I'll need to be even stealthier, but I'm confident we can do this without being seen.

This starflame is your armour.

As I continue from witch to witch, they seem to be growing more alert. Their eyes seem less glazed, their bodies less rigid. Dex must be lifting the thrall.

I raise the starflame in front of an old man. I bring up one hand, placing it in the flame. As I reach for his second, he becomes overwrought.

'Don't touch me,' he mumbles. His eye grow wide, his voice stronger. 'Get away from me.'

He rears back, knocking into the man beside him. The second man stumbles. The space is tight; one person going down could knock over the others like skittles. The second man rights himself by grabbing my arm, the one holding the starflame. It falls from my hand, rolling out of the way.

'What's going on there?' a voice calls in the distance.

I drop to the ground, frantically searching for the starflame.

'You have to hide,' Zenande whispers from down the row.

The ball of starflame is at the feet of a woman. Pushing through the witches, I retrieve it.

'Take this.' Zenande is beside me now. She throws her scarf over my head, hiding my face paint and headdress. 'Keep your face down.'

A beam of torchlight runs through the witches. I hide the ball behind my skirt with one hand and adopt the rigid, blank demeanour of the witches, keeping my face down. I hope the agitated old man has the presence of mind to do the same. There are two of them, the veilwitches checking up on the trapped Market witches. They run the torchlight systematically down the rows. I watch as it falls on Zenande, who is staring dead ahead. The light moves closer to me. It falls on the woman beside me, then rests on me, still looking down.

It lingers a moment, then another, before sweeping away.

'Something's not right,' one of them says. 'Better call Salomé.'

'Quick, we have to get out of here.' Zenande is beside me as soon as they've gone.

'Pass this on.' I leave the ball of starflame in a woman's hands. They're limp. 'This starflame is your armour. Pass it on.' She looks at me with a painful emptiness. 'Don't let the veil-witches see it.'

Not sure if she's understood, I take a last look at the witches before stealing to the back of the pen. We have to get back to the fire and warn Dex. I pull off Zenande's scarf and hand it to her.

The cry is loud and unexpected. It's a woman's voice and my heart is hammering when I realise it's coming from right behind the enclosure. Where we'd left Dex.

Turning the corner, I see them. A woman veilwitch, her

hand over her mouth. Skull and Jaco grabbing Dex's arms. Fighting their hold, he breaks away. Skull is both elegant and brutal as he lands a double punch to the gut. They grab him again and drag Dex away.

I'm about to follow when Zenande closes her hand around my arm and pulls me away. She steers me into the nearest bell tent.

'If you go after him,' she says inside the empty tent, 'it's game over for you and everyone else.'

I walk the width of the tent, thinking. I have to find Quinton first. Break the curse. Dex is a veilwitch, and he can fight. He'll be OK. I pace the tent, sorting through my thoughts, when it occurs to me how nice it is inside. There's a Persian carpet. The leather chairs with brass studs. A cedarwood table. The intricate brass lantern hanging from the ceiling.

When I see Inez's candles on the table I freeze.

We're in the Jackal's tent.

In the corner, in a pile of white gauzy fabric, something stirs. I watch it with muted horror before I realise what I'm seeing.

'Kim!' My heart is in my mouth.

I rush over to my mother, who has woken from the sound of our agitated whispering. I fall down beside her, checking her over. 'Kim, are you all right?' With shaking hands I help her sit.

'Savannah?' She leans against the tent wall, weak. Woozy. I stifle a sob. She's here. I found her. 'What are you doing here?'

'We have to get you home.' I glance over my shoulder at

Zenande. She doesn't say anything, but her anxiety is clear. The Jackal could come at any moment.

Kim looks down to see herself wearing her wedding dress. Her eyes have gone all panda bear with streaky mascara and her hair is tangled. My mother looks a little feral. I slip my arms around her, helping her up.

'Where is Quinton?' I look at her well-bitten wrists. I am so relieved she's not wearing the snake bracelets any more.

'I am so sorry, Savannah.' She looks heartbroken, but now is not the time for confessions about being duped by Quinton.

'You have to get out of here,' I say. 'Do you have your phone?' She shakes her head.

'Quinton brought you here? Why?'

'To lure you.' She stands up now and her voice is stronger. 'Savannah, you have to leave. Now. They'll hurt you if you don't.' She clutches my arms. 'I've made such terrible mistakes. Let me fix things.'

'You can't fix this.'

'You go, get away from this awful place. I'll face the consequences.'

'Kim,' I say, frantic now, 'please.'

'Savannah, I let that man into our home. I didn't protect you. Please let me make it up to you.' She's begging, with tears running down her face. 'I'm so, so sorry.'

'If you want to make it up to me, then you have to leave. Now.'

'Savannah, no.'

I'm shaking my head, speaking too fast. 'There's so much

you don't understand. I can't go. Not if I want to save my life. But I can't worry about you too.'

'You're so predictable, Savannah,' says the voice from behind me. I whirl around to see Quinton.

'Let Kim leave,' I say. 'It's me you want.'

And it's him I want. I face him full on.

I feel the screwdriver in my skirt pocket.

The blood of my tormentor.

'Seems like a fair exchange,' Quinton says.

'Let Kim take your car,' I say. He hesitates, then tosses the keys to me. I catch them and hand them to Kim. 'Please, Kim, please go.'

She must hear the desperation in my voice.

'I love you, Savannah,' she says, touching a hand to my face. 'I've let you down, but from here on I will do whatever it takes to protect you.'

'I'll help her get out safely.' Zenande's eyes are on mine and I know my mother is in good hands.

I wonder how much Zenande understands. If she knows she has to get Kim out of the tent.

Before I kill Quinton.

37

COIN

Earlier this evening, as we prepared for the Nightmarket, I googled how to kill a man with a screwdriver. I know exactly where the sharp steel point must pierce Quinton's skin. How hard I will need to thrust in order to make him bleed.

Now, in the quiet tent, I realise how reading about something is nothing like real life. That putting my hand into my pocket, taking out the screwdriver and stabbing it into Quinton's throat will be the most difficult thing I will ever do. That I will never be the same after.

'You decided from the minute you saw me that you didn't like me.' Quinton steps towards me.

'My instinct was right.' Outside the tent, the crowd is getting louder. More people must have arrived for the Jackal's big act.

'You never gave me a chance. You decided I wasn't good enough for Kim and nothing was going to change your mind.'

'You aren't good enough for her!' I yell. 'You are just another small, insignificant man who needs to beat up on a woman to feel big.'

'I never laid a finger on her.' He's angry now too. The noise outside is getting louder, wilder.

'No, you just made her do it herself.' I'm too loud. 'Everything you did was designed to kill her spirit. Why? To make you feel better about yourself?'

I put my hand in my pocket, feeling the reassuring solidness of the screwdriver.

I have to do this now. I must take him by surprise. I will have only one chance. If I don't get it right, he'll be ready for me and I can't overpower him.

It's time to turn the last key. It's time for me to kill my mother's husband.

'Because you're so perfect?' he says nastily. 'You're just a petulant little girl who stamps her foot when she doesn't get her way.' He stalks nearer. 'They all just tolerate you, Savannah. Your aunts, your friends. Your mother, most of all.'

I flinch from the force of his words.

'The truth is,' he goes on, his mouth twisted in a sneer, 'they hate your drama. You drag them down. You think your anger is power? It's nothing. You're nothing.'

I forget everything I read about killing a man. I launch at him, screaming. My anger must give me superhuman strength because I've leaped on top of him, wrapping my bare hands around his neck, and we fall to the ground.

'I hate you,' I shout. He's much stronger than me, of course he is, and within seconds he's taken my hands from his neck. Fisting my hands, I beat them into his face and they're like pesky little flies bothering him. 'I'm going to kill you.'

Then I feel my body lifted off him and the low chuckle of another man.

'Nice girls don't try to kill men.' The man puts me on my feet. I recognise him as one of the witches who'd been enthralled in the wooden enclosure. 'But then you're not a nice girl, are you?' His face hardens. 'Veilwitch.' He spits the word and reaches a hand to help Quinton stand.

I realise what he thinks he sees, a veilwitch feeding on an innocent man.

'You're making a mistake,' I start, but he's never going to believe me. 'This man has hurt me, hurt my mother.' Frustration makes me sound desperate. Like a liar.

'Sure, sure.' Quinton's rescuer stands in front of him, arms out like he expects me to attack again. Quinton takes out his phone, and the man watches me warily.

'You're trying to distract me, so you can use your magic on us.' His eyes narrow. 'I'm not stupid.'

'I'm not a veilwitch,' I say to him, exasperated.

'Sure you're not,' he says. 'That's why you're dressed like one. Horde marks and all.'

'I'm the cursed girl,' I try again, 'and this man is working for the Jackal.'

The man shakes his head and steps forward, letting me know how much bigger he is. 'Burn in hell, veilwitch.'

I want to scream.

'Tell Madison I have her here,' Quinton says into his phone, and he smiles at me.

'You bastard.' I lunge for Quinton again but the man catches me and, this time holding my arms, walks me outside the tent.

'Wait,' Quinton shouts. 'Bring her back here.'

'I don't make a habit of hurting girls,' the Market witch says to me. 'Even veilwitches. So scram.'

Outside is chaos. Market witches are fighting veilwitches.

Satisfaction sizzles through me. It worked. In the night sky, a star falls.

Khulani charges towards the veilwitch candle seller who'd laughed at me earlier today. Khulani doesn't look quite so frail now. He has a stake fashioned from the enclosure walls and he drives it into the candle seller's heart. When Khulani looks up, he's stronger again.

Drawing the blood of veilwitches strengthens the Market witches, I realise. It may be forbidden, but they can't not fight. Not if they want to survive.

Madison, dressed in black leather armour, advances, and I hurry away from the tent door. There's no way I can kill Quinton by myself while she's around. I need to find Dex.

Around me, it's a battlefield. The Market witches must have taken the veilwitches by surprise. Looking around, there are clearly more Market witches than had been inside the enclosure. Many of them have a pattern of lines and stars painted on their foreheads and arms.

A Market witch spears a veilwitch with a braai fork. She leans back, panting.

'Did Zenande bring you here?' I ask.

She turns the fork to me and I hold up my hands. 'I'm with Zenande too.'

'She did,' she says proudly. 'We stayed hidden until the others were released from the thrall.'

I push through the fighting witches. Beside me a woman thrusts a blade into the face of a veilwitch, rearranging the pattern of his horde marks. The air smells of blood and sweat and death. Fear squeezes my heart. Where is Dex?

Then, through the flaming torches, I see him. He's on the oval-shaped stone stage, bound to a pillar. His face is bruised, with swelling around the eye. He's taken a beating.

'Dex!' I rush up the steps and lean over him. I begin working the knots at his wrists. 'Was it Skull and Jaco who did this?' He nods. 'Why did Inez allow it?'

'The Jackal hasn't arrived yet.'

My hands are slick with sweat and I'm making no progress untying the knots.

'Use the athame,' Dex says through dry lips, 'inside my waistband.'

I pull the athame from its sheath and work the blade through the rope on his hands and feet.

'Let's get Quinton.'

We're nearly off the stage when a voice to our left calls, 'You're not going anywhere.'

Jaco. Then ahead of us, Salomé appears.

We back away, and when we turn to run, we're blocked by Madison. Closing in from the other side is Skull.

'Told you we were coming for you,' Madison says. 'And I always keep my promises.'

They're drawing nearer. I pull the screwdriver from my pocket and growl. 'Don't come any closer.'

Madison rushes for me and I'm slammed against the pillar where Dex had been tied. The screwdriver falls from my hand. In my peripheral vision I see Dex fighting Skull while Madison holds me to the pillar. Salomé picks up the screwdriver and pockets it.

Below the stage, the fighting begins to falter. They're watching the stage, watching the Jackal's horde snare the cursed girl.

'Run, girl!' a voice cries out, and I see a Market woman holding her hand over her mouth, her eyes terrified.

Jaco and Salomé stand together at the centre of the stage. They bow their heads and hold out their hands. The stone floor begins to tremble. Stone rises from the ground, reshaping and re-forming until it is a long slab at hip height. An altar.

Dex and Skull are circling each other. I struggle against Madison's hold, but it's like her hand is made of steel. I see the small nod Skull gives to Jaco and Salomé. All three of them hold out a hand to Dex, and he flies across the stage, falling on to the altar. Vines grow up from the hard stone floor and wrap around his arms and legs.

'Dex!'

A new wave of fury surges through me and I struggle against Madison.

'You could just ask nicely.' She releases her hand suddenly and I fall to the floor. Picking myself up, I run to where Dex is trapped on the altar. I try to hack through the thick vines with his athame, but two grow back where one had been.

'They won't hurt me,' he tells me through gritted teeth. 'Find Jarred. Get Quinton.'

'I'll be back for you,' I promise, and turn.

Madison, Skull, Salomé and Jaco are all waiting for me.

'We have instructions to keep you here until the Jackal arrives.'

'Get away from me.' I spit the words, searching for the best escape. On every side of the oval stage, witches jostle against each other. The Jackal's horde is circling closer, seeking to entrap me. I have to take the gap before it closes.

I run. Around the altar, towards the steps. If I can lose myself between the witches, I could get away.

I'm near the steps when Skull grabs me, holding his hand over my screaming mouth.

I am caught. It's happening. Tonight. These are my last minutes. The curse is near its highest point. Death point. Which means the magic has to be strong. I try to feel it inside me. I try to tune into it, to make it work for me. To set me free. I look inside, searching for that tangle. I feel it, Hella's fury. I call it, hold it, throw it at Skull. He staggers back and energy soars through me. I sprint forward.

Then a hand grabs my hair and when it pulls, it feels like my scalp is being ripped off. I cry out with pain and when it clears, Skull has my arms in his grip, pulling me centre stage. How is he so fast? There are too many of them. I can't take them all on, not with my wild lashing out. Tears of rage and frustration prick at my eyes.

'Let her go.'

The voice is strong and assured. Skull turns, still holding me. Across the stage is Zenande, shrouded by the scarf again. She stands in shadows, her face hidden.

'I'll get this one,' Salomé sighs, and struts across the stone stage in her high patent-leather boots.

She's a few feet from Zenande when Salomé stops suddenly, making a strange gurgling noise. Salomé gasps for air, clawing at unseen hands around her throat.

'Salomé?' Jaco says. He rushes to her and as he gets there, she slumps in his arms. It looks like she's dying. How?

Zenande turns to Madison.

'Die,' Zenande commands, holding out her right arm, her hand flexed. Madison falls to her knees, her face a mask of horror.

Zenande faces Skull, flexes her hand and says it again. 'Die.'

His grip on me slackens. I feel him stumble and I scrabble away.

Zenande turns to Jaco, who's still holding Salomé, and makes the same command. 'Die.'

Jaco drops Salomé, his hands flying to cradle his head. He takes two steps then stops abruptly.

'This is for Mama Daline.' Zenande's mouth twists as she speaks.

Madison gasps as she stares at Zenande, then clutches her stomach and vomits blood. Jaco stands eerily still while blood streams from his eyeballs.

Zenande lifts her face to the stars: 'When the Worm decides, your life will end in pain and despair.' Her words rain down on us. 'I have decided.'

Mama Daline's blood curse.

The Jackal's horde has fallen.

'Go find Quinton,' Zenande says to me. 'Break the curse.'

'Don't let the Jackal see you here,' I beg.

I take a last look at Dex, who's trapped on the altar, and then run down the stone steps. I've gone a little way into the crowd when Jarred and Harrison appear. 'Kim's with Solly. We know where Quinton is. This way.'

We're running down the row when I hear that voice I'd hoped never to hear again.

It echoes through the crowd and reverberates through my body. It's one single word, but it's the word that changes everything because it means that she is here.

Enough.

Down the row lit by flaming torches, from between the marquees and tents, the figure approaches.

The Jackal.

Wearing a heavy black robe and furs, her face is part human but mostly animal. Large ears, slanted eyes, sharp cheekbones. The distortion is strangely beautiful. Even I am awed as she stalks towards the stage, witches and veilwitches parting like the Red Sea for Moses.

There she is: Inez. Confident and alluring, as always. Behind her, several stars shoot through the sky. Like fireworks, heralding the arrival of a queen.

As she passes, several witches resume their attack. Khulani swings his stake, jamming it into the stomach of a veilwitch.

'I said *enough*.' This time the voice is deeper, loaded with something *other*.

The Jackal holds out a hand and everyone stops just as they are. Awake, watchful, but only the Jackal is able to move. I try to step forward but my body will not obey.

'Witches of the Market and the Nightmarket, the time has come to end the fight between us. From now on, we will be united. Under my rule.' Frozen faces stare at her as she walks up the steps to the stage.

She gestures with her hand. 'Come nearer.' The crowd takes one, two, three collective steps towards the stage. My legs move too. 'Savannah.' That terrifying voice says my name. 'Closer.' She crooks one finger. Against my will, I walk towards her. When I reach the top step, the Jackal brings her hand down. 'Sit, all of you.'

My legs sink to the stone stage. Everyone gets on the ground. Some sit beside slain witches, unbothered. Witches sit in pools of blood, bearing cuts and bruises. They're breathing heavily, but they sit. As she commanded.

'It is time,' the Jackal says, looking around, 'to tell you who I am.'

She walks across the stage, stepping over the bodies of Madison and Skull. She walks to the altar and runs a finger down Dex's face. 'It doesn't have to be like this.' Her voice is softer as she speaks to him.

'It is time.' She turns to the crowd again. 'Tonight, beneath the falling stars, I will release the magic of the curse and make it mine.'

She looks at me. The Jackal head with its pointed ears tilts slightly. The slanted eyes appear cunning, the animal mouth smiling. She says it again, but with infinite gentleness, like the woman who knew me as a baby. The woman who cared for me, held me when I was upset. 'It is time.'

38

THRONE

The Jackal faces the altar and holds up her hands. The stone at the centre of the stage reshapes again. The altar changes, shifting from a slab to a massive stone chair. Dex is still tied to it, but he's sitting now and the vines snake into his hair, forming a crown. Holding him in place. Beside his chair, the stone builds upon itself until it's a second giant chair, both with the same intricate design. A massive stone chair, with steps leading up to a high seat. Stone strelitzias are carved into the top and arms.

'From tonight, I am your queen.' The Jackal sits on the chair beside Dex. 'This is your prince.'

She waves a hand over the gathered witches, and we can move again.

'Stay seated,' the Jackal says, but doesn't force it. She doesn't need to. Most obey. Only one witch rises and the Jackal tuts, wagging a finger. The witch falls to the ground, unmoving. 'I said, no more fighting.'

I look at Dex. His eyes are on mine, but I don't know what he's thinking. I don't know if the magic that calls to him settles now that he sits on a throne as a prince.

And above, stars fly across the sky. Every few seconds, another stream of white light.

'Come here, Savannah,' the Jackal crooks her finger at me.

I stand up, stepping forward until I'm in front of the Jackal.

'From the moment you refused me,' the Jackal says, in that terrible voice, 'this was inevitable.'

'And I would refuse you again.' I square my shoulders.

'Still, I am grateful to the women of your family.' The Jackal gives a gracious nod. 'For carrying my magic through the generations. It has ripened and matured and—'

'It's my ancestor, my magic,' I say loudly.

She inclines her jackal head graciously. 'We disagree on that, but no matter – this evening will prove it is mine. As a token of my appreciation, I will avenge you.'

The Jackal gestures stage right and there, between two veil-witches is Quinton, gagged and bound. They force him to his knees.

'What will you do?'

'I will kill him, of course,' the Jackal says.

She knows that I've been looking for him. That this is the tormentor whose blood will undo the curse. By killing him herself, she will cut off my last chance to turn the tormentor key.

The Jackal rises from the chair and walks down the steps. She moves fluidly, gracefully. She goes to where Quinton kneels near the edge of the stage. He flinches as she touches his shoulder.

I study the figure standing beside Quinton. Beneath the costume, I think, beneath the magically altered face, is Inez. How can this be the woman who fought to save my aunt, who claimed she wanted to help me? Corrupted now by magic.

'You could have shared this with me, Savannah. You chose death.'

She steps nearer to me, dropping the fur from her shoulders, then the black robe. She's wearing a red dress and the shape of her, the way she moves, is familiar. The animal features are beginning to fade now, and what's human in her face takes a stronger hold.

'You pretended to help me –' I spit the words – 'so you could take advantage of me.'

'I thought that was rather clever actually.' The voice is changing too. She sounds more like a woman now.

'Is this magic really worth your humanity?'

'Humanity is overrated.'

She closes the distance between us, a predator moving to its kill. Her eyes are still jackal, so are her ears, but her skin is human, and her head.

But then I get a shock. It's not Inez's sleek pixie cut.

It's long, thick glossy hair, flowing down her back.

My breath catches.

No.

'All that time you were complaining about Quinton, I was making deals with him.' The eyes change, become less slanted.

364

Golden skin that glows in the firelight. Wide-set, kind eyes, with thick lashes. 'He wasn't hard to persuade. Weak, greedy men never are. Does that make you angry?'

'Yes,' I whisper.

'Does it make you angry that I hid so much from you? Manipulated you into calling a demon?' The mouth changes. Softens into a laughing mouth I know well.

'Yes.'

The anger burns through me. Stronger than heartbreak, stronger than fear.

'Good, feel that anger, Savannah. That means the magic is strong and alive. Ready for me.'

Rosie.

She stands right in front of me, the change complete. Across the stage, on his throne, I see the devastation on Dex's face.

'Rosie,' he calls, still held by the vines. 'Rosie, don't do this.'

I speak quietly, so that only she can hear. 'Dex will hate you if you kill me.'

'He'll get over it,' she replies softly. 'I won't lose him, you know. He's a veilwitch again. Every day he will grow harder with the magic he uses. In time, he'll barely remember you.'

'Then you don't know him.'

Rosie's eyes glitter. 'You think because you hooked up with him that you matter? He'll always choose me. Over Jarred, over you. Now that he's embraced the true magic, we, the twins, will rule the Market.'

'He thought Inez was the Jackal.'

'Inez.' Rosie curls her lip. 'Inez who rejected her magic?

She's not worthy of this honour. When I was a child, my grand-mother secretly made me a veilwitch. She had high hopes for me, but I was a disappointment to her. I was a disappointment to myself. I had almost no gift for magic, so my grandmother stopped trying to teach me.'

She gives me her mischievous smile and it's so familiar, so loved, it's like an arrow through my heart. 'I got her back, though. I stole the family book of spells and none of them dreamed it was me. I was always invisible to them. See, Dex had the talent. I didn't matter. But that little taste my grandmother gave me left me wanting more.'

'So you fixed it.'

'When I decide I want something, I make sure I get it. The first time I extracted magic from a blood curse was while trav-elling two years ago. I've become quite the expert since. I've prowled, I've forged bonds with creatures of the darkness who give me strength. But this blood curse will give me the kind of power I deserve. This magic will make me a goddess.'

'Why?' I whisper.

'You were so lucky, Savannah, and you didn't even appreci-ate it. You've lived most of your life touched by magic. When you were angry, that was your ancestor the Jackal singing with you.' Her eyes shine. 'You weren't *cursed* – you were special.' She's so close now, we're almost touching. 'I was nothing.'

'You were never nothing.'

'Oh, sure. Teachers loved me, parents loved me. I had friends who thought I was *so sweet*. I learned how to be a nice girl. The girl who brings you hot chocolate, who listens to your problems. The girl who obliges. Who strokes your hair during your nightmares. All the while, trying to steal your dreams.' She sighs lightly. 'People want to believe that girls are sweet, obedient. They never suspect that they may be plotting. That they have ambition. Hiding in plain sight, I became the most powerful witch around. And now, I will magnify that strength.'

'Ruling through fear won't make you strong,' I say. 'Anyone can break things.'

'I. Want. More.' She places her hand on my cheek. 'People hate that idea, don't they? That a nice girl might want *more*. I'm so lovely. So lucky. Why would I want more? Understand this: I want, I crave, I thirst, I need. I will have more.

'After I take your magic,' Rosie says, 'I will share it with my brother. We will rewrite the myths.' Behind Rosie, a star falls through the sky. 'Dex and I forgot you once. We will forget you again.'

Rosie runs her hand through my hair.

'Sorry,' she taunts.

All those times I'd told her not to apologise.

Her hand falls to her side. She drops her eyes for a moment, then looks up.

She is awesome to behold. A fierceness sings around her and I wonder how I could ever have missed this power, this blaze.

Hold your anger, Dex had told me. I hold it. I hold it like it's a ball of fire in my outstretched hand. I hold it like a weapon.

'I want to speak to Quinton,' I say loudly. I have to find a way to get close to him. 'Before he dies.'

'Not going to happen.'

In the audience, I see Jarred, edging closer to the stage, Harrison beside him. *Sometimes we need to be bad in order to do good.*

'She can't win.' Dex smiles up at Rosie. 'So let's play her game.' *Let's play a game.* He's trying to tell me something, I think.

'Salomé took her weapon. Savannah can't hurt him, so let her talk. And then,' Dex says, 'I will do whatever you want, Rosie. I'll work with you.' He's now looking at me intently. Then he turns abruptly away and I'm confused. Hurt. He's facing the audience with a stony face. 'I will be the prince to your queen.'

His eyes are fixed on someone in the crowd. My heart picks up as I realise that Dex wants me to follow his gaze. I search the audience, not seeing anyone I recognise.

Then I see her. The woman with the viper tongue.

Words have power here, he'd said to me earlier. *They can be interpreted literally and you'll be held to them.*

'Death is inevitable.' Dex's eyes are now on Rosie's. 'Let her have the closure she wants, before she dies. You are so much stronger than she is, Rosie. If she speaks to him, I'll be on your side. Willingly. For always.'

They have always been so close. He's promised her the one thing she can't refuse.

'I love you, Rosie.' Does she not hear the heartbreak in his voice?

She's thinking carefully, working through ways she might lose. Eventually she turns to me. 'You have one minute.'

I take nervous steps to Quinton. I've lost the screwdriver, but in my pocket is Dex's athame. I turn it over, feeling it warm in my hands.

I can feel Dex's gaze on me, willing me to understand. Another star shoots across the sky.

Quinton watches me with fear in his eyes. He knows. Beneath the gag, he tries to talk to me. To beg me not to kill him. I stand over him, turning my back to Rosie.

If she speaks to him, I'll be on your side.

So I'd better not talk to Quinton. Not a single word. I'm standing in front of him now. I take a breath. I need to do just one thing. A deep thrust of the athame in his throat. And I need to do it fast.

My eyes meet Quinton's. He's crying now.

I think about the monsters chasing me in my home, the veilwitches who tried to kidnap me. About Claw falling into the fire. The visions I saw in the cloudy water. So much torment. So much hurt. I am tormented by Mama Daline in the tunnel, my hand sinking the knife through skin, into her heart. How it shattered me. How I've carried her inside my heart every moment since.

I do not want to carry Quinton in my heart. If I kill him, I will never be free of him.

Hold your anger. The weight of it, as a weapon. I think about Solly saying, *What matters are your actions. Do you cause harm?*

I don't want to cause harm.

I look up at the stars. A shooting star blazes through the

darkness. It's bigger, slower than any shooting star I've ever seen. Persistent.

'Have you said what you needed to say?' Rosie calls. 'You have thirty seconds.' I look back at Quinton.

Tonight, I am angry. But I have no fear.

Quinton squeezes his eyes shut and I make my decision.

I'm sorry. I pull my hand from my pocket. I think of Kim, of Minnie, Auntie Dotty, Harrison and all the others who have loved me so well. Of Dex, how he laughed that night on his bed, him towering over me with the empty whisky glass between us. I think of his body on mine in the pool house, him sinking to the ground at the old zoo. The falling star lights up the sky.

I'm so sorry I couldn't stop it.

We've reached death point. I couldn't escape the curse. I will die before my time. All I have left is to control how that happens.

I won't kill Quinton. I won't let the Jackal have the magic, and so it must return to the stars. And there is only one way to be sure of that. As if the stars are in agreement with me, the flashing light grows larger and larger, a blinding, brilliant ball of white fire streaking through the night.

Malati, your magic returns to you.

With a single wild cry, I bring the athame down. To my own heart.

We're smothered in white light.

The athame breaks skin at the same time as the loud, echoing bang. A violent shockwave knocks me off my feet and I fall. Around me, witches hit the ground, glass shatters, fabric tears.

A loud sound rings through my head. People are crying out, but their voices are muted beneath the ringing. It feels like the world is beating, a steady throb.

I'm lying cheek to stone when the woman appears in front of me. She bends over me, her long black hair touching my face.

It's the dark-haired woman from my dreams. The manifest walks beside her.

She smiles, showing her sharp teeth.

You broke the curse, Daughter. You chose to spare the tormentor's blood, not spill it, and this has turned the last key. The magic can return to the stars. Or it can be yours. Which do you want?

She holds out a hand to me, helping me stand. She runs her hand down my hair, then kisses my forehead, a cold touch. She touches my chest, the shallow cut of the athame, and the skin seals.

The manifest steps towards me, moving elegantly on its four legs. I feel the magic that pulses through it, magic that calls to me. And I realise that untethered, there is a new connection between us. One that is strong. True.

'Mine,' I say.

Then the magic is yours. Accept it, Daughter.

She kisses me again and I feel it at once, the flood of something alive and electric inside me. Warm fur brushes the silk of my skirt.

And then it's quiet. And then it's dark. That high-pitched ringing again, and muted voices.

Slowly, I tune in to the voices. People babbling about a

371

meteor. Dex right there beside me. 'Savannah.' He holds me so close. 'You're OK.'

'I am.' I let out a choked laugh.

'You broke the curse.' He pulls back to look at me. 'Without killing Quinton.' His eyes hold mine. 'I saw what you were going to do. You spared him.' I can see the pain he's carrying.

'I didn't want to. But there has been so much bloodshed, so much violence. I was going to die, and that's all I had left to control. Turned out breaking the chain of violence broke the curse.' Then I look around. 'Where is he? Quinton.'

'Quinton?' He's stalling.

'I didn't say a word to him because I didn't want you serving Rosie. But there's something I really need to tell him.' That I'm not angry with him any more. He doesn't deserve my anger.

'Savannah.' Harrison leaps on to the stage. 'Don't look down.'

Which of course immediately makes me look down.

Offstage, Quinton is sprawled face down on the ground. He is badly injured, his leg at an impossible angle, and his head – I look away.

'He was hit by the meteorite,' Harrison says, pulling me into his arms. 'I saw it coming towards you both. I have never been so terrified.'

Quinton killed by a meteorite. On the night of the falling stars.

'You took my magic,' Rosie shouts at me. I turn to see her storming across the stage. Dex and Harrison both watch her with guarded expressions.

'It was never yours.'

'The Nightmarket is mine to rule.'

I look out at the sea of people, their uncertain faces. The hard lines, the bitter eyes. This is a world I have no desire to rule.

'I want no part of this,' I say. 'But if any of your witches come near the Market again, you will be sorry.' I was born for this.

'Dex,' Rosie calls, her face contorted with fury. 'You promised you'd be loyal to me.'

'*If* she spoke to Quinton,' Dex says. 'Savannah didn't.'

'You're a veilwitch, Dex,' she appeals to him. 'You're drawn to the forbidden, the dangerous. You can't escape that.'

'We've all got a mix within us, Rosie,' he says. Sorrow is etched on his face. 'But I won't choose this. I never would.'

Dex slips his hand in mine. Freda's ring glints. Turning away, we walk down the steps and off the stage. The crowd parts for us.

We walk through the crowd to where Zenande waits.

'Do you accept this Jackal to rule the Market beside you and Claw?' I say.

'Gladly,' says Zenande, a flicker of pride on her face. 'Gladly, Angry Girl. Look.'

I look up at the stars falling through the velvet sky.

'You did it.' Zenande hugs me. 'I knew you would.'

'And we saved the witches who'd been prowled.' I can't help the broad smile that breaks across my face. '*We* did it.'

'Let's get out of here,' Zenande says as Harrison and Jarred join us. We start walking. It's time to leave the Nightmarket.

'I will be stronger than you, Savannah.' Rosie's voice rings out over the crowd. 'I promise you that. I might not have the magic from this curse, but there will be others. I will find them. I will make them mine.'

We keep walking. I feel my eyes slant. The sharpness of my teeth. My senses are assaulted by the smells, the sounds, the magic of the Nightmarket. I can almost taste it.

'I will not be stopped!' she cries.

I've so much to learn. But I will do it. And I will be there to stop every wicked thing Rosie tries.

We walk together through the Nightmarket, past the small fires burning in drums. I hear the sound of padding paws behind me.

Harrison slips his arm around my waist. My handsome, playful uncle with the core of steel. 'Solly went with Kim back to your house. They're waiting for us there.'

We leave the Nightmarket; we drive away from that terrible place. We follow the road back towards the mountain. To my mother. And when we get home, I'm sure to walk backwards into the house.

39

GRAVE

We buried Quinton this morning, and I'm now serving samoosas to funeral guests. They sit on our worn velvet couches, drink from our chipped cups, taken out of storage.

The funeral guests mutter vague words of commiseration. *So young, such a shame.* There doesn't seem to be anyone here who's genuinely affected by his loss. That simple truth makes me feel sorry for Quinton. It is perhaps the only thing that could.

Across the room, Kim is giving a good impression of a grieving widow. Or perhaps she really is grieving. Even monsters can be loved.

The morning after the Nightmarket, for the first time in my life, I watched Kim lose her temper. She attacked Quinton's clothes in a frenzy, slashing his designer shirts to ribbons. She'd screamed and yelled and cursed, until she stopped, breathing heavily, and said, 'Hell's bells, that feels good.'

Kim has found her anger.

And I haven't lost mine. It's there, but it's no longer a snarling thing inside me, prowling and waiting to pounce. We understand each other better now.

There are so many things to be angry about.

I am angry with Rosie. I thought she was on my side. It was all a lie. Her night-time trips to the cinema were a cover for her visits to the Nightmarket. The way she pretended to help me so she could learn Hella's true name. How she placed Kim at risk by making a deal with Quinton. I second-guess everything now: the trip to the beach when she tried to stop me after I summoned the jackal; the protection spell at the old zoo, where she'd stood at the door, secretly overriding Inez with her stronger magic.

But mostly I am angry because I loved her. And she tried to kill me.

Our enmity is entrenched now. Rosaria the Unveiled, they're calling her. And I am the new Jackal. Along with Claw and Zenande, the new Worm, I will lead the Market. We will do things a little differently than the Daughters who came before us. Be prepared to fight dirty, if we have to. We will meet with veilwitches, cooperate with those who promise not to prowl.

Jarred and Dex are already on board. They're moving in together, to digs in Woodstock. Things are rough between Dex and Rosie, and he needs the space, both from her and Inez. I feel both delight and trepidation that Harrison is taking the third bedroom in the house.

'Angry Girl.' Zenande appears beside me. She's been teaching me. History, lore, magic, ritual, everything I need to truly become the fourth Daughter. She stares hard at Inez, who is talking to Minnie. 'I don't trust that woman.'

'I'm not sure I do either.' I wonder if she was as oblivious to Rosie's growth as a veilwitch as she claims. Inez has made amends with her sister and claims not to be practising veiled magic, but I have my doubts.

'Claw really likes you.' Claw is still in hospital, but Zenande and I visit. She's stronger every day and we make plans. We've talked about the problem of Arrow's heir. She's out there, we're sure of it.

'Savannah,' Auntie Chantie says. 'Come help us for a sec.'

As I leave the living room, she pulls me down the passage, to my bedroom. Inside, squashed together on the bed, are Minnie, Harrison and five aunties: Glynis, Chantie, Tietie, Nazeema and Dotty. An ambush.

'What aren't you telling us?' Minnie demands.

'What do you mean, Ma Minnie?'

'You're different. It's the curse – it's gone, isn't it?'

She lifts up my wrist. My skin has cleared completely in the last three days. All the marks have vanished.

'How did you do it?' says Dotty.

Sitting on my bed, I tell them. About our ancestor, how I learned her name through my dreams. About Quinton and how he controlled Kim. How Rosie betrayed us. I don't talk about the Market or Nightmarket but they don't seem to notice the gaps.

'If I could kill that man again, I would.' Auntie Dotty spits the words.

'I'm just so grateful.' Minnie has tears in her eyes. 'It's over. None of our girls need to suffer this ever again.'

'Savannah, you should have told us,' Auntie Nazeema chides. 'Small thing like you carrying such a heavy burden.'

'She had Dex to help. That boy can carry my burdens anytime.' Auntie Dotty raises an eyebrow.

'No,' Harrison groans. 'Stop.'

'Jirre fok, Dot. Must you always?' Tietie says, irritated, and then we're all laughing. Howling. We shut the door so that the mourners can't hear how horribly inappropriate we are. Our laughter is cathartic. It's a laughter that clears out the bad, that brings in the new.

'So, when you bringing your boyfriend, hey?' Auntie Chantie asks me when she's able to talk without giggling.

'He's already here, Auntie.'

I laugh at her surprised face and then skip out before they ask any more questions.

I find Dex outside. He's sitting on the low wall, squinting into the sun.

I sit beside him. 'You OK?'

'Yeah, I guess. You?'

'Yes.' I exhale the word. 'All fine.'

A car cruises by and then slows. The guys inside give me a once-over. The man in the passenger seat whistles. 'Hullo, baby. I like your style.'

I roll my eyes and push off the wall.

'Savannah,' Dex says, but he's laughing.

I walk right up to the car. 'Listen up, only saying this once.'

'I'm listening.' The guy in the passenger seat smiles wider.

'I can do things to you.' I watch as his smile turns to a leer. I lean forward and speak more softly. 'Yeah, that's right. I can do things, terrible things that would give you nightmares for a month. As a bonus, I'll make your little dicks shrivel up until they're totally useless.' I smile. 'Problem is, I'm still learning, so I might fuck it up and do more damage than I intend.'

They look at each other. *She's mad. Befok in the head.*

I bang a hand on the car roof and they jump.

'You better get out of here before you make me cross.'

The tyres screech as they pull away. They look over their shoulders. I'm laughing like a wild woman. Dex's shaking his head at me, chuckling.

'Come on, let's go in. The aunties want to meet my boyfriend.'

I am halfway up the steps when I see her.

Red, gold and black fur, gleaming golden eyes. The manifest. My jackal. She's free, no longer bound to me. But she's chosen me, as I have chosen her.

GLOSSARY

South African English is frequently mixed with words from the country's many languages. The explanations below refer to the contextual meaning in the book.

Athaan: call to prayer; adhan
Bakkie: small pickup truck
Befok: crazy/wild
Braai: barbecue; refers to the grill that holds the fire, the cooked meat/veg and the event
Dagga: marijuana
Doekoem: refers to magic and sorcery (Cape Malay); doekoem is a noun and a verb: the act, the doing, and the person who does
Doos: idiot; there is another more explicit meaning
Duiwels: devils
Ekskuus: excuse me
Fokken: fucking
Gaadtjie: the guard on a minibus taxi who calls for passengers and collects money
Goefed: stoned
Jintoe/hoer: slut; whore
Kak: shit

Kyk die Tinkerbell: look at this Tinkerbell

Loskop: scatterbrained

Mal: mad

Meisiekind: girl; literally means 'girl child' and is used affectionately here

Met die helm gebore: born with the caul; having the second sight

Moerse: big (here: *moerse big*, which indicates very big)

Naaiers: fuckers

Ou vrou: old woman

She's gonna moer him: she's going to kill/hurt him (vulgar)

Skief: skew; askance (variant of skeef)

Skrik: (get a) fright

Sies: expression of distaste/disgust

Stoep: small raised platform or steps, usually in front of a house, like a veranda or porch

Verlep: wilted

ACKNOWLEDGEMENTS

While writing this book, there was collective fury in South Africa about the high rate of violence towards and murder of women. When Savannah thinks, *I've never not been afraid*, she's remembering that recent stats say a woman is killed every three hours. And yet, despite its problems, my home country is a beautiful, amazing, vibrant place and I hope this comes through on the page.

For as long as I can remember, I've wanted to write a fantasy set in contemporary Cape Town, and I am extremely grateful to the three women at the heart of bringing it into the world: Ellen Holgate, who nurtured this book from conception. Genevieve Herr, who helped me find the shape of this story. And always, Claire Wilson.

Thank you my dear friend Virtue Shine of Emerald & Wax for chatting markets and African magic with me – this was so helpful. Thank you my BFFs in South Africa: Naefa Kahn Crookes, Ashraf Johaardien, Catherine Sofianos, Emma van der Vliet, Martha Evans – for the stories, for magic, for answering random questions, for everything.

Thank you Sally Partridge for reading, your support means so much. This book covers some tricky terrain and I'm grateful to Nadia Davids, who helped me while getting started. I'm also grateful to the sensitivity readers in the later stages: in SA, thank you Mapule Mohulatsi for engaging so completely; thank you Jasmine Richards and the other readers for your insight and wisdom, which helped me think through what I wanted this book to say.

Again, huge thanks to the staff at Bloomsbury, especially

Emily Marples, Jessica Bellman, Alesha Bonser and everyone else who works so hard to bring this book to readers. I am grateful to every one of you. The cover is extraordinary – thank you Jet Purdie and Seth Pimentel.

And always my family, especially my three sisters (my stars), my three sons, my husband Cathal. Deirdre Seoighe for talking me through burns, both real and fictional. My nieces – Zadie who let me check in about Cape teens, and Tracey for enthusiastic chats about jinn and doekoems.

A shout-out to the women I've called 'auntie', family or otherwise. The aunties make Savannah feel safe and loved, and I could write this because I've known it too.

There were many resources that I found invaluable in my research, including online academic papers, the Iziko Museums Slave Lodge website, and visiting the permanent exhibitions at the Lodge in Cape Town. A good starting point was *Slavery in Dutch South Africa* by Nigel Worden, and for anyone interested, there is a wealth of information about slavery in the Cape.

Thank you to my fellow writers who've been so wonderful and supportive – it means everything; it's quite awesome to have writers whose work I adore say lovely things. Thank you everyone who shares the love of books on social media, those I've been fortunate to meet in person, and those I've met online. And, with all my heart, thank you readers for picking this book up and letting it visit a while in your head.

While editing, I lost my dad, our CCV, to cancer and my last thank you is to him, for paving the way, for letting me dream, for believing.

DON'T MISS THESE SPELLBINDING THRILLERS BY MARY WATSON

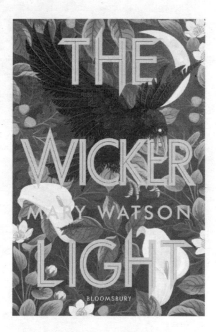

'*The Wren Hunt* rings with ancient, subtle magic, masterfully transmuted into words. A tale that gets into your bones'

SAMANTHA SHANNON

MARY WATSON grew up in Cape Town during the apartheid years and did her Masters in Creative Writing with André Brink. She won the Caine Prize for African Writing in 2006 and appeared on Hay Festival's Africa39 list of influential writers. Mary now lives in Galway with her family. *Blood to Poison* is her third novel for young adults and the first rooted in her South African heritage.